THE DUPLEX REPORT

Robert J. Richey

ISBN-13: 979-8-9883142-1-9 (Digital)
ISBN-13: 979-8-9883142-0-2 (Paperback)

Book Cover by Robert J. Richey.
Planet courtesy of PIRO4D via Pixabay.
Space background courtesy of Placidplace via Pixabay.
Space station created with the assistance of DALL-E 2.

Library of Congress Control Number: 2023908578
Printed in the United States of America

To my wife. You remain the best part of me.

TABLE OF CONTENTS

CHAPTER ONE

Prologue

In the mid-2020s, a syndicate of global leaders met in secret to discuss the fate of humanity—in particular, its exponential growth and its impact on the environment. The mass of earth suitable for human habitat was shrinking, a result of renewed interest in government controlled procreation and an ecosystem which had thrown in the towel. Something had to be done, so the powers that be—*if you'll forgive the pun*—conceived a plan.

The new world order bureaucrats gave birth to an initial concept: twelve self-sustaining space stations each capable of housing ten thousand citizens, including food growth and processing, living and recreation quarters, work cells, power and water distribution, and station administration, contained in structures the size of ten orbiting supertankers named, tritely enough for the twelve signs of the zodiac. Their construction was supposed to take forty years.

The plan was never to house the entire population of Earth. Not only would that be impossible given the allotted time, few believed there were that many humans worth saving. A consortium of government-funded scientists concluded that the optimum number of humans required to rebuild civilization without inbreeding was one hundred thousand—more than one man and a woman made from his rib, but far fewer than the number remaining on the planet.

The project experienced delays right out of the gate as leaders of the free and not-so-free world argued over details. The biggest issue was deciding how to allocate space in space. China and India were in agreement for the first time in history, advocating a model in which station populations mirrored the planet's. By the beginning of the talks, each country had close to 2 billion people, so why shouldn't their orbital residents represent 37 percent of station capacity? This had the effect of pissing off the rest of the world, who argued that an Asian's inability to keep it in their pants did not entitle them to a higher number of extraterrestrial residents. It took several years to reach a compromise—India and China would see a larger portion of their citizens given roles on the stations, but not commensurate with their current population.

The Second Great Pandemic changed everything as the need for the stations, already plagued by delays, took on new life. Governments, which initially conceived and funded the plan, relinquished their authority to rich global benefactors only too willing to assume responsibility and staffing. Most of the influence occurred behind the scenes where politicians remained figure heads while the newly formed technorati leadership made decisions. They argued that TwoGP's impact and the resulting animosity toward Asia, where the second virus originated, necessitated a new plan. Calling themselves The Council, they championed an algorithm, an artificial intelligence developed by a team of socially inept, game playing nerds to select the right people for station Roles.

I was born a few years after Initial Population Integration, or IPI as it's now remembered—the phase one ten-year baseline staffing of the first twelve stations. Phase two, the fifty year period following IPI, would see full station migration. Although my memory of the details is sketchy—*I was a child, after all*—the stations needed resources from Earth while topping off the population. However, once complete there would be little need for continued migration. There were contingencies to ease the suffering of those still alive on the planet through station innovations in zero-gravity food processing, water production and power planning, but it was a stop gap measure. Anyone left behind was doomed.

Some of the people aboard when the first 12 stations were completed, mostly technicians, a few medical personnel, and a small contingent of administrators, remained, but many returned to the surface once they fulfilled their construction contracts. Initial Population Integration saw essential personnel—the Council and their families, scientists, and techs needed for station integrity—migrating aboard first. Once in space, they facilitated the remaining transfer of inhabitants, everyone agreeing to population control measures in exchange for a better life away from a dying planet.

The first Council, the tech elite who assumed the project after the world's governments failed, were titans from social media, transportation, retail, automation, artificial intelligence, sustainability, and data analytics. They believed that genetic and cultural diversity were as important as the Roles needed to sustain life. The code they developed, the algorithm, remains a mystery to all but a few insiders; however, the result was undeniable.

Since people had to be productive, few politicians were afforded space when IPI finally kicked off eight years behind schedule in 2075. Ethnically diverse, educated people from the sciences, engineering, technology, arts, and humanities were recruited, enticed by a chance at humanity's future. A walk around the station is like floating in a pot of intelligently designed human goulash. There is a little of everyone on board—Africans, Asians, Russians, Westerners, and even a few Pacific Islanders thrown in for good measure—as well as doctors, scientists, botanists, engineers, technicians, writers, visual artists, and anyone else deemed necessary to a healthy society.

The initial delay turned out to be a boon for the stations, giving designers time to perfect a number of technologies. Although food gummy production remained a few years out, 3-D printing became a mainstay—everything from station components to non-living organic material. Genetically modified fungus producing high energy vitamins, glucose and proteins was used to supplement station build crew diets during construction. Renewable hydrogen energy provided a means of powering shuttles into space. These leaps meant stations could be smaller and house the same number of people, five supertankers instead of ten.

The new tech Council was not about to share their advancements with those left behind. They'd witnessed the destruction the human race was capable of and would not be party to prolonging the planet's agony. Who can blame them? A person might be reasonable, but a people led by elected representation are selfish, greedy and narcissistic. Politicians cannot be trusted to act outside their own self-interests. They were doomed to perish with their constituents on Earth.

There are hundreds of thousands of people spread across the eleven remaining stations, each consuming resources and generating value-add in a delicate balance of life and death. Sometimes the see-saw shifts, throwing off the stations equilibrium. When that happens, someone has to make tough decisions—reset the scales. That's where I come in.

CHAPTER TWO

The Collective

Ocasio meets me suited up at the airlock. He wanted to talk somewhere private about what he described as a "win-win for the both of us." I suggested PA5 above the containment field. The outer platforms are the most secluded places on the stations.

The internal cameras and airlock security on the doors bracketing the platform are easily bypassed. The security system triggers an alarm only when access is unauthorized, and the cameras are there to review after something happens—there are not enough people to staff watching them full time. In any case, it's easy enough to modify the logs to show only one egress if you know someone on the system security team. I'm covered on both fronts—authorized access *and* a friend on the inside. There are no external cameras, although they are on order, requisitioned after the last suicide.

It's well past midnight and both of us are wearing gravity suits with encrypted comms borrowed from the airlock storage locker. The containment field less than ten feet away is humming a meditative melody, but it's doing nothing to calm Ocasio. His stammering makes him sound less coherent than usual and there's sweat beading on his forehead even in a climate controlled suit. He has to stay clean during rehab—I suspect most of this is a combination of detox and nerves.

"So, Derek, I suppose we need to discuss your alternatives," I say, knowing full well there aren't any.

"I was hopin' we could do something about the rehab," Ocasio says, sounding like a child with marbles packed into his cheeks. His inexperience with zero-G and the drugs leaving his system are causing saliva to collect in his jowls. "I got things that I can share. I just can't do

200 hours in 'group'. There's gotta be a way outta this."

Group is shorthand for group therapy sessions, a painfully boring process during which most people drink the cool-aid, say the right things and are eventually considered rehabilitated. I turn to rest my elbows on the railing, watching as Ocasio apes my movement, his right elbow only an inch or so from my left.

"You know Derek, I have a lot of responsibilities on this station, but they don't go unchecked. It's not like I can lobby to alter someone's sentence without good reason."

The forlorn look Derek is sporting screams of desperation. "Please," he implores. "There has gotta be somethin' you can do."

"Well, Derek, I don't work in abstract. What is it you think you can trade for this leniency I'm not sure I can negotiate?" I'm not in a hurry and I am mildly interested in whatever story Derek plans to proffer.

"I know people who can get stuff. Rations and stuff," Ocasio stammers. "Like alcohol and extra food."

"Derek, why can't you be like almost every other Cit? A productive, contributing, non-draining member of society?" The question is rhetorical, of course. Derek will never assimilate.

"What? Become a member of the mindless hive? No thank you. I took the same batt'try of exams when I was sixteen as everyone else, enrolled in the Station Role Bid process, suffered academic evals, and ranked choices on the dream sheet. I wanted to be an Orbital Sheriff's Deputy, or an engineer, or maybe even a Psych like my ma. You know what the algorithm returned with? Waste tech! Can you believe it? My SR Bid score matched me with Waste Reclamation Technician! I'm not repairing shitty pipes for the rest of my life."

Derek is exaggerating. The algorithm returns a list, not a single Role. I'm sure Waste Reclamation Tech was at the top and that is where Derek stopped reading. But he had choices.

"You don't have to follow the recommendation, you know," I counsel. "It's rare, but people do select Roles outside of their Bid score."

"And we see how that turns out," Derek replies, shaking his head. "No way I'm risking random reassign when I fail their arbitrary training."

He's right about the consequences of not selecting within the suggested roles. The process is designed to match interest with aptitude and usually does a pretty good job. But if someone selects outside of the algorithm and fails to meet expectations, they'll be randomly re-assigned, usually to an unpopular SR. But in Derek's case, what could be less popular than poop pipe repairman?

"So you chose Waste Rec Tech, which you don't actually spend much time doing because you're always in trouble. That makes sense."

One's Station Role is only a matter of pride, not money, which means there is no financial advantage to being a doctor versus a technician. People take time off to decompress, but there aren't any vacations. Where would one go? Another station? They are all essentially the same and flying between them is about the least exciting thing to do up here. Stay-home vacations—reading, virtual sightseeing, and gaming—are popular. There are no cars, no furniture stores, no clothing outlets. People walk everywhere, Habitat Units come pre-fitted based on family size, and everyone wears the same uniform. Pretty much everything is provided—healthcare, food, power, water, lodging, education—it's all issued, regulated and rationed. And there's the rub. When people have everything they need, they crave the things they want or of which they want more.

The black markets formed not long after Initial Population Integration. The stations are a closed loop system designed to provide for the needs of the population without outside intervention…or internal discord. Maintaining the peace with a comparatively small judicial system, few officers, and an almost non-existent detention center requires a citizenry satisfied with their lot and accepting of regulations on consumption, procreation, and entertainment. For the most part, people accept the limitations, but only because they can supplement needs with wants from outside formal channels.

The Council provides plenty of food gummies and hydro-fountains, as well as a small allowance of carbonated alcoholic beverages, but one needs to be creative to find things like liquor, music, and, if I might be so bold, sex. Black markets afford the opportunity to trade station Allotments—food, hydro, alcohol, uniform, cleaning, gaming, movie, sense-dep, power, labor—for the little things that make up the difference between survival and living. Want additional alcohol rations but don't need as much power? Trade power allotments for a bottle of bootleg hooch. Need a post-binge oxygen increase in your Habitat Unit? Barter gaming credits for an oxygen insulator. Unmentionables feeling a little underappreciated? Swap labor for sex. Station Allotments sufficiently sustain the approved family size, but life is a lot more fun with bootleg bourbon.

This is where Ocasio comes in. His attempts to exploit the black market exceeded his abilities. In other words, had he limited his pleasure to himself instead of impacting others by stealing their stuff, we wouldn't be discussing how he might contribute to my own personal gain.

"Maybe I shouldn't have accepted the first Role the algorithm offered," Derek sighs and for a moment I think he might take some personal responsibility for his decisions. But true to form he adds, "If it wasn't for my parents, I wouldn't be here now offering up their future."

"How do your parents fit into the black market?"

"Pharma," Derek answers without looking up from the containment field. "I can get pharmaceuticals from my ma's supply."

"What kind of pharma?"

"Uppers, downers, 'daties,' psyches, you name it, I can get it," he replies, his eyes brightening with the possibility of a trade.

Downers are easy enough to get, as are the Psychedelics. Pretty much anyone with something to trade can get them on the black market. But the 'daties,' those are rare. 'Daties' are synthetic sedative-hypnotics, capable of rendering whoever takes them compliant and forgetful. Remember those old movies depicting Las Vegas hypnotists and a stage full of people all clucking like chickens? Same concept. If you're around when someone takes one, you can control their actions and they will only remember what you want them to remember. Best of all, it's undetectable in the bloodstream, breaking down into carbon dioxide exhaled into the atmosphere over a period of a few hours. Unfortunately, they are tightly controlled and only available to psychiatrists.

"I can get most of those on the market," I reply.

"Not the 'daties' you can't. Those suckers are controlled. But my ma has a supply."

"So what you're telling me is I should be having this conversation with your mother."

"No, the pharma's in my ma's office. She's uh..." He looks out toward the planet, considering what to share. "She's a bit of a freak."

I'm silent, waiting to see if Ocasio will elaborate on his own. It's an awkwardly long minute before he continues.

"Well, not in a bad way. She just has needs and things between her and my pop aren't so good. So she keeps a supply on hand for some of her patients. Well, for her *with* some of her patients. Nobody gets hurt. In fact, it probably helps a lot of them."

"Derek, relax," I assure him. "I get it. Who hasn't been in that same situation? Wanting to help someone while extracting a bit of personal pleasure."

The problem is I need Derek to commit suicide in order to introduce Mick Finn to his future, or lack thereof. How can Derek facilitate access to 'daties' if he's just thrown himself into the charged field array? I just don't see how the two goals are compatible. But perhaps…

"How do you propose we get access to your mom's stash? It's not like you can walk in and take the pills. The minute your biometrics scan it's going to flag you as an offender."

Ocasio's reply without hesitation tells me he's already figured all this out. "No, my ma will just give me what I want?"

"And why would she do that?"

"Cuz I got photos. Photos of her with patients, see." He types a few characters into the ComLink on his wrist and up pops photos of his mom a few inches above the device.

Indra Ocasio is a handsome woman. In her mid-fifties, I suspect, based on Derek's age, with short black hair, a naturally tan Indian complexion, and an insatiably active appetite based on the sheer number of pics in Derek's library.

"So how do you see this playing out, exactly? I can't have you getting pharma from your mom, then shuttling it over to my office."

Derek considers his options for a long moment, looking down at the planet. I can see the gears spinning. Just as I'm about to suggest it, Derek comes to life.

"Oh! I know. I'll transfer the photos to you and you can get them directly from my ma. It's not like she's ever gonna say anything. She'd be risking her reputation." Derek's response is almost gleeful.

This just might work. The photos pretty much guarantee access to whatever Dr. Ocasio has in inventory. But it's also a path I've not taken —a step in a direction not at all legit. I accidentally chuckle at my own hypocrisy, willing to kill for the cause but hesitant to commit extortion.

"What's so funny?" Derek asks.

"Okay," I sigh. "You transfer the photos to me and I'll check it out. If there are no issues, I'll pull some strings and see about having your rehab commuted."

Ocasio thinks about it for all of a half second. "Okay, okay. It's a deal," he says, typing into his ComLink to transfer the photos. "But you have to know that my ma's not a bad person. She just has… needs." He finishes the transfer and leans his elbows on the platform rail, a long sigh of relief echoing through the comms.

That was the last thing he said. He didn't see my arm behind him, or feel my hand lift him over the rail and shove him toward the array. He didn't have time to switch off encrypted comms and activate general broadcast. He simply drifted, repeating something that sounded like "what?" or "whoa" or perhaps "what the fuck?" There was no sound when he made contact, no smoke, no thunderous crash accompanied by a barrage of electrical charges. It was rather uneventful. One second a young man in a gravity suit stood above a charged field array, the next a slimy blood ball lay upon the access panel on the other side. I really didn't expect much, but this was just downright disappointing.

CHAPTER THREE

Jason Plumin

The sign on my desk reads, 'Jason Plumin, Station Representative.' I love my job, but seeing the worst station citizens is not for everyone. Doctors, analysts, techs, administrators, scientists, migrants, they drink too much and run down the hall naked, steel virtual reality allotments, make politically incorrect comments, deface walls with graffiti, break into offices and urinate on desks, hack news broadcasts and air pornography, and sneak into airlocks for a few minutes of weightlessness. Most make their one minor mistake and move on, others are repeat offenders, a few commit serious crimes. It's a grind, but it's never dull.

"Hi Henry, got the Ocasio case, huh?" I ask, placing my hand over my heart.

Henry follows suit, his right hand covering the area just above his sternum, "Hey there, Plumin. Yeah, Ocasio. Don't suppose we can work a deal before we get in there?"

Derek Ocasio is a 23 year old Indo-Hispanic male, black hair and brown eyes from his mother, a temper from his father, and a third-time offender, this time up on B&E—court slang for breaking and entering—he's Monday's first case. Henry's job as Derek's Personal Representative is to make Derek look as much like a victim as possible without making it seem like he can't rehabilitate. He does this by highlighting Derek's abusive past (if one exists), his forced placement in an unselected Station Role (if that's what happened), his conciliatory demeanor (which Derek is lacking), and anything else he can pull out of the ether to show Derek is not a habitual offender devoid of hope. In Derek's case there isn't much to work with.

"I don't think Derek is the best candidate for rehab," I reply disingenuously. "Personally, I think re-homing is the answer. Unless you know of some mitigating circumstance not previously presented?"

I'm posturing, of course—teeing it up for Henry to provide mitigation while teasing the idea of sending Derek to the planet, which I don't think is a realistic option in Derek's case, but part of this dance is leaning in with my best foot.

"That's BS. You know expelling him won't stick. You don't have a compelling enough argument, which will just get you a referral upon Council review and a mark for over sentencing. That of course presumes the judge finds him guilty, which isn't guaranteed. Plus..." Botha pauses long enough to scroll back several swipes into Derek's file. "Plus, I've got this over-arching mitigation letter from his mother from two years ago."

Henry is a solid PersRep. Not outstanding, but consistent. In his late fifties, he remains fit and attentive. His pressed uniform bears a worn Ghanian flag, a gift from his parents before departing for the stations. I can picture him younger, a youthful close cut, jet black afro, taught ebony skin and bright idealist eyes ready to save wrongly accused residents from being deported. These days he seems less enthusiastic, his passion replaced by a graying crown, cracked hands, and a thousand yard stare currently scanning Derek's file for the letter.

Derek is a constant reminder to his father, a physicist, and his mother, a psychiatrist in one of the Aries Med labs, that children don't repair broken relationships. Such were the stories at the time of Initial Population Immigration. Young scientists thinking they're in love and realizing too late those feelings were the result of biochemical reactions were offered opportunities to relocate for a better life aboard one of the savior space stations. They weren't going to turn down the offer just because the marriage wasn't the fairy tale they'd hoped. Then nine months later and '17 hours of unmitigated agony,' according to a character statement Ms. Ocasio submitted in support of her son, Derek came screaming into the world—well, into the space—and the Ocasio's learned favorable outcomes have less to do with genetics than concerted effort.

"Yeah," I respond, "and he has two priors. He wasn't just caught with the stuff from the most recent robbery, he had a stash of trinkets from previous reports. The letter from mommy isn't going to cut it this time."

"Come on, Jason. You know as well as I do the Judge is not going to sentence a Gen to deportation for stealing a few worthless souvenirs."

The stations have been around long enough to sire an entire generation of people known as Gens. They've never lived on Earth, never even seen the CAZ or the Open Lands other than on station news where stories about unchecked crime, disease, violence, worsening food, medical supply shortages, and stringent government regulations scares even the toughest Gen shitless. Which is why re-homing is reserved for the most severe cases.

"And you know as well as I do," I fire back, "that there aren't enough mitigating circumstances to keep Derek from being found guilty. He's being charged with two counts of Station Code 142.0, Resource Hoarding, one count SC-162.2, Burglary, non-violent, and one count of SC-156.0, Excessive Aggression for what he did to that Orbital Sheriff's deputy. He's lucky that deputy wasn't allergic to urine or we might be looking at an SC-178.0 charge."

"Murder," Botha replies. "You're seriously reaching. That charge has never been leveled aboard the stations. Why not just tack on Unauthorized Procreation? At least then expulsion is mandatory."

There are surprisingly few people violating station laws. Don't get me wrong, it's enough to remind me of my own superiority, but it's not excessive. Most people are caught doing small things, violent crime is unheard of on the stations. A common violation might be the purchase of bootleg alcohol and the subsequent making an ass of oneself. The black market is a necessary part of blissful station life, but when it's compounded by bad behavior, I get involved.

The Station Rep's job is to determine how voraciously to pursue sanctions against Derek, and then represent the station's citizens in court before the judge. It's a little like being a prosecutor was in the early twenty-first century, except there is no jury, just me, Derek's representative, and the judge. I meet with the defendant and his Personal Rep to review the defendant's record, only Derek decided not to show this time. It's not a big deal—I've already met Derek on two other occasions, I can make a decision about sanctions without another conversation. StaReps have a great deal of latitude in this respect, so long as we remain within the guidelines, defer to rehabilitation over deportation, and justify our decisions under judicial review. Judges are the jury, deciding guilt or innocence—StaReps hand out punishment.

"True," I say, glancing up from Derek's file with a smile. "If only I could prove he fathered a child without proper approvals. Then re-homing would be a no brainer. But you're right, I have no desire to sit through legal re-education. The thing is I'm seriously sick of seeing Derek Ocasio. I know his file forward and back. So, while I can't expel him, I can stick him in rehab for so long he won't remember his name when it's over. Give me an alternative."

Henry considers my request while scrolling through a few more Derek pages. "Can we at least agree Derek does not meet the statutory requirements for deportation? He has not accumulated multiple infractions, demonstrated a consequential negative impact on station society, or displayed a disinclination for rehabilitation. The founders designed our legal system to be more tolerant than the system they left behind—despite your personal preference to see more repeat offenders stripped of their citizenship."

It's true. If it were me, I'd re-home everyone who couldn't figure it out after three violations—someone like Derek, for example—but I also recognize there is no way the decision will be upheld.

"Sure. We can agree to…most of that," I say, allowing Botha to spy my childish grin.

Henry rifles through his messenger bag, retrieving an envelope. "How about a letter from Brandi Mikkelson?"

I know Brandi. She's a relatively new PersRep of some notoriety, having represented in her short tenure a number of people who were retained rather than re-homed after committing comparatively serious or habitual offenses. She also has the lowest recidivism rate on the stations—well known for turning fifth and sixth chances into productive Cits.

Henry hands me the letter, which reads, "Please accept my personal assurance that Derek Ocasio will not reoffend. I have a position for him within my office and am certain he can become a productive Cit." It's signed Brandi Mikkelson, Personal Representative, Aries Office.

The judge will not consider the letter from Brandi in determining guilt, but it is applicable to pre-meets. If I disregard it entirely, I'll hear from the ethics board and have to justify the decision to the Aries Ambassador and possibly to the Council. Since I wasn't seriously considering re-homing Derek anyway, Brandi's plea gives me some wiggle room. If Derek breaks bad, it's on Mikkelson.

"Very well. In light of Derek's new found opportunity, the people might entertain a lengthy but comparatively truncated stint in rehabilitation services combined with his mandatory attendance in a role at the Personal Rep's office. Was this cleared through Station Role Admin?"

"As far as I know, SR Admin agreed to the reassignment," Henry replies.

"Okay, then," I nod as the judge motions us into her office.

"Greetings, Ms. Ryan," Henry begins.

"Hello, Judge," I say as we take seats opposite her desk.

"Hello gentlemen. What do you have for me today?"

Ryan's office is like every other on the stations. The 24-by-30 inch metal desk serves as a base for a virtual monitor and keyboard, with a moderate amount of room for a photo or other personal item, which are absent in Ryan's case. The ashen top and legs blend with the white walls and the judge's tan uniform like a James Bland painting, the prudent use of color blurring the lines between the elements and creating an almost meditative feeling. The walls are devoid of personal touches, as are all shared spaces, and the grey floor gives the impression of absorbing the desk legs. The only stand out visual is the judge's mop of curly, red hair resting playfully upon her shoulders, a fiery sun against a vanilla backdrop.

Judge Ryan's reputation is built on two decades in the Role, but it's easy to mistake her time on station as less. She's in her fifties—a fact I know only because I asked once after a case—but her petite, fit frame and good genes give her the appearance of a woman ten years younger. She moved aboard Aries station during the latter years of Initial Population Integration, accepting an SR as a judge at a time when there was little need for one. Her first thirty years on the planet give her a perspective that is quickly becoming extinct as the IPI group ages into retirement and death. She approaches every case devoid of bias, exuding the calm, collected, emotionless control of a professional gambler. She's a pro in a way that defines the word.

"Your honor," Botha starts, "my client pleads guilty pending confirmation from the StaRep that re-homing will not be a sanctioned option."

"Well, Mr. Plumin?" the judge asks, her eyes reflecting the words on the virtual screen hovering between us. "How about it? Shall we give Mr…" Ryan pauses for a moment, allowing the 'R' to trill as she reads the screen, "Ocasio. Shall we give Mr. Ocasio a third chance?"

"Your honor, based on Ms. Mikkelson's reference, as well as Derek's other previously presented and documented mitigation, the station agrees with Mr. Ocasio's proposed reassignment to the PersRep's office. The station further orders 200 hours of rehabilitation services to be executed in coordination with the StaRep's office."

Ryan rapid-taps keystrokes on the virtual keyboard. "Very well. Mr. Ocasio is found guilty and the StaRep's finding of rehab is logged. Is there anything else, gentlemen?"

Neither I nor Henry have anything. "Okay, then get out of my office," Ryan adds with a wave.

We both thank the judge and I follow Botha out the door. "Have Ocasio call my office and we'll set up a time to discuss the rehab. Sooner rather than later."

"Will do," Henry replies.

"And tell Brandi I said good luck with Derek."

CHAPTER FOUR

The Collective

We live in a cold, brutal space. The extra-vehicular uniform I wear insulates, but doesn't stop the chill shooting down the back of my neck or the involuntary tremble that follows. I feel the inky black cold even though my EVU keeps me at a comfy 72 degrees. My shuddering shoulders remind me of my grandfather, a boy standing over a chilly camp fire on a frigid Manitoba morning, the wind biting his pink cheeks and blasting through his lightweight, Goodwill jacket. I've only seen it in photos, but the chill I feel now is as real as his snowy winter.

A year ago it would have been nerves, but now I'm certain it's the vast deadness. When I first started, every encounter brought butterflies. That feeling vanished months ago and with it anticipation. Standing here tonight, ready to rid myself of yet another assbag, I feel only resolve and the chill.

I'm marveling at the planet when Finn beckons me over in a voice bracketed by static. "You really need to see this!"

There's no reason to yell, not out here. Sophisticated tech in our EVU suits trap our voices, algorithms process them, and high-powered repeaters transmit the results at a pleasant 60 decibels. Everything but the screams, provided you time it correctly.

In stark contrast to old photos, Earth in 2103 looks more like a brown clump of dirt than a miraculous marble. Governments played kick the can with the climate until it was too late, forcing a dying planet to its grave along with the human race. Best case: life on earth ends in 200 years. Then it's up to the stations to begin reconstitution—another thousand years restoring the planet's habitability after those left behind are extinct.

"Seriously, this is the best one, yet!" Finn calls, waving an arm as if attempting a hook shot.

The final nail in mankind's coffin was hammered toward the end of 2043. We should have learned after the First Great Pandemic in 2020, OneGP. In its aftermath countries contributed their best and brightest scientists to an international team, vowing to put aside political, social, and economic differences all in the hopes of staving off global annihilation. Lofty goals soon overcome by ego and national agendas. All of that government-private sector cooperation to produce a vaccine and establish distribution channels and the best we got was a promise to be better prepared next time.

So yeah, big surprise, governments were shocked when TwoGP hit in 2043. Nobody could decide if it originated in China or India, but anti-Chinese sentiment over unfettered global expansionism and strong arm investment in developing nations saw most fingers pointing toward east Asia.

The West may have suffered disproportionately as a result of the first virus, but Asia paid the price for the second—TwoGP wiped out a third of the Indo-Chinese people. Combined with mortality in other countries, Earth's population dropped by 20 percent. The reduction wasn't enough. Massive spending during the first pandemic combined with hoarding during the second forced suppliers to clear cut large tracts of land just to keep up. It wasn't long before groups formed, proclaiming themselves police and making decisions about who was worthy and who was not. Any tolerance for civil disagreement went the way of environmental protections as society devolved into near total chaos. The only way to save the planet was to wipe out humanity. People acted as a virus, the irony of which was lost to most.

"If you don't get over here before the cleanup crew arrives, you're going to miss it."

Michael Finn, or Mick to his friends, doesn't even notice the planet anymore. He's an old school cop with 143 days to retirement, so he likes to remind me, the number slightly smaller every time I see him. We've been called to another suicide, a common occurrence on the stations. When I say *we*, I mean Mick. He's the Deputy in town. I'm just here for an unsanctioned ride-along before Mick retires. I insisted I needed a taste of normalcy. Mick thinks the jellied remains of dead people after they toss themselves into hyper charged containment fields is the definition of 'normal.'

In addition to being a twenty-two year Orbital Sheriff's Unit veteran, Mick is also a self-righteous, arrogant pig with little respect for those he serves. He doesn't suffer the same space-chill in his gravity suit, which is bloated to threadbare, his 240 pound frame pressing against the fabric like he's wearing a swimming pool donut around his waist. These days he'd never qualify for migration, but 20 years ago the genetic screening process wasn't quite as selective. He likes to brag about how he's worked "three or four of these losers just this year," after throwing themselves into this same containment field. It's a very popular field for suicides.

"Stop looking at that giant turd. There is nothing to see on that shit show of a planet."

It's not a total shit show. Born from the confluence of riots, disease, civil unrest and lawlessness, a few areas within Canada, Australia and Iceland exist as Cooperative Autonomous Zones, within which they manage some semblance of control and comparative civility amid food and water shortages, pollution, and overcrowding. There is even a leadership structure that regulates life—what we on the stations call a benign dictatorship. The various CAZ Senates trade in what few raw materials remain—drugs and alcohol being the most popular—which, although the stations don't need them, certainly make life aboard more comfortable. In exchange, the stations process materials in order to stretch their utility and provide for the greater population density found within the Zones until full staffing is complete.

"At least it's not the Open Lands," I reply.

"The O-Lands? Are you kidding? If the CAZ are the anus of the planet, the Open Lands are the brown stains left behind after a bout of raging diarrhea."

Mick is colorful that way.

"They're an untamed pit of contaminated food and water supplies punctuated by disease and disorder." Mick adds. "When I was a kid we trekked through that shit for days—always at night, never while the sun was up—scrounging scraps from the dead and trying to avoid the roaming bands of poll workers. That's what my old man called 'em. They'd station themselves at makeshift guard shacks, stopping people on their way to the zone. The heartless fucks would take your shit, then slice you from stem to stern without bothering to see if what you were carrying was worth the effort. That was forty years ago. I can't imagine what it's like today."

I've never been there myself. But Finn says he remembers.

"Probably shitty." I reply, starting my lumbering, graceless walk-bounce toward where Mick stands on the platform.

"For Pete's sake," Mick comments as I reach him. "What is wrong with these people? Ball up and get over it already. The stations are not the OLands. Fucking loser suicides."

I don't need a better look at the bloody goo dripping below the pulsing charge, I was here when he went over. But I pretend to be interested because Mick is not going to throw himself into the Aries containment array.

CHAPTER FIVE

Brandi Mikkelson

"Being a Personal Rep is exhausting," I say out loud as I load another ten pounds on one end of the barbell.

"Brandi, you're an idiot," Alex comments in a familiar tone. "You've got the easiest Role on the stations."

Alex isn't the brightest bulb in the room, but he's certainly one of the nicest and you couldn't ask for a better personal trainer. "What do you know, you basically work out for a living."

"Exactly!" exclaims Alex. "That's how I know. I work with people all day. Being a PersRep is easily in the top five best SRs."

Alex has a point. The last three years since selection haven't been the worst—those would be the first 25. Thank Ganesha or Odin or whoever created this chaos for giving the last PersRep an undiagnosed heart condition. One day I'm defending hookers in the Canada Autonomous Zone and the next I'm preparing mitigation for a kid caught sniffing demineralizing solution. Yeah, Alex might be right, but I'm not going to tell him that.

"Shut up. Do you have any idea how difficult it is to create a back story that is both endearing and hopeful? People's lives depend on me making some rando Station Rep believe the idiot sitting in the next room is regretful and can be rehabbed. I spend my days writing fiction for an audience of one."

I slide in beneath the bar, positioning it parallel to the floor on my upper back and plant my feet a bit wider than shoulder width. This is going to be a personal record, the most weight I've ever squatted. "Now shut up for a minute and let me do this."

"Abs tight," Alex reminds me. "Focus on your core."

I take two deep breaths and close my eyes, picturing the entire movement from start to finish. I feel my abs tense, like pulling a slip knot around my midsection, and imagine my hips moving back, knees maintaining their alignment. I see my body breaking parallel, hips below knees, weight on my heels, then I power drive up, chest high, knees locked, core stable.

"Wholly crap! 295 pounds! That's a new PR!" Alex announces for all to hear. "You're fast becoming a real badass."

Alex is being generous, of course. He can squat twice that, but I'd be lying if I didn't agree with him—I am becoming a badass. And to think just a few years ago I was lifting sandbags in a one room flat where the closest thing to a personal trainer was the mugger who tried to steal my ComLink. Back then it was a matter of survival. These days it's all fun.

"Well, I've got to keep in shape somehow and cardio just sucks," I comment.

"So what is that, like 2.5 times your body weight?" Alex asks.

I give him a wry look. "Not quite, ass." Alex smiles, knowing I'm right. He is an ass and the nicest guy on the stations.

In fact, Alex is as close a friend as I have on Aries, even though he's a Gen—a first-generation, station-born Cit. His father died in the Canadian CAZ before his mother migrated in 2076, baby Alex a pea-sized, single-cell organism waiting to become my personal trainer. When is mother died in child birth, a supportive advocate adopted him and guided him toward a career in health services. The work fits Alex's 6 foot, 2 inch Eastern European frame and the mop of sandy blonde curls that he holds back with a retro, orange cotton headband underscores the role. But despite being stronger than a programmable cargo loader, he wouldn't harm a fly. We don't spend a lot of time together outside the HMC, but if I were to want to spend time with people—which I don't—Alex would be my first choice.

"Hi Brandi. How's it going?" The familiar voice brings me back from my last-lift adrenaline high. I look around and spot Jason Plumin on his way to an elliptical.

"Hey, not much. You?" I reply.

"Good. Just here for some workouts. You know. Gotta stay in shape," Jason replies, flexing his arms in a faux bodybuilder pose, then flicking his right bicep with a smile and head tilt that suggestions there's still some work to do.

"In your case it couldn't hurt to add in some weights. With all that time on cardio about the only thing you'll be able to do is run away," I fire back as he climbs aboard the machine.

"Who's that?" Alex asks.

"That's Jason Plumin, one of the Station Reps I write fiction for. Do you know him?"

"Nope," Alex replies. "I can't say we've ever met. Seems friendly enough, though. Maybe he'd like to join us?"

"I'm not sure power lifting is his thing."

I've known Jason since Role training and worked with him opposite cases for over a year. We're a small crew of PersRep's, but the Station Reps office is larger, so we don't always work the same issues. I'd consider him a friend, far behind Alex, but ahead of the random dude serving up suds at the cantina. He's bright, funny and usually fair, but he does tend to be a bit dramatic when it comes to sentence recommendations. Plus, he's mildly good looking, if you like the average build, six foot, somewhat entertaining style that accompanies a full head of lightly salted, clean-cut, jet black hair.

"We've worked a couple cases," I add, bringing Alex up to speed. "He's thorough and seems to know what he's doing—you know, not a total idiot. I get the impression he thinks he's just a little bit smarter than the rest of us. Still, nice enough, I suppose."

"I don't believe I've heard you say that much about anyone, like *ever*," Alex jibes. "Could this be love sprouting?"

"Not quite my type. Although the rumor mill has it he's someone's type."

"Do tell," Alex replies with a nod.

"It's nothing, let's just drop it."

"Ooh. Testy," Alex jests as we load another 40 pounds on the bar for his lift. "Are you sure you're not pining for some skinny?"

"You're an ass. You know that?"

CHAPTER SIX

Jason Plumin

"Mr. Plumin, can I have a word?" Tom Mitchum calls as I walk by his office on the way to my own.

"Sure."

"I've got an opportunity for you, Jason" Tom says, a slightly devilish grin creeping in. Tom is in his late 50s, a tall, tan, youthful build in contrast to a gray mop of hair betraying his years and experience. He's fit, but not bulky, with a slight pooch where an otherwise skinnier version used to sit.

"An opportunity, huh. That's never good," I reply, my own boyish grin betraying a playful acceptance.

"Are you're aware of the suicides this year?" Tom asks.

"Sure." I reply. I know there were suicides, they publish them every couple weeks, but they don't necessarily stand out as significant.

"Well," Tom continues, "they're putting together a committee to investigate. Apparently, the Council wants to make sure everything is above board."

"How does this become an opportunity for me? He asked, trepidatiously," and I did ask trepidatiously.

"They're assigning three people to a committee. A PersRep, a law enforcement type, and someone from the Station Rep's office. I'll give you three guesses who the StaRep is," Tom smiles.

I've always liked Tom Mitchum. He's been aboard since at least 2080 and was already well-respected when he migrated. Before on-boarding into a Station Rep slot he was a Sheriff's Deputy, first in the lawless Open Lands and then in the Australian Autonomous Zone when it formed. He's smart in a way that doesn't make other people seem less so and he'd bend over backwards to help someone else, anyone, really. Even his name is cool. Thomas Ansel Mitchum after the guy who did all the landscape photos. Saying no to Tom isn't an option.

On the other hand, I can't help thinking this is another exercise in wasted time. Researching suicides is like studying the flavor of recycled water—I'm sure there are reasons for variations, but in the end, we accept that it all tastes pretty much like water. Suicides happen, but confirming them as suicides isn't going to impact their frequency. Every few years the Analysis Lab will study causes, which are well documented, but the rate is built into the algorithm. What's the point of a special team?

"Of course, I'm honored," I smile, rolling my eyes. "Which LEO are they assigning to the team?"

"A woman from the OSU," Tom reads from his screen. "Deputy Kami Lee, do you know her?"

"No. Is she new?"

Tom punches a couple keys on the keyboard. "Yeah. She's only been a Deputy for about a year. Apparently, they think she's destined for good things. Here, take a look."

Tom taps a command on his virtual keyboard forcing it into a two-sided display so I can read the profile.

"Wow, graduated at the top of her class…a year early if those dates are correct." The record indicates she was born a year after her parents migrated. Her father was a botanist and mother an engineer. Apparently, the parents are no longer on board. I wonder what happened to them?

Tom clicks though to another screen. "Looks like mom died in child birth. She was 42 when she and Mr. Lee migrated to the station in 2081. Father was…56. He died in 2093, age, uh…68. Doesn't mention cause of death. Pretty common if it was not suspicious. Maybe suicide? But that would be listed."

"That would make her about…"

"21, or ten years too young for you, Mr. Plumin" Tom adds with a grin.

"It worked for her parents."

Tom scrolls down a bit further. "And there's an older brother working in the Aries Farms. Botany apparently runs in the family. He was born in 2071, before the parents migrated."

Ever since they perfected the formula for gummy supplements, the Aries Farms have become a bit of a misnomer. Really, they are small labs used for experimental vitamin supplementation and 3-D hybrid seed printing, should the planet ever recover enough to replant. But I get Tom's preference for remembering things as they were.

"So a young, over-achieving OSU Deputy with almost no experience, an older brother, and dead parents. I'm sure she'll be fun. Who's the other member?"

Tom reverts back to single-sided, leaving me with a view of blurry pixels in the shape of a screen.

"A PersRep, Brandi Mikkelson."

"Nice," I say, reflexively.

"You know her?" asks Tom.

I quash my excitement before answering. "We've met, had drinks, you know. Great reputation."

Tom smiles, "Great reputation, huh?"

I have to admit, I'm not unhappy about spending time with Brandi, even if it is part of a worthless suicide review. We already get along and occasionally spend time together after adjudicating cases, but we're not exactly what I'd consider close. Based on what I know about her—which is little—she doesn't spend much time with anyone outside of lifting weights at the HMC.

Responding to Tom's smirk, I push my face through the digital screen and add, "Yeah, she's got a solid reputation...in the PersRep's office."

CHAPTER SEVEN

Brandi Mikkelson

I bite down on the protein lozenge, hoping to crack it between my teeth before our one o'clock staff meeting. It wouldn't do to be sucking on a hard candy while discussing pending cases, but I need the boost after lifting and the sweet lozenge is more palatable than astringent chewables.

The Health Maintenance Center is a short walk from the office. Alex's rather salient points about the best jobs on the stations might be spot on. I can fit in a hard core couple hour workout just before lunch and make it back to the office in minutes. Through corridor M11, up to level K, right turn off the elevator and I'm greeting our annoyingly perky intern.

"Welcome back, Brange," Anna says. She's sitting behind a small desk typing alternatively into her ComLink and the virtual keyboard on her desk. I presume she's texting her boyfriend on one and screwing up a case file on the other. I hate when she calls me Brange.

"Thanks. Is the meeting still a go?"

"Yep. Five minutes until lift off."

Anna is a Gen, a first generation Cit. She has no idea what the world is like except for what she's read and been told by her parents who were probably trying to scare her into behaving. Don't screw up or you'll be sent to the mean, nasty planet to fend for yourself. It's a good tactic.

Her isolation aboard Aries has created a cute, flighty, sandy-blonde girl with limited perspective. She'll finish school later this year when she turns 16, at which time she'll have to complete a dream sheet and decide on a Station Role. Apparently, Anna's mom knows our Inter-station Managing PersRep, so she gets to experience Rep life part-time until she tests out of primary. She doesn't seem interested in much beyond her boyfriend's messages, but when the ISMP saddles you with a naive adolescent to learn the ropes, well, that's what you do.

"Are you joining us for the fun?" I ask, remembering she was conveniently absent from the last two meetings. Anna looks at me for a moment like I've got three breasts, her head cocked to one side reminding me of clueless puppy memes. "The meeting. Are you joining us for the staff meeting?" I repeat, slower this time.

"Right?" she replies, making her statement sound like a question unasked and as of yet, unanswered. "No. I'm meeting my boyfriend for lunch."

Of course. If her scores allow her to be a PersRep, I'm going to need to rethink the efficacy of this program. "Okay. Have fun," I reply. *Don't get pregnant,* I think heading into the conference room.

"Hi Brandi," Henry Botha greets, placing his hand over his heart. The old-school Cits are big into formality. "The meeting is just about to start."

"What's up, Henry?" I mimic the hand gesture for Botha's benefit.

"The usual. I delivered your letter to Jason."

"How did that go?"

"Fine. Plumin did his usual bit, posturing for deportation. Too bad it..."

The VizD comes to life, Marta's booming voice cutting Henry off before he can finish.

"Okay people, let's get this damn thing started. We only have a few items to review but I'd like to leave time for Q&A, should anyone have intelligent questions. I see Phil is missing. One of the Gemini clan make sure he's not dead. Mikkelson and Botha, you look like you're sitting in each other's lap. When is Aries command going to get you a bigger space?"

Our conference room *is* small. The illuminated ceiling provides plenty of light, but the grey table and chairs sit in stark contrast to absolutely nothing. The walls are a steely metallic instead of the alternative white, reflecting the light in all directions and giving us the look of sunbathers in one of the outer rim compartments. There are four chairs at the round table, but only three are useable during these staff meetings. The fourth sits at the end of the table with the wall-mounted video display behind it. Sitting at that end during a call leaves the party on the VizD looking at a large, angled head off to the side. Hence Botha and I crowding together so Marta can see us both.

"It's a good thing there are only two of us or…" I start before being interrupted.

"About that, we're working on getting you additional staff," Marta pipes in. "Two PersReps on a station with almost ten thousand Cits is ridiculous. I realize it's currently a workable caseload, but the Analysis Lab is projecting an uptick as the first Gens come of age. We're negotiating with SRB to move our posting to the top of the list, but their pushing back. I've gone over their heads to the Council and expect resolution soon."

"Bullshit," I whisper to Henry as I fake a cough. The plan to add a PersRep has been around since I migrated. First it was application errors—Marta not liking the way Henry used 'happy' instead of 'glad' in the initial posting. Then it was Station Command arguing other priorities. Marta leveraged her self-importance to move it from there. Now apparently, it's the Station Role Board—another opportunity for our supreme leader to wield her boundless influence. I'll believe we're getting another body when I see it craning it's neck to see the visual display.

"Anything you can do is much appreciated," Henry replies trying not to sound like too much of a sycophant.

"Well, it's one of my many jobs—keeping my people sufficiently staffed. I'm here for you all." Marta pauses for a moment, probably hoping someone else will recognize her sacrifice.

"Okay, then," she continues. "First order of business. The Council is issuing some revs to the practice of transiting to-slash-from the planet. And I quote: Only those with a valid TransPass and departing from their home station will be allowed on the shuttles. New passes will be limited to official business, mostly trade discussions and the transportation of people from the CAZ to the stations and—in case anyone is planning on royally fucking up—from the stations to the planet. Anyone caught attempting to access the planet from a non-home station will be subject to judgment. This is designed to curb the black market trade on the stations while not being overly cumbersome to those with a legitimate need to access the CAZs."

It's designed to make sure only the Council and their friends profit from the black market, I think to myself.

"Second, anyone transiting between stations must now avail themselves of one of the newly designed inter-station passes, also called ISPs. There have been some reports of people transiting to other stations and not returning. The new ISP is stamped with a maximum length of stay. Should someone want to remain on another station, thus upsetting the delicate life balance, the OSU can track them down, stun them, and return them to their SoR."

Yeah, I think, *people transit to other stations all the time…and they don't return because they are dead. There were twenty suicides on Aries last year, not all were Aries Cits.*

"Should there be…" Marta continues before being interrupted.

"Um, what's SoR?" asks someone on Virgo station? It must be someone new, because I don't recognize his face, which is now filling the Viz for all to see.

"Station of Record," answers Marta. "Please hold your questions until the end. Lastly, we've seen an uptick in suicides over the last twelve months. I'm still waiting on the exact count, but the Council is forming a committee to look into them, starting with this last one, a Michael Finn."

My heart almost stops. "When did Finn die?" I whisper to Henry without moving my lips.

Henry raises his hand to hide his mouth and whispers back, "Early this morning. Collecting evidence from the Ocasio kid."

"I can see you Mr. Botha," Marta chides. "Putting your hand in front of your face doesn't actually hide the fact that you're having a conversation."

"It's my fault," I respond. "I hadn't heard about Finn. Henry was just bringing me up to speed."

After a moment of silence, Marta continues, "That's all for the major announcements. Are there any intelligent questions?" There's silence while we all impatiently wait for her to wrap it up. "Okay, until next week. Remember, mitigation is the heart of the second chance." Our voices echo through the VizD in a digital chorus as everyone recites the family motto.

"What do you mean 'collecting evidence from the Ocasio kid?'" I blurt out the instant the screen goes blank.

Botha looks at me like I've asked a question for which I should know the answer. "Derek. Derek Ocasio. He killed himself last night. Jumped into a containment field. Where have you been all morning?"

Derek *and* Finn?

"Henry, how many suicides have we had in the last year?"

Henry thinks for a second before answering, ticking the names off on his fingers. "Oh, I'd say maybe twenty or thirty confirmed, not counting accidental deaths."

"Is that trending high?"

"Nope. Pretty standard, really," Henry replies.

CHAPTER EIGHT

The Collective

"Seriously, there is actually less of this guy than usual," cries Finn. "Do you think he was one of those 150 pound locker stuffers?" That's Michael Finn's term for weaklings, wimps and other less physically endowed members of his gender. Finn tells a story, the same story, in fact, every couple months about shoving Tommy whats-his-face into his locker two or three times a week during grade school. "You need to be able to take care of yourself, because nobody is going to do it for you." The irony of his position in public safety is lost on him.

I look around, admiring my choice of locations and knowing it probably won't last. Despite five suicides here in the past twelve months, including Derek, station security had yet to install cameras on the platform in EVA Bay 5. The other four Extra-vehicular Activity Bays all have cameras, although they remain absent above the containment fields. Maybe it's by design? Leave one bay camera-free so people committing suicide do it in the same place every time—cleanup is always in the same spot. The Council then uses suicides to diversify the gene pool. Every person that dies is an opportunity for a couple to have a child or for someone to migrate from the planet. Death begets life.

I walk up beside Finn on the gangway. He's quite a bit bigger than me, his suit making him seem more so. "That is quite the mess," I say. "Who do you think he was?"

"Just another loser," Finn rifles back. "Good riddance. I'll need to grab a sample to identify him. Want to do the honors?"

The honors, in this case, means climbing through the rail and dipping a portable sampler arm—a little like a long, skinny turkey baster—into Ocasio's blob to collect blood for analysis. A more svelte person could do it from the platform, but Finn's girth prevents him from getting the right angle. We could go below and open the doors, but that means the mess falling, or floating rather, into the complex, which then requires clean up. Alternatively, we can wait until the maintenance crew shuts down the field. They'll do the cleanup from the outside and Finn can grab the sample he needs for identification. But he's old school, shift ends three hours from now at 07:00, not an hour after maintenance comes on duty at 08:00.

"There is no way I'm taking this opportunity from you, not with five months until you retire," I jest, surprising myself with my sincerity.

"143 days, partner," Finn replies, simultaneously smiling and slapping my back harder than he needed. "Okay, then do me a favor and grab hold of the back of my suit."

Finn moves into position straddling the middle railing bar, his left arm extending the portable sampler into the blob. I take hold of one of the straps on the side of his suit, giving a tug to reassure him that I have a good, solid hold. He can have the sample in half a minute, one quick squeeze and release on the bulb.

I had played this moment in my head a dozen times, scripted each step, imagined every detail. The almost imperceptible hum of the comms systems, the feel of the EVA suit straps in my hand, the force needed to encourage Finn to fall, where to hold in case he reaches back for me, the time required until he contacts the array.

I shove hard as Finn is at maximum reach and the scene evolves just like it had in rehearsal. Finn, already off balance, rolls to his left from the railing. His gravity suit functions as designed, pulling him toward the outer panel—one can't discount quality engineering. He manages to look toward me and for a moment I think I see something. Is it fear? Confusion? It doesn't matter. Just like Ocasio, Finn enters the charged field array a 240 pound man and exits a bloody pool of goo.

A thought occurs to me as I admire Finn's remains. He actually got early retirement. I wonder if he appreciates what I did for him? Obviously not in his current state. But if I'd mentioned I had a plan to get him to retirement 143 days early, I'm sure he would have been all for it.

CHAPTER NINE

Brandi Mikkelson

Anna calls from her desk, having returned from her extended lunch with her boyfriend. "Brange, you have a message."

"From who?" *And stop calling me Brange. My name is Brandi, you idiot,* I think to myself.

"Marta. She said she tried your ComLink but it was DND."

Yeah, because I was in a meeting with her and didn't want the damn thing vibrating in the middle of a riveting discussion about Council policy changes. Hence, Do Not Disturb, as in, do not disturb this boring meeting.

"What do you suppose that's about?" Botha asks.

"Literally no idea," I reply, my curiosity peaked and not in a good way. "Can I use the conference room? My desk still feels claustrophobic compared to pretty much anyplace on the planet."

"Sure," Botha nods, "but I want details."

Henry leaves and I dial up Marta on the VizD, remembering to switch off Do Not Disturb on my ComLink in the hopes someone will interrupt us.

"Hello Ms. Mikkelson. Been awhile," Marta says after swinging her chair around. I start to explain my absence, but she cuts me off. "Don't worry about it. Excuses are like assholes, everybody has one and I don't want to hear from any of them."

Straight from the asshole's mouth. I'm not the only one who thinks so, either. As near as I can tell via my informal straw poll, most people only pretend to like Marta rather than end up on her shit list. She's ruthless and awful, tanking more opportunities than cancer for those who she doesn't like. She's also an unapologetic gossip, sharing the most inappropriate personal information about everyone, like or dislike, with those on her golden list. Luckily, I'm one of the trusted and I intend to stay that way.

"What is it you wanted to talk about?" I ask.

"As I mentioned," Marta continues. "The Council is setting up a committee to examine suicides and other seemingly odd deaths. They've asked for someone from our office and knowing how interested you are in new opportunities, I volunteered you."

"Can't you give it to Henry?" I snap back, "He's been…"

Marta cuts me off. "Yes, he's been around a lot longer. No, I am not going to assign Henry."

I'd like to bitch slap her every time she interrupts me. She thinks just because she manages a bunch of PersReps she can do whatever the hell she wants. She's only in charge because she was one of the first aboard and helped establish the legal system back in the day—she secured her Role by outliving her peers. On the planet she'd be just another short, heavy set, Hispanic bureaucrat with jet black hair and a witch's gray streak that runs from her forehead to the end of her braided pony tail. Instead, time-in-grade guaranteed her the role of tyrant.

I heard a rumor when I first migrated that her husband committed suicide shortly after they arrived. I have no idea if it's true, but it wouldn't surprise me. There were so few people on the stations at the time, she probably couldn't find a replacement, and now in her late sixties—although her exact age remains a mystery—nobody is willing to put up with her shit. Except for me, of course. But even I don't want an assignment to special projects.

"But there are only…" I start and end as Marta interrupts, again.

"Yes, two of you and this will take you out of circulation," she lectures, bringing my ire to a boiling point. "Listen, it's only for a week, it's my decision and it's done. You'll meet with the other two committee members tomorrow."

"And who are they?" I ask, half not wanting to know the answer and half wishing I'd stayed in bed this morning.

"Someone from the Orbital Sheriff's Unit and…"

CHAPTER TEN

Jason Plumin

"So, Jason, what has the Station Reps office got you on these days, besides the Ocasio case this morning, I mean?" Cecelia Ryan asks as she roles onto her side of the bed.

"I've got an *opportunity*," I say, adding air quotes.

"That sounds ominous."

"Yeah. I'm assigned to a team investigating suicides on Aries, if you can believe that," I answer while trying to catch my breath. This is our usual Tuesday night meeting in her HabU, as opposed to the one we had in her office this morning with Botha to dispose of the Ocasio case. It's been a regular occurrence every week for the last six months. No matter how many times I ask, Cecelia doesn't want a commitment, says I deserve someone younger, someone with less baggage and fewer years. I'm a little more flexible on the topic, but we both enjoy the distraction.

"I don't get it, Jason. Why look into suicides? They're an accepted norm for fuck's sake. The price we pay for not being on the surface… like stale air and treated water," Cecelia comments, her Aussie CAZ attitude peppering her usual Judge's lingo with expletives we don't hear except from migrants. She pulls the sheet up just past her naval, allowing the sweat on her chest to air dry.

"Agreed," I reply, pushing myself into sitting and reaching for the bootleg bourbon we poured into a shared glass. "But apparently the Council thinks the number is out of the ordinary."

I float the glass over Cecelia's lips, offering her a sip. She rolls onto her left elbow and takes the whiskey. I watch in awe as she takes a sip, catching a droplet on the side of the glass with her tongue, then pauses for a moment before swallowing. If the liquor burns going down you can't tell from watching Cecelia drink.

"How many are we talking?" She asks, handing me back the glass.

I take a sip, letting the warm liquid flow down my throat until I can feel it in my chest. "I'm not sure. I thought I read there were like 30 last year, but I'll find out tomorrow at the meeting."

Cecelia lays her head on the pillow and reaches under the sheets. "Thirty suicides per sub 10,000 Cits might have been a lot a hundred years ago, but it's par for the course on the stations," she says, her gaze into my eyes unbroken as I begin to harden.

I follow her curves, the sheet hugging her hips, her small breasts untested by age, her alabaster skin contrasting with her short, red, shoulder length hair matted from sweat and sex and the pillow, matched by the strawberry curls between her legs. In the warm glow of the HabU lights, her eyes, virescent and inviting, blend with her fiery features and slight, freckled skin to betray her Irish genes.

"Whatever it is not, I know what it is." I say, the words becoming troublesome as the blood rushes to other parts of my body.

"Yeah. What's that?" She whispers.

I tilt the glass toward her lips and she lifts her head enough to sip a bit more whiskey, rolling it around her mouth before swallowing.

"It's a chance to get in front of the Council—be known. Maybe make my way into a Clerk role."

Cecelia pushes herself up, straddling my hips and pressing my shoulders into the wall. "Jason," she says, taking the bourbon and setting it on the nightstand. "I appreciate your ambition, especially on Tuesdays."

: CHAPTER ELEVEN

Kami Lee

Kami Lee. 02:00. EVA Bay 1. Info about suicides.

I reread the encrypted message off my ComLink as I arrive at the Extra-vehicular Activities Bay. It's not signed—digitally anonymized, which takes connections or skills—and untraceable within the comms ecosystem. Feels like Council, but there's no need for anyone on the Council to contact an Orbital Sheriff's Deputy anonymously. Which leaves, what? Someone Council-connected who wants to remain anonymous? A high ranking station manager? An Ambassador?   A hacker?

Enter the EVA bay.

The message arrives midway through my list of possible senders. I eye the bay controls for a moment, wondering if anyone's ever been inside without an EVA suit when the outer doors accidentally open. I don't recall anything from Role training or primary school, but that doesn't mean it hasn't happened. It's something the Council might keep secret for fear of panicking the masses.

I depress the button on the electronic display and sense the tactile feedback built into the wall-mounted unit. The inner door whooshes open, the computer generated sound momentarily lowering my anxiety as designed—like a baby's pacifier or a thick, warm blanket. Everything on the stations was developed with a purpose. Otherwise, the door would slide open in silence and I'd hesitate before entering the bay.

Enter the EVA bay.

The repeated message arrives while I'm still considering my options. The inner wall controls are the same as those on the outer wall, except they have primacy, meant to keep someone on the outside from inadvertently activating the evacuation sequence before whoever is inside is ready. There'll be an alarm and a two-minute delay if the outer doors are opened from the panel outside the room, plenty of time to deactivate the process. I wonder if it's possible to hack the system and bypass the inner control panel, but discard the thought as unlikely. The number of safeguards in place to prevent accidental opening is ridiculous, right? I step into the bay.

The next message reads, *Close the door.*

I've come this far. If someone wanted me dead—and I can't think of any reason someone would—there are easier ways. Besides, there hasn't been a murder on the stations since…well, there's never been a murder on the stations, actually. I don't want to be the first, but I tap the controls anyway. This time the artificial whoosh does little to calm my anxiety.

The EVA bay isn't large, twenty feet long and ten feet wide with four suits hanging along one wall and various gear along the other. The outer door at the opposite end appears firmly shut, not that I'm leaving the internal panel to check it out. If it weren't sealed, I presume I'd hear something, a high-pitched whistle or another indication of air evacuating into space. I have no idea, really, since I'm not an EVA Tech and have never been outside the station, but it's what people say happens when there's a hull breach.

"The suicides are not what they seem."

A robotic voice echoes from the comms box on the wall next to the control unit. I briefly glance through the small window into the main chamber, but see only an empty corridor.

"I'm not there," it says in even tones.

Instinctively, I look toward the camera in the near corner.

"Yes, I'm watching you."

Viewing someone on a station camera isn't easy. Cameras are installed only in very specific areas, where safety trumps privacy. We live in a closed, communal society where personal space is guaranteed in the Articles of Incorporation. Someone with this kind of access is either very high up or hacked it, which also isn't simple and does nothing to narrow my list of possible senders.

"Then where are you? And how did you manage an anonymized message to my ComLink?" I ask the camera.

"That is not important. What is important is you are assigned to a team investigating suicides on Aries and I have information about those suicides."

"How do you know that? I didn't even know until this afternoon."

"Again, not important. Focus Kami. Suicides."

Focus Kami, I think to myself.

"If you know about the team then you know we haven't met, yet."

"You will meet tomorrow and discuss a plan. Your partners in this endeavor will not be convinced there is anything to investigate. In fact, you'll find the number of suicides on par with previous years. There will be little reason to think anything or anyone is behind any of the suicides."

"Except you. You know something."

"I suspect."

"You *suspect*?" I emphasize, unconvinced.

"I believe the number of suicides should not be as high as it is."

"And why is that?" I ask.

"Initial Population Integration was almost thirty years ago. The Council understood some migrants would lack the ability to adapt to the close quarters, artificial air and few natural surroundings. An acceptable level of suicides was predicted, as was an eventual decline as generations were born on the stations and Cits acclimated to the new living conditions. Despite an entire generation coming of age there hasn't been a drop in the number of suicides."

"Wait, so because people haven't adapted at the rate the Council predicted there must be another explanation? Some metric didn't turn green within the prescribed timeframe, so we need to investigate? Honestly, I'm not sure I'll disagree with my two partners tomorrow."

There's a long silence, long enough to make me wonder if he's logged off. The only group connected enough to make murders look like suicides is the Council, but they are also the last people I'd believe capable of killing. I've been onboard almost my entire life and the Council has always made decisions to the benefit of the Cits, without question. And yet here I am responding to anonymized messages on an encrypted channel and listening to a modified voice in Bay 1, all indications of someone with Council-level access.

"Are you still there?" I ask.

"Yes."

"Let's say you're right. What is it you want me to do?"

"Do your job. Investigate." The response is cold, even for a robot.

"And the other two people on the team? What about them?"

"I have no information about their involvement other than they were selected, like you, by the Council. But you can't share this conversation with anyone. You'll need to figure this out on your own. You can't trust anyone until you know the truth."

"And if you're wrong?" I ask.

There is another lengthy silence while I look into the still empty corridor.

"I'm not."

CHAPTER TWELVE

Jason Plumin

"You want coffee?" I ask Cecelia as she tentatively crosses the heated floor into what would have been a kitchen on earth but is now simply an integrated part of the HabU experience. The mornings after Tuesday nights are a touch of comfort mixed with bittersweet future, a bit like the sugar I add to the two cups from the wall-mounted machine. There's little need for HabU food prep when almost everyone eats communally—if you can call chewing a couple food gummies eating—but we maintain a few traditions, like integrated coffee and tea dispensers. Cecelia doesn't care for tea, something I discovered after our first night together.

She must have changed in the middle of the night. Sleeping naked is not Cecelia's thing, although I get the feeling it was when she was younger and perhaps a bit more carefree. I didn't notice her get up last night, but the pajamas look good, her splashing red hair a fiery auburn against the white.

"What time did you get up?" I ask.

"Not long after," she replies, tentatively touching the hot mug to her lips. "I had a few things to do."

"I didn't feel anything."

"Then I must have done a good job," Cecelia says smiling over the cup.

"Are you heading to the cafeteria later? Maybe we can get together this evening?" I ask, pretty sure of the answer.

"I don't think so. I pulled a pass and a week's rations. I've got a lot going on this week."

An overly solitary existence is socially discouraged, which is why

Cecelia needs the pass to spend multiple nights away from the community. She'd be fine for a couple days, but soon after she'd find a Welfare Specialist at the door asking questions about her mental state, followed by a rather lengthy report detailing how her desire to avoid people might be a manifestation of anti-social behavior complicated by a lack of physical stimulus. This all culminates in a non-binding recommendation to attend one or more groups filled with the people you were trying to avoid. If I sound like voice of experience, it's because I've been there.

I migrated to the stations with my parents in 2078, during IPI. Even at eight years old, I understood the significance of leaving the planet and it's disease, decrepit quarters, and the fear your child might get knifed on the playground. The stations offered opportunities, clean facilities, and few worries, all worth the tradeoffs—smaller living spaces and gummies in place of solid food.

My parents, Evacuation Specialists, were responsible for maintaining the various ingress and egress point on the station. Both died the year I bid for Station Rep. Something went wrong during a routine airlock upgrade causing the door to cycle. The rumor mill suggested it was on purpose, they overrode the safety blasting both of them into space. It's possible, I suppose. I don't recall them ever being truly happy on Aries. But the OSD ruled it an accident.

A few years into the Station Rep role I'd had enough of people's mistakes, so I holed up in my room for a few days with a handful of food gummies, a bottle of bootleg vodka, and an intent to game until my eyes bled. That same week Hardcore Studios released a major update to their new massive multiplayer game *Universe Unfolded*, along with an inter-station competition to see whose team could control the galaxy. Two days later I was knee deep in a mission to annex Saturn from a rogue alien civilization when a WelSpec buzzed my HabU to make sure I was okay. I'd neglected to get the required permit.

It wasn't a breakdown. I didn't want to kill myself—only those assigned to defend Saturn and deny us our rightful victory. As ironic as it sounds, I just needed a little space in a tiny space. The new downloadable content served up a plausible and enjoyable reason to disconnect. I'd spent years supplanting dreadful memories of the planet with a few softened by time. I didn't want to go back, no way, but there was a sense, an illusion of having room to grow without the routine of station life. I just wanted some alone time and a chance to kill the invading Pisceans.

We make our way over to the bed. "So, today's the big day, huh?" Cecelia invites with just a hint of sarcasm while extending the dinette table in place of the now stowed bed. Cecelia has a single, as opposed to the 12-by-20 double HabUs reserved for those with a child. There is precious little room, so most things serve more than one purpose, the bed becoming a dinette when people aren't sleeping…or having sex.

The table also doubles, or triples as a desk. Hidden within the tempered glass surface are terminals—one for a single or two if you're legally coupled. When activated, one can work at the table or project the image onto a larger visual display. The rest of the HabU houses ComLinks, wireless, under-surface charging stations, a wall-sized VizD for station broadcasts, the obligatory coffee, tea, and hydro dispensers, and various areas to store the small number of personal items allowed on board. It's a brilliant use of space in space.

"The big day?" I wonder, confused.

"The suicide review board. Your big chance to impress the Council. The beginning of the end of our Tuesday nights."

"Oh, yeah." I reply as I activate the visual display. "We have a meeting this morning."

The VizD pops to life just as a broadcaster is finishing a review of protocols to follow in the event of a sun spot. Of the five VizD options, Info—the latest station news—is the most popular, second only to Games. Entertainment comes in a close third. It allows users to select digitally entertaining, pre-approved fictional cinema produced between 1930 and 2032, the year the last movie was made in Hollywood and the breakdown in society started to impact personal gratification. Scenes is rarely used. People find the visuals of earth less inspirational and more depressing than the designers hoped. Comms —video communications—became obsolete with the ComLink upgrade two generation ago. It's also possible to buy a chip from a guy on Gemini and get a few pirated stations from the planet, but it's not worth the ass pain if you're caught boosting.

Usually news on the stations isn't very exciting. There are occasional stories about the planet, usually how screwed up it is, clips of station system status, and feel good stories about station life. There's no weather report because the weather doesn't change in space. There are no talking heads discussing politics or climate change—neither of those exist on the stations. If there's an emergency the VizD powers up automatically to share important information, like when there's a solar flare requiring sheltering within a radiation containment zone. Otherwise people don't expect to see much. This morning is different.

"Did you see…" Cecelia starts before noticing the broadcast on the VizD. A pale newscaster with dirty blond hair and a smile at odds with the story announces the suicide.

We have another death on the stations. Sometime early this morning, Nigel Birmingham, one of the original migrants and designer of the station Health Maintenance Centers, hung himself from the showers behind his office. A Cit found him early this morning after completing a lengthy cardio session.

"At first, I was shocked. One minute I'm running through the virtual woods of old Deschutes and the next I'm staring at this naked guy in the shower. His body was all shriveled, like someone had soaked him overnight in water—at first, I wasn't even sure it was human. Then, when I poked his…"

The reporter interrupts before we hear what the witness poked. *No one was seen coming or going while he was at the HMC. His death is being considered a suicide by the Aries Orbital Sheriff's Unit. They're asking for anyone with information about Mr. Birmingham or his mental status to contact them.*

"See," I say. "Another suicide."

"Yes, but it's a suicide," Cecelia retorts, unashamed of sounding a bit callous.

"The Council wants a review and I'm going to give them the best damn review they've ever seen."

"How long is this exercise in futility supposed to take?" Cecelia doesn't look up from whatever she's reading when she poses the question.

"We have a week to present initial findings and a few extra days for the written. We're only looking into the most recent ones, those from this calendar year. We're supposed to present preliminary findings Tuesday, one week from yesterday."

"Honestly, that seems like more time than you need," Cecelia adds.

"Oh, don't get me wrong. I think it's total BS. I can't imagine anything coming of this. But I'll take the recognition. I'm sure I can parlay this into a Council Clerk role, or even a station Ambassador."

"Ambassador, whoa? It's going to be awful challenging keeping up this relationship if you're jetting off to Council meetings and negotiating scientific policy on the planet. I'll be lucky to have you once every couple months," Cecelia says, her foot rubbing the inside of my leg beneath the table.

"Oh, don't you fret about that. I'll make time to meet with my constituents, especially the ones as adept at wielding their influence as you. There is no way I'm letting Tuesdays slip away."

There's a brief silence as we both consider whether we've taken the conversation too far. Cecelia occasionally lets go, allowing her feelings to peep through, but she quickly returns to practicality.

"So, who's on this suicide team?" she asks, taking a sip from her cup.

"A newer deputy, Kami Lee, and that PersRep, Brandi Mikkelson."

"Brandi, huh?" Cecelia replies, lifting her gaze from her ComLink so she can see my reaction, her foot stopping between my legs just above the knee.

"What's that supposed to mean? 'Brandi, huh?'" I playfully protest.

Cecelia smiles, "I'm just wondering if our weeklies are going to become bi-weeklies even sooner than your planned Ambassadorship?"

"Please, I'm too busy. My caseload is unyielding. You're not the only Judge I see." I realize immediately what I said, even without Cecelia's *'Is that so'* glance. "You know what I mean."

"I'm just saying," she replies, her foot sliding into my crotch. "She's attractive, engaging and the right age, gender, and intellectual demographic. If she turns out to be something more than an investigative partner, it's fine by me. Just leave Tuesday's open."

"You can be exhaustingly analytical sometimes," I note, rolling my eyes.

"What time is your meeting?" she asks.

"A couple hours...11:00."

"Good," she says, standing and reaching for the bed switch. "Then we have some time."

CHAPTER THIRTEEN

Brandi Mikkelson

"He's late," I call to Botha.

"Only a minute," replies a young, peppy twenty-something girl with jet-black hair tied into a pony tail extending to the middle of her shoulder blades. "Hi, I'm Kami Lee, OSU."

"Brandi Mikkelson. Nice to meet you, *kay-me*," I say, making sure I caught the pronunciation correctly. I can't help notice she's uncommonly tall for an Asian, probably three inches taller than me and I'm five-four. She has a distracted smile and slender, edged lines visible even in her standard issue tan uniform, none of which changes my rule about disliking everyone on first meet.

"I guess I should make a mental note about being tardy," Kami says, glancing at her ComLink to check the time.

"I was talking about Plumin, the Station Rep. He's late."

"Only a few minutes," Kami comments, taking the seat across from me at the table. "What do you do when you're not keeping track of time?"

She's still sporting a cutesy simper, perhaps an attempt to disarm potential critics. It doesn't work. She reminds me of Anna and the entitlement of Gens and their carefree, born-in-space, spunky station-baby attitude—sheltered to the point of coyly annoying. A decade more experience and a planet-side education have earned me the right to be impatient with anyone I choose, but especially sarcastic tweens. I consider for a moment how much trouble I'd get into if I pop her in the mouth and whether her smile might fade on impact, but decide to take her remark as playful—which I hate more than sarcasm—and leave it lie for now.

"Work is my life," I reply, sardonically. Kami looks hurt. "How long have you been a Deputy?"

"About a year. It was my first choice on the dream sheet. I know almost everyone gets their first choice, but you never know. There are stories. People who didn't place for the role they were hoping, or whose preferred choice was further down the list. They might spend an entire career doing something they hate. OSD was an excellent fit for my scores and all, but there's always that chance you'll get number two or three, which I would have been perfectly happy with, but Deputy was number one. Probably all luck."

Kami's answer and more pointedly her lack of brevity leaves me afraid to ask another question. I can't tell if her teenage chattiness comes naturally or is an attempt to over-compensate for a personality trait for which she was not endowed, like faking extroversion. In my experience, the skinny, athletic types with no expertise tend to drone on because they have little else to offer at this stage of life. I can't imagine she's even any good in bed.

I realize I've missed my opportunity to circumvent the conversation when she glances briefly at her ComLink, then continues.

"You know, he is a little late. I wouldn't call it rude, necessarily. What do you suppose is keeping him? I suppose it could be something important. Is he normally late to meetings, because I can understand a couple minutes, but it's been almost five minutes now and we have a fair amount to do."

"I've worked with Jason a few times and he's always late and it is *always* annoying," I pipe in when she takes a breath.

The first case we shared was about two years ago. A woman had picked up over-ration bootlegged booze and run nude through the stations chanting, "Take me naked freedom!" It took Deputies almost an hour to corner her and another ten minutes to wrap her in a blanket. She'd been on board for 14 years, migrating with her parents when she was 12. Space, or perhaps a lack thereof, finally got the best of her. It happens sometimes with people who migrate as children. They've seen the world, but don't remember the hardships as vividly, their young minds replacing trauma with happy coping memories. They can have trouble adapting. I'm surprised she didn't commit suicide.

I argued mitigation on the basis of her track record and an exemplary employment history within the Astro-Physiology Lab. It was her job to design new and interesting ways in which people might adapt to life in space—ironic, I know. She redesigned the evacuation suits to include an exoskeleton which keeps the whole thing from crumpling. Before the structure was incorporated into the suits, people transitioning from zero-G to the gravity field on board and vice-versa ended up with everything from bruised shoulders to broken collar bones. She also developed Spongy Keys, a faux electronic keyboard incorporated over the digital keys on the ComLink, thinking people wanted something soft to touch. It didn't take off and I left it out of the argument.

Plumin was decent about the mitigation—a short stint in group and nothing more. He didn't even put up an argument. The judge, an attractive red head named Ryan, found her guilty and that was it, done and done. It didn't make sense until I learned Plumin also migrated when he was a child. Maybe we'll find him running naked through the corridor someday, or lying dead in his HabU after realizing all those buried memories were bull and the confines of space are more confining than he realized.

"I wouldn't worry about it, I add. "He's never more than a few minutes behind schedule."

"Oh, good," Kami replies.

Before she can formulate the rest of a response, I add, "Jason and I have adjudicated a number of cases and spend a bit of time afterwards in the cantina. His tardiness notwithstanding, he's generally a decent Station Rep—smart, jovial, not hard on the eyes, you know the type." *Although I doubt she does know the type.*

"That's good to know," Kami replies and stops. I get the feeling she's becoming more comfortable, allowing a bit of silence to take root rather than filling every minute of air time. Perhaps my initial impression was off—it might have been nerves.

"Either way," I say, "he's late. Perhaps we should start without him."

CHAPTER FOURTEEN

Jason Plumin

"Thanks for joining us, Jason." Brandi Mikkelson greets, her sarcasm shining like the light at the end of a tunnel. She and who I presume is Kami Lee sit on adjoining sides of a table in the small, non-discreet conference room where a large VizD blankets the opposite wall.

"I can't believe I'm late. That never happens," I say, adding my own dash of snarkiness. It's difficult to feign genuine regret. Rarely do Tuesday nights become Wednesday mornings with Cecelia. I'd like to think she is warming to the idea of taking the relationship to the next level, but she was pretty clear this morning when I brought it up. *Can we please move on…and I mean to the bed, not in our relationship.*

"Nice to see you, Jason. It would have been nicer fifteen minutes ago," Brandi replies.

I wonder if she'd be more forgiving if she knew why I was late. I'm guessing not, based on the rumors. I have no problem with her sexual orientation. In fact, it's tacitly encouraged to some extent on the stations—same sex couples never have unauthorized children and can always procreate with donor supplies. Plus, she's a great PersRep. I wouldn't necessarily refer to her as easy going, that CAZ-borne attitude follows some people aboard when they migrate. But she's far more forgiving of the victims of station life she defends than I am. I'd be lying if I said I don't also enjoy her edgy, acerbic wit, even when it's aimed in my direction.

I just think it's a bit of a shame for those of us heteros still looking. Brandi isn't a super model, but she's got something. Dark brown hair waving just below the shoulders, matching brown eyes and combination sexy-serious smile, slightly turned up at the edges when she knows she's got one on you, it's disarming. It makes her seem playful, even though Brandi is anything but. Sure, at a lean 5-foot-4 she could probably bench press me, maybe even break me in half. I take it back—maybe her sexual orientation is for the best.

"Yeah, sorry about that," I reply with a smile that I hope won't give away my secret. "I was in the middle of something and couldn't tear myself away."

"I'll just bet," Brandi replies.

Wanting to dissipate some of the tension, I ask, "Is that someone new at the front desk? The perky blonde who doesn't look up from her ComLink while asking questions? She seems a little young to be working intake at the PersReps office."

Brandi glances over her left shoulder at the receptionist. "Yeah, she's interning. Hasn't graduated, yet. And if by young you mean disinterested, you'd be correct."

Brandi's known to be a little hard on interns. The joke among the community is if Brandi likes you, it's only because she hasn't worked with you. But in this case, I get the feeling her disdain is warranted.

"Well, at least you have some help around here, you know, keeping track of everything."

"Right. Help. That's exactly how I'd describe it." This time Brandi's trademark sarcasm is unmistakable.

"Um, hi. I'm Kami. Kami Lee," says a fit woman with pony-tailed black hair across the table. She stands briefly, indicating the standard greeting with her hand over her heart, a sign she was either born on Aries or migrated very young.

I make a mental note, it's *Kay-me*, not *Cam-me*. "I'm Jason. Jason Plumin from the Station Rep's office. Nice to meet you." I repeat *Kay-me* in my head, hoping to associate it with a physical feature or some inanimate object to help me remember, but nothing comes to mind.

I take a seat across from Kami and to Brandi's left and lay my MiniComp on the table. Brandi and Kami do the same, tapping them to activate the terminals. I notice none are upgraded, all three last generation HuangWei Technologies MiniComp Model A5 portable laptops with virtual touch screen displays and tactile keyboards, all packed into a pocket-sized, two ounce form factor. HWT, formerly a Chinese company, is now the sole supplier of technology aboard the stations.

I press my index finger against the A5 and watch as the digital keyboard appears and the virtual screen flashes open—a greeting on the screen welcome's me, *Hello Jason.* The computer boots to the main screen. Security measures are DNA-based, I could have laid my Johnson on the thing and it would have booted up, but given present company it didn't seem prudent. "So, where are we?" I ask.

"We've got what the Council considers an excessive number of unnatural deaths so far this year. Eight to be exact," Brandi replies. "Apparently we need to investigate them."

"Nine as of last night," Kami pipes in. "A designer at the HMC. I'm heading over there after this meeting."

"Nine doesn't seem like a lot to me," I add. "If we trend that out, it only puts us at about 30-40 for the year. Okay, so maybe slightly higher, but that includes accidentals, right?"

"Are you running the investigation at the Health Maintenance Center?" Brandi asks Kami, ignoring my question.

Kami smiles. My guess is she's picked up on Brandi's implication about her experience and age. Kami looks to be quite young—I'd guess early twenties, but Asian Cits can appear far younger than they are.

"No, I was asked to stop by since I'm on this team. Since the Council's involved, the OSU wants to make sure everything is done by the book."

"Did you know him? Birmingham?" I wonder. I expect Brandi to say yes, since she's a regular at the gym.

"I served as his Personal Rep about six months ago."

"What did he do?" I ask, surprised.

"He took photos of adults in the locker room using a portable, ceiling-mounted camera. It seemed like it was going to be a pretty big issue, Violation of Article I: Privacy First. Then someone from Gemini called explaining there was compelling mitigation. I never got the details—I was just instructed to meet with the Station Rep's office and everything would be handled. Before I had the chance, I heard another Rep, someone from outside Aries, had already cut an acceptable deal and discussed it with the judge, so my part was over before it began."

That's odd, I think to myself. It was uncommon for Station Reps from other stations to work cases outside their space, and I've never heard of one offering mitigation, that's the PerRep's job.

"Do you know which Rep or which station?"

"No. Above my pay grade, apparently," Brandi replies with just a hint of derision.

"What did Birmingham get?" Kami asks.

"Um…" Brandi starts, tapping something into her MiniComp.

"Probation? Group? I'm not exactly sure. The file isn't available."

Admittedly, I'm interested, but not sure I want to dig any deeper. The whole thing smells like Council. Besides, he committed suicide, making the entire discussion moot. Unless…

"Were you in any of the photos he took?" I ask, unable to control my own satirical grin.

"That would be unlikely," Brandi replies, slyly. "Birmingham preferred men."

"Crap. Was I in any of them?"

Brandi's eyebrows raise and I wonder if we didn't just have a moment, but I let it go.

"Maybe we should head over together," Kami says, clearing her throat. "Our first case review."

"That should be our general game plan," Brandi follows. "A review of the nine identified cases, along with a scrub for any commonalities, and interviews of associates."

"And links to other stations," Kami adds.

Starting to feel left out, I offer, "And a review of personnel records?"

Kami looks around the room at the blank walls and VizD, "Can we use this as a base of operations?"

"It shouldn't be a problem," Brandi answers.

"We should probably make a list of the suicides and 'suspicious' deaths and divvy up the work." I throw in a set of air quotes around the word *suspicious* for affect.

Kami glances at her ComLink, "Perhaps later? We should get over to the HMC before they clean everything up."

"Sounds like a plan," Brandi and I both say simultaneously, giving each other knowing looks like we're part of an inside joke that doesn't actually exist.

CHAPTER FIFTEEN

The Collective

Nigel Birmingham is an ass. Not just because he is creepy in a way that makes me want shower after talking to him, but because his obsession with taking photographs of naked males in the gym is indicative of deeper personality defects. How someone like that ends up on the stations is a mystery. I'm going to enjoy killing him, not that I can't say the same about everyone else. They all deserve it.

In Birmingham's case, as in every other if I'm doing my job, it's a matter of planning. I know about his fondness for men and cameras, the former inconsequential and the latter a dip into the murky pool of voyeurism. But when my anonymous handler sent me a file describing his other flaws and his overwhelming influence, well, add that to his extremely light sentence from the photos and the decision was made—he will be a satisfying removal from the station population. Once settled on the idea, I just needed him in the right place at the right time with an offer he considered too good to pass up.

Nigel, any chance you want to get together later? I have a proposition. He's surprisingly easy to manipulate for someone so depraved. See, his latest indiscretion was not his only one, nor even his most vile. He'd taken to blackmail for sex, boys and girls. So, when I dangled access to certain easily manipulated targets, his interest piqued. Being the greedy, freaky fuck he was, I was surprised it took as many months as it did to convince him.

Birmingham lived a charmed life. Selected for the stations early in IPI, he formally immigrated in the beginning of 2076. The son of a wealthy British politician, he'd made a name for himself as a fitness guru to the technorati who paid a lot to keep from looking like global warming had been having its way with them for the last 40 years. His mother's connections as a whore—excuse me, politician—kept him in front of all the right people until in his mid-thirties when he was asked to design the station fitness regimen and facilities. He moved aboard Aries, responsible for the HMCs on every station. His mother wasn't invited.

Health and fitness are priorities on the stations. During the early years of selection, you could migrate and be a little soft around the edges. They were desperate back then and finding people physically fit, emotionally stable, mentally robust, and intellectually high performing was like searching for an honest man in Gomorrah. Since health problems drain resources, people were encouraged to maintain a sound mind-body balance, but encouragement rarely works without incentive. Eventually, a decision was made toward the end of IPI and the rule was codified: Only persons meeting both physical and mental standards would be allowed to migrate to the stations. In other words, fat people need not apply.

It's not as dystopian as it sounds. Nobody is expelled for being overweight. Everyone is genetically screened nowadays, so there is little chance anyone is going to plump up after migrating. Plus, people want to be healthy and we all have the time. HMC allotments are as prolific as rations. Everyone eats right—not that there's a choice with those gummies—and everyone, *literally everyone* spends time on fitness. It's like the 1980s aerobics trend, only with less hair and no leggings.

"So, what did you want to discuss?" Birmingham asks as I enter his office. "And so early in the morning. I'm intrigued."

I remove my cap and tuck it into the pocket at the small of my back. "I think it's time we move our relationship to the next level. We both have needs and I think we can satisfy them together."

Birmingham grins, "Do tell." He gets up and moves around his desk, leaning on the edge and folding his hands in his lap. I can't help wonder if he's hiding something he doesn't want me to notice. He's dated, 63 according to his file, but in good shape. His hair, cut close, is still a light brown with just a touch of silver along the edges. He's not small, over six feet, and lean in a way that announces he cares about his looks more than most. His uniform fits well without revealing too much or too little. I imagine him sitting on a Council in some far off star system commanding underlings dressed in togas to do his bidding. His face is clean and cut with geometry in all the right places.

Birmingham's responsibilities give him unfettered access to inter-station travel, a rare luxury among the population. It's rumored he keeps lovers on all eleven stations, from Aries to Virgo. He'd probably have one on Leo, too, if he could figure out a way to get on board the burned out hull without drawing suspicion.

His ability to travel is what makes Birmingham influential. He knows people throughout the station system—ambassadors, Council members, department heads, station management, lab administrators. He leverages his inter-station Cit access to get people what they want, who then get him what he wants. According to the file, he's been playing at this since before he migrated. There are few he hasn't befriended.

There's little risk in killing Birmingham compared to the other so called suicides. Sure, he's protected by someone, or perhaps more than one someone. He's been able to run unencumbered for decades, trading a travel pass for favors. But I think most will be happy to see him go, happy to sacrifice one supply chain for another less likely to expose their proclivities. His death may piss a few off, perhaps a Council member or even someone in my chain. But nobody is going to risk exposure by pressuring an investigation. No, he'll die assisting the cause with little fanfare.

"Here's the thing," I start. "I can get you access to the people you are most interested in meeting. Not just digital access, either. The real thing." *Of course, I can't get him access to shit and wouldn't even if I could. But he knows my Station Role and can use his imagination to fill in the gaps.*

"And how are you going to do that?" He proffers.

Shit. I guess he can't use his imagination to fill in the gaps.

"You know my SR. I meet people all the time in need of favors, people willing to trade. It's not rocket science, it's economics." I don't want to give him any more than necessary. For one thing, I don't actually have details. Can I get him access to willing young men? Sure, if I want to. I know plenty of people who wouldn't mind spending time with a distinguished, older pedophile asshole. But the thought of helping him in any way forces a tiny bit of vomit into my throat.

"And what is it I can do for you?" he asks, his hands shifting over his crotch.

"You have unencumbered access to the other stations."

"And what is it you need transported between the stations?" Birmingham shifts, his left foot now crossed over his right.

"Let's just say our needs are not so dissimilar."

"I'm actually more flexible than people think, if you know what I mean," he replies. "Preference does not overrule access."

"No," I say, confused, "I don't know what you mean."

"You know, I enjoy seeing you in the gym. You should come more often, maybe in the evenings." The more excited he becomes, the less he can control his body language. He uncrosses his legs, allowing his feet to extend a bit further from the desk. I watch as his shoulders ease back, pushing his chest forward until his cupped hands become uncomfortable and fall to his side, exposing the erection he's been concealing. When he pushes off the desk to stand, I'm torn between menacing and commanding. In either case, I'm going to need him compliant for this to work. He's too big a man to go toe-to-toe. I should have stopped in to see Ocasio's mom today.

After a moment, Birmingham moves toward me, sliding his hand behind my head and pulling my lips toward his. Instinctively, I pull back, hoping he isn't scared off by my hesitation. "Wait," I say, just before our lips touch.

"I think we should confirm our compatibility," he says, so close I can feel his warm breath on my lips and smell the sweet odor of candied dust from the food gummies and boozy poteen from his liquor ration. He inhales, drawing in a full, metered breath that pushes his chest to mine, allowing the prolonged exhale to span the silence. His eyes are narrow, his pupils dilated, and I can feel his heart pounding against my chest. It's not confidence, it's concern. He's attempting to feign control of a situation he knows might break bad, wondering where this is going and whether he's made a huge mistake. He doesn't know it, but he's given me the opening I need.

I take a step back toward the door. "This way," I say, turning to leave his office. I don't look back. I don't need to. I can hear his encouraged footsteps, feel his anticipation on the back of my neck.

We walk down the hall to the shower room. The HMC is eerily quiet this time of night, peaceful and humming with the sound of machines and potential energy. Like runners set to explode at the start of a race, it's as if the station can sense what's about to happen, pleading for the pistol and the gates to swing open.

Birmingham follows me into the shower room, allowing the door to swoosh closed behind him. His uniform does nothing to hide his excitement. I step toward him, forcing my hand onto his cock and placing the other on his shoulder to hold him at bay. I want him to know who's in charge. This is my world. I created this moment and he will not take it from me. He is owed nothing but justice.

His breathing increases, shallower. His eyes shut and his head tilts back as I move around him, allowing my right hand to glide forcefully over his crotch. I can feel him pulsing, giving up on control and embracing acceptance. He doesn't notice me pull the paracord from my pocket. I press my body against his back, feeling his head tilt further, begging for what is to come. I almost laugh out loud when I notice the tiny specs of dandruff on his collar. I consider dragging this out, prolonging the power, but I know it's almost over.

Birmingham lets out a long, throaty sigh as I squeeze his balls, his face pointing toward the ceiling, and I know it's time. When I slip the knotted cord over his head and around his neck, he doesn't even flinch. He just whispers, "Yes."

I grip the cord with my left hand and pull, gently at first as he begs for more, my other hand still massaging his crotch. He notices too late my knee in the small of his back, the noose tightening around his neck, his chest pressed against the wall. I can't tell if he's confused or scared as his hands reach first for his throat and then for me. He's strong, but off balance, unable to gain leverage and fading fast.

I drive my knee forward, pulling with my left hand and bracing my right on his shoulder, levering his bent legs and the pronounced arch in his back. I've killed enough people. I understand the dynamics. But the silence always surprises me. The classic movies show a violent struggle, the victim fighting for their life, furniture breaking, a glass knocked from the counter and crashing against a tile floor. But the reality is slow and smooth—one quiet, calm, controlled instant. And in that moment, the second between life and death, the only thing real is my heart trying to cleaver itself from my body. Then it's over.

I hoist his lean body up high enough on the wall to tie off the paracord to the shower head. They'll say he was depressed, even though there's no solid evidence. People who commit suicide are always depressed about something and the people around them are always surprised. They invent signs—trips to other stations, late hours alone in his office, secretive calls during the day, missing minutes. They should have known.

I take a step back, admiring my work, prideful and...something else. A new feeling, yearning, no, arousal. I didn't think it was possible, but there's no other word for it. It's warm and exciting and confusing—a whirling tornado of emotional high watching him hanging against the wall. I reach into the front of my jumpsuit, down into my underwear and find it damp. Shame should accompany my surprise, but no. I feel strong, powerful, unstoppable.

I spray the DNA neutralizer into the air as I back out of the room, giving a last glance at Birmingham. His back is flat to the wall, legs straight out in front of him, hanging from the cord like a marionette waiting to be placed into service. Everything is perfect.

The HMC is still buzzing when I walk into the main bay, potential replaced by the smell of cleaning solution, the chill of recycled air, and muted beeps. Tomorrow it will be bustling with activity, but tonight it's mine. I want to jump on a tread and run a few miles, but I can't. I can only revel, having created an opportunity for someone else.

CHAPTER SIXTEEN

Kami Lee

The door to the HMC slides open as we approach, revealing an OSU deputy assigned to police incoming and outgoing traffic. I can't remember his name for the life of me. Karl something, uh, Polish, I think. I'll wing it.

"Hi Karl. How's it going?" I say, confident I've confused him with someone else.

"Hey Kami. You working this one?"

I'm surprised he remembers my name. I've only been with the Sheriff's unit for a year. I'm not sure if that's good or bad. We're not a huge crew, but there are enough deputies spread across shifts that it would be easy to forget someone's name you only met once. Case in point, Karl's last name continues to elude me. At least I got his first name right. Otherwise, I'd need to revert to an exhausting mix of apologies, awkwardness and self-deprecating, hopefully humorous excuses.

"Nah, just here on behalf of the Council," I reply. "Some special project. What's the story?"

Karl nods toward my two comrades standing behind me.

"Oh, sorry." I turn half a tick and make introductions. "This is Jason Plumin, Station Reps office, and Brandi Mikkelson, PersRep. They're here to help," I say, shooting them a smirk and hoping they get the joke.

Karl nods, "Nice to meet you," then turns back toward me as if the small gesture will keep Brandi and Jason from overhearing his answer. "It looks like your standard suicide, nothing special or out of the ordinary, but you'll have to check with Kornel in the showers for the official report. He's examining the body now."

"They decided not to shut the place down, huh?" I ask Karl, motioning toward all the people working on their fitness.

"Nope," Karl replies. "No need, really. This stuff is so common, people don't even bat an eye anymore. Just the showers are off limits until they're done. Or you're done."

"Okay. Let's catch up on the way out. I want to see Dr. Kornel before he finishes the prelims."

I shoot a beckoning glance toward Jason and Brandi and head toward the shower room. I overhear Jason and Brandi thank Karl as they pass.

We have to walk along the length of the HMC parallel to the activity to get to the locker room. It's buzzing with people and sweat—weights clanging, cables clicking, feet thumping against treadmill platforms—it sounds like a factory floor, except these assemblers are producing wellness. The only silent section is a room in the far corner where three people are doing yoga. We pass as they enter downward dog, their butts in the air, tiny calve muscles twitching. One of the participants follows us as we pass behind them, his eyes tracking us from the inside of one knee to the other.

"Are you a yoga girl, Kami?" Brandi asks.

"Sure. But not in here. Too many people. Yoga is for the HabU, not the HMC."

I pause as we leave the main corridor and enter the hallway, noticing the door to the locker room on the left and another, probably Birmingham's office, at the end. "How about you?" I ask.

"A bit," Brandi replies. "Enough to keep from becoming unrecognizable."

"Shit. She's strong as an ox." Jason chimes. "I've seen you lifting. You're in world class shape."

"You obviously put in a little time at the gym, too, Kami," Brandi says, ignoring Jason. "I've seen you doing circuits and running—fast and graceful."

"Yeah, a bit," I reply distracted as we enter the shower room.

The communal shower room is a small, clean, unadorned circular facility. The entrance is at the end with the only straight section of wall, the door sliding closed after we enter. It makes a sound like a mother comforting her child—a gentle, 'shush.' The arching white wall bends around from one side of the entry way to the other, divided up by half panels that start a couple feet off the floor and terminate at neck height.

They are made of a rigid polycarbonate, also white. Between each set of dividers is a shower head with a small button, a shoulder height soap dispenser fed by reservoirs within the walls, and a waterproof drawer that slides out to dispense absorbent microfiber towels, about two-feet long by one-foot wide.

Nigel is laying on his back in the middle of the room, shriveled, pale and lifeless. There is a small bit of black line, perhaps paracord, tied to one of the shower heads and another small pile on the floor. Other than the body, the room is impeccably clean. Hospital white walls, white stall separators, even the drain is white. The entire place smells like the med lab, sterile almost to the point of nauseating. I glance up at the sanitizing unit mounted to the ceiling and wonder if it's been working overtime.

"Don't worry," a familiar voice calls from my left, possibly noticing my raised eyes. "It's been temporarily disabled. It won't resume normal operations until we clear the room." In his mid-sixties, Dr. Kornel Lento, the chief medical examiner and one of the medics assigned to Aries walks over and kneels beside the body.

"Hey Doc. How's Bhavna?"

"She's good. She'd love to see you more often," Kornel replies. "She's trying to get me to take up Cribbage or some such nonsense. Forty years and she's still preoccupied with relationship growth. Keeps telling me we'll become stagnant if we aren't constantly recreating ourselves."

"Well, growth is good, Doc," I reply. "We're just here on a Council project looking into suicides on the station, which I presume is what we're seeing here?"

Kornel glances up with a big, toothy smile, "Looks like."

One of the first migrants during Initial Population Integration, Kornel is quintessential IPI with his laid back manner, the Canada patch on his uniform, and jowled cheeks below a full head of unkempt gray hair like someone dunked him into a wash station. He has deep, blue eyes and an unpretentious style that immediately puts people at ease. He's the most grounded person I know, which is in no small part because of his wife, Bhavna. Together, they've served as my de facto parents for the last ten years.

Kornel is what's known as an Advocate, someone assigned to raise children orphaned on the stations. He knew my father when he died and volunteered when my brother didn't step up, seeing me through the four years leading up to SR Bid and into OSU classes when I turned 17. I'm sure he's a little disappointed I selected Orbital Sheriff's Deputy outside the Bid recommendations, especially since I matched for any of the physician subs, but he's never shown it. His only advice at the time: "It's a risk selecting outside the top few pairings, but then what isn't."

Bhavna is Kornel's rock and the closest thing to a mother I've ever known. As a couple, they're old school, having met on the planet, dated and married all before migrating, no genetic review required. Even aboard the stations people are free to marry who they choose, but getting a procreation permit to have children is another story. If a genetic marker comparison determines a degree of relatedness greater than third cousins, the only way for a couple to have children is through randomly selected In-Vitro Fertilization. Still, it's a shock finding out your significant other is a blood relation. I've heard stories of people committing suicide and even self-selecting deportation back to the CAZ.

"In all my 67 years, almost half on this very station, I've never seen a body or site so clean," Kornel says without looking up.

"Did the sanitizer run last night?" asks Brandi, glancing up at the ceiling and then back toward Kornel.

"As soon as the body cooled," Kornel replies. "I'm Lento, doctor and resident suicide confirmation specialist." He offers a gloved hand to Brandi.

Brandi examines Kornel's hand like it's attached to an alien life form. "Sorry Doc," I chime in. "This is Brandi Mikkelson from the Personal Reps office."

"My apologies," replies Kornel, touching his hand to his heart. "I'm old school in the worst ways."

Brandi places her hand over her heart to return the familiar greeting. "I thought the sanitizer wouldn't run if someone was in the room?" she asks.

"Well, that's partially true," replies Kornel, "as long as the someone in the room isn't dead."

"They're infrared," Jason says stepping forward. "Hi, Jason Plumin, Station Reps office," he says, holding his hand out toward Kornel. It's weird and unexpected, reaching to shake someone's hand, but not to Kornel who grasps it with a clap.

"That's right," says Kornel. "The lights turn red as a warning prior to the unit activating, but if someone is in the room it won't initiate, it just notifies the manager and logs the delay. In this case it didn't run until 01:00. We know if Mr. Birmingham was in here at the time, his corpse's detectable temperature was below 95 degrees Fahrenheit." Kornel pauses for a moment before adding, "And of course, it wasn't moving."

"Yes, but why would it activate at all at that point? Nobody was using the shower so there was nothing to clean," Brandi mentions.

"The sensor detected Nigel in the shower when he committed suicide, didn't it?" I ask. "Triggering the cleaning cycle to begin as soon as he left" I step around Kornel to get a better look at the body. "Normally, the cleaning would have abated until after the first use the following day. But since it recorded a presence, it activated as soon as it sensed the person exited the room."

"Right again," says Kornel like a proud parent whose daughter just aced an exam.

"Is that why he looks so, um, dehydrated?" asks Jason.

Kornel looks back toward the body. "Oh, this withered, wrinkled look? Yeah, that's the result of the chemicals in the sanitization process, as well as two to three additional cleanings."

"What?" Brandi asks, surprised.

Kornel smiles as if preparing to teach a child some big life lesson. "It appears when the room was sanitized it heated the body to a point within the detectable range for the sensor, triggering another cleaning cycle, then another and another until our intrepid gym-goer arrived this morning for his post-cardio cleansing."

I recall from today's news report that Birmingham committed suicide early this morning. "So we announced the TOD before we had the sanitizer logs?"

"Again, spot on," Kornel replies. "The sanitizer kept raising the temperature of the corpse, so we couldn't use it to determine time of death. Best we could do is check the time between the last cleaning yesterday and the first cleaning this morning. Theoretically, he could have committed suicide any time last night. It's entirely moot, anyway. He committed suicide. What does it matter what time he did it?"

"Except for the multiple cleanings and the fact that he looks pickled," Brandi comments.

"Except for that," Kornel adds. "Since the wash cycles are logged and given a constant rate of cooling, we can determine TOD based on when the cycles started repeating with some regularity. Which means he committed suicide around 01:00, give or take."

"You're sure about the cause of death?" asks Brandi.

"Did you find him like this?" I interrupt, ignoring Brandi's evil eye. If I know Kornel, he wasn't about to let the question go without some sarcastic comment. He doesn't like his expertise being questioned.

"No, we cut him down. He hung himself from that shower head, there, where the paracord is hanging," Kornel motions toward the length of thin rope hanging from the wall. "Can't tell if he took anything beforehand, but as I said, who cares?"

Jason walks over to the shower head, flicking the cord with his finger and setting it gently swinging. "I don't suppose you're planning to conduct an autopsy?"

Kornel looks at him oddly. This time I'm too late to stop him. "Do you know something I don't? Because if there's evidence to suggest this is something other than suicide, I'm happy to consider it," he concludes, not hiding his aggravation. As an afterthought, he adds, "What Council project did you say you're on?"

"We're just rounding out a review of suicides for the Council," I say, feeling a need to step in before this devolves further. "It's nothing, really, but an autopsy on this one in addition to the standard toxicology would be helpful. I know it goes beyond the usual screening SOP for suicides, but we don't want to be accused of not being thorough."

"For you Kami, anything," Kornel says with a smile.

The smile is short lived, vanishing a second later when Jason asks if Kornel shot any photos of the body before cutting him down.

"We only shoot photos of crime scenes," Kornel says, looking up toward the ceiling exasperated. "Since suicide isn't a crime, well, you get where I'm going with this."

"Yeah, no photos," Jason answers, which seems to piss Kornel off even more. "Can you at least describe the scene when you found it?"

"Yeah, in fact I can. You'll be able to read it in my report as soon as I finish the autopsy." Kornel's response is terse to say the least.

"Any chance I can get a few minutes with the Doc?" I ask my teammates, hoping to diffuse the tension.

"Of course," Brandi says, circumventing Jason's reply. I'm grateful. "Let's meet up at the office at 16:00 to finalize a game plan," she adds.

"Sounds good," I say, shooting her a *thank you* glance she acknowledges with a nod.

Jason looks disappointed. I suspect he wanted to ask more questions, but I've seen the Doc like this. Any patience he has fades fast when he thinks people are questioning his competence, especially from someone who's job is doling out punishments for being human.

I'm taken back to last night's conversation in the EVA bay. What if it wasn't a suicide?

"Kornel?"

"Yes."

"Is it at all possible this wasn't a suicide?" I'm careful in my word choice. It's doubtful he'll react the same with me as he did with Jason, but the only evidence I have is a voice on the other side of a door.

"Possible?" Kornel shifts into a cross-legged position on the floor next to Birmingham's body. "I suppose anything is possible. The problem is how would we know?"

"Perhaps the killer, if there was one, left marks on the body? Signs of a struggle?"

Kornel points toward the sanitizing unit on the ceiling. "Except the body's been cleaned. I'm guessing three or possibly four cycles overnight, high pressure, better than 120 degrees F. Cuts would stand out like a sore thumb, but the cleaning process would effectively eradicate any bruising."

"DNA?" I posit, knowing the answer.

"Seriously? We'll be lucky to find *his* DNA, much less someone else's. I doubt there'll even be DNA in the room. Not that it would help. Hundreds of people are in here every day."

Kornel stands, stretching a stiff back into a 5 foot-8 inch frame not much taller than my own. His breath smells like coffee—it's the first smell other than sanitizer I've noticed since entering the room and I find it oddly relaxing. "Maybe we'll get lucky," he says, arching his back until I hear an audible pop from his lower spine. "But don't get your hopes up. I doubt it'll show anything more than suicide. All things being equal, the simplest answer is usually the correct one, or something like that. I mean, you don't *suspect* foul play, do you Kami?"

"No." It's not a lie, exactly. I'm not sure I trust the robot voice from the Evac Bay.

"Good. Because there's never been a murder on any of the stations. Never. Ever."

"I know," I sigh.

There's a long pause as I consider Kornel's last statement, which broken when he switches the subject.

"How's, um, nobody?" He's referring to my relationship status. "Anyone under consideration?"

"You know me, always considering."

"Well, better to be sure than jump in head first. But don't take too long. At some point time overtakes plans leaving nothing but regret."

Kornel and Bhavna never had children of their own, a choice Bhavna said they made prior to migrating and one I think causes some remorse. The Council forbids Cits from procreating without a permit in order to manage growth—they call it Atmospheric Population Control. It's an environmentally distributed conception inhibitor, gender neutral birth control released into the ventilation system, dosing everyone aboard, until a procreation permit is issued to conceive, at which point the couple—or sometimes just one of the couple in the case of In Vitro—receives pharma to counter the effects of APC. Cits migrating from the planet agree to the measure, and I suppose I tacitly agreed, as well. I never really gave it much thought until Bhavna mentioned it during one of our talks, a hint of melancholy similar to Kornel's as she explained that by the time she and Kornel seriously considered children, they were too old to obtain Council approval.

I watch as Kornel takes measurements of the body and wonder why he never defied the rules. As a doctor and one of the earliest aboard, he had some leverage and it's easy enough to get black-market pharma to counteract the APC. Given his Role and history the Council might have made an exception to the mandatory deportation rule. Maybe he didn't want to risk it. Knowing Kornel, he would have volunteered to be the one deported, leaving Bhavna and the baby aboard Aries.

Kornel walks toward the shower head where the paracord dangles. "He was hanging here, his derriere a couple feet off the floor, back against the wall, and his legs straight out in front of him," he says, tracing the description in the air with a pencil. "He must have just tied the cord around his neck and the shower head and sat down until he passed out. It would have been painless, but still…"

"Still what?" I ask.

"You really have to want to kill yourself to keep from standing up. It's not like he was swinging and couldn't reach the floor. It screams suicide…maybe drugs, too, though." The way he tapers off at the end, I can't tell if he's talking to me or himself.

"Who found him?"

Kornel pulls a notebook from his front pocket and flips a few pages in. He's definitely old school—pencil and paper. "Sam Michnak. He's a minor. Hasn't even completed the SR Bid process, yet."

I type the name into the log on my ComLink. "Where do you get those things?" I motion toward the spiral bound pad.

"I have my sources," he says, smiling.

"You know those are bad for the environment, right?"

Kornel closes the notebook and returns it and the pencil to his breast pocket. "The environment on Earth? When that becomes a priority, I'll stop using paper. But at the rate things are going, I'll be dead long before then."

"Do you think it's worth examining the water recycler?"

"Maybe after the first cleaning," Kornel replies. "But there's been so much washed down it'd be like looking for a specific grain of salt in the ocean."

"I'm sure I have no idea what you mean."

"I mean the multiple chemical cleanings diluted any potential evidence."

"Now why didn't you just say that? What about cameras? I didn't see any cameras in the hall or outside."

"Privacy First, remember?" He replies just a bit more sarcastically than I expect. "This is supposed to be Utopia. Can't have big brother spying on all the idealists."

"Right," I acknowledge. "You know, Nigel's been around a long time. Who do you think will replace him?"

Kornel grins, "You know I can't share that information. As a member of the Migration Selection Committee, I'm not allowed to discuss who is or is not being given an opportunity to migrate."

"Oh, don't be such a stickler. I'm not asking for a name, just an idea."

All stations share the same overarching immigration policy. The Council determines the criteria, such as the genetic protocols to rule out obesity, chronic health disorders, and transmissible diseases, as well as standard operating procedures for recruitment and working with the Zones. Factors such as population demographics and needed Roles feed into the algorithm, which optimizes station viability. The individual station five-year plans then become part of the collective policy, which is reviewed and adjusted annually based on current data and forecasts.

"Well, if I can't trust an OSU Deputy and adopted daughter, who can I trust?" Kornel playfully nudges my shoulder. His smile is disarming in a good way. "Between the two of us, the push over the last couple years has been females," he continues. "We've been instructed to select women where candidates are equally qualified."

"Uh, isn't that somewhat anti-algorithmic?"

"Perhaps, but it comes from the Council."

"The Council rather than the algorithm is dictating gender? That's a bit out of the ordinary."

"Listen, this is all highly classified." Kornel says, looking around the empty room.

"I can't do my job if I don't know what's going on."

"This can't make it into any report. No notes. No recordings. Understand? This could get a lot of people…"

"Deported?" I interrupt.

"No! I was going to say it could get people into trouble. You can't even share this with those other two, the Reps. Do you understand, Kami?"

Kornel seems genuinely wary, more so than I've ever seen him. I nod my head in concurrence.

"No, say the words. You'll keep what I'm going to tell you to yourself, no matter what."

"Okay." I hold my hands up to assuage any concern. "I'll keep it to myself. I won't tell anyone."

Kornel pauses for a moment, seeming to consider whether my assurance is enough, then steps closer as he explains in a whisper, "The Analysis Lab produced a report a few years ago titled, *The DupleX Defect*. It analyzed the affect living in space was having on the population. They found a correlation between births and an increase in the percentage of males—more boys are being born than girls. The radiation in space is greater than on the planet and it's affecting female reproduction. X chromosomes cannot combine, so they mutate from X into Y's post fertilization. If we can replace with women, it should give the scientists time to figure out and correct the problem."

What? I can't believe what I'm hearing. "So we're giving preference to women during replacement selections hoping it will give them time to fix the problem?"

"We're not simply selecting females and hoping for the best." Kornel pulls his head back, insulted. "The algorithm is set up to replace male deaths with males and females with females. The Council decided before IPI to limit the number of birth permits to allow for migration… they thought it would maintain population diversity in the long term. But the gender birth rate anomaly set everything off kilter. A higher male population trickled into increasing numbers of males dying and being expelled, thus more male migrants. The Council recognized the trend and established protocols to immigrate more women, especially those with female children or genetically predisposed to birthing female babies."

Kornel is a practical physician and a scientist, he must understand just how this sounds. Selection is supposed to be unbiased, based on SR needs and genetic screening for disease, not someone's gender or the likelihood they'll produce girls instead of boys. If anyone found out about the Council manipulating the process and the reason why, people would freak out. Then a thought occurs to me.

"How far off are we? I mean, how bad is the disparity between males and females?"

"Well, the last report indicated only 45 percent of the current population is female. The birth rate anomaly is much worse, almost nine-to-one. In 80 years, there will be twice as many men on the stations as women, two-thirds of station inhabitants will be male. Another 40 years and the ratio will be three-to-one and it's not just on Aries. All the stations are in the same boat. Some are doing slightly worse, others better, but the trend is the same across the board."

Kornel puts his hand on my shoulder and I reflexively pull away. His disappointed look leaves me regretting the move.

"Considering we've been at this for more than twenty years," he continues, "and we only implemented the female selection preferences three years ago, I'd say we're doing pretty good."

"Jeez, it's a wonder I'm still single. I have my pick of excess men. If I hold out for a few more years I could end up with two or even three boyfriends," I quip. "How did this go unnoticed for so long?"

"It's just not something we were looking for in the beginning. We monitored overall births and deaths by gender. But the presumption was always that the ratio of male to female births would mirror that of Earth, some years trending male, others female, but balancing out in the end. The focus was always on replacing deaths with the same gender. It was two decades before anyone started looking at the disparity at the birth level and realized we'd been managing ourselves into oblivion." Kornel pauses for a moment, perhaps noticing the look of disbelief I'm attempting to quell.

"The medical field," he continues. "At least the one's in the loop, as well as the scientists working on a fix are confident they can solve the problem before it becomes untenable. As long as we have the planet for repopulation, we can always reverse the trend once there's a solution. There have been a couple almost leaks, people who found or figured things out, but the Council shuts them down before it becomes mainstream. If it ever got out, there would be chaos. People want answers, not questions, especially in space."

I recall the conversation in Bay 1 and wonder if I should tell Kornel. He deserves to know if someone on the Council is pulling strings. But I'm not sure the two issues are connected—two X and the suicides—not without evidence. I'm not even sure there is a suicide issue. Just because a faceless, anonymized voice suspects the suicides are not what they seem doesn't make it so. If the suicides are just suicides and Kornel tells the Council, whoever is feeding me information on the sly could be exposed. If there is a connection, it could stir up a whirlwind of cover ups. I'm fond of neither option without knowing how deep this falls.

"Are all the stations in agreement? Has this policy been implemented across the board?"

"The Ambassadors from each station and the Council proper unanimously agreed to the plan three years ago. There's really no other option, other than returning to the planet, which is a death sentence." Kornel pauses for a moment allowing me to digest the information. "There are exceptions, of course. We're not selecting *all* women."

There's a long silence, me considering what this means and Kornel probably regretting telling me. "It's the right thing to do, Kami," he finally says. "At least for now."

I'm not so sure.

CHAPTER SEVENTEEN

Brandi Mikkelson

"What are you watching?" I ask Jason while we wait for Kami in the same room in which Marta volunteered me for this BS committee.

Jason looks up from his ComLink for the first time since he arrived. "Just reviewing the footage we collected after the HMC this morning. I'm telling you, Brandi, there is absolutely no good angle here—nothing showing anyone coming or going."

"Privacy First," I chime. "Privacy is most valuable when it is scarce."

"Yeah, I remember the lesson in primary school." Jason clears his throat before continuing in a voice between a baritone and one scarred by too many years breathing unfiltered Autonomous Zone air. "The founding Council recognized the need for personal space. It is for this reason Article I codifies, 'The Stations, which by design result in intrusion into almost every aspect of life, will hold the privacy of Citizens tantamount and as such shall protect the right of every Citizen to engage in daily life without intrusion.'"

It's a pretty decent impression of the virtual history lecture, I think. We attended the same lessons as migrants that Jason learned in primary school and received the same digital cheat sheet—Station Articles of Incorporation and Subsequent Amendments: An outline of policies, rules and regulations governing station society. I presume the founding Council members, after creating what they believed was a communal Eden of common goals and shared interest, figured there needed to be some trust or people might revolt. Life aboard the stations is comparatively idyllic, but it is also an assault on Citizen liberties—procreation control, rationing, movement limitations, habitat assignments, Role testing, and absolute Council autonomy to name a few. Their concession, a healthy respect for personal privacy, is meant to dull the sting of restrictions and give a sense of control to Cits over at least one thing in their lives. Privacy First.

"You know Birmingham is just a suicide, right?" I ask, convinced, but also fishing for Jason's opinion.

"Of course," Jason responds without looking up from his ComLink. "This entire effort is a huge waste of time. But when the Council calls…"

"Yeah, the Council. Do you think they actually believe there's an issue? I mean, how could they? Has there *ever* been a murder on the stations?"

"Nope," Jason replies, now looking up from the small screen on his wrist and shaking his head. "And we won't be casting doubt on that stat with our little investigation. But they'll expect a comprehensive review nonetheless. Speaking of which, do you have the list of suicides from the coroner's office? The one's were supposed to include?" Jason asks.

"Yeah. Nine in the last three months." I tap out a couple quick commands on my ComLink and swipe the list onto the wall mounted visual display.

Jason examines it before speaking, his hand stroking his hairless chin. "Nine seems a little high, especially since we're only a week into the second quarter, but not enough to worry about. A normal year will see around 32 per station."

"So we're trending toward 36, a slight uptick," I calculate in my head. "About twelve, um, twelve and a half percent."

"That doesn't seem like much to me," Jason comments. "Do we have any data on trends over the last few years? Has the suicide *rate* been going up or down?" Jason taps something into his ComLink in what I think is an attempt to answer his own question.

"I'm not sure. What does the screen on your wrist tell you?"

Jason shoots me a sly smile, his head cocked like a puppy. "It says the number of suicides on Aries held steady at about 30 until about three years ago, then increased. The years 2100, 2101, and 2102 saw 35, 37, and 36 suicides, respectively."

"Okay, so an increase that has held steady for the last three years."

"And appears to be holding for 2103, as well," Jason adds, glancing back up toward the list on the visual display. "I see Nigel Birmingham, Michael Finn, and Derek Ocasio are the last three."

I note the list also includes:

Vincent Jepus
Nicholas Kesik
Candace Rogala
Neil Palau
Gotthard Hong
Hannah Bonikowski

"Yeah, Ocasio was odd. Didn't see that one coming," I comment.

"And Finn, of course." Jason adds. "That just proves this review is a bunch of hooey. Finn was an accident, right?"

"I believe, but I don't have access to the official coroner's ruling, yet." Then, remembering Jason's terse exchange with Dr. Lento, I add, "By the way, what's with you and the coroner? Seems like there's some history there."

"Not history," he replies, still examining the list. "I just don't care for doctors. Highly overrated in my opinion." There's a brief pause before he asks suddenly, "Wait. Did you think I was a little harsh?"

"Actually, I thought the exchange was fun to watch." I leave out my assessment of Lento, his need to have his methods respected and an air of medical superiority shining like Venus at dusk.

"No, seriously. I'm usually pretty good about keeping my opinions to myself. Did it seem like I didn't respect him? Or did he just overreact to my questioning him?"

He sounds seriously concerned, like the answer might alter what he believes about himself.

"You were fine. I didn't get anything from you. Besides, he deserved it. It's not like we need doctors much in space."

"That's my point," Jason adds. "We don't need doctors. People are genetically screened prior to migration and quarantined before entering the population. There's virtually no disease, no health issues —save the mental ones—and pretty much anything that does pop up is corrected by the Med AI. No more waiting weeks for appointments and hours in a waiting room for five minutes with some doc who probably graduated with a 'C' average. I can access the Med AI from my ComLink, authorize a scan, and within seconds have a prescription for my hangover or pulled muscle or whatever else is wrong. I suppose if I break a bone or have an appendicitis, I'll have to visit the Med Lab, but the AI does all the work—diagnosis, surgery, post-op— the doc just audits the computer's decisions. And how often is the AI wrong? Never, that's how often. Have you ever heard of a case where the Med AI made a mistake?"

"No, I can't say as I have."

"Exactly!" Jason exclaims more excited than I expect. "M.D.s are a throwback to a time before the stations, resigned to feeding samples into computers and pronouncing suicides."

"Agreed," I offer, enjoying this deep dive into Jason's opinion pool. "Unless you're dead or need surgery there is no reason to visit a doc."

"That's why a doctor's primary duty is to act as coroner," Jason quips. "People like Kornel, IPIs, can't let go of the past. My guess is he'll give Nigel a full physical before the autopsy just to make sure he's actually dead."

That makes me chuckle.

"Do we have Roles?" Jason asks, switching gears rather suddenly and turning back toward the screen. "Migration or birth dates? Because other than knowing five of the people on the list, I'm not seeing any commonalities in the names."

"You know five people on this list?" I ask. "Which ones?"

"Well, I didn't necessarily *know* them. Nigel's case, the one you worked, was handled by our office. I also worked on Derek's issue, and who didn't know Mike?" He asks, rhetorically. "You worked on Derek's case, too, didn't you?"

"Sort of," I reply. "It was Botha's case. He just asked me to write a letter. But I did know Birmingham and Finn."

"Then there's Nicholas Kesik and Neil Palau," Jason continues. "Our office handled both of their cases, so I'm familiar with the names."

"What were their issues?" I ask.

"Nick was caught distributing bootleg booze to a minor and Neil…" Jason's eyes float upward in search of a memory. "I think Neil made complaints about a doctor that ended up being unfounded. I want to say, uh, defamation? But I'd have to check the records."

"So, we have nine names," I summarize. "Men and women, four of whom had broken some station law. We should probably check on the others—see if there are other criminal histories."

"Well, we know Finn isn't in that group," Jason notes. "He was OSU. Do we have Roles for the others?"

"It's a pretty diverse group," I say as I pipe their SRs onto the visual display next to their names.

Nigel Birmingham - HMC Designer

Michael Finn - OSU Deputy

Derek Ocasio - Cafeteria Helper/Conditional SR

Vanessa Jepus - Astrophysicist

Nicholas Kesik - Historian
Candace Rogala - Nutritionist
Neil Palau - Station Operations Analyst
Gotthard Hong - Author-Fiction
Hannah Bonikowski - Water Reclamation Technician

"Ocasio worked in the cafeteria," I add. "Until his re-assignment on conditional SR to our office, and you know about Birmingham and Finn. Then we have an Astrophysicist, a Historian, a Nutritionist, a Station Operations Analyst, one Author, and the last one worked as a Water Rec Tech." I catch myself reciting the list even though I know good and well Jason can read it from the screen.

Jason considers the list, having returned to stroking his bare chin. I notice I'm staring at him and look away reflexively, but not before catching his eye, a slow burning desire to fill the silence overwhelming me. Jason does me the favor.

"I don't know," he says. "We're going to need more information. There isn't anyone on there that stands out as a huge surprise suicide. Not that I'd suspect any of them *would* kill themselves, but there's no reason to suspect they wouldn't."

"Except Finn," I mention. "Finn is the only person I'm surprised to find on the list."

"Yeah, what the hell," Jason comments. "He was about to retire and move on to some volunteer role."

"The reason it looks out of the ordinary is because it is out of the ordinary." Kami's voice from the doorway catches us both off guard. She continues around the table, taking the seat she occupied earlier.

"Well, if it isn't someone else's turn to be late," Jason replies, a flirty lilt attached to the observation.

"I stopped by the OSU offices on the way over," Kami explains. "I needed to confirm some information about Finn. Besides, why should you be the only slacker in the group."

"Oh, now I'm not only late but I'm a slacker, huh?" Jason shoots back, causing Kami to dip her chin, but not before I notice her faint, blushing smile.

This time I'm sure, he's fucking hitting on Kami. Not that she's complaining. No, she seems to be enjoying it.

"Um, mind if I ask a question?" I interrupt.

"Of course not," Kami answers, a normal shade returning to her cheeks.

"Why is Finn's suicide out of the ordinary?"

"Because," Kami starts. "Michael Finn did not commit suicide."

"I knew it!" Jason exclaims.

"*We* knew it," I add. "But he's included in the list. Why is he on the list if he isn't a suicide?"

Kami pivots away from the screen, making a show of angling her body toward me and not Jason. "It's a clerical error. That's why I'm late. When I left the HMC I remembered he was listed as a suicide and wanted to see if it'd been corrected in the system."

"Well, apparently not," I reply, hoping the hint of sarcasm finds its way to the correct set of ears.

"Apparently not," Kami replies, seemingly unaware of my dig. "But it's been corrected now."

"If it wasn't suicide, what was Finn's official cause of death?" Jason asks.

"The official cause of death is listed as 'circumstances beyond one's control,'" Kami answers, pivoting toward Jason and a friendlier voice.

"So…it was an accident," I clarify.

"Correct," Kami confirms without making eye contact.

"What exactly accidentally caused his death?" Jason asks.

"A Charged Field Array," Kami says, enunciating each word as if it's a punchline. "Finn was investigating Derek Ocasio's suicide out on Platform Alpha 5, PA5, above the containment field. We knew it was Ocasio, but needed a sample for positive DNA match and to analyze for contaminants. Finn decided he did not want to wait for cleanup and climbed out on the platform himself. He must have lost his grip and fallen into the array."

"Ouch," Jason says. "Wasn't he nearing retirement?"

"Yeah. What a waste," Kami shakes her head. "Another deputy just finished collecting Ocasio *and* Finn's samples—this time they waited for the custodial crew. Results showed no outside environmental factors, other than the environment of space, of course. He should have followed protocol, waited for the cleanup team to open the doors, then collected the sample from inside the station."

"And what time was all of this?" I ask.

"An hour before shift change," Kami answers.

"Wait," I add. "So, Finn did an EVA, by himself, above a charged array, just so he wouldn't have to wait around for the cleaning crew?

"Yeah," Kami replies. "Like I said, a waste."

"How close was he?" Jason asks.

"Apparently too close, because he fell into the field array," I reply, noticing the smile hidden behind Jason's hand.

"143 days," Kami pipes in, seeming not to appreciate my sense of humor.

"Five months," says Jason. "He was almost there."

"Did you know him well?" I ask Kami.

Kami pushes the chair away from the table far enough to cross her legs. Sitting there with her back straight as a board, feet tucked beneath her thighs and knees splayed out to either side she reminds me of an old statue of Buddha I once saw in the CAZ—the skinny one where he looked miserable, not the fat, happy one. Her flexibility notwithstanding, the position makes her seem too young to be a Deputy.

"Not well," Kami replies after getting comfortable. "Nobody under the age of 40 knew Finn well. He didn't have much respect for newbies, or the system, or the Council, or anything he found lacking for that matter, and he wasn't shy about voicing his opinions. But it wasn't personal. You had to know Mike."

"Yeah, Mike was a prize," Jason adds. "No shortage of disdain for the things he didn't agree with. Add to that a healthy dose of cynicism and a pound of loyalty to his friends and you've got Mike in a nutshell."

"Right?" Kami replies, adding an inflection at the end to make it sound like a question when it's really not. "Sounds like you knew him pretty well."

"Definitely," confirms Jason. "We've been friends since I first joined the StaRep's office almost 10 years ago."

"Well, I wouldn't know," I throw in. "I've never met Finn."

It's common for Station Reps to meet with investigators, but Personal Reps rarely have a need. Jason would have known Finn from any number of cases. It doesn't surprise me they were friends.

"Is there anything else about the list that stands out?" Kami asks, glancing back at the visual display.

"Not that we noticed," Jason replies. "Although now that we've dropped Mike, we're left with eight suicides instead of nine."

"Eight is better than nine, I suppose," I add. "It leaves us hitting below average by year's end."

"We should probably divide up some of this work," Jason adds. "No sense in all of us chasing down the same information. As I see it, we should at a minimum review the contaminant records for each suicide, interview next of kin, talk to any friends and coworkers, pull criminal records, and loop back with Kornel about the autopsy. When will he be done with that?" Jason asks, turning toward Kami.

"Tomorrow afternoon. I can touch base with him and pull any criminal records. I'll also take Hong and Bonikowski."

"Okay, I'll take Finn and Ocasio," Jason volunteers. "And…Palau, since you're already talking to the doctor about Birmingham."

"That leaves me with Jepus, Kesik, and Rogala," I volunteer. "But do we really need to do anything with Finn? Technically he's not part of the suicide club."

Jason glances again at the screen, "Probably not. But that leaves me with two."

"No problem," Kami notes. "You can help me with Hong or Bonikowski. I'll also pull the contaminant records when I see Kornel and send over a list of any criminal files."

Jason suggests meeting here Friday afternoon to touch base and catch everyone up. It's a time commitment on an already tight schedule, but we'll want to make sure we're on the same page.

We all nod in agreement, a signal the meeting is over. I've got just enough time to meet Alex at the gym. "See you Friday," I call, pushing my chair toward the table.

I head immediately for the door and am almost out of earshot when I hear Kami ask Jason, "Do you want to meet for a drink some time to discuss the other two after you finish with Palau?"

Hmm.

CHAPTER EIGHTEEN

Kami Lee

I'd planned to meet with Kornel first thing, but it took longer than expected to pull all the suicide files. Once you walk into an Orbital Sheriff's Unit after being assigned to a super-secret committee, the entire office wants to know about it. So many people said, "Kami, let's grab coffee," you'd think I'd been appointed Aries Ambassador to the Council. As it is, I consumed enough caffeine this morning to power a small craft half way across the galaxy.

I'd like to blame the delay all on curious coworkers, but I'd be lying by doing so. I really need to see Parker in records for help pulling the information we need. Except the Records Deputy isn't the most likable person in the Unit. The frequent interruptions between the front door and Parker's room in the back allow me time to mentally prepare for what's to come.

"Enter and be judged," Parker's voice booms from the other side of the door after I knock.

"Good morning, Parker," I say with as much enthusiasm as I can fake.

"What can I do for you, intrepid space person?" He says in a voice that sounds like he's narrating a documentary about time travel. "Oh, Kami. It's only you."

Parker is short, shorter than me by a couple inches at least, which forces him to peer around instead of over the physical monitor mounted atop his adjustable height desk. I once made the mistake of suggesting he upgrade to one of the virtual 8k models with multi-side screen sharing and transparency mode, which resulted in a twenty minute dissertation on the drawbacks of a disposable society and its impact on the planet. Since then I keep my opinions about his office to myself.

"I need to pull some records," I reply, setting the coffee I brought him on his desk. Parker doesn't get coffee for others. It doesn't work that way.

"Ah, I see," he says, eyeing the cup conspicuously. "Do you know how much coffee I've consumed in my 82 years?"

I think I'm going to find out.

"26,208 cups. In my day, we started drinking it as fucking children. It was one of the safest ways to get clean water—boiled. In fact, it's probably the reason Parker still doesn't miss a fucking beat. You'd be wise to consider that. When the spoiled little shits being raised on the stations these days are my age, they'll have regressed to sucking their thumbs simply due to a lack of caffeine."

"Cheers," I say, holding up my cup and ignoring the 'spoiled little shits' comment meant for me.

"Do you know why I'm here?" Parker asks.

In fact, he's told me this story several times. He was the oldest migrant during Initial Population Integration and is currently the oldest person on the stations still working in their original Role, and the Council came to him and nobody else when they needed a records management system, leaving Parker with more self-proclaimed connections on the Council than anyone I know. Usually he peppers the story with expletives and questionable allusions to people of a variety of faiths, ethnic backgrounds, and complexions, wrapping it up with an off-handed remark about how I'm lucky to be from Asian stock, where they birthed them smart and motivated. But I don't have time to listen to it today.

"Yep," I interrupt before he can begin the tale. "You're here because *you* are the best at finding nuggets in the records system. Which is also why I'm here—I need some nuggets found."

There's a short pause as Parker considers whether the compliment is sufficient payment for skipping his story. I'm pleasantly surprised when he peeks out from the side of his monitor.

"Well said, young padawan," he comments, a wrinkled smile forming an instant before his head disappears once more behind the screen. "What information might I mine for you today?"

"I've been assigned to a team…"

"Yes, I know," Parker interrupts. "You're looking into suicides.

Everyone knows and everyone knows it's a waste of time. Another Council effort to prove to the Cits that they care. Honestly, we don't need that kind of proof. What we need is to finish staffing and sever ties with the planet. We need to be self-sustaining and to let those still below finish killing themselves so someday we can rebuild. But since that's not happening and this is, why don't you tell me exactly what you need so we can put this behind us."

Parker's comments don't shock me. People aboard the stations generally fall into one of two camps: the Parker 'let them die' contingent or the more compassionate 'we should keep helping as long as possible' folks. The former group makes up a larger portion of Cits and are usually older. They lost the people they loved or sacrificed them when they migrated. They've seen the CAZ and in a few cases the Open Lands and have a real-world understanding of where the greed, fraud, and political divide is heading. To them, it's not a matter of *if* the population of earth with die, but when. Given that, why prolong the inevitable.

By contrast, the smaller number of Cits who want to continue to help the Autonomous Zones either migrated very young or were born on the stations. They have no current firsthand experience with the planet-side population, the unsustainable rate of consumption, and the disregard for the environment in lieu of survival. They only see people, *our* people, and believe we have a duty to help. I tend to agree, but then I was born on Aries.

"Of course," I reply. "Here's the list." I tap a command into my ComLink and send Parker the names. I can't see his face behind the monitor, but am assured he's reading it when he finally replies.

"There's an Orbital Sheriff's Deputy on here."

"Yes. The Council wants every death during the time period in question reviewed."

"Fine. I'll have it in an hour," Parker says, still not bothering to look out from behind his screen.

I stand there for a moment, wondering if we're done. After a few seconds I say thank you and walk toward the door. As I'm about to exit, Parker adds, "Kami. This is a bunch of shit. We've all lost people. It doesn't mean there is something wrong with the system. Some people just can't cope no matter how good they have it. Remember that when you're seeing clues where there aren't any."

I can't help but wonder if Parker's referring to my father or just simply a statement as the door soothingly whooshes shut behind me.

CHAPTER NINETEEN

Brandi Mikkelson

The next time someone says, *'Hey Brandi, I've got an opportunity for you,'* I'm heading for the nearest door. I had three suicide interviews to do for Kesik, Jepus, and Rogala, and only finished the first two. Grieving family and friends want to talk it out ad nauseam. No surprise—all evidence suggests both were suicides.

"How's the suicide thing going, Brandi?" Henry's sitting across from me, a body with a virtual monitor for a head tapping out mitigation on his laptop.

"Fine. I'm just behind. Had three interviews for three different suicides and only got two done."

"And?" Henry asks, still looking at his screen.

"Nothing unexpected," I reply, adding my notes to the virtual case file. "Nicholas Kesik and Vanessa Jepus both committed suicide. Shocking. Need to get the Rogala one done before tomorrow, which means another late night."

"Well, that's good news, right?" Henry's headless voice asks.

"I suppose. I was hoping for some excitement. Instead, I got Jepus, an astrophysicist suffering from depression, and Kesik, a savant Historian. You'd think someone who understood as much about our history as Kesik would know that bootleg liquor and distribution to minors is both ill-advised and has been a crime for over a hundred years."

"He was cited because he got a couple kids drunk?" Henry asks, unconvinced.

"No. He was cited because the two minors combined their liquid courage with Art 101—they drew dicks on the doors of several Aries

HabUs. The two boys gave up Kesik without a fight. One count purchase and distribution of booze to minors using food allotments."

I review my notes, noting how young Kesik was when he committed suicide, and that he didn't leave a note or video log. He was a Gen, born to two station Techs on Aries in 2082. His coworkers described him as smart, funny, outgoing, and brilliant when it came to designing History learning components for the virtual environment. The Team Lead at the Education Lab pulled studies from the archives showing student success rates before and after Kesik joined. The change was dramatic. Test scores jumped an average of 8 points following the deployment of the modules he authored. He apparently had a real knack for developing virtual content that resonated with kids in the 10-16 year old demographic.

"I wonder what role the booze played in his success?" Henry asks, this being the closest he comes to sarcasm.

"Either way, it's not a reason to commit suicide. The thing is, everyone was surprised when he did it, but there's no evidence it was anything but. Here he is."

Henry glances at the photo of Kesik I ported to his monitor, a blue-eyed, blond haired man in a neatly pressed tan uniform holding a placard, 'Historian: Class of 2101.' He's sporting a wide, captivating smile and the nicest teeth I've ever seen. I'm not sure why I focused on his teeth. Perhaps because they were so perfect—perfectly sized, positioned and blindingly white, like they'd been digitally enhanced to the point of looking almost fake. I asked one of his coworkers about the teeth, a middle-aged man named Jon who authors some of the science modules. He confirmed that Kesik's teeth really were a sight to see.

"Good looking kid," Henry says. "Nice teeth."

"Yeah, and no traumatic history, either. He was in decent shape physically. Uneventful childhood, both of his parents are still alive and working. He took the role in which he ranked highest, completed SR training in the standard three years, and didn't have any odd personality quirks, unlike the coworker, Jon, who kept referring to me as 'deary'"

"That's creepy, even to me," Henry notes.

"Seriously. The thing is, to a person—even creepy Jon—Kesik was the least likely to kill himself. One coworker even suggested they were surprised it wasn't the Jon guy. All indications are he was well-adjusted and successful."

"Take it from someone who's seen more of these than he'd like," Henry starts. "We don't always know the reason people commit suicide. If the physical evidence indicates he killed himself and there is nothing to suggest otherwise, then he killed himself. It would be different if it weren't as common as it is aboard the stations."

"Yeah, I get it. I'm not trying to convince myself. I know he did it. It would just be nice to have a note or something."

"You know that's not common, right?" Henry asks.

"Yes, dad." My reply sounds more acerbic than I mean. If Henry notices, he doesn't let on.

"How did he do it, anyway? Pills?"

Pills are a common way to commit suicide on the stations. They are easily acquired on the black market, and the quality of the ones from the market is superior to those from a Med Tech, meaning a quicker and less messy death, or so I'm told. Even someone who doesn't understand how the black market works—although I have no idea who that might be—can get a prescription for something with enough potency to extinguish life. Although you can't physically assist someone in committing suicide, the legality of suicide extends to those providing support in furtherance thereof, so one can simply ask a doctor. But most medical professionals will try to talk people out of it.

The problem with pills is they're messy. It's not uncommon for the suicid'ee—or is it suicid'er? Whatever—it is not uncommon for the person committing suicide to vomit all over themselves, leaving a chunky detritus for the clean-up crew. Of course, the dead person doesn't really care much at that point, having self-expelled to heaven or Valhalla or wherever one believes one goes when they die.

Hanging is also popular among the suicide crowd. There are a number of places with sufficient height on the stations to hang oneself, the deceased Mr. Birmingham a case in point. What his choice lacked in originality, simply sitting down until he passed out, it made up for in effectiveness. In some cases, perhaps most—I haven't witnessed enough hangings to confirm—the person relieves themselves upon expiration, again, leaving a mess for cleanup. Such was not the case with Birmingham, since the scheduled sanitization process did its job long before anyone arrived. Again, no originality but kudos for location and timing.

Come to think of it, most methods involve one expelling their insides. I'm told it has something to do with the human body losing control of everything from bowels to bladder once the brain is dead.

Some people think it's the soul not wanting to transcend with a bag of shit, a thought I find mildly entertaining. The idea of an afterlife and some sort of judgment is as outdated as politicians and anyone who subscribes to such fantasies is setting themselves up for major disappointment. Science tends to trump blind faith in space—religious nutbags and their proselytizing are rare.

There are almost no guns on board save for a few in the Defense Section, which means no self-inflicted gun shots. High speed projectiles are not things you want on space stations They tend to ricochet off the inside of someone's skull or miss their mark during last second reconsiderations, punching holes in vital systems. Frankly, I doubt anyone would use them even if they could, given the level of communal consideration, but best not to test human nature.

Some people choose un-suited airlock openings because they consider them painless and leave no mess for loved ones or sanitation crews. The problem is nobody knows exactly how long it takes the brain to quit registering the excruciating pain of rapid decompression, O-2 evacuation from the lungs, exaggerated body bloating, and the boiling off of every ounce of exposed liquid. There is no reason to risk agony at the end when there are plenty of quick, effective, and more popular suicide methods. Charged field arrays, timed environmental suit oxygen discharge, electro cerebral conduction, and good old fashioned wrist slicing with the assistance of drugs to block pain receptors each result in what is believed to be a comfortable, if not in some cases instantaneous death. Plus, with all the safety protocols in place to prevent accidental outer airlock door openings, one needs an insider or specialized skills to override the program and force an evacuation. Not everyone has the technical acumen to kill themselves in an airlock.

"No pills," I reply to Henry. "Kesik took advantage of his drinking problem, consumed copious amounts of laced bootleg booze until his body shut down. The tox screen came back with excessive amounts of alcohol synthesized with downers probably purchased from the black market just for the occasion. By the looks of his photo at the end, he'd been getting the majority of his calories from a bottle."

"At least he died doing what he loved," Henry says, deadpan.

"Agreed," I quip back, considering our shared callousness. Henry and I both migrated from the planet, a place people try to leave. Station life is idyllic compared to the best Earth has to offer. If we are a little crass when referring to suicides by people who probably weren't stable to begin with, it's because we've seen the other side. Far more people per capita commit suicide on the stations than on the planet, which is fine with me. Every suicide is an opportunity for someone like me from the surface to make a better life in space.

CHAPTER TWENTY

Jason Plumin

The screen on the outside of the Analysis Lab flashes my name when I touch the scanner, *Jason Plumin*. Neil Palau was a station Operations Analyst when he committed suicide—earning him the first suicide of the year on Aries. I drew him because the A-Lab isn't far from Cecelia's office, giving me a chance to pop in and say hello. Unfortunately, she wasn't around and nobody seemed to know where she'd gone. All's the better, I suppose. It's not Tuesday and she can be picky about unannounced visitors.

I'm desperately trying to treat this thing, this study with an amount of interest commensurate with its importance. I'm failing. The suicide rate is what it is and no amount of investigating is going to change that. People kill themselves on the stations and I can't say I feel much for them. There are a lot of people on the planet hoping to someday migrate and if someone wants to open a spot for them, so be it. It's harsh, but not if you think about it from the point of view of your average Cit in the CAZ. To them, Neil Palau's death is a chance at something better.

The A-Lab is actually several labs connected by a series of corridors housing everyone responsible for monitoring and analyzing station systems, processes, demographics, dynamics, and integrity. Accordingly, there are many here who prefer working with information over people. Economists, engineers, statisticians, and of course data analysts monitor, tweak, analyze, and report to the Council about potential trends and predictions. They basically keep everything running now and into the future without turning wrenches. When physical intervention is required, they call in the techs.

This section of the A-Lab houses Station Systems and Operations Analysts. It's like every place else on Aries—tiny, cramped, and mostly impersonal with only a few small remembrances adorning individual workstations. The walls are cold white, the desks metallic gray, and it smells of disinfectant mixed with despair and a hint of worry. The Station Systems Analysts scrutinize station status—orbit, velocity, sun burst impacts, ambient radiation, burn requirements, oxygen consumption, community dynamics, and the population algorithm—as well as ancillary systems. They are responsible for monitoring Aries for anomalies and dispatching crews to correct them before they become problems that kill thousands of people.

As much as the SSAs are the firefighters, the Station Operations Analysts are more strategic planners, recording baseline dynamics and providing recommendations in the form of detailed analytic reports to the Council so they can make informed decisions. At any time, there are dozens of variables for an SSA to balance in order to keep the stations running smoothly, but Aries as a whole only requires minor tweaks based on input from a small number of SOAs.

There are no windows in the Station Analysts lab. Windows are reserved for living quarters and the common areas where people congregate off-hours. Along the side walls are workspaces for two analysts sitting side-by-side, a total of four people in the room at any time. There are usually three System's Analysts and one Operations Analyst on duty, except during third shift when all four seats are occupied by SSAs. Filling the far wall are six substantially sized screens mounted side-by-side, three across and stacked two feet off the floor up to the ceiling. They display the status of various station dynamics and systems and allow Analysts to push visuals from their local display to the main wall. It's pretty impressive, not unlike what you'd see in classic crime fighting TV shows from the early twenty-first.

Rather than isolated cubicles, there are six-inch tall dividers separating each workstation pair. A product of the movement away from offices, they're meant to encourage collaboration between and among analysts. Instead, they merely keep other people's stuff from creeping into your space. Sitting in a room all day staring at monitors with three other people hoping to catch some random event before it destroys life aboard Aries is not what I consider a sublime existence, with or without tiny barriers to stem the tide of a coworker's detritus. I can't decide if placing people who score high on the introvert scale in such close proximity is ironic or not.

Not that being a Station Rep is all glamor and intrigue, but at least I have my own office and meet people. Sure, they're people who've broken laws and committed sins against their station brethren, but people nonetheless. It's better than sitting in a room all day pushing a desk mate's personal items back over the mini wall, leaving the room to pass gas, eyes bloodshot from staring at my best friend, a HuangWei Technologies virtual screen. Standing here now makes me want to conjure up a big fart just to see everyone's reaction, since they're not allowed to leave the room unoccupied. "What do you call a clean analyst?" a friend once joked. "Baptized." No wonder Neil committed suicide.

"Hi, I'm Jason Plumin from the Station Reps office. I'm here to talk about Neil Palau?" I announce to three startled sets of wide, bloodshot eyes lodged into three slightly disheveled heads. Apparently they hadn't noticed me enter the room, despite its small size.

"*Who* are you?" A stocky man with gray hair asks in what I take for a surly tone. He's in one of the Station Systems Analyst seats along the left wall. Neil Palau's wife is an SSA and unless she has extremely masculine features, a deep voice, and an excessive amount of hair, she's not in the room. I'm actually pretty happy about that—a conversation with the widow around her coworkers could prove awkward for both of us.

"Jason. Jason Plumin, from the Station Representative's office. I was hoping to ask a few questions about Neil Palau." I speak slowly, hoping they'll understand. It seems like they don't have much human contact.

Another analyst, a slightly tan man who looks to be about thirty despite his prematurely receding hairline, replies, "Oh, of course. Aarav mentioned you might stop by. I'm Patel, but you can call me Pat."

Pat comes off confident in his response, but I can tell he's uncomfortable. Perhaps it's the way he never fully turns to face me or how he keeps fidgeting with his fingers, like he's been out digging ditches and can't seem to get all the dirt from beneath his nails. His eyes are dark brown and punctuated by thick, black eyebrows hell bent on growing into a single brow. I wonder inwardly if he's plucking the space between to keep them at bay. Pat is tall, evident even though he's sitting, and keeps glancing back at his PC with the occasional, tentative look at his partner in the next seat.

The woman sitting next to Patel is young and attractive, maybe 22 years old, tops. Her long blond hair extends to the middle of her shoulder blades and is wrapped together in a pony tail that swings carelessly across her left shoulder when she swivels her ergo-chair in my direction. Her skin is pale with just a touch of pink and for some reason I imagine her in a bikini on a beach under an umbrella watching the Karate Kid do jump kicks atop a pylon. Her face is imperceptibly pocked, the result of an acne problem during her youth, no doubt. When she speaks, she lowers her head slightly, attempting to minimize eye contact.

"I'm Annie," she adds in hushed tones. "I've only been aboard since February, after Neil…well, you know. I didn't know him."

"Still, you might have picked things up along the way. I'd appreciate if you'd stick around," I say, hoping to reassure her that her presence is helpful despite what appears to be an obvious desire to vacate the room.

The first guy, the surly one, is a Systems Analyst named Glen. Although he's thickset, big-boned and graying, he's not overweight, presenting as more of a stocky wrestler than a portly librarian. His squat, powerful build makes it difficult to discern his height, but he's definitely shorter than Patel. When he introduces himself, he places his hand over his heart in the more formal greeting of the stations, which tells me he's been aboard for some time, I'd guess since station inception or shortly thereafter. His voice is gruff and the mop on his head matches his tone—a medium length, curly feral thatch placed atop a round ball, dense rings falling over the tops of his ears and long, silver bristles having dropped onto his upper lip.

I take the empty seat, rotating it around so I can see everyone and flip on my ComLink to record. "How well did you know Neil Palau?"

"Pretty well, I'd say." Glen is the first to offer an answer. "I've known him and his wife for over 15 years, since they first migrated. It was a package deal. We needed a Systems Analyst and an Operations Analyst and they happened to apply *and* be together. Back in those days we were looking for married couples because they were more likely to have children."

"Did they?" I ask.

Glen looks at me confused. "Did they what?"…and in my mind I hear, *you moron*. I let it slide.

"Did they have children?"

Glen's eyes widen and the ends of his bushy mustache curl upward.

"Oh. No, they never did, actually. They were pretty young when they were selected and I guess there was some trauma on Neil's part. Neil never mentioned specifics, just said they'd decided that kids weren't in their future."

Glen glances back toward his monitor before returning to the conversation. "Sorry. I'm watching all systems until Susan returns. Where was I?"

"They didn't have children because of a trauma."

"Oh, right. Yeah…I mean, no." His bushy, gray brow furls like I'm not keeping up. "I don't know if the trauma was the reason, I think it was medical. But Neil was also dealing with something from childhood. Anyway, they didn't talk about it much, but you pick things up over the years."

"Was he seeing someone for whatever problem he had?"

"I'm not sure," Glen replies, "I don't recall him mentioning anyone. Probably a better question for Susan. That's his wife." Glen adds the last point with a hint of a smirk, as if he shared some secret information.

"How about you, Patel? Did you know Neil well?"

Patel still isn't facing me. His body is contorted so that his right shoulder is pointing in my direction, his back is facing the wall of communal screens, and his hips are toward his workstation. It's a feat of yoga dexterity I don't possess.

"You can call me Pat," Patel reminds, still picking at his fingernails. "Neil never talked about trauma. Of course, I haven't known him as long as Glen. Only about eight years—since I migrated. But we didn't sit next to each other, so there's that." Pat taps the mini-wall with his left hand as if to make sure I know what he's talking about.

"There's what?" I ask.

Patel stutters for a second, trying to figure out how to explain the comment before settling on, "Well, that's, um, like an expression. You know? It doesn't actually mean anything." Then he turns back toward the screen, stopping briefly to check out the back of Annie's head. I give him a nod to acknowledge his answer and decide to leave it rest.

Annie hasn't said anything since the introductions, but she does seem interested. She hasn't looked back at her Viz once. I can't tell if she and Patel are a couple, but if so, she is not aware. His interest is abundantly apparent, with the sneak peeks and head tilts, but she hasn't so much as accidentally eyed him. I decide to engage her a bit, if nothing else to keep her on the Neil information team.

"Annie. You didn't know Neil, but you took over his work. Anything strike you coming on board in his place?"

Annie starts rotating her chair back and forth in small movements, taking her time to answer. "Nothing really. I took over most of his projects after migrating and completing the abbreviated Role familiarization session. All the projects I assumed from Mr. Palau were in order."

Annie describes how she migrated as a replacement for Palau since there wasn't anyone immediately available in the Role pipeline. She was an analyst in the CAZ, responsible for monitoring changes to life support and sustainability systems, conducting impact studies relative to those changes, and recommending solutions to mitigate future issues. The problems are many and longevity on the planet is finite, making Annie's job in a CAZ demanding, thankless, and ultimately futile. Her word choice strikes me, though. "You assumed *most* of his projects? Which ones didn't you assume?" I ask.

"That's a question for Aarav," Glen blurts out. When he sees the confused look on my face, he adds, "Our *Supervisor*."

I ignore him and turn back to Annie. "Do you know which projects Neil worked on that weren't passed to you?"

"Only one. He was responsible for GBRs...I'm sorry, Genetic Balancing Reviews. It's where we analyze the genetic differences among births and deaths over time and compare those to what the algorithm expects looking for any variance greater than a set of upper and lower control limits across any number of genetic factors." Annie's innocent smile and flushed cheeks betray her satisfaction with the explanation.

"Who does the GBRs now?" I ask.

"I'm not sure," Annie replies, furrowing her brow and tilting her head upward as if the answer might be floating in the air above her.

"I told you, that's a question for Aarav," Glen adds. "He is responsible for all analytical functions on Aries. He's the one who would know who was assigned to which processes and projects."

"Thank you, Glen," I sigh. "That's super helpful." It's as much sincerity as I can muster. Glen doesn't notice the dash of sarcasm, sitting back into his chair and lacing his fingers behind his head in satisfaction. "Other than the trauma for which he was or was not seeing someone, can anyone think of *any* reason Neil would want to commit suicide? Was he acting strange around the time of his death? Did he make any odd comments?"

"I can't think of *any* reason *anyone* would commit suicide," Glen answers, again. "It's a coward's way out. After all, how bad could things be? We have this great, space-borne platform to call home, absolutely zero worries as long as systems keep functioning and there isn't an errant asteroid, and every modern convenience known to man —coffee makers, meal gummies, health facilities, recreational spheres, entertainment, and the best view ever. You can't even tell just how fucked up Earth is from here. What could possibly be happening in someone's life to make them want to kill themselves?"

Glen is sincere. You can hear it in his voice. He really loves this place.

"While I don't share all of Glen's beliefs, I agree with him on the suicide point," Patel adds, half-rotating back toward me. "This place is a damn site better than the surface and I'll be…"

"Well, not everyone's brain works the same," Annie interrupts, shutting Patel down and causing him to lower his head and start cleaning under his left index fingernail. "Some people just have problems adjusting. I agree the stations are far better than Earth, even the CAZ, but some people just need the right kind of help."

"Not me, missy," Glen adds. "I've been on here since about the get go and I haven't ever needed help adjusting."

As much as I enjoy watching the dynamics between Annie and Glen, and Patel's utter disappointment at being rejected, I'm hoping to get out of here before I start having suicidal thoughts of my own, and I still have to find Mrs. Palau and Aarav, the supervisor. "Let's stick to Neil, okay? Did Neil give any indication he was considering suicide?"

"No, no, no," Glen responds. "Neil never said a word. There were no *indications* he was going to off himself," he adds, punctuating the word 'indications' in air quotes with his stubby fingers.

"He was a bit quieter than usual the last couple weeks," adds Patel. "But I wouldn't call it out of the ordinary. He still did good work and managed his time. He even worked a little overtime, commandeering a seat in the Economics Lab…they're down one body right now."

"And that wasn't abnormal?"

"Not really" Patel responds. "He'd been doing it for the last couple months. Some project he was working on for the Council."

"Did he mention the project to anyone else?"

"He didn't mention it to anyone," Glen adds again, unable to contain himself. "We just knew he had a project. Sometimes the SOAs are asked to conduct analysis on a specific issue of long-term interest to the Council. It's very compartmentalized, all need-to-know, but that's because if the wrong people found out they'd assume there was a problem when there isn't one. People are generally stupid, jumping to conclusions rather than waiting for the data."

"So he didn't discuss…"

"Hey Susan," Glen says as the door swooshes open. "This is Jason something, here asking about Neil's suicide."

Glen is really starting to annoy me.

Susan Palau, Neil's wife according to his file, stands in the doorway for a moment, I presume digesting Glen's pronouncement or considering why I'm sitting in her seat. The other three just stare at her, probably wondering if she'll lose her shit and break down. After an uncomfortable silence, I introduce myself with a bit more tact than Glen and ask if she'd mind talking for a few minutes somewhere more private. I can't help but notice the disappointment in Glen's eyes when she suggests Aarav's office, the lab supervisor.

We walk down the corridor in silence, Susan leading the way past a four-way intersection and toward a small room at the end of the hall. Her short, straight, jet-black hair is peppered with a few strands of gray at the roots and brushes against her shoulders, swaying gently back and forth with each step. It looks healthy from the back, although I think I notice a small thinning spot toward the top. Her uniform is neatly pressed, showing off a trim 5'6" build punctuated by curvaceous hips that seem slightly out of proportion to the rest of her features. The etching on the door reads, Aarav Ericsson.

We take the two seats on the same side of the desk and swivel to face each other. Aarav's office is plain and gray, not a single personal touch anywhere. His desk is clear and looks like it's been recently wiped clean, except for a small stamp in the corner closest to the wall that reads, "HWT X1." I'm instantly overtaken by a bout of jealousy, wondering how a lab supervisor rates HuangWei Technologies latest hardware-software combo and I'm still lugging around an old A5. There is no justice on the stations.

According to Neil's file, Susan is 38 years old, the same age as Neil, or the same as he would be if he hadn't committed suicide. Her perfectly cut, black bob and bangs frame a round, pretty face with a small pock mark on the left cheek that resembles a dimple. She reminds me of a robot from an old Sci-Fi movie, one of those films made when every futuristic female had bangs.

"So, what is it you want to know Mr. Plumin?" Susan asks, deciding to skip the formalities.

"I'm very sorry for your loss," I start. I look down to make sure my ComLink is still recording, then ask as tactfully as possible, "Was your husband having any problems around the time of his death?"

Susan takes a deep breath and exhales slowly, a hint of a frown appearing on her face. "Let's just call it what it is, a suicide. He committed suicide. And in answer to your question, no, I am not aware of any problems he was having that would have driven him to commit suicide."

"Nothing at work? Coworker issues? Boss? Anything?"

"No, nothing. None of those. He was actually doing really well at work and loved his job. It was a lot of pressure, of course, predicting problems that might wipe out all life on Aries, but he enjoyed the responsibility and was good at it. If he were having problems with anyone at work or with the job, I would know. We worked a few feet from each other every day for the last eighteen years. We spent virtually every waking moment together. If there was anything bothering him, he would have talked to me about it?" Her eyes start to water, but she seems to toughen up rather quickly.

"I understand he was working on a project for the Council, something that took up some time after hours. Do you know what he was working on?"

Susan shifts to her left and crosses her legs, which makes me wonder if a lie might be forthcoming.

"Only that it had something to do with genetics, a look at genetic diversity and equilibrium. We didn't talk much about work outside of work, there's enough of that in the lab," she replies, sounding a little defensive.

"So, he never mentioned any details about the project or why he was working extra hours?"

Another shifting movement.

"No, I told you. The Council assigns projects to SOAs on occasion and those projects are quite siloed. Analysts are not allowed to discuss them, even with other Analysts, even with their spouses. He only shared the basic premise, not the details. Yes, it kept him at work late sometimes, but it wasn't stressing him out. It's the nature of the job— sometimes we need to work a few extra hours to get things done on a tight deadline. I don't understand what all this questioning is about, anyway. Why are you so interested in a suicide?"

Now it's my turn to take a deep breath. I'd like to tell her that I'm not actually interested in Neil's suicide, not even a little bit. I'd like to tell her that I was assigned to this team to look into what appear to be perfectly normal occurrences given people's confinement in space and close, constant interactions, and I don't believe for a second that any of these suicides are even remotely suspicious. But then I remember Glen mentioning a trauma.

"It's just a routine review. The Council orders these on occasion to make sure there aren't any links—especially since they are not routinely investigated."

"I see," says Susan. "Well, there aren't any links here."

"Glen mentioned Neil might be seeing someone for some type of trauma. Something that kept you from having children?"

Susan crosses her arms and sits back in her chair, which she's started to swivel back and forth. "Glen's a nosey busy body," she replies. "And he thinks he knows everything that's going on with everyone. I'm sure he didn't get that information from Neil, and I definitely never told him that."

"So there wasn't a trauma?"

"No, well yes, sort of, but not trauma and it had nothing to do with why we didn't have children, that blowhard. We didn't have children because we didn't want children. For fuck's sake, have you seen those little bastards? They smell bad, make a huge mess, grow up to despise you, and finally, when you've given them everything, they just want out. I can't understand why anyone would want kids. Don't get me wrong, I appreciate the propagation of the species argument, but it wasn't for us.

"If anything, Neil was better adjusted than most. He was involved in most of the high profile, confidential studies over that last fifteen years. There was always something coming up and it was almost always a priority. I know the Council doesn't talk about it like that, like there are ever really priority studies, but usually when they want something they want it yesterday. It's not an easy job. But he'd taken some steps to make sure he was maintaining balance. The fact those didn't pan out the way he'd liked and he still maintained a good attitude is a testament to his resilience."

"So he *was* seeing someone for work-related stress."

"I wouldn't call it 'stress' exactly," Susan snaps back. "He just wanted to talk to someone, someone dispassionate who wouldn't be inclined to share what he'd told them. But that only lasted a short time and he quit and was back to normal. Besides, that was three months before his suicide—three months of zero indications there was anything wrong."

Susan drops her chin as her eyes start to well up again. I give her a minute to compose herself before asking if she knows who Neil was seeing.

"Yeah. That quack doctor, Ocasio."

"I take it you weren't a fan?"

"Absolutely not! There was something going on with her, something during their sessions." Susan stops swiveling and sits upright, crossing her hands on her knees. "He couldn't remember any of the discussions with his counselor. He would come home feeling better and talk about having met with Dr. Ocasio, but then he couldn't remember details. I'd ask what they talked about or what about the session made him feel better, and he'd give me a blank stare. Then there were the dreams."

"The dreams," I ask?

"Yeah. He said he was having these erotic dreams, sex with a faceless woman…that's why he filed the complaint. They got worse with each visit and they were freaking him out. He was sure she was drugging him or hypnotizing him, but he didn't have any proof. That's why he was referred to the Station Reps office, *your* office…they said he was making false accusations without proof. They said there was no evidence, no other witnesses, and nobody else had come forward, so it must be a lie. Neil never lied in his life. He was a good man, until he wasn't."

I let that hang for a moment, not wanting to interrupt Ms. Palau's train of thought. She'd just unloaded a lot and I got the feeling she was teetering between breaking down and kicking me out.

I know about Neil's problems. The violation wasn't minor, defamation as I recall, but he didn't have any priors or a history of combative or confrontational behavior, which likely influenced the sentence—probably just an apology and commitment to discontinue whatever he was doing to defame the other party, which was apparently Mrs. Ocasio. What are the odds she files a complaint against Palau, Palau commits suicide, then months later Ocasio's son also commits suicide?

"Anyway," Susan starts up again, having recomposed herself. "It's not like any of that had anything to do with his suicide. All of that was done a couple months before he killed himself. He was in good spirits leading up to his death. He seemed fine."

"When did he stop seeing Dr. Ocasio?"

Susan thinks for a moment, "It was late October. It had nothing to do with him killing himself in January."

My mind wanders back to the project Neil was working on before his death, the one that wasn't reassigned to Annie when she took his place—genetic rebalancing. I jot a quick note into my ComLink to touch base with Mrs. Ocasio, hopefully tomorrow. I'm sure it's nothing, but I need to close the loop.

"Sometimes there aren't any indications beforehand," I add. "People can have problems nobody knows about." I again let the silence settle before continuing. "I'd really like to thank you for your time. I can't imagine how difficult this is for you."

"Yeah, no problem, right? It's just another suicide. The station will keep spinning, food gummies produced, oxygen consumed," Susan says, pausing for a moment. "Nothing changes."

Susan looks toward the door and I wonder if she might be considering the same way out as her husband. "If you're heading back toward the lab, can you tell Glen I'll be back in about 15 minutes? I need some time to process."

"Of course," I say, standing to leave. "Again, I'm sorry for your loss." It's trite and untrue, but it's the only thing I can think to say.

CHAPTER TWENTY-ONE

Kami Lee

I detect a faint whiff of cigar as I press my hand to the bioscan reader on Dr. Kornel Lento's office and watch my name appear on the digital read out above it—Welcome Kami Lee. When the door swooshes open, he's sitting behind his desk, shoeless, feet up and a book in his hand. The culprit, a slightly sweet smelling cigarillo, sits balanced on a homemade void-filtering ash tray struggling to tame the smoke. It's a vice he refuses to give up, like real pencils and paper to take notes, except this one can get him into trouble.

"Where do you get those?" I ask after stepping inside the small, white-washed office.

"Get what? Books? It's not like they're illegal. Not yet," Kornel replies.

"You know what I mean." I give the air two quick sniffs for affect. "You could get in a lot of trouble having those on the station, not to mention what will happen if someone finds out you've been burning them onboard. And where are you getting fire?"

Kornel knows as well as I do there are few things that result in automatic expulsion: murder, rape, oxygen system sabotage, and especially fire. There's never been a murder or rape on the stations, or any attempt to tamper with the oxygen supply. But there was a fire.

"Leo was almost twenty years ago, Kami," Kornel retorts, not bothering to look up from his book.

"Yes, but it burned the entire station and killed thousands of people," I say as visions of the training reels role through my memory. Leo was the first and last station fire.

Early migrants were not accustomed to life in space, often believing they could combine it with some Earth-friendly vices. The Council predicted as much and instituted a number of rules to keep hazards off-station, such as banning liquor, food, tobacco products, hair spray, and anything one might burn. As I recall from the film, one or more migrants disregarded the warnings, smuggling aboard, among other things, candles and matches for use in a religious ceremony. Combustion failsafes didn't detect the fire soon enough. Emergency bulkheads sectioned off the station into smaller, self-contained units, but it was too late.

There was a rescue mission and plenty of drone video of dead bodies in black corridors. Leo was only fifty percent staffed at the time, about 5,300 people. Those in the sweet zone, compartments insulated from space by another room but not so deep within the structure they couldn't be reached, were the lucky few. Responding teams tried cutting through barriers that separated space from the air keeping occupants alive, or drilling through meters of cooled molten metal, but the sudden evacuation of oxygen and the resulting structural degradation caused fatal instability.

The teams rescued 113 Cits from Leo. Some of those whose Roles were unfilled elsewhere repopulated to one of the other eleven stations. Others were expelled back to the surface. A few volunteered to return to the CAZ, the planet preferable to the possibility of burning in space—a pretty telling narrative of the horror on Leo given the state of affairs on Earth.

Not long after, the Council set strict search and seizure protocols for immigrants, followed by a first time since inception temporary hold on Privacy First to search quarters. Cits were offered an opportunity to turn in their banned items or face severe penalties. Most complied willingly after seeing the devastation—doors soldered shut by heat, video of people burning alive, agonizing screams of faceless specters running from the horror, melting metal covering families as they cowered in an evacuation bay, children gasping as toxic fumes seared their lungs, audio of the din echoing from unreachable survivors banging on bulkheads, images of Leo's burned hull floating in space like a black, mangled Claddagh ring.

"Dammit, Doc! Fire can get you expelled. You know that better than anyone!"

"Oh, chill out," Kornel replies. "I took precautions. It's not fire. The burning is chemical-based. It generates enough heat to keep the tobacco lit without producing actual flames. It doesn't taste the same, but it's better than nothing."

"No fire?"

"No. No fire. Happy now?"

"No, not really. I'd rather you just quit."

"Kami, I don't expect you to understand. You've lived aboard Aries all your life. It's what you know. But there is a bigger universe out there full of experiences some of us still enjoy. We're afforded so few vices, hanging on to this one at my age is how I survive."

"The Council can still deport you if you're caught. Your 'it's chemical-based' argument won't replace the damage the smoke does to you or your fellow Cits. And as a doctor, you should know better."

"Well, then we'll have to keep this secret, won't we," Kornel says, punctuating the statement with a wink.

I sigh, resigned to accepting the situation for what it is. He's not going to change for me or anyone else.

"Can we move on?" I ask.

"Sure. What is so urgent?"

"I don't suppose you finished the autopsy?" I take the chair across from Kornel after realizing I've been standing in the doorway with my arms crossed the entire time.

"I said I would, didn't I?"

"And?"

Kornel sets the book down and presses his index finger against the desk, causing a virtual screen and keyboard to appear in front of him. "Sorry to disappoint but there is nothing remarkable to report."

"Wait. You have an HWT X1? How is it you get the best HuangWei tech and I'm still using an old A5?"

Kornel smiles, pretending to stroke the top of his virtual screen. "I get these the same way I get the cigarillos."

"Still, I'd really like to know how they decide which Roles are upgraded first. I'm carrying a PC everywhere I go while you get HWT's fully virtualized platform embedded directly into your workstation."

The new tech recognizes the DNA of a user when they touch a surface, presenting them with their own laptop, preconfigured based on their preferences and usage. The virtual screens are flawless, and best of all, the keyboards provide tactile stimulation while typing. Something to do with electromagnetic resistance to human electrical patterns. Whatever it is, it's a huge upgrade to the A5.

"What are you complaining about?" Kornel quips. "The A5 fits in your pocket for Pete's sake. Besides, until they roll out the X1 station-wide, I still have to lug my A5 if I want access from outside the office. Luckily, it's rare I need access anywhere but here, which allows me to carry more important things, like pencil and paper."

"I guess I'll just have to wait patiently…until they roll them out to the people doing the real work."

"Napoleon Hill said, 'great things are born from great sacrifice,'" Kornel notes with another of his signature winks. "Now if we could return to the autopsy." He taps a few keys on the virtual keyboard and starts reading the results. "There were trace elements of an anti-inflammatory in his blood, but nothing out of the ordinary. He was in pretty good shape and I expect there was some pain in keeping that way." Kornel scrolls a bit further down the screen, "There was also some bruising—again, consistent with the suicide."

"Where was the bruising?"

Kornel scrolls back up the screen. "It was on the lower back, just above the right buttock at about L4/L5. Consistent with the way he was hanging. It probably happened when he sat into the wall after wrapping the paracord around his neck. It would have taken a minute or two to lose consciousness, during which his lower back would have been pressed against the wall and remained there until we cut him down the following morning."

"I didn't think bruising could occur post mortem?"

"Well, it's rare, but not entirely abnormal. Either way, it's presence is inconclusive. The blood could have collected prior to death or after, or been exacerbated after he died."

Kornel shifts the display so it's visible from both sides so I don't have to lean in to see the photos.

"So the bruising isn't out of the ordinary. What about the location?"

"As I said, the lower back would have been pressed against the wall for some time. Just because there isn't bruising in other contact areas, like the upper back, doesn't mean it isn't normal."

"Yes, but the bruising is only on one side of the lower back. Was he twisted when he hung himself?"

Kornel appears to considers this for a moment, reviewing the notes and photos on the screen. "Perhaps it occurred when they cut him loose? In any case, there's no indication anyone else was in the room at the time of death. Granted the body was scrubbed clean from the sanitization cycles, but given the lack of evidence to suggest otherwise, the most plausible explanation is he killed himself."

Most days I'd agree with Kornel outright. Cits don't kill other Cits on the stations. But that robotic voice from the airlock bay seemed convinced. What was it he said? *I believe the number of suicides should be lower. It is being artificially elevated.*

"Okay, I get it. A lack of evidence is not evidence of a crime. What about the anti-inflammatory?"

"What about it? It was one of the NSAIDs, probably Naproxen," replies Kornel.

"So you need a prescription for it. Can you look to see if he had one?"

Kornel scrolls through the screen again. "It doesn't appear so. But they're easy enough to get on the Market. As I said, there was probably some muscle pain keeping in the shape he was in."

"Anything else in the tox screen?" I ask, doubtful Kornel overlooked anything.

"Nothing."

"What about the body? Anything other than the bruise stand out?"

"Nope. As I said, if it looks like a suicide and smells like a suicide, it's probably a suicide."

"I guess it's a suicide then," I reply unconvincingly. "But why now? It's not like any of his previous issues were coming back to haunt him. Everything was mitigated and closed. He wasn't being expelled or anything. In fact, the way I hear it, he avoided any serious repercussions."

"What issues?" Kornel asks, not knowing about Birmingham's closed file.

"Nothing. Just part of some discussion we had yesterday. I just don't understand why he'd choose to commit suicide now?"

"Who knows? Perhaps there was something going on behind the scenes? Maybe he's been hiding his depression or was recently dumped. Heck, it could have been something in his past, something from childhood he just couldn't keep buried any longer. It could be anything. The fact remains, everything points in the same direction."

Kornel taps his desk again and the virtual screen and keyboard disappear. He's got that look, the one that says he'd like to talk, confirmed a second later when he asks if this could be about more than Birmingham.

"What do you mean?" I ask. I know what he means. He's referring to our conversation yesterday at the HMC about the DupleX paper and manipulating the algorithm.

"I share information about the Council and today you're desperately searching for a nefarious motive to a suicide."

"I'm not *desperately searching* for anything. I'm simply asking questions. The conversation we had yesterday has nothing to do with me doing my job." I'm fired up in my delivery, but I want to make a point.

Kornel looks at me for a minute before responding. I'm not sure if he's assessing my anger or considering backing off until he finally spits it out.

"So instead of seeing the evidence for what it is you're fishing for facts that fit your narrative. That's not how you were raised to think. Consider the facts without inserting your own bias. Why is it so difficult for you to accept? People commit suicide and sometimes, oftentimes we don't know why. You can't solve every problem or answer every question…and you're not going to figure out why your father committed suicide."

"I get that!" I snap, but he deserves it. We haven't talked about my father in years and it has nothing to do with what is happening now. At this point I just want to put this to rest. "But here we have a Council," I start, yelling. "Manipulating an algorithm to make up for an anomaly they didn't predict and a suggestion these suicides…" I stop myself before mentioning the voice outside of Bay 1.

"A suggestion these suicides what?" Kornel asks.

"Never mind." I'm still not sure I want to share this with him.

There is a lengthy pause as Kornel waits for me to explain and I delay hoping he'll drop it. He breaks the silence with a question, "How are you holding?"

He's not just asking about my day, he wants to know how I *feel*. He's wondering if I still wake up every couple weeks in a panic after a lengthy conversation with my father's corpse. He wants to know if his decaying body still asks why I didn't do more to help when he was alive. He's concerned I'm going to end up one of the people under review by the next suicide committee. We've moved on from my almost slip to another subject I'd rather not discuss.

"I'm fine."

Kornel gives me a look, one bushy, gray eyebrow raised, leaning forward in his chair. He's known me long enough to know when I'm uncomfortable and lying and this is one of those times. Being an advocate isn't easy, taking over for a parent, raising someone else's child. The appointment is supposed to last until the minor enters role training, but in reality, the relationship and responsibility last a lifetime.

The thing is I *am* fine, mostly. I've grown used to the nightmares and restlessness, the questions without answers, the morning guilt. I don't walk about wondering whether it's worth it to stick around, to gut it out for another seventy years or more just to end up dead in space like everyone else.

"Why do *you* think people kill themselves?" I ask.

"So, you're not 'fine,'" Kornel replies.

"I am fine," I quickly retort. "I'm just thinking about the investigation. We're looking at nine deaths, eight if we discount Deputy Finn and the charged field array. They all have one thing in common—someone, presumably a living, caring, loving human being, came to the conclusion that suicide was an option. Not just *an* option, but the *best* option. They decided they'd rather end life than continue. Let's say we determine all eight people committed suicide, unaided, without intervening circumstances. That means, by extension, the 30 to 40 suicides we see every year are normal as well. We're still left with the question, why? What was so troubling that they saw death as the only way out? What pain drives that much conviction?"

"Kali, the Analysts on eleven stations have been asking those same questions for years. I'm not sure we'll ever have an answer," Kornel replies. "People do what they do for their own reasons. Sometimes it's drugs or loneliness or perhaps despair at what they've lost. Often there are signs and the people who knew them best are left to wonder why they didn't see those signs when it might have mattered. We can't blame ourselves for the deaths around us. Your father wouldn't want you blaming yourself."

I take a deep breath and hold it for a moment, allowing the slow, audible exhale to relax my shoulders. I'm not sure if it's the thought of my father or a subconscious attempt to distance myself from this discussion, but I suddenly remember I'm supposed to meet with Jason to discuss teaming up on an interview. I tap out a quick IM asking if he wants to get together tonight.

"Kali, you can't hide from what you feel."

"It has gotten easier since his...well, you know," I finally reply. "It's been almost ten years."

Now it's Kornel's turn to lean back and draw a deep breath. "Your father was a profoundly spiritual man. When he lost your mother, something inside him disappeared forever. He missed her so much and living without her was far worse than the alternative."

"But *we* were here. Me and Christopher. We needed him." I glance down, partially because I don't want Kornel to see my eyes turning to watery pools, but also because Jason responded confirming 18:00.

"And yet here you are, an Orbital Sheriff's Deputy looking into suicides on behalf of the Council. You're not cowered in a corner waiting for life to give you a sign. You're living, breathing, thriving in a world created to be better than the one we left behind. Nobody will ever be able to tell us why your father committed suicide, but we can choose how we remember him."

"Can we?" I ask, remembering the dream from a few days ago.

"You're still having the nightmares." It's a statement more than a question.

"I'm not going to kill myself," I say, deciding not to confirm his suspicion.

"I didn't say you were. I'm just concerned about your wellbeing."

Kornel scribbles something and tears the page from his notebook, sliding it across the table. "Here."

I reach for it hoping it's something I can use to sleep or at least forget, but instead there's a name. "Who's is this?"

"A friend and Psychiatrist."

"You want me to see a mental health specialist?"

"You have questions I can't answer and quite frankly, neither can you. What's the harm in speaking with someone who might be able to help? Make an anonymous appointment, just one if you like. If it's not helpful, you've only wasted a couple hours."

I consider the name on the paper for a minute and eventually relent. "Okay," I say. "And thank you. Not just for this but for everything."

"No problem," Kornel replies. "All part of being an awesome Advocate."

CHAPTER TWENTY-TWO

The Collective

There are two means of replacing the station population: permitted births and migration. The former is used for deaths the AI can predict, while the latter is for unplanned endings—the one's I facilitate. According to Council Directive 2082, all persons selected for migration as well as those born on the stations agree to harvesting—collecting sperm and eggs and storing them for future use. The Cooperative Autonomous Zones also provide material as part of the standard trade agreement. After the Fertilization Lab screens samples, those not selected due to a genetic abnormality are discarded. Nobody asks where the unused samples end up, possibly the Food Processing Lab. I'm sure those are just rumors.

When a permit is approved, a couple's genetic material is combined and implanted into the female using a process called In Vitro Fertilization. If a same-sex couple wishes to have a child, they can petition to use someone else's sperm or eggs. The only real complication to IVF is if both partners are male. In those cases, a surrogate is recruited to carry the baby to term. Surrogates are pretty easy to find on the stations—Cooperation Equals Success, Article Two. I've heard it's possible to bring a surrogate aboard from the surface for nine months in the off chance one cannot be found on board, but I've yet to meet anyone who went this route.

The only people prohibited from having children are singles. Never in the history of the stations has there been a solo Cit granted a child permit. The decision was made early on that children should have two parents, at least at birth. The policy also results in an extremely low separation rate, since it is nearly impossible for someone to get a second child permit. A person commingling with someone who already has a child won't be granted a permit for more children, lest children or grandchildren, unaware of their shared family tree, hook up later in life. Combined with other safety protocols, like genetic screening to determine relatedness prior to IVF, the population avoids becoming overly inbred.

IVF seems archaic, but there aren't any alternatives. The Council experimented with fertilizing material in tubes and growing babies in pods without anyone carrying a child. The results were disastrous. Infants would develop severe deformities mid-term—extra organs, tumors, lymphatic defects—necessitating premature termination. In two early cases infants survived incubation without issue, but the lack of human stimuli in utero resulted in destructive, anti-social behavior so severe they had to be deported. Incubating within a machine prevented them from bonding with humanity.

Births are used to fill planned deaths, but until the algorithm learns the cycles—which I've heard may take a generation or more—migration makes up for the unplanned terminations. People die of all sorts of non-age-related things every year: faulty bay door crushes, accidental field array decompositions, rapid decompression, accidental alcohol-pharma overdoses, simple falls, anaphylactic reactions to station-borne environmental factors, overexposure, and of course suicide. When one person departs, a Migration Selection Team authorizes a recruitment from the planet, kicking off the evaluation process. So every time I do my job, the MST does theirs—selecting a replacement. Which is why I'm visiting Indra Ocasio.

I made the appointment for Thursday morning hoping to check it off my to-do list early. One of the great things about Privacy First as an overarching principle is the protection it provides where doctors are concerned. The concept goes beyond a prohibition on medical professionals disclosing information about patients, it gives people the ability to schedule appointments anonymously. There is no tracking mechanism within the system to determine who met with whom. In the 25 years since IPI there have only been a couple cases where this proved to be problematic, none involved fatalities.

There are exceptions, of course. One cannot tell their doctor they are going to kill someone or disclose plans to vent all the oxygen into space, otherwise the Duty to Inform clause takes precedence. Under DTI, responsibility to the community overrides one's right to privacy, giving everyone, including medical professionals, an avenue to disclose personal details acquired during a session. But this happens so infrequently and the actions and plans falling into this category are so narrow disclosure is rarely an option—even planned suicide isn't reportable unless it will result in harm to others. In fact, the potential punishment for unauthorized disclosure is a major deterrent in itself.

Richard Ocasio—he left a few minutes ago—is a Physicist whose duties in the Navigation Lab keep the stations from dropping out of orbit or flying off into space. It's one of the more time consuming Roles. Genetically he's Hispanic IPI, which is why he changed his first name. People who migrated from the planet in the early days were compelled to conform to a certain ideal. Racism was still a thing, even as late as 2070, making name changes common among some groups. So Ricardo became Richard as a child and never went back.

There was little pressure for people from the Indian subcontinent to change, having by the mid twenty-first century established themselves as far more integral to most societies . The second great pandemic of the early 2040s, TwoGP, created a need for labor across the globe, a shortage many in the world's growing economies were happy to fill. But the West needed educated people, not *any* people, and only two countries had an educated populace able to answer the call for the newly needed supply—China and India.

Both China and India were hit hard by TwoGP, but remained powerhouses in the educated persons supply chain with people not only trained but willing to immigrate to the West. The talent shortage in places like Europe, the United States, and Canada meant more opportunities for skilled Chinese and Indian labor on the stations. The station selection algorithm does not take into account one's lineage, only where one resided at the time of selection. By supplying masses of people to western countries, China and India could essentially stack the deck and ensure more people from their countries were selected.

Unfortunately, China had burned too many bridges throughout the world with its push toward global dominance, policy on investing and extortion, and penchant for sequestering information. The previous quarter century saw Chinese aggression against neighbors, rampant spying, and unchecked theft from virtually every country on the planet. Their complicity in the creation of the first virus and the devastating impact it had on the world's economies pushed them into infamy, but it was their annexation of Mongolia, Taiwan and North Korea, as well as their attempted invasion of southeast Russia after TwoGP that scaled their fate. China would maintain their station representation, but governments didn't want any more of the communist country's people than necessary. They did, however, welcome the Indians.

The massive Indian migration saw hundreds of millions of people from the subcontinent, about 50 percent of their remaining population, welcomed into countries with few restrictions and plenty of opportunities. Indians were generally likable, intelligent, good natured and most important, they assimilated into the societies into which they joined. They often took western spouses and adopted western cultural norms. They immigrated already speaking their new country's language, usually English, something the Chinese couldn't offer even if they hadn't been such global assholes. Soon, Indians were ubiquitous in the U.S. and Europe and their DNA filtered into the general population like salt into the sea. It wasn't long before the Indian genome became a majority stakeholder on the stations.

Indra came aboard with her husband, Richard, in 2080. The child of an Indian doctor and a German physicist, Indra trained in the US-Canadian CAZ, first as a medical doctor and later specializing in psychiatry, an underappreciated field of endeavor on the planet but prized on the stations. A 2092 study titled, *Considerations for the Elimination of Psyches Aboard the Stations*, determined that eliminating the Psyche station role would result in a fourfold increase in self-inflicted deaths. The role Psyches play within the medical services cannot be understated.

Technically, Mrs. Ocasio is assigned to the Science Lab, but she doesn't actually report there. The bulk of the activity taking place in the lab is performed by scientists working on station-wide problems. Water acquisition, nutritional deficiencies, ergonomic challenges, radiation exposure, communal living complications, and physiological evolution all fall under the Science Lab. Even predictive studies, like what to do if a super-heated comet passes too close to the station, or how we compensate for a sudden and prolonged decrease in oxygen content, fall within the Lab's purview. They are basically responsible for predicting the worst things that can possibly happen and coming up with solutions we hope we never need to employ. And while there are psychiatrists conducting analysis—examining anonymized patient records, administering controlled studies, interpreting data from the mandatory annual psychological tests administered by the Analysis Lab—most Psyches work from their HabU in a space expanded to include an additional room for serving patients. Someone walking into a lab either works there or is a patient, but visitors to a HabU might just as easily be a friend, an inspector, a technician—or even a lover.

Mr. Ocasio is a predictable workaholic with a consistent track record in the Nav Lab. A call to the lab coordinator confirmed that Ocasio arrives every day at 08:00, coffee in hand, ready to abate station disaster. He doesn't break for lunch or to kibitz at the cafeteria, working throughout the day and into the evening until leaving at 19:30. There's no telling what goes on before or after work, but Derek implied his parent's home life was respectfully distant and physically stale. My appointment, an initial meeting, is scheduled from 08:00 to 10:00—a *get to know you and figure out your problems* session.

I notice her HabU has a print reader as opposed to the standard DNA Identification Pad on most other HabUs. I prefer the latter touch-less sensor over the former print-based system for the lack of having to actually touch anything, but the upgrades are slow to roll out. Both are biometrics, meaning they'll scan either my palm or finger print, or in the case of the ID Pad, the DNA present in tiny airborne particles as I pass my hand in front of the reader.

The upside to living on the stations is the utter lack of serious crime. Although HabUs are locked by default, common areas like the HMC and most offices, labs, and workspaces are unlocked until placed in secure status by an occupant. Occupied, unsecured offices don't require any interaction, simply stepping up to the door activates it and allows one to enter. However, secure rooms on Aries require biometrics to enter, which either opens the door or alerts the occupant within. The downside to station life is each of those entries is logged with the user's personal ID and a date-time stamp. If you know the right people, it's possible to alter logs. Of course, a simpler method is to knock—eliminating the need to modify the record.

"Hello. Please come in," Indra says, a disarming smile and arm wave pointing me toward her office.

She offers up coffee, but I really don't need any more caffeine. "No thanks," I reply, cordially. "I've had enough to keep me up for a month."

We move into the next room and she nods for me to take a seat opposite her. It's easily the most comfortable, sedative chair I've ever sat in. It's tan, like the station uniforms, I presume as a means of avoiding contrast and inviting calm. The cushions are of some type of memory foam covered in a soft faux lamb skin, and there appear to be shock absorbers beneath the seat. I'm sitting upright, but I could recline if I wanted, laying me flat as the dead. I catch a glimpse of Ocasio while inspecting the chair.

"The controller is here," she comments, tapping the top of her tablet. "Built into the screen. I can adjust firmness, position, and temperature if it's uncomfortable."

"No need. I'm fine."

The chair in which Dr. Ocasio sits is also not standard fare for an Aries office. Not quite as elaborate as mine but the same uniform tan, it looks like it was built for someone who spends a fair amount of time sitting with other people. A hand-sized platform extends from an arm off the right side where a disk lies flat on the surface projecting a virtual screen into the air above it. The entire set up is angled slightly to one side, allowing patient and doctor unobstructed views of each other. It's far more elaborate than the chairs in other offices.

A quick look around is enough to realize the room is also atypical. Most spaces on the stations are drab white, lacking personal touches or any sense of ambiance. People who migrated from the planet will occasionally add to their HabUs, but since space is limited, it is usually only with some small reminder of the past. Even the Cantina, which lays claim to the best piped-in music, has steel furniture and an off white floor surrounded by white walls with only a few VizDs to break up the landscape.

Ocasio's office though small is customizable, designed to enhance the therapeutic process. The walls and ceiling are modulating verdant shades of forest green and aquamarine, starting with a light hue in one corner and colorizing across the space. The shift is subtle and reminds me of the ocean videos from before people polluted them. There is a barely detectable pulsing sound, like a muffled heart beat most people probably don't even notice, and an aroma of vanilla or perhaps brown sugar, unfamiliar to anyone born on the stations but soothing nonetheless.

"Is that cookies I smell?"

"Yes, as a matter of fact it is," Ocasio replies. "The room responds to the patient in an attempt to provide a calm, comfortable atmosphere conducive to sharing."

"It can tell what I think?" I ask, concerned.

Ocasio smiles. "Not exactly. It takes readings—heart rate, perspiration, exhalation, pheromones, temperature—and processes the data to determine optimal colors, sounds and fragrances. Most people find the same smells, sights and sounds soothing with only slight adjustments. The key is not triggering major emotional shifts." She pauses momentarily to observe my reaction before continuing. "I can adjust anything that is distracting." She slides her index finger along the top edge of her virtual tablet to punctuate the statement.

"No, it's fine, just unexpected," I say, bringing myself back into focus and wondering how I didn't know about these rooms. I would totally have made up a reason to see a Psyche if I'd known about these rooms. "So, how does this work?"

"Well, since this is your first session," Ocasio starts. "We have extra time. We'll spend some of it getting to know each other and discussing any concerns you have with the process. There's usually time for a brief session if you have something you'd like to discuss today. Then we'll set out a schedule for the future. It's flexible, you drive the process. I'm more of a guide." She pauses momentarily as if about to say something that's proven unpopular in the past. "It often helps if people share their name."

I'm not startled by the question. I expected it. There is no requirement for me to tell her my name, but people are people and want to know who they're spending time with. I politely decline the offer, but ask if we can revisit as our relationship develops. Dr. Ocasio seems okay with this and moves on.

"Perhaps we'll start with you telling me a little bit about yourself," she says.

I have about two hours before her next appointment. Two hours to convince Ocasio to give me the pharma her son, Derek, promised. I'm not here for my mental health—I'm the sanest person I know. But the game *is* half the fun. It would be a shame to waste an opportunity.

"Well, if I'm being honest, there's not much to tell." *Therapists love it when you start a sentence with "if I'm being honest." It's a sure sign the next thing they hear won't be the truth.*

"I'm sure that's not true," Dr. Ocasio expectedly counters.

I sit for a moment in a state of what I hope is perceived as contemplation.

"It's okay," prompts Dr. Ocasio. "There's nothing you can't share here. This is a safe space.

"I guess there is something. But..." I trail off.

Ocasio doesn't reply. She allows the silence build. I presume at some point her patients become uncomfortable and continue, which is what I do.

"It's not a big deal. I just...I'm uncomfortable around women."

"I see," Ocasio says, tapping something onto her screen. "So you don't engage positively with women?"

"Maybe. But not, *exactly*. I mean..." I let it hang, allowing Dr. Ocasio to do what she was trained to do—draw tentative patients from their comfort zone.

"What do you mean?" she asks.

"I mean...I *engage* all the time. I'm just not sure *how* I connect is... healthy."

She types a bit more into the tablet before responding, "What about how you connect to women do you believe is unhealthy?"

"Well, I think, um..." *I avert my eyes, scanning the room in what I hope looks like embarrassment and regret.* "I think I'm addicted to sex."

Dr. Ocasio glances from the screen, her deep, umber eyes like pools of spilled ink inadvertently divulging a secret. "There are worse things than promiscuity," she offers. "In fact, sex can be a healthy release and a method for feeling close to other people. It's only a problem if it becomes destructive. Do you feel your propensity to engage in sexual intercourse is destructive in some way?"

"It's the *only* way I engage...all the time. I'm with a different woman two, sometimes three times a week. They aren't relationships. It's just fucking. Hours and hours of sex."

Ocasio leans almost imperceptibly forward, her body betraying interested anticipation. Her black hair, cut short on the sides and spiked on top, remains kempt when she runs her hand through it. She lets her fingers glide along the back of her neck, flowing down the front and brushing against her breast before coming to rest in her lap. I notice her chest rise and watch as her full, dusted-rose lips outlined in black part to taste the air, pausing at the top of the inhale in what I assume is her attempt to maintain control.

I meet her eyes and whisper, "I can get women to do things they wouldn't normally do—things they wouldn't even conceive of doing with others."

Ocasio's mouth closes as she swallows and I swear I can hear the warm saliva slide down her throat. She's not typing anymore. "Well, that isn't necessarily bad," she says, tentatively. "So long as it's consensual."

"Oh, it's all consensual," I offer, still whispering.

"You don't have to tell me if you're uncomfortable, but," Dr. Ocasio hesitates. "What sorts of things are we talking about?"

Ocasio leans into her chair, fingers poised to tap out notes on her tablet. She's almost begging for details in the way a teenager hounds his friend for more. I don't think she's going to try to sleep with me. According to her son, Dr. Ocasio's proclivities revolve around drugging her patients and she hasn't offered me anything. Perhaps it's too soon and she's waiting for a future session? I'm a little hurt, but it doesn't matter. It's not why I'm here.

"It's hard to describe," I say. "I'm, um, I'm just not comfortable putting it into words." I pause long enough to see her disappointment. "But I have photos."

"Photos?" she asks, surprised.

"Yeah, women let me take them. There isn't anything seedy about it. If you don't want to see them, that's fine." I'm going for a defensive tone, but may have missed the mark.

"No, no," Ocasio responds a bit too quickly, abating my fears. She seems to recognize her enthusiasm and sits back in her chair in an attempted course correction. "I didn't mean to imply anything. Of course we can take a look…you know, to get a better understanding of what's troubling you."

Derek Ocasio was right. His mother has needs and those needs combined with years of training, curiosity and experience are driving her to dig deeper. I sigh, as if committing to the process, tap a command into my ComLink and swipe across, sending the photos Derek shared cycling one after the other into the space between us. Her attention is fixed on the images, but I'm not sure she fully comprehends what she sees. She just stares, leaning further forward, her bottom lip sucked between her teeth. We're several pics into the montage when her eyes widen, her face morphing from erotic interest into blushing embarrassment punctuated by appalled disbelief.

Dr. Ocasio's breathing shifts suddenly from deep and controlled to panting—quick, short breaths threatening to overtake her escape. Her dark eyes, made more so by dilated pupils, dart around the room in search of meaning or perhaps waiting for someone to crash in and throw her in restraints. She seems to want to speak, her mouth moving without the aid of sound. I decide to say something before she passes out.

"Take your time," I say, calm and relaxed and hoping to keep her on track.

"How…" she trails off.

"It doesn't really matter. What does matter is what we are going to do about it."

"What…what do you want?" Ocasio says, still looking at the photos, voyeurism overruling fear.

I tap on the ComLink and the photos disappear. Ocasio jolts back, suddenly startled by the lack of virtual barrier between us. I lean forward to match her retreat, locking our eyes. "I want benzo."

It takes her a moment to comprehend my request. "Benzo? Benzodiazapine? What for?" she asks, suddenly looking exhausted.

"Good, you're familiar with them. I assumed you would be, given the photos. About a dozen should do for now."

"A dozen?"

"Look, it's not complicated," I explain, sounding perhaps a bit too harsh but feeling she needs someone to take control right now. "You give me the pills and I promise not to share the photos with anyone." *However, I might check them out myself from time to time,* I think to myself.

"It's not that simple. They are tightly controlled. I have to account for all of them. What if there's an audit?" She asks in a panic, struggling to gin up a reason to avoid giving up the pills.

She has a point. The synthetic form of Benzodiazapine is highly controlled, requiring increased reporting and periodic audits by the central Pharmaceutical Service. They're engineered more powerful and lack the addictive qualities and side effects found in their predecessors. The optimum dosage is also comparatively small, and it breaks down quicker in the bloodstream, leaving no trace after a couple hours. But what choice does she have? She's been using them herself, so she must already have considered the possibility of detection and figured out a way around the issue.

"You're obviously using them on unaware patients. How do you handle audits now?"

Ocasio looks shocked at first, as if I've accused her of something unrealistically insulting. But her body language quickly changes as the reality of being outed sets in.

"Placebos," she finally whispers, her head falling to her hands. "I have a supplier who makes them look like synthetic Benzodiazapine, but they're actually placebos—ineffective and inert pills."

I give her a moment to absorb her situation before restating my request for the daties.

"What guarantee do I have you'll delete the photos?" She asks, raising her head from her hands.

"Oh, no guarantee whatsoever. I have no intention of deleting them. They're an investment."

"An investment. Right," she mutters.

Ocasio taps something into her ComLink causing a drawer to open from the empty wall behind her and extracts a small, white packet. She stares at the pills for several seconds before reaching forward to hand them over. The look on her face and the offer of the pills like a little girl proffering her last cookie tells me she's resigned herself to the transaction.

I take the pills and give them a shake. There are twelve small, white tablets, each with a logo stamped in blue. There is little else interesting about them. Just that small blue logo, a picture of a closed eye, or perhaps a rugby ball. It's tiny.

Ocasio slumps back into her chair. I'm sure she's hoping this is over, but I've got other plans.

"How do I know these are real and not the placebo?"

"What?" she asks, startled from wherever she'd mentally transported herself.

"Real. How do I know these little pills are the correct little pills? You've already mentioned you have a supplier for copycats. These could be the fakes."

"Well, you could take one," she says, and I think I detect a fleeting grin.

"How about you take one, instead?" I ask, peeling back the zip locked bag and dropping one of the pills in my palm.

"I…I'm not sure that's a good idea," Ocasio says.

I smile, nodding toward the pill. Ocasio sits upright, back straight, looking at my palm. For a moment I'm not sure she's going to take it. I quickly run through my options if she chooses not to comply. Just as I'm considering a more physically proactive approach, she pinches the tiny tablet between her fingers and places it on her tongue.

If it's the real thing she'll develop the telltale droopy eyes described in the article I read. Within a few seconds the drug, pumping through her bloodstream, will create a sense of euphoria. We stare at each other for a moment, her probably wondering how this will end and me waiting for the signal to proceed. It doesn't take long—as if finishing a grueling, high-intensity race, her shoulders relax and she fades into acquiescence.

"Indra, how are you?" I ask.

"I'm good," she says without emotion.

It worked. She's not actually out, just highly compliant. In fact, the way I understand it, she's totally aware of what's happening, she just can't resist, nor does she want to. She'll follow suggestions and respond to questions honestly—one of the perks of benzos is an inability to lie. I decide to test the hypothesis, "Indra, do you know who I am?"

"Yes," she replies, still emotionless. "You're the one with the photos of me with patients. You blackmailed and drugged me."

"And this doesn't bother you?"

"No."

She will remember all of this, the entire interaction, unless I replace the memories, which I plan on doing before leaving. But as long as I have her attention, I might as well enjoy myself. I lean over, my mouth a few millimeters from hers. I can feel her breath on my lips, slow and intense, an inviting smell of dark cherries and vanilla. I lean into it, sliding my tongue into her mouth, meeting hers as she tilts her head imperceptibly to one side. It's warm and wet, driven by passion to play forbidden games. She's reacting, as if I'd suggested without having to speak the words.

I stand, my hand moving behind her head and pulling her up to me in one motion. She seems to be *responding,* as if it's her idea. She unzips her tan uniform down to her waist. The zippered edges hang from her breasts baring a flat, tanned stomach above a dark patch of curly hair. I do the same, allowing the one-piece to drop to the floor before stealing another long, wet kiss.

I'm a little surprised when she gently pushes me away, forcing me back into the chair. The thought the drugs might not be working creeps in, but when Dr. Ocasio peels the uniform from her shoulders, I remember what I'd read about people under the influence of benzos. She reaches a hand between her legs, but not before slapping me in the face. It catches me off guard, causing me to wonder if the Benzo's are all hype. Then she sits on my lap, her knees on either side and her left arm on my shoulder gripping with just enough force as to be both painful and erotic. We move together, ebbing and flowing, touching and stroking, the passion building until we are both covered in sweat.

CHAPTER TWENTY-THREE

Kami Lee

I'm here…Kami :) See you soon.

My text is short, a passive-aggressive attempt to let Jason know I'm early to our date, er, meeting. I just hope Jason's early, too. It didn't take nearly as long to interview all of Nigel Birmingham's friends and family as I thought it would. I figured those interviews would at least drag out into evening, but he didn't have any family on board and the few people who knew him didn't refer to him as a friend. In fact, most seemed to struggle with even modest personal details about the man. The terms *nice enough*, and *sure, he was okay* rolled off the tongue as if rehearsed. I've got one more interview right before our catch-up tomorrow, but I doubt that's going anywhere.

Hopefully Jason's not in an interview of his own, otherwise I might be sitting here alone for a while, not one of my favorite things to do. It's not loneliness, quite the opposite. I could read alone for hours in my HabU or nestled into a corner of a visually immersive recreational sphere. But the cantina is exposed. There is a chance someone will notice and want to talk. I have no problem faking my Type A at work, but after hours I just want to take off the mask and retreat into a space with fewer people.

My ComLink buzzes and I see it's an IM from Jason. *OMW. Order me something with at least 3.2 percent alcohol.* He punctuates it with his own smiley face. After a hundred years, a 7G rollout, and attempts to automate the process—voice-to-text interfaces, blink-to-text glasses, and the radical thought-to-text chip implant movement in the late 2050s which resulted in a dearth of awkward moments—we're still using simple, economical and energy efficient instant message for communication. I text the order from my ComLink to the Cantina.

I haven't had time to review Jason's file—Parker included both his and Brandi's with the suicide studies. It's not protocol, but Parker is old school thorough and suggested knowing was better than not.

The stand out surprise about Jason is he's not a Gen and he's quite a bit older than me. I presumed we were both born on the stations, but Jason migrated with his parents in 2078 at the age of eight.

I've often wondered what it's like for child migrants, stepping off the shuttle that first day into artificial gravity and manufactured air, everything new, shiny and clean, no graffiti or loud industrial noises punctuated by sirens and the occasional screams day and night, devoid of the eye watering brown haze and polluted miasma weighing on Zone-dweller lungs, small red and green lights flickering on the walls like it's Christmas every day, the faint, almost imperceptible hum beat programmed by the designers to provide a rhythmic calm. I've been told there is not even a discernible odor aboard the stations compared to that of the planet. Normal for those of us born aboard and otherworldly for migrants.

According to his record, both Jason's parents were Geneticists in the Science Lab in the Canada-United States Cooperative Autonomous Zone, Roles they also filled aboard Aries. Jason was born comparatively late for the time—both parents, George and Alyssa, were in their forties. If I had to guess, Jason is the reason they applied for migration. Most planet dwellers didn't apply after a certain age unless they had children—the CAZ was no place to raise a child, even after they sealed the borders.

"Two?" the Cantina Tech asks, setting two beers on the table.

"I'm quite thirsty," I say with a smile.

He gives me a look, something between a *ha ha* and *really?*, then heads back toward the dispensing station. I take a sip, trying to remember my primary school lessons about the formation of the Cooperative Zones. As I recall, the three Zones—CAN-US, Australia, and Iceland—formed with a single mission: development and staffing of the stations. There was a transition of power as big-tech Council members left in 2075 and the politicians took over, pushing the CAZ into increasingly chaotic leadership. If Jason's parents applied after his birth, which makes sense based on their genetic marker collection date, their age would have put them lower on the waiting list, even with the future productive child boost. In any case, they appear to have gotten out just in time—by 2079 the Zones had destabilized, crime and food shortages were rampant, and housing was over-crowded and dilapidated.

One thing we have in common is both our parents are dead. It appears his died in their seventies. At least they got to see him grow up.

"Hi there," Jason says, shocking me from my reading trance. "Looks like I owe you another apology for being late."

"It's not a problem, I'm getting used to it." I smile to highlight the joke and immediately regret it. I'm not a teenager.

"Is that mine?" Jason asks, nodding toward the only unaccompanied beer on the table.

"Yep. One Peg as requested."

Jason takes a healthy swallow followed by a long sigh, like he's just dropped a heavy pack to the floor. "There is something about a beverage brewed from yeast, sugar, and grain that makes one feel alive again."

"Plus, it's the only legit alcoholic drink we can get outside the Black Market," I add.

"Yeah. Thank heavens for the enterprising botanists who figured out how to combine 3-D printed ingredients into an infinite number of carbonated flavors, smells, and colors. If not for them, we wouldn't have free—so long as your allotment doesn't run out—3.2 percent beer. Cheers," Jason says as he raises his glass.

"Peg: It's what Orbiter's drink," I add.

"Oh, that's good. You remember the slogan."

"Kornel used to hum it. The advertising stopped long before I was born."

"Speaking of which," Jason asks. "Did the good doctor come through with the autopsy?"

"He didn't have much more than when we met with him. Negative on drugs, other than a low dose pain killer. No physical evidence suggesting anything but suicide. I also pulled all the criminal records and contaminant reports on everyone who reportedly died 'suspiciously,'" I say, punctuating the word like an idiot with my fingers.

"Anything interesting?" asks Jason, ignoring my sophomoric air quotes.

"Not really. None of the suicides had toxicology done except for Finn, and his was not a suicide *and* it came back negative. I haven't finished plowing through the criminal reports, but doubt I'm going to find anything out of the ordinary. Still, I suppose it's worth checking. How about you? You had the Palau interviews today, right?"

"The interview was a non-starter. Met with Palau's coworkers, his boss, his wife. None of them had anything interesting to add. He committed suicide—even his wife, Susan, thinks so," Jason replies. After a short pause he adds, "I'm not sure about any of this. It seems like a huge waste of time if you ask me."

"You've been around longer than I have, is this normal? Does the Council routinely review suicides as *possibly* suspicious?" *No air quotes this time.* "Suicides have been around since the stations were initially populated, right?"

Jason takes another long drink before continuing, "Excuse me," he chuckles, stifling a burp. "Yeah, this is new. I don't recall anyone ever questioning whether the number of suicides in a given year was abnormal. Perhaps someone in the Analysis Lab did a study and found anomalies and the Council thought it best to assign a team. But they didn't assign an analyst, which suggests they're ticking a box somewhere to turn some metric green. Nothing I've come across so far, other than the number of suicides being *maybe* slightly higher for the first quarter, convinces me there is anything going on."

"That's what I was thinking," I say with the conversation in the EVA bay and Kornel's revelations about gender inequities nagging me. "But still, perhaps there's something we're not seeing."

"Sure. We should probably keep an open mind, right?"

His pause before replying and the way he hid his face behind another gulp of Peg makes me wonder if he's humoring me. I guess I don't blame him if he's skeptical. Heck, I'm skeptical despite what I've been told, which isn't much—a voice with suspicions and a doctor with a reasonable explanation. I'm about to ask Jason if any of the people he interviewed about Palau mentioned current population studies when he breaks in.

"So, what's your story? Graduated from Role training early, youngest Orbital Sheriff's Deputy in station history, and already assigned to a special project. Is there not a single black mark? Untamed youthful indiscretions expunged from station records? A history of rebellious abandon with a more experienced professor?"

Apparently, I'm not the only one whose done their research. "No, nothing like that. No hot-wired shuttles or allowances spent on bootleg booze. What you see is what you get."

"Come on, there has to be something. Some little imperfection?"

I consider for a moment telling Jason about my mother who wrote the initial code we use on our ComLinks. Christopher's memories, eleven years older, remain in a sort of stasis—a young boy with a caring, protective mum who read bedtime stories, applied hugs and encouragement in equal measure, and who's dark side sent her into days of silent solitude where she wouldn't eat or interact with anyone. Since she died in child birth, mine, my memories are entirely derivative, the product of stories told by Kornel who wouldn't dare speak ill of the dead.

There is something horrific about the number 11 in our family. Christopher was 11 when mum died and our father died 11 years later. Not that he was much of a parent. Kornel says father was ill-equipped to raise two children on his own—it just wasn't part of his skill set. It's not part of Christopher's skill set, either. He at least had an excuse, he was only 22 when father committed suicide, barely out of Station Role training and pursuing a career in the Botany Labs. I was sent to live with the Lentos per father's request. The difference in our ages, Christopher's station adaptation issues and growing black market business, and his drift toward solitude left us with less and less in common until we finally settled on our current scheduled visitation—me texting him every couple weeks and him not replying. Occasionally I deviate and go looking for him in the B-Labs, forcing a hug on him after an awkward, one-sided conversation.

None of that is casual drink conversation, so I decide to err on the side of brevity.

"Well, it would be an over statement to say Kornel is super pleased with my Role selection. But that's about as good as it gets when it comes to issues."

"Dr. K doesn't like you being an Orbital Sheriff's Deputy? What the heck? Does he not like law and order?" Jason asks with a broad smile suggesting he's kidding.

"I think he'd have preferred I select something ranked in the top three spots. He would never say anything, of course, but every once in a while, I catch him glancing at the OSU patch on my arm with this wistful look. You know, like he wishes I'd done more."

Jason nods, holding his reply just long enough for me to appreciate his timing. "Could you have done more?"

"You mean could I have been a doctor or scientist or something? I don't know. Maybe."

The answer is 'yes' and I know it. Humility and honesty are the cornerstones of the Lee dynasty and questions about self tend to put them at odds. Just as father was ill-equipped to raise two children, I'm ill-prepared to boast about myself. It's not a lie. I don't know for *sure* if I could have done something else because I never attempted any other role.

"What were the top three career fields from your SR test?" Jason asks, unwilling to let it go.

"Okay, I'm going to tell you," I say after an audible sigh. "But don't judge me. Promise?"

"Promise," Jason replies, putting his hand over his heart.

"Medical-Research, Science-any, and Astrophysics." I pause, then quickly add, "But right behind those were station Window Washer, HMC Sanitation Tech, and Pet Robot Trainer. And don't think I didn't seriously consider the last one. The chance to work with robots instead of humans becomes increasingly appealing with each passing minute."

Jason laughs out loud, causing me to laugh, too. It feels good. It's been a while since I've made anyone laugh and even longer since I've laughed *with* someone.

"Well, if it makes a difference, and there's no reason it should, I think it took a lot of guts to go off script and select Orbital Sheriff's Deputy. Not everyone has the courage to follow their dreams... although I think the odds of success were in your favor."

"Thanks," I say as the Cantina Tech delivers two more Pegs.

"So is this working?" Jason asks.

"Is what working?"

"My flirting. I'm not very good at it. Kinda hoping we're hitting the mark here."

Flirting? Of course he's flirting, you dork. He didn't show up to talk cases. He's interested and I'm slipping into awkward.

"Yeah. It's, um, good. You're flirting, I mean. It's nice. Like, sweet and all. Is mine working? The flirting, I mean?" *I sound like a moron.*

Jason laughs again. It's unforced, spontaneous, causing my shoulders to drop and what I presume is an idiotic smile to stretch across my face.

"Yeah, although I think you're more out of practice than I am," Jason replies.

"Here's to being bad flirts," I praise, raising my glass.

Jason taps his mug to mine and we both take a swig. I'm not sure about him, but it gives me time to formulate a coherent sentence versus the babble that spilled out last time.

"What about you? What's your story?" I ask, not wanting him to know I reviewed his file.

"There's really not much to tell. We migrated when I was a kid, two parents, both loving, passed, and no siblings I'm aware of."

"What made you choose the role of Station Representative?"

"Not sure. At first it was the chance to work with people. Then, as I continued down the path, I realized it's not so much Cits I enjoy, but the law. I really enjoy being part of a process that defines in a major way how we coexist."

"Wow, that's deeper than expected."

"Ha! A little too much 3-point-2 beer, I think."

"How about something lighter? Like, what is your fondest and least happy memories from when you migrated aboard?"

"Oh, that's an easy one. It was the HabU. Our unit in the CAN-CAZ was bigger, but what a dump. We were the first to occupy our Aries HabU and its hidden beds, integrated gaming system, and on demand video. All of a sudden, we had access to every video game, movie, sit-com, and late-night episode from the late twentieth and early twenty-first centuries at our finger tips—way better than the 24/7 propaganda news network on the surface. I didn't get any sleep the first few weeks aboard. Even the station news—upcoming communal events, station status reports, important reminders, policy changes, public Council meetings, helpful wellness suggestions, reminders of why you don't want to return to Earth, the occasional averted disaster—all-in-all a pretty benign feed. The Council *really* scored with this eight year old when they archived the movies and TV shows from their childhoods."

"That's some testimonial," I praise. "Admittedly, my own memories of childhood do not include a glowing review of station digital entertainment. My father was all business and the Lento's never watched the Viz except to see the news. I feel woefully unprepared for any discussions about historical pop culture."

"Well, we might have to do something about that."

"Oh, definitely," I reply, hoping I'm not blushing as much as I feel I am. "And the least fond memory?"

Jason thinks for a moment, evidenced by the pause and his thoughtful glance up and to the right. "I suppose that would have to be the food gummies. I remember the CAZ importing nutritional gummies from the stations as supplements because of the waning food supply, but they weren't a mainstay. We mostly ate whatever real food was available. But on the stations, gummies are it. No need for sit down meals—how long does it take to eat a couple gummies? For a while my mom insisted we meet at the table every evening and chew our gummies together. But eventually she dropped the pretense. The only thing she never quite quit was morning coffee—the nectar of life as she put it."

"I think your mom and I would have gotten on quite well."

"I'm sure. It sounds like you both shared a genius level IQ."

I take a quick drink of Peg to hide the rush of blood to my face and the accompanying pink cheeks. I'm sure Jason notices, but he doesn't say anything—just takes a long swallow of his beer and looks around the room.

"What are you looking for?" I ask.

"I'm just wondering how many people in here get to carry a CSW *and* a pair of Autonomic Restraints."

I chuckle, patting my left hip where the Contactless Stun Wand sits hanging from a loop on my uniform.

"Ever use those for fun?" Jason asks.

"I'm considering it now, in fact."

"Well, if you need to practice, I'm your guy."

"Unfortunately, a hit with a CSW sucks. In addition to a nasty headache and acute dehydration, it's been known to put an immediate end to flirting."

"Yeah, it doesn't sound nearly as much fun when you say it," Jason says, making an involuntary nose crinkle that I find adorable. "Do the Restraints cause headaches and dehydration?"

"Not that I know of."

Jason smiles. "Perhaps we can find out later."

CHAPTER TWENTY-FOUR

The Collective

Mrs. Ocasio's reaction to the Benzos was far better than expected. She was compliantly autonomous in a way I did not anticipate. Part of me wishes I could have left her with a piece of our time together, a Thursday tryst to brighten her Friday morning. Given her proclivities, she might have enjoyed a souvenir of our time. But I couldn't trust she wouldn't tell someone.

Implanting a new memory was fairly straightforward once she explained the process. I simply had to rewrite our time together, replacing the Benzos and coitus with an alternate reality. First, she deleted the anonymous appointment I made—a precaution, since it's easier to create a scene where Ocasio chills out than one where she has a patient session with corresponding discussion topics, triggers, diagnosis, recommendations, and future appointments. Details are a necessity in her profession. Most people remember events in broad brush strokes, allowing the mind to fill in the gaps. But as a therapist, she'd be immediately suspicious if she couldn't remember the session minutiae.

I replaced our 90 minutes with free time—a rare commodity for mental health professionals on the stations—and an opportunity to get caught up on news of the day. She learned the outcome of the CAN-US CAZ elections, a new food gummy supplement being developed with the added benefit of adding color to otherwise space-bleached skin, and the date of the Council's next open meeting. There was also another small attack from the Open Lands to balance out the good news and reinforce the reason we prefer the stations to that shit show of a planet.

It took more time to add details to the story than expected, which left me bumping up against her next appointment. I set the mood lighting back to its original, pre-me setting, shifting the chair slightly and making a mental note to get one for my HabU. The door cam showed the corridor empty, so I ducked out feeling pretty good about the outcome. It was a fine piece of work—neither my first nor last.

I've been taking care of the algorithm's inadequacies long enough to have racked up quite an impressive record. Whereas women made up 40-to-50 percent of the suicides on Aries prior to my joining the team, that percentage is down to under 15 percent. For every male killed, a female was recruited and those are just Aries numbers. Add in the other stations and our clan is well on its way to filling the void between algorithm and DupleX solution and its only been a few years.

It's not all business, not for me at least. The goal is to stem the gender imbalance until someone figures out a way to reverse the effects of space on female reproduction. But nobody knows how long that's going to take, not even the Council, forcing us to operate as though this is a long term effort. The thing is, I rather enjoy it. The killing, I mean. There's an excitement to the hunt—target identification, recording habits, learning motivations, manipulating actions and emotions. Sometimes I'll even meet with victims several weeks before termination just to get to know them, to make a personal connection. There's an adrenal warmth to the final outcome, like being wrapped in a heavy blanket while staring into space. It's sensual.

My own journey started several years ago with a chance meeting, or so I thought when I was too naive to imagine anything else. I'm a sucker for bootleg booze and well-timed flattery, something my recruiter must have known. She was older, over 50 when we met, her sleek lines and beaming smile undimmed by time. Her fitted, one-piece uniform highlighted slender curves and toned muscles, transforming the harshly lit doorway into an Edouart silhouette. I felt a bit self-conscious watching her walk toward the bar.

It wasn't her stunning seductiveness and compelling charm that swayed me, although she was most definitely beautiful in the way refined, experienced women become when they dispense with the pretenses of youth and embrace their vitality. It was a presence, a prominence held in the ether by power earned and deserved. I was overwhelmed by her laugh and gentle, sovereign touch—she coaxed from me a passion I'd long forgotten. I was sold on her ideas, her ideals, well before she mentioned the mission.

Soon I was part of a tribe, the Collective, devoted to a single god, the god of preservation. At some point in the late twenty-first, station design and implementation diverged, leaving a gaping hole in the future. The sacred algorithm, the one developed to protect humankind, had an error. Well, not quite an error, but a blind spot amid it's trillions of calculations and permutations. It couldn't fathom an environment where people failed to adapt to the dynamics of space. Over time, the AI would learn and grow, but nobody could predict how long it would take or if its evolution would come in time. Which is where we come in.

Waiting for someone else to take action is not a plan and she knew it. She was in a position of influence, *within* the circle. She could control the flow and the narrative, purifying insight for the masses and channeling knowledge to the right people like water to the fields, growing an elite force capable of stemming the erosion of the human race. We weren't simply killing, we were protecting an uncertain future until a remedy could be forged.

There are precious few who understand the extent of the Collective. I know there are others like me on other stations—as good as I am, I can't be everywhere. In fact, there may even be others on Aries, although the suicide rates would suggest otherwise. But I have no idea when I meet someone in the hall or over vid if they are part of the Collective or simply another uninformed lamb. I've wondered, of course, while talking to people at the HMC or in the cantina. Could they be just like me? But there's no way to tell. Anonymity and compartmentalization are the cornerstones of our oath—it protects us all.

The question is moot, anyway. Nobody is quite like me. We do what we do for the same reason, but there's no way the others enjoy it as much as I do. It takes a true believer, one not only committed to the mission but passionate about the process to embrace the sacrifice of human life. I am all-in, willing to do whatever it takes, Council support or not.

What do those ass bags know anyway? There's only one or two of Councilmembers worth their weight in food gummies. They planned this perfect society, set everything in motion, then when it comes to righting the ship, they lack the fortitude. So they hide behind covert decisions which on their own won't make a bit of difference. One simple call, get rid of some men and recruit more women, and they can't own it.

That's really what it comes down to, making a decision and following through. If we don't there won't be a station population. Everyone on the Council, all twelve people, read the same report from the Analysis Lab. The population dynamics are unsustainable given the effect of radiation on female reproduction and the current rates of replacement for routine, predictable deaths just won't cut it. The only way to buy enough time for the brains to figure out a solution is to increase the number of men dying and replace them with women. It's simple.

The Council had no problem telling most of the politicians they weren't invited to join the rest of us on the stations. Sorry, you cannot pass go, you cannot enjoy a life of luxury aboard a state-of-the-art space station where all of your needs are taken care of and your biggest worry is whether to bring along a flask of bootleg booze to strengthen the 3.2 percent crap at the pub. Who on the Council thought it a good idea to limit the amount of alcohol in beverages aboard the stations? Maybe if they had access to some liquid courage, they wouldn't be so tentative when it comes to making tough choices.

The offspring of tech giants and tycoons of industry are little more than apparitions. Their parents and grandparents were smart, influential, and ruthless, the richest people on the planet during a time of chaos. They recognized the impact politicians were having on economies, climate, and societal discourse and invested in first the formation of the Autonomous Zones and then the stations. They weren't afraid to make difficult choices for the benefit of the greater good—who to include in development, how to house people in the CAZ, where to allocate food supplies, when to seal off the Zones, and who to leave behind on Earth. But their children and grandchildren rely on an Algorithm to determine their fate. They are descendants of the best and brightest, but one doesn't need smarts to govern, one needs merciless abandon.

I'm not sure anyone at my level in the Collective knows which Council member is leading the effort and providing aerial support for our operation. Perhaps a son of one of the founders or a granddaughter? Someone who remembers the stories of their elders about what it means to be responsible for millions of lives. A lone fighter among the congress responsible for balancing our campaign across all eleven stations, providing high cover until a solution can be found. A single soul willing to make the right choice for the sustainability of the human race.

That's the beauty of the arrangement—everyone is a semi-autonomous cell unto their own. There is a risk one person gets caught, outing the next in succession, taking the entire Collective down like so many dominoes. But the possibility is remote. Only the recruiters know true names, and I'd suppose our lead on the Council, but maybe not. I don't even know the name of my recruiter, only that she isn't on Aries. And there are no records—no orders, dates, positions, or any other identifying information. It's worked this way since the beginning, a single directive, limited contact, occasional target assignments, encrypted channels, and four rules: only kill men with problems, unless it's absolutely necessary to kill a woman to protect the program; all deaths need to look like an accident or suicide; don't get caught; and if you get caught, you're on your own.

I relish the lack of direction. I'm free to take out whoever I want and as many as I want, so long as I follow the rules. There are no quotas, no minimums, no meetings or metrics, no reminders to stay on track, no monthly summary reports, no boxes in a spreadsheet to turn green, and no end of year roll-ups. Simply find the males who don't fit in and remove them from the equation, the Council does the rest through station policies. They've already adjusted the replacement percentages of women and men and altered the selection protocols, we're just giving them an opportunity to put the new ratios in place.

The lack of guidance also means a lack of feedback. Am I taking out the right people? Are we making an impact, sufficiently stemming the tide and buying time for a fix? I like to think if I were fucking up I'd hear about it, or end up a suicide myself. I don't think they would leave me in the dark if I weren't doing the right things.

I'm told most people ask how long we need to do this. Nobody really knows. The scientists will eventually figure out how to compensate for the radiation damage, the Council will adjust quotas based on the new data, and sometime afterward we'll get the order to discontinue over our ComLinks. But I'm not looking toward that future. I don't care how long I need to keep going. This means more to me than a simple mission. It's an opportunity to make a difference, contribute, serve the citizenry by ridding them of those who don't fit in. And if I'm being totally honest, stalking and killing turns me the fuck on. It's authentically sybaritic. How long do I need to do this? Shit. More like, sign me up.

When names are passed directly, they come via anonymous, encrypted channel to my ComLink. They flash on the virtual screen for

several seconds while reviewing a file or watching a media update—
like Neil Palau's did—and vanish just as quickly. It happens so fast one
might even be forgiven for missing it. The names don't come with
instructions. We're supposed to know what to do.

I didn't know Palau personally. I'd heard he was censured for
making accusations against a therapist, the same Dr. Indra Ocasio who
supplied the Benzos, in fact. Defamation is a big deal on the stations,
one's reputation being the lifeblood of relationships and commerce, so
I was surprised when Palau received zero rehab time, his only
punishment being an apology and promise to stop. It wasn't until
much later, while building out his profile, I found out the real reason
he ended up on someone's shit list.

Palau was a workaholic who spent almost all of his time either in
front of a Viz or with his wife, who also works in the Analysis Lab. As
a Station Operations Analyst, he was always involved with some
special project, and routinely on quick turn-around assignments from
the Council requiring short-term bouts of long hours to meet
deadlines. If the Council was interested in something, deadlines were
generally short.

SOAs all work on different projects, either assigned by the Council
or self-directed based on analysis, observation, or some wild theory.
Mr. Palau's studies didn't overlap with other SOAs—each SOA
operates as a single, separate analyst. After compiling what digital
footprints I could find, I surveilled Palau for several weeks, eventually
settling on an at-work, after hours intervention—among the few,
predictable times he and Mrs. Palau weren't together. Outside of his
normal shift he used his supervisor's office. It was preordained.

Lemborexant is an exquisite sleep aid, easily obtained from the
station's less legitimate corridors by people suffering from insomnia. It
has all the benefits and few of the side effects of the barbiturate-based
drugs, like hallucinations and suicides—although the latter would be
handy in this case. The newest, highly refined versions of Lembo are
fast acting, resulting in almost immediate syncope. It's recommended
you take it when you are lying in bed, lest you not make it there before
transitioning to the horizontal.

There was a remote chance of a post-mortem. They aren't routine in
suicides, but better to plan for the possibility. Insomnia is common on
the stations, the ubiquity of electronics and faux lighting interfere with
melatonin, and not everyone can handle the supplements. Palau was
working a lot of hours, had a tendency toward isolation, and was

seeing a mental health professional. A medical examiner would take his these into consideration.

His wife might claim Palau didn't take drugs, but it didn't really matter. He could obtain Lembo from the black market. Anyone who's aboard for more than five minutes knows how to get things from the market, and someone who's been aboard for fifteen years knows more than most. They'd figure he just didn't tell her about the meds. If Mrs. Palau didn't know Mr. Palau was considering suicide, she wouldn't be expected to know her husband was scoring.

We actually had a nice chat before he took his own life. I told him I was working on a story about couples who migrated together and the challenges of co-working spouses. At first, he demurred, saying he was too busy. But when I mentioned the opportunity to talk about children, he warmed up to the idea. Apparently it was a hot button topic between he and Susan—him wanting to apply for a permit and her not wanting anything to do with raising another human being in space. She was fine with migrating, but drew the line at bringing new life aboard.

We talked only briefly about his duties. As expected, he was reluctant to discuss specifics, mentioning only in generalities his focus on human factors systems and processes aboard Aries—things like psychological effects of space and confinement, post-migration adaptation, impacts of social interactions on station populations, effect of physical activity on societal well-being, long-term station sustainability, and, he added tentatively, genetic rebalancing. Those two innocuous words were why he was targeted.

I got bored after about an hour, having drifted into a discussion about how he loved his wife and how much they had in common and how his job bit into their personal time and that even though she didn't want children, it was a sacrifice he was willing to make for her happiness. Blah, blah, blah. It was all so droll. "Very noble," I commented, searching for a way to wrap this up. "I think I have everything I need."

His disappointment at the suggestion our time was coming to an end was a surprise. Apparently he'd been working a ton of hours with little human contact and I assumed little intercourse of late. Perhaps he just wanted some company? Especially someone who cared less about his work and more about his personal dynamics. Even nerdy, awkward introverts need human interaction. But I had to move on. There were things to do and it was getting late. Besides, my door doesn't swing in his sexual direction.

I reached into my left pocket and palmed the tiny syringe filled with enough Lembo to put half the station to sleep. The tiny injectors were designed to be painless, but fell a bit short in practice. "Thanks for your time," I said, offering my hand.

Palau looked confused, probably wondering why I didn't use the standard station greeting with my hand over my heart. It was a gamble, I know, but I hoped, given how long he'd been on board, he might be nostalgic enough to appreciate a handshake. Worst case, I could just tag him on the arm and hope the fast-acting drug kicked in before I had to restrain him. I was hoping it wouldn't come to that though, since it might result in suspicious bruises. The gamble paid off. Palau took my hand with a reminiscent smile.

When I cupped my left hand over his right and injected the Lembo, he pulled back reflexively. For an instant I thought he was going to yell, or say, 'What the fuck?' But he did neither of those things. His initial look of surprise quickly morphed into recognition. With a slight nod of acknowledgment, he sat back down into his seat, then laid his head on the table. I got the weird sense he'd expected this to happen.

CHAPTER TWENTY-FIVE

Jason Plumin

"Good morning," Kami mutters, still half asleep. "I'm glad you stayed, Jason."

I glance at my ComLink on the retractable night stand and notice the time—06:00, too early to consider getting up. I'd rather just lay here hoping our night at the cantina getting plied on 3.2 percent Pegs topped up with the bootleg hooch I smuggled in wasn't a contributing factor in last night turning into this morning. It definitely helped loosen up memories of her mother dying during child birth, her father committing suicide and a drug dealing brother. She's a lot more complicated than she lets on. I'm definitely going to remember the bit about the brother in case I ever need a new source for high quality Pharma.

I wondered about the father since his suicide isn't recorded in the official record. Her story about finding him and Lento fixing it is a little disturbing. Suicides are pretty common—zero stigma surrounding them even ten years ago. But a person in Lento's position hiding an official finding isn't supposed to happen. Messing with data throws off the algorithm, leading to biased, misinformed decisions and algorithmic adjustment errors. There are a lot of things one can lie about on the stations, but data isn't one of them. It's like tinkering with the Holy Grail of station dynamics.

"What time is it?" Kami asks, nuzzling her back up closer and pushing her bare bottom into my hip.

I roll over onto my right side and wrap my arm around her waist, gliding my hand over her stomach and between her diminutive breasts until it wraps over her shoulder. Her warm skin is soft and taut with fine muscle fibers, like one would expect of a twenty-year old whose job demands a certain level of fitness. It would be a mistake to call her skinny. Her lean, sinewy figure, chiseled shoulders, sculpted arms and molded back betray a woman at peak performance.

"It's still early," I say. "06:00. Relax while I get us some coffee."

I slide out, leaving behind the warm bed for a long walk across a brushed metal floor to the coffee dispenser. The floor's heated, but compared to two bodies between the sheets it feels cold beneath my feet. I spot my uniform between me and the beverage center, stopping long enough to pull it up to my waist and wrap the arms around my hips.

Kami asked about the Palau interview last night and I was less than forthcoming. I mentioned it was uneventful, touching on his relationship with Dr. Ocasio, but omitted any information about the Genetic Balancing Reviews. We know about his conviction, but not the GBRs or his connection to another suicide, even if only tangentially through his association with Derek's mom. I could have told Kami and suggested we interview Indra Ocasio together. Apparently, I'm okay sleeping with her *and* withholding potentially relevant information.

In my defense, there wasn't really an opportune time to bring it up. The Palau interviews came up early in the evening, long before we decided to return to her HabU, and by the time we got here we weren't discussing much of anything. There wasn't time to mention the genetic rebalancing project, was there? Now it's the next morning and the moment is lost. *So stop thinking about what you didn't tell her and press the buttons for the coffee.*

Every HabU is pretty much the exact same design. There are small differences based on family size, and sometimes people who work from their HabU have a slightly different configuration, but the important functions are all exactly the same in precisely the same place. It's reassuring knowing if I wake up in a strange bed, I'll be able to find the head, hydration station, and coffee dispenser without stubbing my toe. A few steps and a couple short minutes and we have two, hot caffeinated beverages to wash away any guilt I might have about last night.

"Here ya go," I say, handing Kami the cup with the haft pointing toward her. "The mug is hot. Be careful." I know the mug is hot because I carried it from the beverage station to the bed in the palm of my hand so Kami could grab it by the handle. Who says chivalry is dead in the twenty-second century.

Kami sits up, pressing a button on the wall next to her to transform the headboard into a backrest, then props the pillow against it for added support. Once she's comfortable, she reaches for the mug, cupping her left hand around the side for warmth. Another couple seconds and it would have been decorating the floor. I watch as she pulls it close to her face and inhales deeply, letting out an audible, satisfied sigh, as if the smell alone comforts her. I shuffle around the other side, perform a single-handed untie of my uniform letting it slide to the floor, and slip beneath the sheets.

Kami is sitting with the covers around her waist, her petite breasts exposed to the comparatively cool room causing her nipples to harden, which in turn causes me to harden. When she pulls the mug to her lips to take a careful sip, she presses her forearms against her breasts to warm them. After swallowing she says, "Last night was fun. Did I say anything embarrassing?"

"Not embarrassing for you," I reply. "But then again you're not the one who was under all the pressure to perform in the face of a genius."

She laughs. It's carefree, like someone just starting out in life, untempered by one-night stands and major mistakes. "You did just fine. In fact, better than fine. Let's just call it genius itself."

"Seriously, you were pretty chatty, but in a good way. It took a lot to share the information about your father's death and Kornel. I really appreciate it."

Kami blows into the mug before taking another sip. She's thinking about something, perhaps regretting having shared as much information as she did about her father and the doc. It's during these awkward silences I start to wonder if I should break in with a joke. My procrastination pays off.

"It's not something I normally discuss on a first date," Kami finally replies. "It tends to ruin the moment." She glances over with a smile and I wonder if she's expecting some confirmation that the moment was not ruined.

"Well, obviously it didn't affect anything," I say, nodding toward where my erect penis lays hidden beneath the sheets. "It's life. As difficult as it might sometimes be, it makes us who we are."

"And what's happened to make you who you are?" Kami asks.

"Me?" I sigh. "I've lived as close to a charmed life as one can hope. I'm an only child, so no sibling issues to contend with. I can't blame anything on my amazing parents. About the only thing missing was a dog, which is probably best. Having one would have made me far too responsible an adult."

"Are your parents still around?" Kami asks, having forgotten that part of our conversation from the night before.

"No. My father died in 2091 and my mother passed about three years ago. They lived long and happy lives, both aboard Aries and on the planet. No regrets that they ever mentioned."

Kami's eyes widen as she figures out this all sounds familiar. "Oh my god, you totally told me that last night, didn't you?"

"Your advanced years must be starting to affect your memory." I say, playfully.

"I'm so sorry," she says, pausing for effect. "But at least memory loss is something you're familiar with, given half your life is about over."

We both chuckle and Kami puts her left hand on my leg beneath the covers.

I can't remember the last time I was this comfortable around anyone, especially after such a short time. Don't get me wrong there were plenty of women, especially in my twenties when I wasn't nearly as picky. But lately nobody seems to click. I've grown tired of looking for the right person. Nowadays, if it doesn't develop organically—a chance meeting, an introduction at a friend's birthday party, presenting the station's side to a red-headed, Irish judge—if it doesn't just happen it's probably not going to happen. Cecelia is the most intimate relationship I've had in years and as she's so fond of reminding me, she's almost twice my age. She has no intention of taking away my chance at fatherhood.

I'm a shit. Here I am in bed with Kami and thinking about Cecelia. Maybe I should I tell her about Kami. It's not like she hasn't been honest about her feelings and our future. Our thing is casual. It is an opportunistic mutual appreciation based on shared interests with someone who isn't a complete idiot and enjoys great sex every Tuesday night. She's said often enough she doesn't have a problem with me meeting other people…as long as I keep Tuesday's open.

On the other hand, I can always tell Cecelia later if this ends up as something more. Besides, my guess is Kami is probably damaged given her history. It's just buried a little deeper where one-night stands can't find it. Not that I don't like her and last night was awesome, not to mention this morning. But the likelihood is either she'll move on because of her own issues, or she'll figure out in short order just what an asshole I am, bringing whatever developed to an abrupt end. Until then, Cecelia does not need to know anything.

"Are you thinking about something important?" Kami asks, having noticed my metaphysical departure from the bed. Let's just add 'intuitive' to the ever growing list of her attractive qualities.

"Just formulating a plan for my day. Are we doing the Water Reclamation Tech interviews this morning? What was her name?"

Kami thinks for a moment, tapping her ComLink to bring up the file. "Hannah Bonikowski. Yeah. I set up a meeting for 08:30 to meet with her boss. Her parents aren't on board and there's no significant other listed in her file."

"Was she a migrant or…"

"No," Kami interrupts. "She was a Gen, born on Aries. Young—only 20 when she committed suicide."

"What's so funny?" Kami asks, noticing my one-sided smile.

"Aren't you 21?"

Kami gives me a shove with her shoulder, almost spilling what's left of my coffee. "Yes, I am, as a matter of fact."

"So you referring to her as young, isn't that a little ironic?"

"I'm an old soul. We geniuses are like that—the downside of having highly advanced brain function. We may be ten years apart physically…"

"Um, twelve years, but who's counting?"

"You might be twelve years older, but we are intellectually and psychologically in the same decade," she says, giving my thigh a pinch.

"Plus, I'm in awesome shape," I add. "Which might actually make me younger than you." I say, playfully pinching her back, only a lot more gentle than the bruise-inducing one she just delivered.

"Is that a fact?" Kami replies, setting her empty mug on the nightstand. "Let's see just how young you really are."

As she reaches her hand between my legs, I think to myself, *that's going to leave a bruise.*

CHAPTER TWENTY-SIX

Brandi Mikkelson

Brandi, Friday, 09:00, find a private VizD.

Our Interstation Personal Rep Coordinator, my boss, the demanding bitch that she is messaged me. Marta's actually the boss of all the PersRep's. She acts like she's endowed with awesome authority and incredible power, like she's responsible for keeping Cits breathing or the toilets flushing instead of just coordinating the activities of a couple dozen people whose job it is to make excuses for bad behavior. Sure, we can be a rambunctious bunch, our days bleeding into afterwork games of checkers and late nights with a good book, but for the most part we manage to stay out of trouble and get done what we need without anyone watching over us. Calling her a *Coordinator* is a bit like calling a CAZ sanitation tech a Garbage Manager.

Most annoying is Marta's need to constantly remind us of her superiority. 'It's my decision.' 'I am responsible.' 'I have to decide.' 'I am going to need...' I once witnessed a briefing she gave to a PersRep class. There were more "I's" describing her career than there were in the audience. In Marta's mind, she is both hero and martyr—her accomplishments the result of initiative and her limitations a sign of people intimidated by her intellect quelling an otherwise gifted bureaucrat. In truth, Marta is just a bully with a predictably narcissistic need for approval and feeling of power. But she does like me.

I think I'm one of the few who listens to her bullshit without calling it BS. She'll talk to me about other people's problems, idiot Council policies, ignorant department heads, even peers she finds unfairly promoted before her. I know things about other PersReps I'd prefer not know. I listen patiently and agree with her when she starts in about being the victim of patriarchal station dynamics, and in return for not mentioning that half the Council and close to 60 percent of everyone in station management are women, she doesn't fuck with me. I am her first choice for preferred assignments as long as I answer when she calls and turn my monthly stats in on time.

It was tough when I first migrated. I'd listen to her shit, get frustrated and want to beat the crap out of her. Eventually I realized all the self-promotion, self-pity, and attempted intimidation was Marta's way of dealing with a life spent without accomplishment. She's worked an entire career, fought her way to the lowest rung on the middle management ladder, and watched her husband die—or more likely commit suicide, who could blame him—all to end up responsible for a bunch of people who don't need any direction whatsoever. So I started placating, nodding my head a lot, and agreeing with her even when she was obviously wrong. Soon I was brought into the fold, part of the inner circle, selected for choice assignments and her preferred ear for the latest gossip about coworkers, Council members, and anyone else who crossed her. Still, I wouldn't be the least disappointed if she ended up in a malfunctioning air lock without a suit.

Which brings me to our PersRep meeting room, a small, non-descript, three-walled metallic grey space with four utilitarian chairs and one VizD on the wall waiting for me to dial up Marta. This is going to take well-over an hour, cutting deep into my HMC time with Alex.

"Hi Marta," I say with as much enthusiasm as I can muster. "You're looking especially clever this morning." *If I don't add a little sarcasm, she'll think something is wrong.*

"Don't be an ass, Brandi. I look like a POS. I've been up all night slamming decaf like it's H2O and confirming intel streams to make sure my people are covered in case there are any big issues. It's a constant battle taking care of my direct reports and making sure they don't fuck anything up. One accusation of misrepresentation can bring the entire establishment down."

Marta is on a roll this morning.

"Well, we appreciate all you do." This time I decide to leave out the scant smile in favor of sounding sincere.

Marta looks away for a moment before replying. "I'm not sure about everyone, but the people who matter care, which is why I wanted to meet this morning. I want to make sure you're in the loop rel-to a couple of your teammates on the suicide crew. This thing isn't exactly SOP and I don't want anything coming back to bite me in the ass."

In addition to the self-promotion she wears like a day glow jacket and a flair for the dramatic, Marta enjoys both expletives and acronyms. 'Intel streams' is simply *information*, 'rel-to' is *relative to*, and 'SOP' is *standard operating procedure*. I'm not sure if she appreciates the efficiency or is just trying to sound ITK—in the know.

"Suicide crew? Is that what we're calling it now?"

"Well, just me so far," Marta replies before noticing the bandage on my right cheek. "What the holy hell happened to you?"

"Nothing. Just a freak accident while running the botany lab late last night."

"A freak accident?" asks Marta.

"Yeah," I reply, realizing I'm not going to get out of this without an explanation. "I was running the botany lab—I like to sprint it once a week late at night when there's no one else around. Anyway, a panel came loose from the star dome and landed right in front of me. It missed, but a piece ricocheted up from the floor and tagged my cheek. So basically a non-event."

"A panel came loose? Like by itself?"

"That's what I'm told." *Although walking Marta through it makes me reconsider. The techs mentioned it was the first they'd heard of something like this happening across the stations.* "It was normal wear. Luckily, I was in a hurry. I usually stop where it fell because it has the best view of the earth but there was a solar flare last night—I opted to keep going to catch it on the other side. Had I rested where I usually do, you'd be on the hunt for a new favorite PersRep."

Marta's eyes soften as she fakes the compassionate look I've seen her use on others right before telling me how stupid they are. "Well, I'm glad you're okay...and speaking of people being okay, did you hear about Marcel Reddy, the PersRep on Taurus?"

Marta moves on from concern to gossip faster than anyone I know.

"Apparently he decided to screw some Tech's wife without asking the Tech's permission. She was up for something minor, bootleg booze purchases resulting in an embarrassing strip tease in one of the Taurus cantinas or some such bull, and rather than attending rehab for a few weeks, she decides banging Reddy is a preferred penance. Of course, he can't persuade the Station Rep—whose name escapes me right now, a real idiot—he can't persuade the StaRep to give up the rehab, so the

Tech's wife, who is also a Tech in one of the Dynamics Labs, decides to call me complaining how Reddy took advantage of her. I spend an hour on the phone with the girl—and get this, she and her husband just applied for and received an SBP…" *That's Marta-speak for Screaming Baby Permit,* "…so they're looking to have a baby, although why anyone would want one of those, I have no idea."

"Did you talk her out of it?" I ask, hoping to move this along.

"Of course. She wants a kid and her current husband is her best shot. Reddy, another idiot, but *my* idiot, sure as hell isn't about to settle down with some Tech who'd sooner sleep with him than sit in group for a few hours. I felt bad for her…" *Marta didn't feel bad for her, not even a little,* "…but reality is a bitch."

"Thank goodness we have you covering our asses," I comment.

Marta either ignores or doesn't hear my sarcastic response.

"Then I had to talk to Reddy. Do you know him?" She's trying to feel out whether Reddy is a friend and how much she can editorialize. Even if Reddy and I were besties, I wouldn't tell Marta. Doing so would mean missing out on her description of the conversation.

"Not really. Just the name."

"Well, he's about the most arrogant SOB ever. Thinks his shit doesn't stink. It was a pleasure knocking him down a couple pegs—well deserved lesson in humility I was happy to administer. I doubt he'll be so quick to stick his dick in the next Tech who wants to avoid a few weeks with IIG." *Idiots in group.*

Marta maintains a general disdain for men. It's odd, considering she was married and by all accounts, at least according to those who knew them when they were together, they had a solid, femme-dominated relationship. To hear people talk, Marta was definitely in charge, but she was also in love. Her current attitude toward the male of the species—contemptuous liars who are intimidated by powerful women and believe they deserve every opportunity without sacrifice—fuels her drive to open doors for her female subordinates, provided they've done nothing she perceives as a slight, like questioning one of her ill-conceived decisions. I, with my conciliatory agreeableness and vagina am in the category of trusted female comrade, and Marta is the mother I never wanted but will tolerate as long as I get what I want.

"Jeez, I'm not sure I could ever do your job." Which is true in so many ways.

"It's not so bad," she couches. "You'll make a great SPR someday."

'SPR' is supervising PersRep. Not an actual title, but close enough.

"I wanted to let you know, one of your suicide teammates reached out to someone close to the Council yesterday."

"Which one?" I ask.

"Plumin, the Station Rep."

I consider for a moment whether I should lie and tell her I know so she doesn't think I'm without sources, or act surprised and validate her position as supreme information broker. I decide the latter is better for her ego and my career.

"Do you know who he talked to?"

"Apparently he's trying to meet with one of the C-clerks on Saturday. I have a friend and former PersRep close to the Council. We were discussing how station politics have changed. Things were a lot more straightforward back in the day. None of this touchy-feely we need to consider everyone's emotional investment prior to making a decision crap saturating today's Council. I have no idea how we don't implode. Anyway, one minute she's complaining about how these days any friend of a friend can ask questions about Council business and the next she's dropping Plumin's name."

C-clerks—again, not a real title but one Marta coined—are usually assigned to the Council from other Roles. The transfers are temporary, lasting 24 to 36 months in order to give the transferee a broader exposure to the station big picture. Clerk opportunities go to those the Council feels are movers and shakers—'blue flamers' in station vernacular, rapidly rising stars. They've generally expressed an interest in moving up in the station hierarchy, perhaps into station governance, high level operations, or policy development. They aren't eligible for Council membership any more than I am—those seats being held by formerly wealthy and still influential big tech and business heirs. Occasionally, Council Clerks will become careers unto themselves, with a few Clerks remaining part of Council dynamics for decades, but it's rare.

"You might just want to ask him about it," Marta continues. "You know, put him on the spot. Find out why he's talking to someone about Council business when he should be looking into suicides. See if there is anyone else he's meeting offline."

Marta pauses for a moment, as if considering other options.

"On the other hand," she says methodically, "maybe wait to see if he brings it up on his own. If he doesn't mention it, he's definitely hiding something. I wouldn't put it past his type to gaslight you, cutting you out entirely so he can take all the credit. They'll be expecting prelims on Tuesday, right? Not that anything's coming of these suicide reviews. I'm surprised it's taking as long as it is. Just don't get wrapped up in his BS. You have your own reputation to consider. This can be a door-opener for you if it's done right."

"We've come up with nothing to suggest these suicides are anything more than suicides." I say, reassuringly. "I'll see what happens at the meeting later and then maybe talk to Jason after."

I can see Jason framing his effort on the team to leverage a promotion, he's not going to sit as a Station Rep his entire life. But he's always been pretty straightforward. Unlike Marta, I don't mind giving him a shot at telling us before jumping to conclusions.

Marta glances down at her wrist and taps something into her ComLink. Multitasking is one of her strengths, or so she reminds people when she's tapping away instead of listening. The awkward pause ends when she finishes. "I was reading through a couple of the reports. Did you know the Ocasio kid and Palau have a connection?"

"Are you following up on me? Don't trust me?" I ask, forcing a playful grin as if I'm kidding, which I'm not.

"Of course not! I'm just looking out for my people. I don't want you caught off guard. Not everyone cares about playing fair on life's football pitch. I'll be damned if I'm going to let whatever comes of this suicide thing reflect badly on you or me," she says, not returning my smile.

"Well, that's good to hear," I reply, still smiling, lest she think I'm serious, which, again, I am. "What is the Palau-Ocasio connection?"

"Apparently Palau—he was an analyst, right?—Apparently he made a complaint about the Ocasio kid, the one who committed suicide. The kid filed a defamation claim as a result. Palau couldn't prove his allegations, so they sanctioned him. Definitely too light a sentence for something as important as smearing someone's name without a shred of proof or a single witness."

I recall something about Palau's conviction, but nothing about Derek Ocasio. I tap a couple commands into my ComLink to check my notes. During our Wednesday meeting Jason said Palau was convicted of defamation because he accused a *doctor* of wrongdoing. Marta's got the Ocasio part correct, but she's totally dished on the victim. Palau knew the *mother*, the psychiatrist, not the son, and accused Indra Ocasio of wrongdoing.

I consider correcting Marta, but can't find an upside. I'll gain a momentary feeling of superiority, but it could piss her off. It's not that she has a lot of people she considers friends, but I don't really want her holding one of her epic grudges, either. Best to just let this one lay.

"Palau accused Derek Ocasio of something in public? I wonder what it was?" I ask, hoping to sound genuinely surprised.

"Who knows? But whatever it was he couldn't support the accusations." Marta pauses to send another text before continuing. "But it's weird they're even connected. They both knew each other, had a disagreement, and both committed suicide. What are the odds? You have to ask Plumin about it. Find out what he knows. His office worked both the Ocasio and Palau cases. He must be at least tangentially familiar with them. It's not that big an office for fuck's sake."

"Agreed. I'll see what I can find out at the meeting this afternoon."

"I'll be busy the rest of the day," says Marta while glancing down at her ComLink. "Let's debrief on Monday. Send me an invite. I'm sure I'll get more intel after Plumin meets with the Clerk. My Council POC said she'd keep me up to date." Without waiting for me to respond, she signs off and the screen goes blank.

Jason didn't elaborate on the link between Palau and Ocasio. It's possible he didn't know Indra Ocasio was the doctor in question, especially if it wasn't his case. But why would he reach out to someone on the Council? Did he discover something in one of the interviews? I like the guy, but Plumin is a pretty high performer with a reputation as someone going up, not down. It's possible he's hoarding information, positioning himself as the unofficial head of our team. If he thinks I'm gonna to sit back and watch while he takes control, he's crazy. I'm lead dog on this sled.

Shit. Now I'm starting to think like Marta.

CHAPTER TWENTY-SEVEN

Kami Lee

We were late to interview Hannah Bonikowski's boss. Jason was good about it. I think his exact words were, "Kami, I can handle the interview if you'd like to ease into the day." Not condescending, just caring with a small side of snarky. But he must have realized at that point no amount of meticulous planning was going to make up for another twenty minutes in bed. I have to believe it was worth it for both of us.

Afterwards we split with a firm commitment to touch base later. Shouldn't be too difficult, given we'll see each other this afternoon at the team meeting. But I'm thinking we won't be grabbing each other's asses in front of Brandi. It's a little too soon to be acting all boyfriend and girlfriend. It was one night, not a commitment. We're not lesbians.

I probably should not have discussed so much about my father and Kornel last night, but Jason didn't dwell on it. There was no residual awkwardness working its way into the naked morning-after where our bad breath and bed head already filled out a graceless agenda. Still, it would have been better if I'd left *Kami Lee: An Autobiographical History of Death and Coping* off our pre-coitus reading list. Nobody wants to hear about parental suicide and sibling trauma when they're considering whether to sleep with someone.

I like Jason, but I'm far too practical to be smitten. He seems like a genuinely nice and interesting guy, the only one I've met in quite a while, which is surprising considering Kornel's news on Wednesday about men outnumbering women. The growing gender disparity should have improved my odds. Jason doesn't even seem to have any baggage, unlike your's truly. No parents or siblings, Advocates, obtrusive family friends, not even a virtual cat. I don't think he's even considering a commitment. Available, handsome, funny, smart, stable and happy—what's not to like?

Still, it was a good idea to leave out Kornel's revelation about gender-biased migration selections, not to mention the voice in the airlock. I'm still not sure how I feel about mucking about with the algorithm, even if it is to make up for deficiencies, and I'm even more at odds with not telling the population at large. The Council's decided people won't be able to handle the news, which is more than ironic considering they tout only bringing the best and brightest aboard. If everyone is so enlightened, then why the secrecy? People are smarter and more considerate than they think. We should be allowed to make the decision as citizens, or at least understand the problems and options. Either way, there's no need to tell Jason just yet. It would simply get Kornel into hot water if Jason ends up not being the person I think he is. Maybe I'll mention it on the second date. Ha, ha.

Hannah Bonikowski's boss, Siddarth Brown, was a non-starter. Sid —he insisted we call him Sid, mentioning he's more Gen than migrant at this point—talked more about his own time on Aries and the challenges *he's* faced than Hannah's suicide. His life story would need to be filed under *Break In Case Of Insomnia*. He mentioned Hannah had become withdrawn lately and less satisfied with her role as a Water Reclamation Specialist.

"It's not a glamorous job," relayed Sid, "but without someone repairing the filters, we'd all die of dehydration." The statement sounded a bit self-aggrandizing.

Sid heard from a couple of Hannah's friends that she stopped attending social gatherings in the weeks before her suicide. There were no indications of drugs, other than the plastic container found next to her on the bed after she overdosed. There wasn't a prescription, so they assumed she traded for them on the black market. Her account was low on cantina and food credits, which made sense if she didn't plan on needing them. Everything pointed to suicide, just like the others.

After the interview Jason left for the gym, which is where I planned on heading, as well. Instead, I'm on my way to see Sam Michnak about Nigel Birmingham. He was the last person to leave the HMC prior to the estimated time of Nigel's death, and the *only* person I wasn't able to interview yesterday during the round-robin. Sam texted during the Bonikowski interview asking to meet this morning.

A quick records check revealed the basics about Michnak's time on Aries. He was born onboard in 2088, making him a Gen like me, but six years younger, so still in primary ed. His SR Bid score won't come out until next year, just prior to completing a dream sheet, followed by the move to SR-specific training the year after. At 15, this is basically his last year to be a kid before he's forced into major life decisions.

His parents, both alive, are migrants who boarded with the last of the IPI recruits in 2085. His father, Vivaan, definitely has some Indian heritage, or someone in the family really loved the culture, but it's hard to say about the mother. The only clue was her first name, Karitas—possibly Northern European or maybe Icelandic according to my ComLink. No clue on Vivaan and Karitas Michnak's last name, probably Vivaan had a non-Indian father, which was common after the second global pandemic in 2043. TwoGP added a lot of Indian spices to the melting pot.

Sam's father works in the Energy Tech role where he spends most of his days maintaining power generation and distribution equipment. It's a respectable gig, not overly stressful, unless the power goes out. His mother's role is Communications Tech, working in the Aries station Control Center, the SC2, routing comms between Aries and the other stations, or Aries and the planet, depending on her current assignment. Neither had anything derogatory in the system. Model Cits since the day they migrated.

Sam asked if we could meet at the gym, but I suggested one of the OSU outposts. Aries population density makes it difficult to find privacy outside a personal HabU, so the OSU keeps rooms throughout the station big enough for four people and a table, just in case someone needs to interview a witness or temporarily detain a Cit. Detentions are pretty rare—where is anyone going to hide on a space station, it's not like you can just commandeer a shuttle and fly away, or hold up in someone's HabU. There are protocols, processes and technologies to circumvent disappearing Cits.

Witness and subject interviews can happen anytime for any number of reasons, criminal and non-criminal. The OSU is tasked with investigating all of the standard crimes, as well as anything the SC2, station Ambassador's Office, or Council deem appropriate in support of the Analysis Lab. Last month I interviewed half a dozen people as part of an A-Lab study into the impact of lighting adjustments on attitude and productivity. Analysts are good with data, less so with humans.

I'm a few minutes early and consider texting Jason while I wait for Micknak, but decide against it. As cute as it might be to touch base with a suggestive emoji, he could misinterpret and assume I'm *that* girl, the clingy, needy, friendless, I-love-you-after-one-night chick who maintains a tentative grip on reality—even if at least one of those is true. I really need more friends.

The ceiling illuminates in a soft glow when I enter, revealing a small, empty room. The only identifying feature is the two-line etching on the outside wall adjacent to the door notifying all who enter that this is an OSU Meeting Room - Authorized Personnel Only. There are four chairs, two each sitting on either side of a metal table extending out from the wall opposite the sliding door. Their round bases, swiveling seats, and tilting backrests are not designed for comfort. The walls are gray, lacking even the slightest blemish and reflecting enough light to keep the underside of the table from being enveloped in shadow. Built to eliminate unnecessary distractions, it is by design the most boring room on Aries.

I recognize Sam Michnak from his photo. He arrives just as I'm settling into one of the metal chairs. Since it's just going to be the two of us, I move the two chairs on the other side of the table into a distant corner. The two remaining seats I turn to face each other, forcing Sam and I to sit on the same side. This isn't a confrontational interview—I want him comfortable and relaxed, without barriers between us. Near Sam's chair I place a disposable can filled with drinking water. Despite our technological advances, we still haven't figured out a means of hydration that doesn't include water consumption—although the water reclamators make on-demand production a simple process. Sam takes the seat next to me.

"Hi Sam, I'm Kami Lee from the OSU. I understand you want to talk about Nigel Birmingham," I say, offering my hand over my heart.

Sam looks young, even for his fifteen years. His slightly tanned skin, likely a product of his Indian heritage, is punctuated by dirty blonde hair, hazel eyes, and a developing, chiseled jaw. He's not tall, maybe just shy of 5 feet 10 inches, and his lanky build leaves his uniform looking unfilled. A lot of his slight features may be the result of youth. In the gym, I doubt I'd even notice him, but in this tiny room I can't help extrapolating out and wondering what a few years and a dedicated strength training program might do for his contours and profile.

"Hi," Sam replies, swiveling the chair in my direction. "Thanks for meeting me."

He's soft spoken and doesn't make eye contact. Is it nerves, or is he bashful? It's hard to tell. I tap my ComLink to begin recording.

"Why don't we start with why we're here," I suggest, turning my chair to face him.

"Okay," he replies again.

This might take some encouragement to get him going. Sam isn't exactly a fountain of chatter. "Sam, you texted me. Why don't you kick it off?"

Sam sets his left elbow on the table and rubs his forehead. "I'm just not sure. If this gets out it could be awful. Things get around, people talk. Is there any way you can keep this between us? Do you have to record this?"

I'd like nothing more than to assure him anything he says will remain confidential, but since I don't know what he's going to tell me, I won't make that promise. I explain as clearly as possible why I can't guarantee the information will be kept secret. What if he has information Birmingham was murdered? What if he's the one who killed him?

"Until I hear what you have to say, I can't pledge to keep anything confidential."

"What?" Sam looks genuinely surprised. "No, I didn't kill him. I don't even know who did, if anyone did. I just know he was an asshole. The dude was a pedophile, probably many times over. He's been screwing people on the stations for years. I'll bet there were dozens of people who wanted him dead, including me, but I didn't kill him. Not that *anyone* killed him. Maybe guilt finally got the best of him and he offed himself." His initial hesitation has turned into an unstoppable train of thought.

"Sam, slow down," I whisper, touching his forearm. "Just tell me what you know and everything will be fine."

Sam's chest rises beneath his ill-fitting uniform enough to fill it. There is a momentary pause, like he's considering whether to exhale, as if doing so will blow to the surface a memory he's tried desperately to bury. When he finally lets it out, it's slow and in hushed tones. Sam explains how he's known Birmingham for six months, since just after his 15th birthday. Birmingham was there the first day, during his first trip to the gym. His parents discouraged physical training for its own sake. Sam was allowed to play any of the virtual sports, but they feared him over doing it with the weights at too young an age. He just wanted some bulk. He seemed on the verge of breaking down, his voice quavering, eyes gleaming with tears.

"Which sports did you play?" I ask, hoping to keep him on subject but distracted.

"Soccer and La Crosse. You know the big arena in the Education Center, the one on level Q?"

I nod, knowing exactly where it is. I spent most of my youth hiding out in that arena.

"I used to play there Friday nights," Sam continues. "It's not exactly the real thing—virtual balls, electronic sticks, simulated goals—but there's still a lot of running. I'm tall, but not super strong. So, when I turned 15, I basically begged my parents to let me go to the HMC. If they ever find out, I'll never hear the end of it."

"Did you meet Birmingham at the HMC?"

"Yeah, he was there the first couple days. I wasn't sure who he was at first. Then a couple weeks later he told me he was in charge of all the HMCs on every station. He said he had an inter-station pass and could get just about anything. He knew everyone.

"Like the third day I'm there he comes up asking if I want some help. I'd been using the Virtual Trainer, you know? It's pretty simple, extracts all your biometric and DNA data from the ComLink, processes it through the algorithm, and spits out a series of guided workouts based on the results. Except if you're under 17, it doesn't allow you to pick your goal—it just assigns you to the general fitness category."

I'm also familiar with the Virtual Trainer, having spent a fair of time with it at the HMC growing up. If you're an adult, you can choose a goal, like power or strength, or a program like bodybuilder, strength-endurance balance or cardio conditioning, and the VT will program your workouts basically forever. It updates based on your macros—calorie intake, protein, carbs, perceived exertion, volume, VO2 max, heart rate, blood pressure—all pulled from your ComLink's perpetual biometric scans and consumption data. You don't have to enter anything manually, it adjusts for each session. You just show up. It's genius, really. I still use it to program my health.

The VT has some built-in safeguards. It won't allow someone to train to damage. Instead, if it senses you're overdoing it, the VT will alert the HMC on-duty attendant who will have a long discussion about the potential pitfalls of overtraining and possibly refer you to a Welfare Specialist for further evaluation. Another built-in safeguard limits resistance training in the young before they are physically fully developed. It's this latter restriction Sam is referring to. If you're 17 or older, you can choose to disable the VT—personal responsibility taking primacy over guided common sense. But as a teen, you're stuck until you leave for role training. The Council looks at that period, the two years between age 17 and completion of the shortest role-training course, as the Pre-Citizen Intermission. PCIs are granted some freedoms of Cits—like use of a VT without child restrictions—and limited on others, like alcohol consumption, until they turn 19.

"So Birmingham offered to help?"

"At first, yeah. He said he could bypass the VT so I could train like a PCI. I knew it was illegal, but I really wanted to do more than the VT programmed workouts. So I took him up on his offer, which ended up being total bullshit," Sam said, more anger coming through than regret.

"Why was it bullshit? He couldn't hack your ComLink?"

"I have no idea because he never did it. He kept pushing me off. He'd say he'd do it next week, then come up with an excuse, like the Council was dropping a new security update, or they were updating the VT, or he had to visit one of the other stations and wouldn't be back for a week. The point is he took and took but never delivered. That's the fucked up thing about it…"

Tears fill Sam's youthful, hazel eyes like a glass until they overflow, single streams running down each cheek and falling into his lap. He wipes them away with his sleeve, but it doesn't help, the damage is done. His lean, boyish face is now a soppy, red, puffy mess of regret and shame.

"What did he take, Sam? What did Birmingham take?"

Sam explains through bouts of sobbing that Birmingham promised to trade a ComLink hack for certain sexual favors, favors the boy was willing to perform so long as nobody ever found out. Every week for almost half a year they'd meet in Birmingham's office and the boy would perform oral sex on Birmingham and every week Birmingham would promise the ComLink hack was forthcoming. Sam was young, innocent and sheltered from the horrors of the planet that until now we believed didn't migrate on to the stations. Ours was a better place, a sanctuary and Birmingham ripped that from this boy.

Birmingham was true to his word on one front, he never told anyone about his relationship with Sam, most likely because it would have gotten him deported from the stations. It's one thing to snap a fcw photos of adult males—people in the right places can mitigate what was described as a first time offense—but it's something else entirely to coerce a teenager into performing oral sex in exchange for an illegal hack. Birmingham threatened to expose their relationship and Sam believed him.

"Sam, it's not your fault." I hope I sound as convinced as I am, but there is little consolation in knowing you made a horrible decision. "You can't go through this alone. You have to talk to someone."

"I can't!" Sam blurts out, lone tears turning to uncontrollable sobs and gasps for air. "It's bad enough…this is all going to come…out. I'm a…pariah. My parents…friends…there's nobody."

Sam buries his face in his elbow on the table. I watch as his body convulses, short deep breaths punctuated by audible whimpers and scratchy sniffles. I can't just leave him like this—he could end up on our suicide list. I also don't want to make it worse by bringing in someone else. Then I remember the page from Kornel's notebook, the one with the name of a psychiatrist.

"Sam, what if I told you I can probably keep your name out of this? Maintain your anonymity?"

Sam looks up from the table, his eyes bloodshot, imploring.

I don't see why I can't keep him out of the report. It doesn't serve anyone to know Sam's name, only the details of Birmingham's depravity. Birmingham is dead and Sam has an alibi, so what would it hurt to keep his name out of any discussion?

"That…would be great," Sam says, the wave of sobs ebbing.

"There are a couple conditions," I add.

"Anything."

I slide the sheet of paper with Dr. Ocasio's name on it across the table.

"I'm going to put a biometric trace on your ComLink to monitor for anomalous behavior. You're in a pretty shitty state right now and until you talk to someone, I don't want you doing anything irrational, like committing suicide. Once you see this doctor, she can remove the bio-trace." Even Sam understands the privacy issues surrounding doctor-patient relationships.

"Of course," Sam agrees. "I'll make the appointment right away."

Sam stands, wiping the snot from his nose with his sleeve and placing his hand over his heart. "Thank you so much. I can't tell you how grateful I am."

I mimic his greeting. "No problem. Call me if you need anything or if you can think of anything else."

The door shushes shut behind him and I punch the codes into my ComLink to set a bio-trace. This would normally be a preventative measure until we meet with a WelSpec, but I'll get an alert if he hasn't scheduled the meeting with the psychiatrist in the next 24-hours. It's not a violation so much as an exaggeration of current policy to initiate a bio-trace without also setting up a WelSpec appointment, but it's better than letting him go without any follow-up. At least I'll get a notification if his behavioral patterns change.

I desperately want to believe there is something more to Birmingham's death in light of Sam's story. Perhaps someone found out and killed him? Or tried to blackmail him and it went bad? There wasn't any evidence of another person in the locker room, nothing on camera or DNA. It's possible it all got washed down the drain, but everything still points to suicide. No, most likely Birmingham killed himself, seeing no way out when a blackmailer approached him. He would have known the inevitable ending to his story, as well as realizing he'd last all of five minutes on the planet. None of the Autonomous Zones would take him, leaving the Open Lands his only option. The idea of being dropped in the middle of the lawless OLand would be enough to convince almost anyone to consider a quicker and far less painful way out.

I just can't believe at Birmingham's age Sam was his first victim. Someone had to have known about his degenerate hobby and provided high cover—but from where? The Council? A clerk? Perhaps I'll start with his last infraction. Brandi said he had help with the photos, someone offering mitigation beyond what a PersRep could add. Otherwise his sentence would have been stiffer.

CHAPTER TWENTY-EIGHT

Jason Plumin

"Hi Jason," the receptionist calls from behind her conventional, gun-metal table, a digital screen hovering between her and the outside world. What is her name? Starts with an 'A.' Ali? Avery? She's working on an HWT X1 with its all-virtual monitor and synaptic response keyboard. I'm jealous. How does a receptionist in the PersRep's office rate the latest and greatest and we're stuck with these old school carry-alongs? I get that soon the entire station will be outfitted and I'll be able to ditch my A5, but the priorities are all out of whack.

"Hi. How's it going?" Crap, Amber? Anna? That's it! "How's it going, Anna?"

She's multitasking, tapping into her ComLink, glancing back and forth at the virtual screen, occasionally typing into the computer-generated keyboard and attempting to greet people entering the office —and doing a piss poor job at all of it.

"I'm, it's good," she finally says, the mix of tiny words forming in her almost-adult brain.

"You're due to graduate soon, right?" I ask, not actually caring but feeling a need to make small talk.

"I get my scores at the end of this year, then I'll be moving on to SR training."

"Wow, that's thrilling," I say, trying not to sound as indifferent as I am. I can't imagine what she'll be ranked highest in. "What Roles are you most interested in?"

"Well, it doesn't really work like that, does it?" Anna replies in a condescending tone I imagine she uses with her parents. "I get my scores and ranked list and choose whichever are at the top. The scores tell me what I'm interested in."

I consider reminding her she has a brain and it seems a shame to leave it on a shelf while life presents options. In the two times we've met, she's struck me as an uninformed, sheltered teen, lagging behind her peers in almost every category. Her ever-changing hair color—it's got a purple tint today—delicate features, and overly pleasant, bubbly personality leave a cloying taste after each interaction. I see her sampling experimental food flavors or testing the flow from water reclamators until she finds a mate, applies for a baby permit, and brings the next generation of nail painting, mascara-wearing underachievers into space. Of course I could be wrong, it might just be her youth.

"Besides, it's just a Role," Anna finishes. "It's not like picking a significant other, is it?"

Nope, it's definitely not just youth.

"Well, good luck anyway," I add, turning toward the conference room. "Maybe you'll get one of those flex Roles, where you train in four or five fields before being called to serve the Council."

"Wait! Is that a real thing? That would be great!"

I'm a few minutes early and not surprised to find Brandi at the head of the table typing something into her MiniComp. I take the seat at the other end, setting my A5 down and pressing the biometric reader to activate it. We shouldn't need the Viz today, so I don't much care if it's behind me. Plus, I'd rather not sit across from Kami—it makes the chance for inadvertent glances too great and I'm not sure anyone, especially Brandi, need know we spent last night together. As the pocket laptop springs to life, I mention to Brandi her receptionist thinks she might score the 'flex role' during Bid, maintaining my serious Jason face during air quote deployment.

"And who gave her the idea such a thing was possible?" Brandi asks without looking up from her screen.

"Unknown."

"Great," Brandi sighs. "Now I get to spend the next week explaining how there isn't a 'flex role' on the stations and she'll have to choose just one. It's like being a mother…scratch that, an older sister to a child whose friends just told her she could be a supermodel."

"It's tough being responsible for another human being at such a young age," I quip. "Especially one as innocent as Anna. I figured you'd have tuned her up by now—taught her the difference between fact and fiction."

Brandi stops typing and looks up from her screen and for the first time I notice both the bruise on her cheek and that she looks tired—like she didn't get enough sleep and skipped breakfast. It's not a look I've seen her sport, but before I can comment she continues on about Anna.

"It's exhausting. She's interested in nothing, spends all her time texting, and can barely figure out how the virtual case file system works. On top of that, she's Marta's friend's daughter—purportedly a well-connected friend. So all of this is a favor to get her some exposure to the legal system, I presume so she doesn't do anything stupid in the future because she *certainly* doesn't have the mental capacity to actually work in the field." Brandi pauses abruptly, perhaps because she's said too much or because she notices the startled look on my face.

"What?" she asks.

"What the hell happened to you?"

"It's a long story."

"And?"

"A panel came loose and almost killed me this morning. Okay, it's not a long story."

I've never heard of a panel coming loose. "A panel? What panel? Where?"

"I'd really rather not discuss it," Brandi replies, her eyes having returned to whatever she was working on before I interrupted.

I decide in the interest of coworker harmony to leave it be and return to our previous subject. "Well, don't worry about the Anna stuff. It's our right to complain about the high maintenance people in our lives."

"And who do you have in your life?" Brandi asks.

"Well, nobody, actually," I add. "I only said that to make you feel better. You're basically the only person I know in this situation. However, I'd estimate you're handling it better than most—not that I have anything to compare it to, of course."

Brandi laughs, punching a key on her MiniComp like she's hitting send on an email she's spent too much time drafting. Her laugh is infectious, causing me to smile in unison. Growing up in a CAZ made her a little rough around the edges and imbued a solid vein of sarcasm down the center of her personality. But she can be fun when she lightens up.

"How does your receptionist rate the new HWT X1 with the improved cloud processor, virtual anywhere keyboard and motion-sensitive screen? I'd expect we'd have it before she would. Damn, I'd expect the guy who programs the showers at the gym to have one before your receptionist."

"Did I mention she's the daughter of someone important?" Brandi quips. "Apparently her parents have it already installed on their HabU surfaces. A quick call to the techs in the Computing Lab explaining how it doesn't make sense for her to carry an A1 MiniComp to work when she already has access to the X1 virtualization at home is all it took. The next thing you know a tech from the C-Lab is retrofitting her tiny table for the latest and greatest. Anyway, stop whining. It's not like you'd know what to do with all that excess capacity if you had it. It takes you twenty minutes to punch in the station's orbital vector address."

Now it's my turn to laugh. "That's a little harsh, don't you think? It's a long address."

"Oh, and my boss has a new name for our team," Brandi adds. "The suicide crew."

At first, I can't tell if Brandi's joking or not. Marta has a reputation and it's not for her sense of humor. She can be a bit of a know-it-all, glory-hound bully. I had the misfortune of attending a seminar she spoke at during Role training over ten years ago. I had no idea the PersRep program had so many eyes in it: *'I wrote the book on Personal Representation.' 'The entire program was going nowhere until I migrated.' 'I have more responsibility than anyone on the stations.'* Thank goodness for Marta, without her the stations would stop spinning and fall from orbit.

"Well, it's kinda catchy," I say. "The suicide crew. It's like we're part of a secret Council program designed to eliminate dissent and maintain the peace, except in our case it's more about making sure we don't screw up our careers."

"Are you hoping to parlay this into something bigger? A Council role perhaps?" Brandi asks, fishing for information. Can't really blame her. She's still young, only three years post-migration and likely considering long term options.

I'm not thinking much will come of any of this, but like I mentioned to Cecelia, I wouldn't mind parlaying the exposure into a role with the Council. I'm not going to tell Brandi that, at least not yet.

"Not exactly. I like what I do and wouldn't mind sliding into something with more perspective in five or ten years, but this effort will be long forgotten by then. Besides, nobody wants Jason working with the Council."

"You can say that again," Kami offers as she enters the room, taking one of the seats on the side of the table between Brandi and I. "By the way, did you know Anna thinks there's a 'flex role?' Someone needs to have a serious talk with that girl."

Brandi gives me the evil eye, imagining a long and difficult conversation with Anna about the realities of the Station Role Bid process and how I shouldn't be taken too seriously. That charming guy from the Station Rep's office is okay, he just doesn't know when to stop having fun at other people's expense. Without breaking her glare, Brandi welcomes Kami to the suicide crew.

Kami smiles, "I like it. It's got a ring to it. Bold yet secretive. Too bad it's only going to last until Tuesday. Our deadline is four days away and I've got pretty much nothing from my end. And what the heck happened to you?"

Brandi takes a deep breath before explaining to Kami what she told me a few minutes earlier.

"Are you sure it was an accident? I mean, what other explanation could there be, right? But seriously. Are you sure?"

"You're not the first to ask that question," Brandi confirms. "Which is actually disturbing considering where we live. But yes, I'm assured it was an accident. Now if you two are done with my face, perhaps we can move on to suicide crew business?"

"Okay, now you're just saying it to see if it sticks," I quip.

I spot a grin creep across Brandi's lips before she starts up again.

"We might all be heading in the same obvious direction here. Why don't you kick it off, Kami?" Brandi looks in my direction, "Unless *Jason* would like to explain how we're going to incorporate the 'flex role' into our suicide report."

"Nah," I reply. "Let's shelve that idea until you accept the Aries Ambassadorship."

Kami deploys her MiniComp on the austere table, flipping to a file with notes. "Why don't we start with Hong, Gothard Hong, since I didn't actually get to him. I pulled his records and there was nothing out of the ordinary. No accusations or convictions, no disciplinary actions, not even a referral from a jilted ex-lover. Digitally, he was basically boring. I didn't see a single friend in the file review, only a couple distant contacts. I suppose that's not abnormal given he was a writer—they're generally anti-social by nature."

"Hey, I take offense at that," I counter. "I write a bit and I'm social as hell."

"Yeah, a little too social if you ask me," Kami replies before dropping her head, averting her eyes from the contact I hope Brandi didn't notice.

"Um," Kami starts, trying to remember where she left off. "I have an appointment with Hong's parents Saturday…well, tomorrow. Perhaps that will yield some insight, but I'm not hopeful."

Kami regurgitates the Hannah Bonikowski interview we tag-teamed this morning. She describes Hannah's boss, Siddarth Brown, to a tee: a narcissistic, despairing, self-important victim who is still suffering professionally since Hannah's death. Kami also summarizes our belief Hannah likely committed unassisted suicide. She'd been a bit of a recluse in the weeks leading up to her death, becoming increasingly morose but short of triggering an alert for her friends. Her low food and cantina balance without a corresponding increase in consumption or hoarding indicate trades on the black market for the drugs used to end her life. Kami's voice drifts into a whisper toward the end.

"Sometimes space depresses people," I add, hoping to draw attention away from Kami. "It's not always obvious and we can't necessarily help those in need." We all know people commit suicide, that's life on the stations, but there's no debating the impact suicides have on those left behind.

Brandi doesn't seem to notice anything out of the ordinary. She's typing into her MiniComp, looking up occasionally to make eye contact. "Did you happen to finish up with Birmingham?" She says, not noticing Kami's distress.

"Yes," says Kami. "Birmingham's suicide also fits with the evidence. He had no real friends—few people seemed to know him well. He did have access to all the stations and seemed to spend a lot of time off-Aries, but I don't suppose there's anything odd about it since he led station-wide HMC development. Records indicate he was a bit of a lecherous ass, and…"

Kami trails off as if wanting to add something, but seems to decide it's not worth mentioning. This time Brandi picks up on the cue. "And what?" She asks.

"Nothing," Kami answers. "I was just going to say it was odd not to find people who knew him better given his longevity on Aries. I sent a request to the OSU on the other stations to see if anyone there knew him and heard back. Most people knew of Birmingham or had only a passing relationship. Nobody mentioned him being depressed or showing any signs of suicide, but as I said, nobody seemed especially close to him."

"Where was his last trip?" I ask.

Kami clicks a couple times on her virtual track pad. "Looks like he was on Taurus a week before he committed suicide, a routine inspection of their HMCs. Seems it was something he did every couple weeks—visit station HMCs. Nothing out of the ordinary and Taurus OSU already responded to my RFI with nothing further to add."

"Is that it then?" Brandi asks after she finishes typing.

"I had the easy lift," I begin during the silence. "Finn was an accident."

I tell what I know about the Finn case, but there isn't much to say. As Kami mentioned on Wednesday, it was a fluke. I did a cursory review of Mike's records and found nothing out of the ordinary. He was getting ready to retire—his fall into the field array was a shame, really, given how much time he had left. Other than the fact he happened to die in the exact same place as Derek Ocasio, there's nothing else to tell.

I also do a brain dump of the Palau interviews, including the rather lengthy discussion with his wife, Susan, about Neil seeing Ocasio and Susan's theories about Ocasio drugging her husband. Palau's supervisor confirmed Neil committed suicide in the boss's office, where according to his wife and coworkers he'd been spending time after hours to finish a project for the Council. The supervisor, Ken Ericsson, doesn't spend much time with the A-Lab—he described it as a self-guided missile, tackling priorities as they come up and working on various analytic projects. Most of his time is spent with the Electronics Maintenance Team, it requires a bit more hands on prioritizing recurring and unplanned repairs. The only odd issue he's had in the last year was Neil's suicide.

"Palau's coworkers didn't see any signs he was struggling with depression or an inordinate amount of stress at work," I continue. "His wife..." I glance at my notes, "Susan, said he was seeing the mental health pro, Ocasio, until a couple months before his suicide, but also said there weren't any indications he was going to kill himself. She's still pretty broken up."

I decide to leave out the discussion about Genetic Balancing Reviews, the project Neil was working at the time of his death. I'd prefer to touch base with my Council contact, first. It wasn't reassigned to Neil's replacement, which may mean nothing, or may be an indication of its sensitivity. Neil's boss, Ericsson, wasn't aware the

Council even assigned the project to Palau. Station Operations Analysts often undertake self-assigned projects, but it would be nice to know for sure if it was self-directed or requested. Either way, I'm not adding it to the chaff until I have a bit more information.

"I haven't met with Ocasio," I add. "I was actually hoping someone else could handle it—maybe discuss Derek and Palau at the same time."

"I'll take it!" Kami interrupts with a little too much enthusiasm. She seems to catch her gaffe, collecting herself before adding, "I've got some time before the Gothard Hong interviews tomorrow. It's no problem."

I really don't want to meet with Mrs. Ocasio. Aside from the obvious reasons—namely talking to a woman about her dead son is never fun—there are the Susan and Neil Palau accusations. Plus, as pleasant as she is, I just don't need to spend any more time with her. Our comms during Derek's various issues was enough. If Kami wants the interview, she can have it.

"Great," I'm thrilled, actually. "I put in a call to Derek's father, Richard Ocasio. He doesn't want anything to do with any of this. He suggested calling Derek's mother. As he was not-so-politely telling me to go fuck myself, he said his wife is the talker in the family and would be more apt to have information about Derek's state of mind. If you're serious about taking it, Kami, I can meet you later to discuss Susan's accusations, add a little meat to the written report."

"I just scheduled an appointment with her for tomorrow morning," Kami mentions after typing something into her MiniComp

"You don't need an appointment unless you're nuts," Brandi notes, forcing a joke into her delivery. "Appointments are for people seeking professional help, not interviewing grieving mothers. Which isn't to suggest you can't handle both at the same time."

Kami's face is frozen in wide-mouthed wonderment, probably not sure if Brandi is joking or not. "That's what I meant. I requested to meet."

"Right. Well, with that..." Brandi runs through a summary of the interviews with Vanessa Jepus's and Candace Rogala's coworkers and friends. Candace, a Nutritionist, was a late twenty-first century migrant. Vanessa was an Astrophysicist in the station Dynamics Lab who migrated in 2089. All indications are they committed suicide, both sets of interviews identifying subtle signs of depression and isolation leading up to the end. People didn't report what they'd noticed, thinking it was simply a case of someone having a bad day. They found Candace in her HabU, a drug overdose. Vanessa on the other hand rigged an airlock to open while she was inside. Her body is floating somewhere between Aries and the rest of the known universe.

Perhaps unsurprisingly, suicide by airlock is not very common—it requires one to have some knowledge of airlock protocols in order to reprogram it to open with a person inside. The system detects a body without a suit and locks out the exterior door. There's a manual override, but any attempt to use it sets off alarms in the Aries Control Center giving the crew time to disable the override and trap anyone trying to kill themselves within the airlock. The only way to open it without setting off the alarm is to reprogram it prior to entry, skills an Astrophysicist certainly maintains.

Bodies are not normally recovered in cases of airlock breaches. The process is time consuming, and since the individual is jettisoned at high speed without a suit, they lack a beacon for the recovery crews to track and triangulate. As a result, it's a little like trying to catch a baseball by aiming a canon in the direction of flight, firing a tethered person with a glove, and instructing them to grab the ball before it flies out of reach. A few degrees off in any direction results in missing the body entirely. Thankfully, airlock suicides are extremely rare or we'd be dodging bodies with every shuttle launch.

"Neither of the women had a record," Brandi explains. "Nicholas Kesik, a Gen Historian and the third suicide on my list was convicted of distributing bootleg liquor. It wouldn't have made a case, except apparently Kesik decided to share his find with two underage students who went a little nuts drawing dicks and balls on all the doors in their wing. They gave him up about eight seconds after being detained."

"I don't recall that case? Did you work it from the PersRep's office?" I ask, trying to remember if I saw a file with the words *dicks and balls* in the narrative.

"No. Botha worked it about eight months ago. He said it was a pretty simple mitigation. Kesik didn't have any priors. He was basically a model Cit, spending three years in role training and the last two as a Historian teaching and advising. The students were both about to enter role training and Pre-Cit Intermission, giving Botha some room to argue their age."

"Were there any recent stressors in Kesik's life?" Kami asks.

"Nope," Brandi offers after scanning her notes. "Kesik was well liked by his students, friends and coworkers. Nobody noticed anything out of the ordinary prior to his death. There were some initial questions since he died consuming tainted liquor. But it was ruled a suicide because there was no indication of anyone tampering with the booze."

"So basically they assumed he poisoned himself," I add.

Brandi looks up from her screen, "That's about the size of it. There haven't been any reports of tainted liquor on any of the other stations. If it was a bad batch on the black market, it wouldn't have been isolated to one person. It's possible someone targeted him. But why? He didn't have any enemies. Hence, welcome to the suicide club."

Kami taps the table three times with her right forefinger. At first, I think it's to get our attention, but then notice she's rubbing her forehead like she's got a thought rattling about she wants to nab.

"You have something?" I ask.

"No, not really," Kami replies, tentatively pausing to pin that errant thought down. "Just to summarize, there were signs the two women might have been having issues, but nothing on Kesik, the Historian?"

Brandi considers the question for a moment. I wonder if she's trying to figure out where Kami is going with this. "That's correct."

"What are you thinking?" I ask.

"Nothing. I just want to make sure I understand the facts," Kami replies, still tapping her forefinger.

"Because if you have some theory, now would be as good a time as any to share it," Brandi fires back.

Kami's eyes narrow, almost imperceptibly, and I think I see an instant where she's going to launch into attack mode. But she recovers quickly. "It's not a theory. I'm just making some notes and want to make sure I heard everything correctly."

There is a pause as the women size each other up. I can't tell if Brandi is satisfied with the answer or if Kami wants to explain further. In either case, the silence is starting to get to me.

"Okay, then where do we go from here?" I ask.

"I'll meet with Ocasio and finish up the Hong interviews." Kami replies, typing as she talks.

My effort is mostly over, but I want to be in on the draft report. Better to shape the outcome and highlight my contribution than to leave it to Brandi. "I'll start drafting the report after I find out what the other stations are doing. I think we might actually finish ahead of schedule."

"I'll drop my notes into a cloud doc and you guys can add to it,"

Brandi replies.

I'm pretty sure Brandi's hoping to head off any attempt to cut her out. I concede to the idea of co-authoring, however, the truth is joint reports rarely flow well without an overseer, someone to make sure it doesn't sound like seven dwarves each wrote a different section. Besides, at the rate this is going, the entire report is going to be a single line, *Suicides are up because more people are committing suicide.* The only thing suspicious about any of this is the Council asking us to review them.

"Should we set up a time to meet next week?" I add.

"Let's get everything in the cloud and I'll send an invite this weekend for a Tuesday morning meeting," Brandi offers. She seems to have everything under control. I decide to let her believe as much.

CHAPTER TWENTY-NINE

Kami Lee

"Welcome, Kami Lee. What would you like to view?" An artificial female voice asks as I sit in a chair specially designed for the space.

"I have no idea."

"Please take your time. You have two hours and fifty nine minutes remaining on your session. This can be extended if there is not anyone waiting to use the facility."

The facility is the Entertainment Lab, a series of small single and double occupancy rooms with large screens and domed ceilings for viewing approved historical videos and vintage shows brought aboard by the original Council. I'm in a single with one chair that reclines when I sit, optimizing my view of whatever I choose to watch, which is nothing as I'm waiting for the faceless voice from the airlock. Although I'd rather be watching a documentary, like Die Hard.

"Are you enjoying the show?" A robotic voice asks through the speakers on either side of my head.

"Not especially." I'm not the least surprised whoever this is has access to the EntLab comms.

"You sound annoyed. You really need to relax. Maybe stick around when we're done and view some video footage of early twenty-first century riots."

"Those aren't available." I reply, hoping to sound more angry than annoyed.

"Not to everyone."

"So, you're a Council member. Who else would have the kind of access needed to watch restricted video? Who else can hack into EntLab comms and manipulate Evac Bay systems?"

"I am not and your guessing at my identity isn't going to bring you any closer to the truth."

The reply sets me off to the point I don't want to sit any longer.

"And what is the truth?" I ask, now standing in the cramped space between the chair and the door.

"Sit."

"What?" I'm surprised they know I'm standing.

"Sit."

"Why?"

"There is a sensor in the chair and another in the room. If the chair sensor does not detect a presence but the room sensor does, it will signal for an attendant to check the room prior to initiating decontamination…besides, you need a break."

I consider walking out, which of course I'm not going to do. I can't just walk away from what appears to be a well-connected lead and the robot voice knows it. They needed the airlock the first time to ensure my compliance, but I'm not going anywhere now.

"Okay. I'm sitting."

"I know."

"Wait. Are you watching me?" I ask, looking around the room for a camera. "A camera in here violates the Privacy First doctrine, you know."

"Indeed. Which is why I'm not watching you. There are no cameras in any of the EntLab rooms. I'm monitoring the chair sensor."

The sensor logs? The robot voice continues to surprise with their access. I don't have any idea how one even goes about monitoring EntLab sensors. I want to ask a few more questions, but I'm sure it will lead to nothing more enlightening than being told to focus.

"If you're finished considering the level of access required to monitor sensors, we should move on. We are here for a reason."

"The suicide study," I reply after being dragged from my internal debate. "I don't have anything else. The suicides appear to be just that —suicides. I haven't talked to the others, but I can tell you from a records perspective, there is nothing abnormal. I get the stats aren't in line with projections, but perhaps the projections are off. Maybe the analyst who assembled that particular assessment was an optimist or didn't have enough data to make an informed prediction. Either way, unless the last couple interviews on my list reveal something unexpected, there doesn't appear to be anything to investigate."

"That is all quite interesting, but not why I suggested we meet."

What the actual heck. "Then why am I sitting in this chair?"

"I've done some checking on your partners. You'll want to watch out for them," says the robot voice without elaborating.

"What do you know?"

"Unfortunately, I can't share specifics. Of the two, I believe Mikkelson to be of greater concern. But you should also take care around the other one, Plumin."

"What do you mean *of greater concern*? Is she involved? Is she covering for someone? What?"

There is a short pause—I presume the voice is deciding how much to tell me. When it speaks again, I think I detect a hint of regret.

"I can't elaborate without risking exposure. You'll have to find out for yourself. Do what you were trained to do and investigate."

"That's just great," I say, exasperated. "How do I know I can trust you? You could be dispensing a pod load of BS. The only thing off about this entire investigation so far is you."

There's another long pause as I sit reclined in the EntLab multimedia chair wondering if the robot voice has gone. "Are you there?"

"Yes."

"Well?"

"Can you trust me?" The robot voice asks.

"No! Who are you?"

"I'm not going to tell you that right now—and if you do your job, there won't be a need for you to find out."

"And if I don't? Then what?"

"I'd suggest one of the prescient films from the late twentieth century. Perhaps *The Star Chamber.*"

CHAPTER THIRTY

Brandi Mikkelson

"What the fuck is wrong with Kami?" I ask Jason after she leaves.

"Brandi, language. There are young, impressionable ears listening," Jason smiles, motioning toward Anna who is getting ready to end her day.

"I'm not that impressionable!" Anna yells as she heads out. "And I know the Flex Role isn't real!" As the door shushes shut, I hear her add, "Asshole." Jason hears it, too.

"She's right, you know. You are an asshole."

Jason acquiesces with a shrug, careening to make sure Anna isn't coming back. "I'm just wondering how she figured it out so quick. She must have called someone, right?"

"Probably her boyfriend," I answer. "She's tethered to him via her ComLink."

The conversation with Marta is still fresh, forcing an internal debate. Should I follow Marta's advice and ask him about his meeting with the Council Clerk, or follow her other advice and wait to see if he brings it up it on his own? I'll let it go for now. As long as Marta is still in the loop, I will find out sooner or later.

"So you're meeting with Kami about the Ocasio interview?" I ask, interrupting whatever he's typing into his MiniComp. "Will you be doing that at her place?"

There's a momentary stutter in the keystrokes before he replies.

"It's hard to say," Jason responds, not looking up from his screen. "That would certainly be more private than the Cantina."

His reply is missing the jagged edge of sarcasm I expect. Something about it—the way the corners of his mouth curl upward and he avoids eye contact without trying to *seem* like he's avoiding eye contact—something is definitely going on. They were supposed to meet yesterday regarding the joint interviews. Perhaps yesterday turned into last night and then this morning?

Not that I care. Don't get me wrong, Plumin is nice enough. He's good looking, in the right age bracket, and fairly intelligent. His sense of humor and healthy competitive streak also don't hurt. But there's no chemistry, in or out of work. He's never expressed an interest in being more than casual friends who occasionally get together after hours for a drink. Thank goodness, because I'd hate to test our relationship with an awkward rejection. I imagine being with him would be a lot like kissing my brother, if I had a brother.

"Maybe while you're someplace *more private*, you can ask why she was so excited to interview an MHP." I immediately regret using Marta's acronym for Mental Health Professional.

"Do you have something to ask? Or are you going to keep fishing?" This time Jason looks up from the MiniComp. There's a look on his face, like he's got the answer to the winning game show question and he's about to make millions.

"How *did* it go last night?"

"It went quite well, if I do say so myself," Jason answers with a deepening smile. "And this morning went well, too."

"*Quite well* is not actually something to be proud of. It's not like *earth shattering* or *amazing* or even *pretty good for a first draft*. Maybe you want to rethink your technique?"

Jason laughs, which is what I was going for.

"I figured you'd appreciate the humility, as well as a little discretion."

"Well, I guess the rumors about you seeing someone aren't true."

There's a momentary twitch, a barely noticeable softening of his lips before answering.

"Nope, not in the least."

I'm not convinced.

"So you've never heard the warning, 'Don't shit where you eat?'"

"First of all, this is a space station," Jason starts. "It is impossible to keep from shitting where one eats because we all eat and quite frankly, shit, in the same space. It's not like I will meet someone on another station or the planet and we'll create this beautiful life together."

"Oh, so now you're building a beautiful life together? You've known her for less than a week. She's over ten years younger than you. A couple years ago she was a minor, getting her Role rankings and thinking about her future. What happens in a decade when she starts considering babies? What then?" I notice I sound more jealous than I intend.

"Jesus, that's not what I meant," Jason fires back. "It's an example—focus on the point. We meet people where we live and work, there is no such thing as a chance encounter because by definition we are all here according to a plan. And second, I don't know how shitting where you eat has anything to do with this situation. We had one date, if you can call it that, and neither one of us is attached."

There's that twitch again—a fleeting glance to break eye contact.

"At this point," Jason adds. "It's just two people getting to know each other."

I notice he skips right over the age difference and the babies. I wouldn't consider Jason a bestie, but we've talked enough to know neither one of us ever wants children—one of the few things we have in common. I actually considered being *more* than friends based solely on our mutual distaste for offspring, but dropped the idea almost immediately. He's fun enough to hang out with on occasion and not horrible to look at, but I'm not ready to spend a lifetime pretending to love him or anyone for that matter. Besides, it's obvious he wouldn't be able to keep it between us—look at how fast he caved on the Kami thing.

"I didn't realize this was going to strike one of your dating sensitivity chords," I say, knowing it's probably just going to rile him more. This relationship might easily turn into a shit show, not to mention the blowback as those in charge wonder why I didn't know what was happening, or more importantly, why I wasn't the one hooking up.

"What do you care, anyway? Jealous?" Jason shuts down his MiniComp. I guess he's done with the notes.

"Of you or her?"

Jason stops for a long second, likely assessing whether I'm serious or not. I've heard the rumors—shit, Alex mentions something to the affect every couple weeks just fucking around. A woman apparently can't be intelligent, strong-willed, and physically intimidating without being a lesbian. Just because I can out-lift most of the men on the stations, doesn't mean I like women, which I do, but that's not the point, is it?

Truth be told, I'm flexible on the subject. I don't want children.

Getting stuck raising a gross, demanding, ungrateful little shit who'll blame me for their hang ups when they reach adulthood is at the bottom of my priority list. Which makes long term relationships with men problematic—most of them at some point want offspring. I suppose I could find some widower with a child, but that still leaves me raising a kid, someone else's kid, which would be even worse. I could hook up with someone older, maybe in their late forties or early fifties, but those single guys are few and far between. Not that I want to be with someone fifteen to twenty years older.

The problem is there are more opportunities with men than women. Well, it's not exactly a problem, more a nuisance. A lot of effort goes into identifying a man who might be good in bed, then assessing their willingness to both engage in a casual relationship *and* be discreet. Case in point, Jason, who came clean about Kami under a few minutes of badgering. Which is why, in addition to having a bit of a preference for the road less travelled, women are a good fallback option. No, that didn't come out right. Not a fallback option, just a good option. It's not a second choice, rather two equally adequate choices for which I have a tiny preference of one over the other. I wouldn't give up either, but if I'm leaning in a direction, it's going to be toward the girlfriend six times out of ten.

Not that women are easier to assess. There's still the possibility they'll want a relationship, hoping to bond, apply for the Screaming Baby Permit—*sometimes Marta is spot on with her descriptions*—and get inseminated. But they are generally more discreet about relationships and one-night stands. This is especially true if they're not interested in being with a woman long term.

Yet here we are in the twenty-second century and still a woman can't be with who she wants. Why should I need to choose a partner for the next fifty years, someone I have to wake up with every day, the same bad breath and bed head, scratching and body odor, day after day? Maybe I want different bed head? Different bad breath? It should be okay choosing who I want when I want and I don't want to choose right now. I've had great sex with both men and women—like phenomenal, mind-blowing, passionate, grip the sheets with both hands, sweat dripping from your stomach, if I don't cum soon my heart is going to explode sex. The ability to be good in bed, or bad for that matter, is not genetic.

I'm about to take the question back about being jealous when Jason responds.

"I apologize." He sounds more conciliatory than I expect. "I know it's not the best timing. The truth is I don't know where it's going with Kami. Probably nowhere. It's not like we're making big plans after one night."

Shit, I was ready to unload on him and now he's turned it around, employed the old *apologize to disarm* tactic. If I keep at him now, I'll be the asshole.

"I appreciate you keeping this between us," Jason adds. "Nothing's gonna change in the next few days and the Council will close us down once the report is finalized. We will all be moving on to bigger and better projects long before this thing with Kami ends the way it will likely end."

"Yeah, no worries," I reply without invoking my inner Marta. I don't mean it. I want to remind him he's putting his dick before the good of the team. Plus, I'm still a little pissed he didn't mention contacting someone close to the Council. Not to mention Kami's overtly eager desire to interview Indra Ocasio, which he deflected with a joke about Anna. I feel like I've lost control of this situation—an entirely unacceptable outcome.

Jason doesn't seem to want to talk anymore and stands to leave.

"Let's catch up in a couple days, maybe grab a drink when this is all over," Jason says, pocketing his MiniComp.

"Sure." I reply.

Jason leaves the room. I guess I'll have to rely on Marta for the after action report on his meeting with the Council POC—that's Marta-speak for *point of contact*.

CHAPTER THIRTY-ONE

Kami Lee

Kami, what are you doing?

I'm not sure if this is Saturday morning regret or morning-after hope, but it is definitely a record. The last time I had sex on two consecutive nights was…well, never, actually. In fact, two nights in the same month is just crazy. Aside from that experimental guy during Role training, it's been a lean couple years of adulthood.

Then there's the robot voice's warning. *You'll want to watch out for your partners.* Not much to go on. I mean what's the worst they could be up to? They're not killing people, that just doesn't make sense. If robot voice had actual information Jason or Brandi were killing people, he—or she, it could be a woman with the voice modulation—they would have told me. So what then? What is it I want to watch out for?

It's all a bunch of hooey. Jason's biggest vice is ambition, not murder. He's older, but that just means he's figured out his career and isn't still coming to terms with a bad decision. He's not wondering who he is, where he fits in the big picture, or whether he's made the right call or a wrong turn. Unlike me. I wake up every couple weeks, heart pounding, a sudden sharp breath pulling me from sleep into reality. That's if I can get to sleep. Most nights I'm staring at the ceiling reliving some random moment—an action not taken, the wrong words, something I should have said but didn't. Recreating it, as if there is anything to be done about it now. I envy Jason, lying there asleep without a care. It's admirable being dialed-in to life.

I shouldn't have been so eager to take over the Ocasio interview. I'm sure Brandi sensed something was up—I'll bet she was assessing my stability with every stuttered syllable. I basically shouted with antsy hunger a desire to meet with a mental health professional, ready to wrestle it from anyone who stood in my way. I should have casually offered, then waited for the 'thank you.' *Oh, no problem. I can take it, my schedule's pretty light tomorrow.* Jason would have been thrilled to hand it off without the eager icing on top.

See what I mean. Here I am laying next to a hot guy and I'm reliving a few minutes from yesterday. Brandi can be so pushy. She's not that much older than me, but seems to think she's in a different generation. She's only been on Aries for about three years. Maybe that's it—not enough time to adapt to station life. She hasn't quite learned that there's no need to be a roaring bitch every minute of the day. She's basically taken control of this entire project, handing out assignments and deciding how things will be structured. She really needs to step back and realize we are all in this together. It's not a competition, it's a cooperative.

Jason didn't mention anything odd about my volunteering. He stopped by a few hours after the meeting to brief me on his interview of Palau's wife, or so he insisted right up until we were naked. Any need for posturing fell to the floor with our uniforms. Now, lying beside me, he's certainly not voicing any concerns. I'm sure he would have said something if he'd noticed anything.

I should tell him my concerns about the suicides with him. At first I agreed with Jason and Brandi that this was all goat rope, just another random effort to prove the Council is concerned about our collective well-being. But at least four of the suicides had station infractions: Nigel Birmingham, Derek Ocasio, Nicholas Kesik, and Neil Palau. All of them were in the system and all of them had interaction with both the PersRep and Station Rep's offices. And none of them showed any signs of depression or intent to kill themselves. Not one witness suggested any of the men were having psychological problems. All three women—Vanessa Jepus, Candace Rogala, and Hannah Bonikowski—all three of them showed signs of depression. Their friends and family described anxiety, isolation, and—what did they say about Hannah?—here it is, she became 'increasingly morose.' I recall a study from several years ago suggesting women and men were equally prone to signs of depression. If so, why didn't anyone in the men's lives notice anything. Outwardly, they were all perfectly normal, in some cases even happy, right up until the instant they decided to commit suicide. Statistically, it's just not possible.

Ah, crap. There's got to be something I'm missing. Perhaps robot voice is correct, suicides haven't dropped and it has nothing to do with a failure to adapt. Could there be a link between the DupleX study and people killing themselves? This is going to drive me nuts—but not enough to take my own life.

If I listen to robot voice, I should keep any theories I have to myself until I'm sure. Worst case, Brandi and/or Jason are involved somehow, which I still doubt but why take the chance. Best case, they are going to think I've lost my grip on reality. Sigh. Either way, this stays in my personal log until I have more information.

According to my ComLink I've got about three hours left to get some shut eye—07:00 is early when you've been up most of the night. I'll stop by the office on the way to the Ocasio appointment—excuse me, I mean *meeting*, Brandi—and see what else I can find about the suicides. I should try to confirm if any of the other stations have similar findings. That's going to require a meeting with Parker and more ego stroking. FML.

CHAPTER THIRTY-TWO

Brandi Mikkelson

'Welcome, Brandi' flashes across the virtual screen when I tap the biometric reader on my MiniComp. Nothing more. It's the only way I know for sure I'm on the right system. An important consideration as I sit here researching my colleagues. Jason's secrecy surrounding Council meet-ups and Kami's enthusiasm about interviewing Derek Ocasio's mother left me with my own questions. Which is why I'm pecking away and reading instead of meeting Alex for our morning session at the HMC.

According to his file and various open source reports, Jason has what can easily be described as the most boring life ever. There is a ton of information about his parents migration and him growing up on the station, any nibble of which can get me in trouble for violating his privacy. Luckily, in addition to Alex being a genius when it comes to physical fitness, he's also a savant at hiding in the digital ether. His obfuscation and compilation code executed just after logging on to the Aries mainframe allows me to search without triggering alarms. As far as someone looking at network logs knows, everything is authorized. Not that anyone is going to examine these searches—they won't even be flagged for follow-up. But it's better to be safe than sorry.

I met Alex a few months after migrating. He'd had some problems with aggressive behavior owing to supplement over use and youthful exuberance. After graduating from training as a Physio-Nutritionist, he started working for the HMC as a coach, giving him unfettered access to people during his regular work day and sufficient time to pursue his secondary passion, hacking. I mitigated his circumstances and we became fast friends—my closest friend aboard Aries.

Alex is a Gen, having been born on the stations—it's all he knows. He's never even left Aries. The first case he helped with involved another Gen, a kid caught attempting an unauthorized spacewalk. Alex dug up digital comms from the girl's parents suggesting they encouraged her to live her dreams, not knowing one of her dreams was to walk in space. It was the perfect argument for another chance. Afterward, Alex shared his love of digital anonymity, although he decided to keep to himself whatever hack he uses to covertly access restricted accounts. In his words, "If I share all my tricks, you won't need me anymore." Luckily, my job grants me all the access I desire, I just need to keep the activity from being flagged.

Jason on the other hand has lived a wildly sheltered life. He's never been in trouble, graduated Role training at the top of his class, and has commendations for Fairness in Sentencing and Mitigation Deference. He's never been to the planet's surface or to any other station, which isn't actually odd. His viewing habits tend toward the late twentieth century films—he likes historical fiction and period documentaries. The last book he read was Stan Glendale's *Call Me Pat: A Non-Binary Approach to Cinema*, a criticism of the early twenty-first century progressive movement and the negative impact it had on the movie industry. Not my kind of reading.

Jason doesn't contact many people outside of his professional circle. There are some comms with our office, me and Botha, as well as a few errant Aries Internet Protocol addresses, but nothing out of the ordinary. There are a number of exchanges with judges, Cecelia Ryan most often. I'll bet she's the one the rumor mill refers to, the one he denied fucking on the side. No wonder they're keeping it secret—she's almost twice his age and a judge to boot. Based on all the Tuesday calls, I feel pretty confident Tuesday is their night. Good for her.

This is odd. There's recurring contact on the third Thursday of every month with an IP on Virgo. The Virgo IP he's been chatting with resolves to the main station relay, which indicates someone in a sensitive position who doesn't want to be identified—a Council Member, primary station Control Center, or in this case, probably Jason's Clerk contact. Virgo is a popular station for Council Clerks because of its synchronous, geostationary orbit above the Canadian Autonomous Zone, one of the three zones still remaining on Earth. Clerks sometimes shuttle to the Zones to meet with various politicians, negotiating trade agreements and resolving conflicts. The other two stations, Gemini and Libra, are synced to the Iceland and Australian Cooperative Zones, respectively and also house a number of Clerks. Whoever Jason's contact is, he or she is likely responsible for activities in the Canadian CAZ on behalf of the Council.

I'm not at all surprised to see the recurring comms in the logs, there's rarely a need to travel to another station, even to meet with someone important. The Council almost never meets in person, preferring virtual for security reasons, not that there's been so much as a rumor of a threat in the last 25 years. Station Ambassadors will occasionally shuttle to another station for business, but even that's rare and more of an excuse to travel versus an actual need. There's really nothing to see, every station being basically a mirror image of every other station, but there are sometimes black market goods to exchange. People with a pass can make a small bit by delivering bootleg items. As long as nobody gets hurt or does anything stupid, the authorities don't really care. Besides, an encrypted channel provides more secure communications than an in-person meeting—not even Alex can decrypt Council communications but anyone with a bit of skill, or in my case a friend with skills, can find out if someone is flying between stations.

It looks like Jason's contact goes all the way back to the year he completed Station Rep training. I should pull a list of people he went to school with—it wouldn't be very big—but correlating that with the list of Clerks is problematic. Clerkships are not published anywhere. I can't just ask around, either, setting off alarm bells and drawing unwanted attention. I'll let Marta figure this one out.

If Jason's past is boring, Kami's is only slightly better. She is a Gen just like Alex, born and raised on Aries. She's never been anywhere— the planet, another station—I can't even prove she's seen much beyond the HMC, the Cantina and her HabU. She's only 20, but already decorated for use of non-lethal force to halt a suicide attempt on the shuttle deck. *Seems like a waste of resources to me.* She scored at the top of her class in every category and apparently has an IQ greater than the circumference of the moon. Beyond that her file reads like an abbreviated dictionary—lots of words and no plot.

I notice both her parents died, but there's no cause of death for the father. Normally I'd just assume suicide, but seeing Lento's name as the examiner confirms it. He was assigned to be her Advocate *and* was responsible for filing the record of her father's death. *Manipulating official records is pretty serious stuff, Dr. Lento.* Not enough to get him expelled to the planet, but he'd definitely end up getting spanked and depending on who represents him, he might even be out of the medical program for lack of integrity. The problem is he's pretty well connected—his longevity affords him access to people who can provide all the mitigation he needs.

It looks like Lento's known the family for years. No wonder he became Kami's advocate after her father died. There isn't any obvious Role manipulation in the record and with her scores I wouldn't expect she'd need any help getting into any Role she wanted. What I don't get is her going the OSU route. It's not exactly filled with the best and brightest. She could have done anything with all those brains—station leadership, analysis, medical, even Council Clerk someday—yet she chose to confirm suicides, detain drunk graffiti artists, and help the elderly find their way between the community lounge and the food gummy distribution center. What a waste.

The brother is more interesting than Kami. He apparently has a penchant for developing clean, effective synthetic drugs—highly sought after on the black market. It looks like he's been able to stay in business because nothing's been linked back to his side hustle. Nobody has used his product and stole a shuttle or assaulted a sanitation tech. I'm guessing he's producing something with a delta-9-tetrahydrocannabinol base to relax the mind, making people less excitable without the hallucinations. Most other synthetics have a tendency to produce some unpredictable behavior. The same substance, also called THC, was legalized in the early-to-mid twenty-first century and used to alleviate the boredom and isolation resulting from the second great pandemic. Those were the good old days.

I'd guess her father killing himself and the relationship with her misfit brother probably have a long term effect on Kami's psyche. She's a hot mess of loss, guilt, and questions—it's just a matter of time before all that bubbles over. It's no wonder Jason was able to scoop her up without much effort. The poor girl was probably Jonesing for a good fuck.

It may be possible to use some of this information if things go sideways. And a visit to Kami's brother is definitely in order. Brandi needs a reliable hook up.

CHAPTER THIRTY-THREE

Jason Plumin

I'm standing outside Dr. Kornel Lento's office wondering just how bad an idea this is when I place my fingers on the reader and see my name pop up on the screen, Jason Plumin. I considered all night whether to change my mind. Well, not all night, but definitely during the times Kami and I weren't having sex. The guy lied on an official record when he reported Kami's father's death as natural causes and Kami knows about it. If anyone finds out, they could both end up before judicial review. That might not mean much to someone with Lento's bona fides, but it could sideline Kami.

I didn't mention this detour when Kami and I split this morning. She's supposed to meet with Dr. Ocasio, which freed me up to take care of this. But now that I'm standing here, I'm starting to question my decision. Can I fall back on the *good intentions* argument if this breaks bad? I think so.

The door opens and I step inside just in time to see my image disappear from the virtual display on Lento's desk. He's sitting behind a glossy, gray metal table in an unpressed tan uniform. It's neat and clean, but lacks the fine lines cutting down the legs and arms found on most station suits, leaving me wondering if he or his wife request it that way. Perhaps the starch chaffs his skin, or maybe it's just his way of maintaining a grip on a formerly bohemian lifestyle. It doesn't look staged, but who knows. He's not smiling when he asks what he can do for me, adding, "I've already reviewed the autopsy findings with Kami." His tone tells me he hasn't forgotten our last meeting over Birmingham's dead, acid-washed body.

"I was hoping to talk about Kami, if that's not too much trouble," I reply with my own lilt of contempt. Lento doesn't look surprised. Perhaps Kami's already told him about our getting together? She doesn't strike me as the type to tell anyone anything after only two nights, even her former Advocate. But who am I to judge? I told Brandi the next day.

Kornel's face tells a bifurcated story, first of an arduous life on the planet and later of comparative ease aboard Aries. Disease, food shortages, detritus, lacking tech, close quarters, processed water, intermittent power outages, waste disposal challenges—being a doctor in the CAZ is not an easy life and it shows in the lines etched into gaunt cheeks and a stubble-filled chin. Migrants who come from the Autonomous Zones tend not to lose their edge, even after years on board.

On the other hand, station life has been good for his complexion, giving him a soft, delicate tan rather than the harsh, dry leather of most Earth inhabitants. Although I've never noticed him in the HMC, he's known to walk about the station, presumably his preferred form of physical activity. He also sports a full head of gray, unkempt hair that blends well with the table where he sits. I find myself just a little jealous of his good genetics.

Lento considers my request for a moment, pushing his chair back from the table an inch or so like he's preparing for a fight. "I'm not sure we have anything to talk about. My relationship with Kami is none of your business, whether you're sleeping with her or not." He says it with calm indignation, like a challenge to convince him otherwise.

"I'm not surprised she told you," I fire back. "Well, whether we're sleeping together or not is our business, not yours. Besides, that's not what I came to talk to you about. I'm here because…"

"I don't care what you're here for," Lento interrupts, shaking his head. "And Kami didn't tell me anything, you just did. Now perhaps I should have a conversation with her about her life choices. Seems like she's not making the best decisions, lately."

He's standing now, shoving a small notebook and pencil into his breast pocket as if he's done with the conversation and about to leave. I'm not done. I move a step back to block the door, placing my left hand at shoulder level on the frame. He's going to hear what I have to say whether he likes it or not.

"Here's the thing, I care about Kami…"

"Oh, really?" Lento interrupts for the second time. "After two days?"

"Would you stop interrupting me for Pete's sake?" This man is exasperating. "I'm not the one who knowingly violated station policy and then made Kami complicit by telling her. You did that. Now you've put her in a position where she could lose her job or worse if anyone finds out."

The look on Lento's face changes from defiantly composed to an amalgamation of moderate concern and confusion as he steps back toward the desk and into his chair. The color, previously warm and inviting, drains from his face, fading the tan brought on by years on-planet. He doesn't speak right away, deciding an emotionless stare is a wiser approach. I too let it linger for a moment, having learned long ago the value of silence when trying to elicit information. At least I've got his attention.

"I can't believe she told you." Lento's muted response while looking down at his shoes tells me I've hit on a topic he'd hoped not to discuss with anyone ever. "I was sure she'd keep that between us."

I expect him to be recalcitrant, combative even, not forlorn. He's pretty well connected, far more so than I am, which means he's also got a lot of high cover from important people, people who don't care if he fudged a death certificate years ago to protect a frightened girl. If it were me, the sentence would be stiff. But the chances Lento gets hit with anything more than a slap on the wrist are slim. I'm not sure if that extends to Kami—probably not, but he'd likely tell her to deny knowing anything. But Lento isn't fighting, he's capitulating. It's as out of character for Lento as honesty is in politics.

"Well, I don't care one way or the other," I chastise. "I just don't want to see a promising career destroyed when all this comes out— and it will come out, sooner or later. Somebody you piss off is going to start scrutinizing the data and will figure out you're involved in a cover up. How long do you think it's going to take for them to connect you and Kami, and to realize she must have known, too. I get that it won't impact you with all your connections, but will those same people go out on a limb for Kami? That's going to leave her fighting for herself. I don't care what she's done to this point, she'll be out of the OSU and assigned to some less rigorous Role."

Lento remains silent. I wonder if he's contemplating the ramifications of his decision when he suddenly stands up and moves around the table toward me. "You can't tell anyone what you know. I mean nobody," he demands. "It's not just a matter of censure or some group time, it's a matter of life and death. If anyone else finds out, we're all in deep eff'ing shit."

I'm not sure his fight is back, but I recognize genuine concern when I hear it. Although I think he's being a little melodramatic. Nobody is going to die just because he misreported a cause of death over a decade ago. I mean, seriously, it's paperwork, not…

Wait? I suddenly realize we may not be talking about the same thing. Did Lento tell Kami something else? Something that might get people killed if it were leaked to the general population? What do I do? There's nothing I can do except press on and pretend I know what he's talking about. I want the whole story and at this point I don't even have the Cliff's Notes.

"I'm not walking around with half the information. Either I'm all the way in or I'm going to the…" Who? Who am I going to? If it's huge, it might involve the Council, so threatening to go to anyone on the Council might give away my hand. Then again, if they aren't involved, a threat to report him might be enough to push him over the edge. "… the media. Either I'm in or I'm going to blast this to the underground media." The media is essentially controlled by the Council here on the stations, but there are pirate outlets both here and on the planet. Of course I have no idea how to contact anyone in the underground media, so this is all a bluff on my part.

"You can't do that!" Lento barks back, his eyes widening at the prospect of whatever it is he thinks I know getting out to the masses. "Don't even joke about leaking anything to the press!" He's definitely found his fight. He paces around the tiny, bland room for a second before finding his way back to his chair behind the desk. I can see him weighing how much to share—trying to determine what Kami might already have told me. He's a smart man. I consider for a moment that he might just figure out I have no idea what I'm talking about. Then, without warning, as if he's reached a point of acceptance, he sits down and unloads what he told Kami.

At first I'm shocked, unable to grasp what I'm hearing. A fantastic story of gender disparities and cover ups, DupleX reports and manipulation, conspiracies and desperate attempts to find solutions. The population of the stations, all of the stations, is becoming increasingly male—women aren't having female babies. He's saying the stations, a place designed to save humanity from our misdeeds and mismanagement are essentially unsustainable. Within a hundred years there will be no way to maintain a population on board any of them.

The human race and this grand utopian plan will cease to exist in space. It's a serious *what the fuck* moment and I don't waste it. "What the eff."

Lento's correct, if any of this were to get out there would be mass panic. There aren't a lot of alternatives to the stations. Earth isn't an option with its near depletion of natural resources, global pollution, rising sea levels, and massive fires. The average age of a planet-goer at death has been dropping for decades. Most scientists predict within a generation it will be less than half what it was in the late twentieth century. A planet-wide 35 year life expectancy is what makes the stations so attractive. If this gets out, people will be forced to decide between the stations and a hopeful fix, or leave and suffer the same extinction that is creeping up on Earth's humans. If enough people leave, the cascading unsustainability within the CAZ and on the stations will increase exponentially. I'm no station Analyst, but I know it takes a lot of people to live in space. Orbit, oxygen, sustenance, hydration, and energy all require techs, analysts, scientists, and engineers, and that's just to maintain the basics. I'd guess losing a significant percentage of Cits to the planet would jeopardize everything the Council's built and probably force consolidation and abandonment of stations in order to maintain viability. This isn't a problem, it's a potential doomsday scenario.

"Do you have any idea what this means?" I ask in my best *holy crap* voice. "Will the CAZ even allow people to reverse migrate. As soon as the politicians left behind to run the Autonomous Zones find out life on the stations is no longer feasible, they'll institute a tax for anyone wanting to reintegrate and a selection process for potential returnees. The Council's 50 year minimization of the political class will give way to revenge of the politicians. It will be capitalistic chaos right up until the end of humanity."

Not that the Zone's can accommodate an influx of people wanting to return, I think to myself. Overcrowding, shortages, and violence are already a way of life. They rely on the stations for their food gummy production, space being the only stable environment in which to print and combine the necessary ingredients. Some people will have to stay aboard to keep people alive on the planet for as long as that lasts. Who the heck is going to volunteer for that assignment? If the global pandemics taught us anything, it's that people won't wait for a solution, they'll panic and react to save their own asses.

"There is a plan." I hear Lento's voice like someone is holding their hand over his mouth, tempered and without passion. The muffled tones bring me back into the moment.

"What?"

"There's a plan," he repeats. "A plan to set things right before it's too late."

"A plan? What kind of a plan?" I ask, wondering why he wouldn't start with that information.

"They're working on a solution," Lento clarifies, sitting up, legs curled beneath the rolling swivel-chair and hands crossed in his lap like a child whose been invited to come with their parent to work. "A remedy to correct the female-to-male birth disparity. They're close to a breakthrough—something to reverse the effects of the radiation *and* allow us to program gender in vitro. We just need to manipulate the algorithm for another few years and perhaps a while longer after they develop the vaccine in order to set things right."

Manipulate the algorithm? I must have misheard him. "What do you mean 'manipulate the algorithm?'"

Dr. Lento lets out a long sigh. "We've been selecting female over male replacements, especially women with female children or those genetically predisposed to having girls."

"How effing long has this been going on?"

"Three years," Lento looks confused, leaning forward and planting his elbows on the table. I can tell he's figured something out, an assumption confirmed with his next statement. "Kami didn't tell you this, did she?"

I want to say, *of course she didn't freaking tell me any of this. Are you crazy? She knows the fewer people in the loop on something like this the better. You shouldn't have told her, either. You've placed her in a shitty position. If anyone finds out, we'll probably both be expelled to the surface— and not one of the comfy Autonomous Zones, either, where we can blab to the authorities on the planet. No, they'll drop us in the middle of the Open Lands with no hope, as far away from the nearest CAZ as possible, and that's a best- case scenario.* I want to say all of this, but instead I sit down across from Lento and having spent the last cent of emotion, come clean.

"No, Kami didn't tell me."

"If she didn't tell you, then what in the name of Theodore Roosevelt were you here to talk about?"

"Kami's *father*." I reply, still trying to grasp the magnitude of Lento's big reveal. "You covered up his suicide."

"Shit," Lento says in a matter-of-fact a tone. "You know you can't tell anyone about this. You can't even talk about it with Kami. If anyone got wind of it, overheard a conversation or located a reference within the system, it would be the end of everything. They'd probably deport you both just for knowing, or in the least confine you to solitary until there's a solution in place, which might be a year or more. This is a secret you'll have to keep until it's not a secret any longer." Lento pauses for a moment, I assume for effect but who knows. I only know his next statement brings me no comfort. "Besides, with a little luck we'll soon have a fix and this entire problem will simply disappear."

"And if they don't find a cure? If all this effort and manipulation doesn't fix anything? Then what?" I ask, pretty sure I already know the answer.

"Then I guess we'll move on to Plan B."

"Plan B? What's Plan B?"

"I don't know," Lento acknowledges, looking me in the eye. "But it's going to be a lot worse than what we're doing today."

CHAPTER THIRTY-FOUR

Kami Lee

"Hello Ms. Lee. Come in," says Indra Ocasio, greeting me with her hand over her heart before I have time to place a digit on the sensor. It's like she was waiting for me. She leads me to her office, adding, "I suppose it's Deputy Lee, isn't it?"

"Please, call me Kami."

Dr. Ocasio is Indian, tan, and almost three times my age according to her file, but she looks more like a woman in her early forties than one in her mid-fifties. Her uniform is unzipped a little further than I'd expect for someone in her position, revealing a bit about her figure and personality. I'm not going to read too much into it, but I'd say she's embraced some freedoms afforded those over a certain age. Not that I'm an expert on the subject. Everyone I know over fifty is dead or left mid-century in the mirror a decade earlier.

"Can I offer you some tea, Kami?" she asks, leaving me to wonder whether she's this attentive with all her patients, or if it's the nature of my visit.

"Tea would be wonderful, thank you."

She leaves me to choose one of the two chairs in her rather austere office. I'm surprised to see it looks like every other room on the station with its drab, unadorned, egg shell walls. The chairs are the only stand out feature. I choose the one that looks like it was built for patients and am shocked at how comfortable it is. It sits upright, but has synthetic lamb skin covered ridges along the spine and seat—the sides seem to be poised to warmly hug me.

I'm not sure where to begin with Dr. Ocasio. I've come with two topics: Derek and the Neil Palau accusations. Jason briefed me on his conversation with Palau's wife, Susan, who said Palau thought he was being drugged or hypnotized during his sessions. He'd was having erotic dreams which for some unknown reason bothered him. Being a male, I would have thought he'd welcome the midnight distraction. Perhaps that's not a thing for anal retentive, OCD analysts worried about every thought that passes through their unconscious mind. Either way, it led him to make some accusations against Dr. Ocasio and perhaps contributed to his eventual suicide.

According to the records, the case was pretty straight forward. After Palau accused Dr. Ocasio of possibly drugging him, the doctor went to the OSU and filed her own complaint. Had there been proof she'd drugged Palau or done anything else untoward, she would have been sentenced—possibly sanctioned, temporarily barred from seeing patients, and reassigned to lab work. However, there wasn't any proof, so it fell on Palau for making unfounded—in this case, unprovable—accusations. He was convicted of slander, a pretty serious offense when it involves questioning someone's integrity. Jason asked me to make sure the Palau and Ocasio stories match up.

I suppose being forthright out of the gate is the best course of action. Normally I'd try to be more nuanced, but I don't expect this to be a confrontational interview. Sure, she's connected to at least two suicides —Derek and Neil—and she'll likely be emotional about the loss of her son, but there's no reason for her to lie about Derek now. Mothers don't kill their adult sons, not even in the Zones…not even in the Open Lands, or so I've read. There are killings within families, even some ancient cases of parents drowning their infant children, even mothers, but a mother murdering her adult child is as atypical as anyone being murdered on the stations.

Dr. Ocasio returns with two cups, honey, and a kettle smelling like chai. She presses her thumb against a sensor next to the door and a slim tabletop extends out two feet from the wall, creating an unobtrusive spot on which to place the tray. I notice it doesn't create a barrier between us, probably by design. The last thing a doctor wants is a physical or metaphorical divider interfering with treatment.

"Would you like some honey?" Dr. Ocasio asks before pouring the tea.

"Yes, please." I've never acquired a taste for tea unless I can sweeten it. In fact, I find it tastes like someone boiled grass with wood chips, straining the concoction into cups to serve to people you want to get rid of it quickly. But with a little honey, or in this case synthetic, honey-flavored, capsulized sweetener, it is at least palatable.

The room fills with the scent of spices. The wafting cardamom, cinnamon, ginger and cloves from the tea remind me of my mother, which is totally irrational. My mother died when I was born and I can't remember anyone mentioning her love of chai. But there is also a hint of vanilla and biscuits mixing into the air. I'm unexpectedly relaxed by the aroma and the warmth the kettle adds to the otherwise bland space.

"Is that the tea?" I ask, suspecting there is something more happening.

"Partially," replies Dr. Ocasio with a short chuckle. "I added the smell of bakery. We can't get biscuits, so it's the best I can do to augment the tea. It's built into the environmental controls. If it's distracting, I can disable it."

"No," I say, not wanting to be rude, but also because the smell makes me feel good. "It's fine."

"I only wish we could get milk," Dr. Ocasio adds. "It's impossible to make a real chai without real milk. But there hasn't been anything that produces decent milk on the planet in decades and there's nothing making milk on the stations. I suppose I could request a 3-D printed milk extract from the Botany Lab, but it's just not the same thing."

I take a sip and am instantly thankful she added the honey.

"So how can I help you today?" Dr. Ocasio inquires. "I presume it has something to do with Derek's suicide."

"Do you mind if I record?" I ask, tapping the ComLink on my wrist. "It will add our conversation to the records." *Which are already filled with my notes from the investigation, interviews, and file checks.*

Dr. Ocasio smiles, giving me an acquiescent wave.

"I apologize for having to bring this up again."

"Of course," she nods.

"Did Derek have anything going on which might have contributed to him committing suicide?"

"Derek was not a trouble-free child," Dr. Ocasio sighs, shifting in her seat before continuing. "He had a way of inviting in problems. He didn't do especially well in school, leading to limited options as he neared SR selections. He discovered the black market in his late teens after stealing a country-origin patch from an IPI, someone who'd immigrated during Initial Population. The black market gave him a short respite from the realities of daily life, allowing him to focus on his passions—stealing and trading—but it also opened the door to bigger issues. About the only thing he was consistently good at was getting into trouble. I think he just had a hard time adapting to station life. It's not that he knew anything else, but he had this imagination that would not quit. He couldn't help thinking there was a better life anywhere but where he was at that moment.

"I don't suppose his father or I helped much. We were always so busy, consumed by our Roles. We love our Roles. But I'd be lying if I didn't admit our dedication to work made it a lot easier to overlook Derek, to give him freedom without guidance and then judge when he didn't perform up to our expectations. I suppose it's a little ironic, me a doctor, a Psyche, and I couldn't be bothered with understanding my own child. But look who I'm telling, you've probably seen all of this in his records. Don't let the tea get too cold, dear." She adds the last bit after glancing at my almost full mug.

I take another sip and notice her watching intently. Not wanting to be too insulting, I force down another bigger swallow, emptying half the mug, which she promptly tops off.

"Yes," I reply. "I've seen his records. This is more to get a mother's perspective. Do you recall anything recent? Anything bothering him in the days leading up to his suicide? Perhaps he was acting different? More secretive?"

"Oh dear, secretive was Derek's middle name. He didn't share anything with us. We'd hardly know where he was from one day to the next. He didn't really have any friends, just people he'd met through the market or the legal system. I suppose he was lucky, though. Had he not been rolled into the system, he'd probably be a lot worse off."

Worse off than suicide? I think. "What do you mean?"

Dr. Ocasio picks up the small plate with three honey capsules, offering me another for the tea. I shake my head to decline, but take another big swig of chai to assuage any feelings of guilt I might have for not caring for tea in the first place.

"Shortly after his first, um, issue, he met Mr. Plumin from the Station Rep's office. Mr. Plumin accepted Derek's mitigation and recommended a fairly light sentence—a couple months of evaluation and group support."

Jason didn't mention anything about Derek's previous conviction or mitigation. I know he was involved with the last issue, the one Brandi wrote the letter for, but I wasn't aware there was history. Maybe he didn't think it was relevant?

"Do you know the Station Rep, Jason Plumin?" I ask, not sure which answer I'm hoping to hear.

"Oh, no. We've never met. I drafted a letter on Derek's behalf for the first offense and sent it to Mr. Plumin's office, but a face-to-face meeting was never necessary. Derek just spoke really highly of him—said Mr. Plumin was one of the better StaReps. Had Derek's cases not been assigned to Mr. Plumin, he might have ended up with someone less considerate of his mitigating circumstances."

"His mitigating circumstances?"

"Derek was on the spectrum...the autism spectrum," Ocasio adds after noticing the puzzled look on my face.

"Derek had autism?"

Ocasio shakes her head like a disappointed school teacher. "No, no. He wasn't autistic, exactly. He was diagnosed with pervasive development disorder not otherwise specified. It put him on the spectrum, albeit highly functioning...so to speak."

If Derek was diagnosed with a developmental disorder, he would basically have lifelong mitigation for minor offenses—things like bootleg booze, non-lethal drug use, minor burglary. An asshole Station Rep could assign on a harsher sentence if there were multiple infractions over time and thereby order re-homing, but short of unauthorized procreation or murder, it's unlikely. The station would have to show a total and complete failure to rehabilitate, which in Derek's case might be possible at some point, but not after a couple rounds of rehab. Derek definitely wouldn't have considered it a possibility, which means he wouldn't consider suicide to avoid expulsion.

"His Station Rep, Mr. Plumin, he knew about Derek's diagnosis?"

"I mentioned Derek's diagnoses in my first letter," replies Dr. Ocasio.

"That all makes sense," I lie. I don't recall reading anything about Derek's developmental disorder in his file. It should have been there along with Dr. Ocasio's letter, but it wasn't. There was no mention of a disorder in the case notes from this last case, nor in any of his three previous appearances before the StaRep's office. It could have been deleted, but why and by whom? Who would want to delete a document from Derek's records, especially an indication of a developmental disorder? I suppose the bigger question is who has sufficient access to alter electronic records? The Council? Robot voice?

"I wonder if we might switch the subject just a bit and talk about Neil Palau?" I ask, taking another sip of my tea before Dr. Ocasio has a chance to mention it.

"Anything," she replies.

"He made some accusations. I know according to the records they were unfounded, but I have to ask, were you treating him with any pharma during his sessions?"

"As I mentioned before to the investigators, I never supplied Mr. Palau with any pharmaceuticals. Our sessions consisted of sensory manipulation via sound, sight, and smell, combined with verbal discussions of his past. We did not use drugs to enable his therapy."

Ms. Palau wasn't clear about why Neil was meeting with Dr. Ocasio. Jason suspected it was work-related based on Ms. Palau's statements about recent projects, but he didn't have specifics or any evidence to support his hunch. It would be nice to know exactly why Neil was seeing Dr. Ocasio, if only to confirm any major mental problems.

"And why exactly was he seeing a therapist?"

"I'm afraid I'm not at liberty to discuss the particulars, Kami" Ocasio replies.

"I understand Privacy First, but the man is dead. Certainly you can share a little bit about why he was seeing you and what was discussed during your sessions?" I'm perhaps a bit more blunt than I mean to be.

"No, Deputy Lee, I can't talk about our sessions," Dr. Ocasio replies, sitting up in her chair as if posturing for a battle. "He still has a widow who could be damaged by any revelations."

It's back to *Deputy Lee* I see. "Perhaps you could simply confirm a couple things rather than giving up any private information. Like, was he seeing you due to problems in his marriage?"

The doctor sits silent for a moment, hopefully considering an answer that isn't party line. "No, I can safely say we did not discuss marital discourse during any of his sessions. What I will say is he was under some stress at work. Our discussions centered on a recent project, something to do with genetic balancing, but he wouldn't share the details. I presumed it was something the Council assigned and suggested he request help or more time, but he insisted he could handle it—said it was almost complete." Dr. Ocasio crosses her arms, usually indicating the end of the interview. "And that's all I'm going to say about it."

Yep, we're done.

I hate to leave on a contentious note, so I say, "Thank you for the tea," glancing at what's left of the now cold, sweetened herb-water. "It was lovely. Reminds me of home."

"No problem," Dr. Ocasio replies with a smile, uncrossing her arms. "And I'm sorry about my attitude with respect to Mr. Palau. It's just that some people don't respect the sanctity of the doctor patient relationship when it comes to privacy. Sometimes we need to consider how information will affect a patient's family."

"I understand completely," I say, standing to leave. Dr. Ocasio walks me to the door, which opens as we approach. "Just one more question, if I may?"

"Of course."

"Was there any indication Neil Palau was considering suicide?"

The right side of Dr. Ocasio's lip bending upward into a somewhat devious half-smile doesn't catch me off guard as much as her answer.

"No, dear. There weren't any signs Mr. Palau was considering suicide and given the, um, tenor of our sessions, I can't imagine why he would do so."

"I see," I say, a little creeped out. "Thank you, again, Dr. Ocasio. I really appreciate your time."

"No problem, Kami. I doubt I was very helpful."

CHAPTER THIRTY-FIVE

Kami Lee

A moment later I'm standing outside Dr. Ocasio's HabU with the door swooshing shut behind me and feeling more than a little weirded out by how our conversation ended. Perhaps I'm reading too much into her micro expressions and the allusive lilt in her voice, but I don't think so. She seemed pretty normal up until that point. But I'd swear she was remembering something when she answered, some specific moment or visual—the *tenor* of their sessions. Very odd.

On my way back to the office I tap my ComLink to review the transcription and other notes I've added to the file. Parker was able to pull some historical data and transfer the information to my account. It appears the ratio of men committing suicide has gone up every year for the last couple years. This is quite anomalous. Suicides are committed in relatively equal numbers, some years more men, some more women, but the difference is usually nominal. I set my ComLink to record, hoping to memorialize some thoughts before I get back to the unit.

Normally there are 25-30 suicides per year on any given station. Some say that's too many, but people mostly accept it as the price for sustained life in space. Our total lack of violent crime coupled with a virtually stress-free existence, one devoid of hunger, disease and war, provides the needed justification for so few unhappy and unstable people. Besides, it's less than .002 percent of the population, so the odds are in your favor you won't have issues.

The concern is, if my calculations are correct, that number is set to hit about 40 this year. Of the suicides to date, five of the nine people in our study were male, six counting Finn, which appeared to be an accident. That's 66% and it's only the first week of April. Couple that with the information from Kornel about female reproduction and prioritizing females for recruitment and it certainly seems plausible someone is manipulating male suicides. An increase in male deaths combined with Lento's recruitment board means exponentially more females migrating to replace males.

For an instant the thought of Lento being in on it pops into my head. He told me about the board prioritizing women, but I can see where he'd want to leave out the part about killing men. While his selection of women to replace male deaths is bad, it's done at the direction of the Council. But killing men in order to force selection of females is an entirely different matter. Unless the Council knows and ordered the deaths. Is that even possible? Would the Council be ordering the killing of men to buy time to correct the male-to-female birth mismatch? No, no, no—the Council doesn't kill people. The suicides must be normal. But they're not. Even Robot Voice doesn't think so.

I dial up Susan Palau on my ComLink. She answers immediately.

"Hi, Ms. Palau, this is Deputy Lee from the Orbital Sheriff's Office. I was just hoping to follow up on your conversation with Jason Plumin with a quick question."

"What can I help you with Ms. Lee?" She says, sounding disinterested.

"I was wondering if there is anything more you can tell me about Neil's genetics project?" I leave the question open-ended, hoping she'll fill in the blanks with whatever comes to mind.

"I already explained all of this to Mr. Plumin. He was assigned the project by the Council. Neil did not share details of his projects as it is forbidden by the Council. Not that any of this is relevant, he committed suicide because of the Ocasio woman."

"Thank you, Ms. Palau. I'm very sorry for your loss."

I hastily hang up the phone. So Jason knew about Neil's genetics project and didn't mention it. He knows some of the victims and he's withholding information.

But how does Palau's project fit into all of this, if it does fit into it? It's possible genetics is somehow related to the gender preference selections Lento and his team are making. Did Palau's other coworkers know about the project? Surely someone in the Lab would have mentioned it during their interview, especially if it was taking up an inordinate amount of time or appeared to be having an impact on his personality. Maybe they did and Jason just didn't document it. Maybe

Palau's project led to a conflict with the Council? That just doesn't make sense if the Council assigned it.

I feel a little light headed. Like my brain is working overtime. Stopping, I tap into my biometric output on the ComLink for a health scan. While it's running, I thumb through Derek's file again, looking for Dr. Ocasio's letter. It definitely is not here, which means someone deleted it. Someone who knew about it. Jason had to have known about the letter. But he doesn't have the kind of access needed to delete digital records. The Council does. Which means if a Station Rep deleted Ocasio's letter, he had help.

I click back into the rest of Parker's transmission and see the study I requested this morning, the one produced a couple years ago about suicides. Here it is: *Males and females committed suicide at the same rate, however, men displayed signs of depression and despondence in greater numbers than women, with men showing more overt signals and indicators.* Parker added his own commentary, 'Apparently women are better at hiding their emotional distress in public. Who knew?'

None of this makes sense. This was supposed to be a review of predictable increases in the rate of suicides among Aries Cits. Now there are missing files, suicide increases, zero male indicators, birth discrepancies, gender preferences, incomplete information—a flurry of activity, like ducks feet beneath the surface. I can't see them moving and don't understand the meaning behind the ripples.

Plus, this entire investigation is giving me a major headache and making me a little nauseous. Biometrics shows my heart rate elevated at 132 bmp and blood pressure is 130/90. I'm about to rerun the scan when a message flashes on the ComLink screen: ANOMALY DETECTED. SEEK MEDICAL ASSISTANCE.

The metal corridor wall feels cool against the back of my uniform. I'm definitely flush and my head is pounding. Hands are shaking, light headed. Something is wrong—I need to get to the Med Lab, or some water, or call someone. Who? Jason. No not Jason. Lento. Where is everyone? A tech walking by, grab him. He's looking at me, longer than normal, too long.

"Hour yoo oookaaay?"

My head—throbbing. Gothard Hong. Interviews. Lento and Jason killing men and replacing them with female migrants. Message to Parker: "Pls send Hong, writer." No. Shit, I accidentally hit send. Resend: "Hel…" Fuck. I'm on my back, a fluorescent river winding down the corridor above me. Shit. Focus dammit! Typing…ComLink.

Lento…

CHAPTER THIRTY-SIX

The Collective

The Council assigned three, low-level people to investigate the uptick in suicides on Aries—two Reps and an OSU Deputy. It can't be coincidence that none of them are well-known. Either the Council wants to avoid the publicity these things get when assigning high-level Cits, or they don't think the study will uncover anything abnormal so why waste the time of important people. Why not just assign it to an Analyst on each station? Because those idiots dig like there's treasure at the bottom.

If there were truly anything to worry about, the Collective would have found some way to pass along a warning or guidance. Instead, it's radio silence, not even a recommended suicide. Not even an order to monitor the suicide team. That I'm doing on my own.

It took a while to hack into Kami's private files—she's been a very busy girl with lots of wild theories bouncing around her head. According to her notes, Lento told her about the DupleX report and the impact of radiation on female reproduction. I wonder how he knew? Probably because he's on the recruitment board. He would have questioned orders to prioritize females for migration if he didn't know the background. The Council would have brought in the board to force their complicity and keep them quiet. Of course he agreed—given the choice between helping to stave off the end of the human race and possibly buying enough time to save it, he'd have chosen the latter.

It would have been better had he not told Kami, who is apparently wrapping the news in layers of clues and Cit violations where it can gestate into her current questions about who's involved. One minute she agrees with the idea that this is just another Council effort to cover their asses, and the next she's surmising links between migrant selections and suicides, adding up connections to the PersRep's office, and postulating on the possibility of a secret society bent on killing some for the benefit of others. The girl does have a knack for puzzles.

Unsurprisingly, Kami is starting to realize she can't trust anyone, least of all her teammates. It didn't take her long to spot the links between the suicides and the Rep's offices, both the PersRep and Station Rep. The biggest shock came in reading her thoughts about Lento. She'd known him all her life and there she was questioning what the good Doctor knew and when—a wide chasm to cross considering he basically raised the girl. I decided to intervene before reading her concerns about her beloved Advocate, but this confirmed it was the right decision.

If it were possible to feel anything other than satisfaction about what I've done, it would be for the women I've sacrificed for the greater good. We assist in the death of any male whose name crosses our ComLink on the encrypted channel, but we are supposed to avoid killing females if possible. Have I terminated some people without receiving their name? Of course. I'm a pro, trained to observe, evaluate, and act. I've even violated the no-females edict—sometimes we do what we have to despite the guidance. But those killings are the ones I...regret? No, not regret, that's just plain disingenuous and frankly disrespectful. Pause, maybe? Yes, those killings are the only ones which gave me pause. They didn't die for nothing. Their suicides had meaning, if not in the short term than in the long. Nevertheless, there is a pang of irritation, a bothersome twinge over doing what is needed, a sort of momentary stay if you will, while considering whether those women, having driven us to the intersection of anonymity and discovery, might consider joining the cause as a player rather than a martyr. It is the same intersection I found myself standing while reading Kami's notes, wondering for an instant whether she might be persuaded to make history as an actor rather than a prop.

I've never really liked Dr. Lento. If I could communicate up, I would tell someone he violated his nondisclosure agreement, telling Kami about the gender disparity. Had he not shared information about the Board's female migration bias, Kami might not have connected the rest of the dots. *His* revelations provided her a possible motive, one she would not likely have considered without his help. Her fate is his responsibility and I'd love to throw that in his face.

But Lento is protected. His role on the migration board and his obvious knowledge about the issues sets him off limits, although he doesn't seem to know about the Collective—something I doubt he'd sign on to keep secret. It's one thing to choose female over male replacements, it's something entirely different to take men's lives. Lento's self-righteous attitude peppered with self-aggrandized planetary grit and untouchable bulwarked arrogance may play like an orbiting tough guy, but he has neither the character nor foresight to appreciate sacrifice. Him spilling all he knows about the gender disparity to someone outside the circle makes me want to force his head into a charged field array. Instead, he'll see his adopted daughter become a statistic—the first murder in station history. I can only hope to see his name pop up on my ComLink.

Dr. Ocasio didn't remember my previous visit, a pleasant effect of the Benzos. I knew Kami was on her schedule and since Ocasio has access to all sorts of drugs, she's the perfect tool. This time I dropped the Benzos in Ocasio's tea when she stepped out for honey capsules—her hospitality even with unexpected guests and my sweet tooth served me well. Once she'd ingested enough of the Benzos, it was simply a matter of suggestion—offer Kami tea when she arrives, add enough poison to kill someone twice her size, encourage her to drink it. Inhibitions erased by the Benzos, Dr. Ocasio performed as instructed.

I considered reassessing my decision to kill Kami until after her meeting with the doctor. Perhaps she'd reach other conclusions and I could avoid taking drastic measures. Unfortunately, this meeting presented the best opportunity to stem a potential disaster—I wasn't sure I'd get another chance anytime soon. Worst case, should Kami start to back pedal on her wild theories about the suicides, I'd have killed an innocent. But I had a contingency in case she turned out to be harmless—I'd meet her in the corridor outside Dr. Ocasio's HabU and slip her the antidote. It's aerosolized, odorless and colorless. But as I monitored the interview transcription and her personal logs, I knew I'd made the right decision.

The bigger risk is how the Collective might react. They might question my motives, or worse, my judgement. The first murder in station history, *any* station's history, will draw a lot of attention. I was sure they could handle the scrutiny and positive even a murder would blow over soon enough, relegated to the anomalous behavior of a single unstable individual. There'd be some changes to migration protocols, perhaps additional screening of mental health professionals, but nothing excessively intrusive or long lasting.

Still, the Collective might find my actions overly aggressive and prefer an opportunity to recruit Kami rather than terminate her. Kami just isn't the type. She's too law and order, by the book, idealistic. She would never agree to join the Collective, even if it meant saving her own life. Look how quickly she was able to transition from trusting her Advocate to presuming he was part of a conspiracy. No, she would definitely go to the Council or perhaps even go public with the information just to maintain her sense of order and civility. There was no other way. Kami was getting too close.

One thing is certain, the Collective will ask why I didn't make it look like a suicide. I would have preferred to stick to protocol, but there wasn't time. These things take preparation, lead time, staging, learning routines and preferences, peppering digital data with convenient clues, none of which I could make happen on short notice. I've spent significant time building up a network on Aries to study male candidates identified for repurposing, as well as setting tripwires to be alerted to anyone posing a risk to our work. I couldn't put the entire effort in jeopardy on the hope I'd have enough notice to plan a suicide before Kami told someone else about her theories. A quick solution followed: poison Kami, modify key parts of her personal log to remove any wild theories, insert a few mundane facts confirming there were no indications the suicides were anything more than suicides. It was the best choice—the only choice.

So I did it. I killed Kami Lee and modified her personal logs in violation of Collective protocols in order to save the effort—and I did it without pause.

CHAPTER THIRTY-SEVEN
Brandi Mikkelson

"Hey Brandi," Botha says with his usual optimistic lilt like everything is fine even when it isn't. "I didn't expect to see you here today."

I stopped by the office to pull a few things together and review Kami and Jason's notes before starting a draft of our final report. We haven't discussed any conclusions, save that this entire thing is a huge goat rope. But I can pull together a bunch of the background data into something resembling coherence, saving some time on the back end. Besides, if I start drafting now, it will be primarily my voice coming through to the Council.

"Hi Henry. Yeah, I didn't intend to stop in today, but I wanted to get caught up on some stuff." I go vague. Henry knows about the suicide investigation and has enjoyed tossing out a few barbs over the last couple days. At least I won't have to explain the panel falling and almost killing me—Marta already briefed the entire PersRep team via email.

"The suicide review keeping you busy, I guess." Henry pauses for effect before chuckling. He's sitting at a desk in our shared space adjacent to the same conference room where Kami, Jason and I met yesterday, Kami awkwardly jumping at the chance to interview Derek Ocasio's mother and Jason admitting he's fucking Kami. He's scrolling through something on a virtual display projected from his MiniComp into the space between our two desks. I decide to let the comment lie rather than racket back with an expected snarky reply.

Normally the space seats three, with Anna's desk closest to the entry and Botha and I facing each other a few feet away. There is room to reconfigure and add two more desks, something the Aries management team has been promising for some time, but which has yet to happen. It's not that we're overloaded with work, but another body to lighten the load couldn't hurt. Botha and I are constantly passing cases back and forth and with me on this special team he's taken on the entire load. Another good reason to get this done as quickly as possible.

The additional space in our office is easy to create. The stations are an engineering marvel, with their solid outer structure and flexible internal barriers supported by surprisingly few fixed components. The nature of space—as in outer space—it's lack of pressure, allows for greater flexibility. A rigid skin and sparsely placed bulkheads provide the primary skeleton, while light weight, mobile walls separate internal compartments. One can't just push a wall into a new position, but a call to the Remodel Lab and thumbs up from the Aries management team can get a room reconfigured in a couple hours.

The problem of course isn't space, it's recruitment. Since migrants are usually replacements—except during end of year balancing—the Council would have to approve a reallocation, essentially moving a Role. There are a fixed number of people allowed on the stations, every person fitting into predetermined slots. When Aries was created the people in charge of staffing decided we should have two Personal Representatives, just like every other station. To have the number of PersReps increased, someone somewhere has to give up a Role, which is difficult to justify unless something has changed—improvements in technology making a Role obsolete is the most common.

The Council also prefers both centralized control and uniformity among the stations. If one station has two station Analysts, every other station will have two Analysts. Stations have little autonomy when it comes to Role allocation. In order for the Aries management team to move a body from say the Botany Lab to the PersRep's office—which is actually a crap example since they would never give up a science role for a PersRep, but whatever. In order to have the Role staffing level reassigned, the management team needs to present a compelling argument justifying the variation, which requires a formal study demonstrating how the losing entity won't be affected and the gaining entity will be enhanced. The process is arduous, designed to discourage stations from attempting to deviate from the plan.

Botha doesn't seem to mind our normal workload or picking up my crap during these rare studies, or if he does mind, he doesn't complain. I've never heard him say a single disparaging word about station management, the Council, or the stations. Perhaps because he's seen the other side of things, the planet side before food gummies. He's been part of the post-Global Pandemic recovery periods, witnessed the starvation, experienced migration to the CAZ, and remembers the Open Lands through CAZ walls. He rarely talks about his pre-station life, except to say that if there is too much work it simply means we have job security—which says a lot about what it must have been like before he migrated.

"Henry, can I ask your opinion about something?"

Henry glances at me from behind the virtual monitor. "Sounds serious."

"How well do you know Jason Plumin and Kami Lee? I'm dealing with both of them as part of the suicide crew…um, suicide study, and I find myself wanting to punch them in the head sometimes. Kami can be so quick to jump to conclusions and unwilling to look at facts for facts. I know she's smart, but it's like dealing with Anne, all *on* and ready to go all the time. Jason on the other hand is more realistic, but I get the feeling they're both hiding things, perhaps from each other, but definitely from me. I think Jason's planning to spin this study into an opportunity, perhaps as a clerk or even a station Ambassador. Kami was also acting weird at yesterday's catch-up meeting. Afterword I got some other info I've got no idea how to process. They're just both so damn secretive and we're supposed to be in this together. I'm not disappointed so much as just pissed and sick of the bullshit."

Henry presses his finger against a reader on his MiniComp and the digital display between us vanishes. "Sounds like trouble in paradise," he notes, a sardonic grin forming on his weathered face.

Henry and I have worked together for three years and while his cheeky smile is totally in character, he's not what I'd call outwardly sarcastic, preferring a subdued, British approach to comedy over something overtly loud and North American. He'll pin the occasional mocking comment on the proverbial donkey at what seems like unexpected moments, but it always comes off as dryly funny, never rude. In fact, other than the errant jibe, I don't think I've ever seen him other than mundanely professional.

Henry's dependability is one of the things I can count on most aboard Aries. He comes to work, plugs away until it's time to mitigate with a Station Rep or Judge, meets with the occasional client, then heads back to his HabU or the HMC at the end of the day. He doesn't drink, not even 3.2 percent Peg. The times I've seen him in the Cantina, which are rare, he is usually alone, reading and sipping something bubbly and non-alcoholic. He's not married—never has been—and as far as I know he's not seeing anyone. Everyone knows him and most would refer to him as a friend, yet I'm not sure the term is entirely accurate. I'm not even sure I'd classify *our* relationship as friendship, and I see him more than most.

In fact, Henry knows me better than anyone on the stations, save maybe for Alex. We don't sit around having deep, philosophical conversations in the middle of the workplace, but you can't spend hours a day with someone without sharing a small piece of yourself. Yet, Henry's never said anything critical or judgy about any of my ideas, sexual or otherwise. I know he knows where I stand on most issues, including preference, procreation, personal mistakes, station management, Council directives, the planet, and anything else that might flash across the news feed. If he has an opinion about me, he keeps it to himself.

I deferred to Henry quite a bit when I first migrated. He had decades of experience by the time I came aboard, having immigrated during IPI and moved into the PersRep role almost immediately. But over the last couple years there's been less need to pick his brain about anything work related. Marta prefers me to Henry, which while occasionally awkward means I get most information directly from her to pass to him, and the majority of the cases aboard are routine and straightforward. Occasionally I feel a little bad watching his light black curls turn gray and new wrinkles accentuate his features, so I throw him a question for which I don't really want an answer just to remind him he's still needed. Unlike now, when I'm seriously hoping he'll give me an enlightened piece of information.

"I'd just like to know who I'm in bed with, if you get my meaning, H."

Henry smiles again, seeming to appreciate the attempt at humor. "Well, I don't know Ms. Lee at all, except by reputation. She's new to the Orbital Sheriff's Unit and only a year out of role training, which I understand she finished a year early. She has a reputation for being bright and motivated, but I imagine her lack of experience might require some patience from Personal Reps with a bit more time and wisdom under their belt." Henry pauses momentarily, assessing whether I picked up the rather large hint he just dropped. "Perhaps she'd be open to a meaningful conversation, woman-a-woman, as it were, to discuss your concerns? You might find you have a lot more in common than you think. If not, then at least you've given her a chance to be part of your process."

Henry runs his left hand atop his curls, sliding it back to rub the muscles of his neck. I wonder if he's trying to decide how much to say, his demur wrestling with an equal penchant for honesty. The question is answered when Henry begins his summation of Jason.

"He's...well, complicated would be the word I'd choose." For Henry, that's like describing the infamous conspiracy theorist and mid-twenty-first century U.S. President Sarah McAdams as mildly misinformed.

"I first met Jason while teaching a section on justice when he was in Station Rep role training," Henry continues. "You'll recall from your fams course that justice aboard the stations is quite a bit different from what it is on the planet. There aren't nearly the volume or severity of crimes aboard the stations as there are in the CAZ, which means justice need not be nearly as harsh or final."

Henry reviews the various reasons for the deviation between station justice and planet justice—fewer violations, less severe consequences, the Council's more liberal-leaning leadership style, improved understanding of cause and effect, the financial and social impact of expelling violators and migrating replacements, and virtually no space to house prisoners. I could interrupt and remind him these are all things learned transitioning from CAZ PersRep to Aries, but it would be rude and besides, Henry's earned the right to make his point via whichever circuitous route he chooses.

"Jason was the brightest Cit in his class, but he could also be argumentative, questioning many of the tenets on which we base our entire legal system. He didn't understand why we don't pursue minor violators with more veracity, such as black market traders and recreational drug users. According to him, if we expelled people in accordance with a statutory limit on violations, something akin to the archaic three-strikes rule of the late twentieth century, we'd be affording exponentially more people in the CAZ an opportunity at a better life. He was correct, of course, the more people we expel, the more people we migrate."

"Yeah," I acknowledge, "but what about the people *around* the violator?"

"Exactly," Henry agrees. "You were paying attention in class. There are second and third order affects. Every person we expel for minor violations, even frequent minor violations, impacts not only the people who know him, but those who know of him—or her, as it were. Loved ones feel the direct loss and society reacts to the variance. Because even though we purport to equally apply the rules, we know from history there is a disproportionate and unequal application in practice. Those with influence are allowed their minor dips into illegality without recourse, while the rest are subject to the harshest penalties. When society sees the powerful circumvent the system and recognizes intolerance among the common people, they eventually lash out. The institutions designed by those at the top to protect those at the top come crashing down."

I remember those courses in PersRep training during indoc after migration. The Council understood the concepts of collateral damage and empathy, deciding during the formation of the stations to decriminalize activities which did not negatively impact others or society as a whole. They provided for extensive leeway in rehabilitating through community service as often as possible. It is more difficult to expel someone from the stations and that is by design.

"Collateral damage and empathy are concepts Jason had trouble grasping," adds Henry.

This is quite the revelation from someone whose penchant for neutrality is rivaled only by his appreciation for the rules. Henry keeps most of his opinions about life, love, people and current events under close hold. His thoughts on the Council are complimentary, on station management he is forgiving, and on the general intrusiveness of Cits tightly contained in a spinning donut he is apologetic. Even Marta, who generally treats Henry like a dog she doesn't have time for anymore, gets nothing but praise for her command of station rules and overall efficiency. The man wouldn't speak an ill word about someone if they bit him on the ankle, so his comments about Jason are shocking.

I think about my own interactions with Jason over the years. None of them would indicate a lack of empathy. "I've always found Jason's actions regarding sentencing to be fair—not leaning toward overly harsh at all."

"It's true," Henry confirms. "Before the judge Jason evenly dispenses corrective actions and adheres to the guidelines. He's not an idiot. He knows his adjudications will be questioned if he's seen deterring from station norms. He doesn't believe it, but he is smart enough to know he needs to follow the rules. I suppose that's what's important in the end—fair, equal and empathetic justice in practice despite one's personal beliefs. Perhaps he's changed? Or maybe he's found another way to slip a bit of his own philosophy into the system."

"Do you think he'd apply some of that philosophy to this suicide study? Maybe try to turn this into something professionally advantageous, like a Council clerk opp?

"Are you asking if I think he'd try to screw you over just to get ahead?" Henry responds. "Sure. Wouldn't you?"

I'm not sure if I should be insulted. Coming from anyone else, I would be. But from Henry, it's more of a casual observation, not judgment.

"I suppose," I reply. "But I'm not going to step on people to get ahead."

"No, perhaps not," Henry adds, making me feel a little better. "You're not really the type to chase recognition. But if it comes, it will be a nice bonus for a few days of effort."

A few days of effort. I need to keep that in mind.

CHAPTER THIRTY-EIGHT

Jason Plumin

Jason, meet in main bay at 17:00.

I leave early for the shuttle bay to meet Sean. Normally we'll talk once a month or so, him catching me up on station business and Council doings, at least the one's he's comfortable sharing, and me summarizing Aries adjudication data he collates in support of Council initiatives. But this time when I mentioned Neil Palau's genetics project, Sean was insistent, "Don't say anything else to anyone. I'll be aboard a private boat originating from Pisces." Sean is pretty level-headed, so the sense of urgency in his voice left me speechless.

Sean and I were inseparable during Role training. We both interned in the Station Representative's office, completed our first years together adjudicating cases, and spent our formative time commiserating about the Council. He's my best friend, despite accepting an appointment to be a sellout Council Clerk.

I didn't know about Lento's gender preference selections when Sean and I talked, only about Palau's genetics study; however, since my conversation with Lento I can't help assume both Palau's work and Lento's are somehow linked. It can't be coincidence. Palau receives a tasking from the Council to conduct Genetic Balancing Reviews— GBRs, as Palau's replacement, Annie, called them—and Lento's team selects women over men for migration. Sean must assume I know more than I do or he wants to find out exactly how much I do know.

It makes sense Sean is in the loop, Lento said the entire Council was on board. Council Clerks go through an intense vetting process prior to recruitment—the Council wants people they can trust for situations just like this. Sean's never shared sensitive information with me, only things that appear in the news a few days later, and I doubt he'd discuss this if he didn't think I already knew. The question is whether he's coming here to warn me, turn me in, or find out exactly how much I know. We've been friends a long time, but he's always struck me as someone who equates the good of the Council with the good of society. He's not going to risk societal breakdown for me or anyone else. I'll have to be careful how I approach the conversation.

The thing is the circle of people who know about and are involved in this effort has got to be larger than anyone hoped. Lento said there were scientists, analysts, and doctors working on a solution or engaged in various mitigation efforts, all to buy time until a correction can be implemented. It's just not possible for that many people to keep something this big a secret forever. Someone had to have leaked information and would have been dealt with quickly and without remorse. Unlike Lento, I do think the Council would kill someone to keep them quiet, but even if I'm wrong, they wouldn't have a problem sequestering them and in extreme cases threatening people with re-homing. They need vigilance to control information.

This is why the suicide reviews don't make any sense. First of all, if the Council was killing people to keep them quiet, there are easier ways than faking suicides. They could simply cart someone off in the middle of the night and deport them to the Open Lands. It's harsh and unlikely, but a far simpler option than fake suicides. Second, the last thing you'd want to do if you were helping people commit suicide is establish a team on each station to start reviewing them. An investigation was sure to reveal Palau's involvement and result in more questions, something the Council had to anticipate. Not to mention, if they had Palau looking into genetic rebalancing on Aries, they probably had people on other stations studying other aspects of the issue, which might also come to light. Why would they order the suicide reviews? Sean will probably have all these answers—whether he's willing to share them or not is another question.

This end of the shuttle bay is quiet, a private docking station set aside for people who only plan to stay aboard Aries for a few hours before moving on to another station or the planet. Usually this means Council business, but it could also be an Ambassador's meeting or a Centralized Systems Review to root out nonconformities in the HMC, food gummy dispensary, Cantina, station Control Center, or one of the various labs. The CSRs are extremely intrusive, examining every aspect of operations, personnel, processes and technology to ensure there are no unauthorized deviations from Council established protocols. The Council prefers predictable standardization over rogue innovation when it comes to the lives of station Cits. Despite major findings being rare, people generally despise Centralized Systems Reviews, so much so they refer to them as station Colonoscopies.

I watch as Sean's shuttle enters the landing bay, guided into position by algorithm-controlled magnets, MagLev for short, and overseen by a Shuttle Specialist in the Aries station Control Center. I watch as the boat settles into position, outer doors seal, and the digital readout flashes green to indicate the room is pressurized and atmospheric conditions are normal. Sean starts down the ramp from the shuttle before it is fully extended and waves me over.

He's an odd duck, Sean. He stands over 6-foot 4-inches tall, towering above pretty much everyone he meets, and has a gregarious streak almost as imposing as his frame. I know he can be serious because I've seen him 'in character' as he calls it, briefing an Ambassador or station Chief. The Clerk-Sean in sharp contrast to the casual, jovial personality on display when among friends. He blames his mother, a hard-scrabble and boisterous red-headed Irish woman, every time his animated persona creeps into a business conversation, forcing him to step back and recover with a trait from his father's refined arsenal. Her deep, blue eyes against his father's jet black hair give Sean an almost anime appearance, like a cartoon descending the ramp.

Sean's old man was Indian, or rather half Indian, migrating with Sean's mother during station construction in 2065—two of the lucky ones allowed to remain on board after their contracts expired. Mr. Ramachandrani worked as an engineer, designing most of the structural aspects of the stations, while Mrs. Byrne—"She were naht goin to give up 'er Irish last name joost because she weren't boern a mahn," Sean quotes in his own accent made thicker by booze. Mrs. Byrne served as a structural tech, bringing her husband's designs to life. They were the first couple to officially have a child aboard the stations when Sean was born in 2070. This was before any of the stations were fully operational. Sean spent his formative years mostly interacting with adults—techs and engineers who had no choice but to embrace the austerity in partially constructed space havens.

Prior to Initial Population Integration kicking off in 2075, the stations were anything but self-sufficient. Scientists were still working on food gummies, although they'd perfected a tasteless vitamin supplement required for anyone choosing space-bound life. Supplies—food, materials, even water and oxygen prior to the reclamators coming online—were transported daily to the stations along with building supplies. Most people involved in the construction phase were single, and although many like Sean's parents were offered an opportunity to migrate, most returned to the various Cooperative Autonomous Zones rather than raise families with a view of the planet.

Sean's parents didn't just raise him, they were his teachers and de facto best friends. They had limited support from video links with exceedingly high latency, the bandwidth prioritized for communications between planners on the ground and engineers in space, which left the bulk of Sean's education to Amel Ramachandrani and Maggie Byrne. His upbringing, punctuated by lessons from Maggie's cold-forged coworkers and Amel's cerebral but adventurous colleagues, equipped Sean with a broad set of skills in everything from brawling to whiskey distilling, drone design to hacking. Maggie used to joke that had Sean not bid for the Station Rep role he'd likely be running the black market.

Sean's parents saw him graduate in 2091, proud their son had chosen a Role as a contributing member of society rather than one selling system backdoors and bootleg booze. We met when we were assigned as each other's Role Buddy, a relationship developed to ease the transition from childhood through Role training and into full Citizenry. We were inseparable, me enhancing Sean's academic grounding and Sean bringing me up to speed on the intricacies of the black market and the dynamics of negotiation. His father died a few years after we graduated, but Maggie lived long enough to see Sean recruited into the Council Clerk cadre, passing away last year. The loss hit Sean hard, but he'd inherited his mother's tenacity, as well as her ability to hold her liquor, allowing him to come through the other side of a dark tunnel—after we'd drunk an entire bottle of black market rum.

I place my right hand over my heart to greet Sean, but he's having none of it. "What the fuck, dude," he says, stepping off the ramp and wrapping me in a bear hug a chiropractor would be proud of.

"Hey Sean. You haven't changed a bit," I exhale forcibly. "What's it been, like, five months since we've seen each other in person?"

Sean releases his crushing embrace, taking a half step back while keeping his hands on my shoulders. He's always been more touchy-feely than me and I think he knows it makes me a little uncomfortable, but he doesn't care. His father wasn't much for physical contact, but Maggie was as likely to wrap her arms around the people she loved as she was to punch those she didn't. If Sean and his mom were together, it was a good bet she'd have her hand on his shoulder or he'd have one of his clubs draped over hers.

"At least five," Sean comments. "We're gonna need to catch up in-person more often."

"Well, you're obviously not staying long," I note, motioning toward the sign that reads: Non-Resident Bay. "And what's with the shuttle from Pisces? I thought you were stationed on Virgo?"

"I wouldn't be here at all if it weren't for you," Sean remarks. "I added a couple intermediate transit points between our call and this meeting in case someone is tracking me...or you. But not here. Let's move this into the Cell."

The Cell is a room in the Non-Resident Bay where those conducting temporary business on the stations can meet with locals or other temps. It's not any more secure than anyplace else on Aries—the Privacy First protocol forbids audio and visual surveillance of Cits without compelling cause. It only seats four around a small table just big enough for MiniComps or the new virtual X1s, making it a little cramped by design, the intent being to discourage long stays. Sean and I catch up on Aries and Council gossip as we walk the short distance across the bay. He opens the flood gates as soon as the door closes.

"Dude, " *Sean likes the word 'dude'.* "What the fuck are you doing messing with Neil Palau's GBRs? And how in the hell did you even come by that information? Do you have any idea how sensitive that subject is?"

I take the seat across the table, my back to the tinted glass windows designed to allow those inside the Cell to see out and block prying eyes from seeing in.

"I get the Council does not want people to know about everything they assign, but then they should not have set up a team to look into suicides. What did they think would happen when we started reviewing Palau's death? It was bound to come out. They're just lucky I was the one who interviewed Palau's coworkers. If it had been either of the other two, who knows where the information would have gone?" I'm still not positive Palau's work is linked to Lento's, but I don't mind floating the implication.

"Are you questioning the Council's decisions? Because..."

"I'm not questioning anything," I fire back. "I'm just saying...ugh, never mind. That's not the point. What are Genetic Balancing Reviews and why is the Council all of a sudden so interested in suicides?"

Sean rolls his eyes and shakes his head slightly from side to side as if to let me know he's disappointed. It's perhaps the longest I've ever seen him silent. After a minute, he takes a deep breath and says, "GBRs are not Genetic Balancing Reviews. They're Gender Balancing Reviews and the Council didn't ask Palau to undertake the analysis. It was a personal project."

Neil Palau's replacement was wrong. Neil wasn't analyzing genetic disparities over time, he was analyzing gender disparities over time. And he wasn't doing this as part of a Council request, he'd taken it up on his own. Did he know about the gender-based selections Lento's team was making? I wonder if he connected enough dots to figure out it was an inter-station problem and not confined to Aries? If the Council didn't request the study, then perhaps they killed him? I pose that last question to Sean.

"Don't be an idiot, Jason. The Council doesn't kill people. They would have discussed his options with him and allowed him to choose the best fit."

"I have no idea what that means, but it sounds ominously vague."

"Whatever, dude. Palau's study was unauthorized and quite frankly, unnecessary," Sean continues. "The Council knows about all the issues Palau uncovered."

"Including the DupleX report and the migration selection committees giving preference to women? How long has that been going on?"

"What the fuck!" Sean snaps. "Where in the actual fuck did you hear that? That information can get you..."

"Killed?" I interrupt.

"No! I told you, the Council doesn't kill people." Sean places his elbows on the table, followed by a lengthy sigh and a defeated drop of his head into his hands. I can't tell if he's frustrated or trying to figure out what to say next until he mutters something I don't understand.

"What?" I ask.

Sean looks up, worry, not frustration painting his freckled Indo-Irish face.

"I said, you can't tell anyone. If anyone finds, they're going to relocate you. There won't be anything I can do."

"How long has the Council known DupleX report? Why are we

investigating suicides?"

"Three years." Sean's answer is immediate and resolute. "The Council has known for at least three years, maybe longer. They established the female selection protocols right after determining the disparity was affecting long term station viability. The problem is serious. If we don't come up with a solution soon, the impact may be irreversible. Even with the change to selecting females for 75 percent of the migration vacancies, we're still doomed. If we don't find a solution, a genetic solution that will correct the ratio of female to male births, within a generation over 85 percent of the station population will be male. Eventually, the human race will cease to exist in space. We will be no better off than those on the planet."

"So in roughly a hundred years Aries is will be an exclusive, men's-only club."

Sean shakes his head. "Not just Aries. Every station is suffering the same fate. The best scientists we have are working the issue. Every migration team is affording preference to females during selection, but even genetic screening for the likelihood of female offspring isn't a guarantee. By the time migrating women have children, the damage is done—their babies are male. The only upside is they're at least confident they'll find a solution before it's too late."

"And these suicide studies? Why are we reviewing suicides?"

Sean sits up for the first time, allowing his hands to fall to his lap. "Several people on the Council thought Palau's death was suspicious—not the circumstances, but the timing. The Council—the entire Council—was aware of his personal project. He'd discovered the secret they've been trying to contain. The DupleX problem was moving the human race closer to extinction. He hadn't gone public, but someone close to his work, someone he trusted, was feeding information back to the Council and reported Palau's intent to leak it to the public."

"Jeez," I say. I'm stunned.

"It's not the end of the world," Sean adds. "The Council voted to bring him into the loop and to be part of the team working on the problem. Palau's reputation for patriotism was as solid as his credentials, so *most* of the Council were convinced he could be brought on board. But then he suddenly goes and commits suicide. There were rumors a Council member went rogue, but it couldn't be proven without an investigation. But an investigation into a single suicide would have looked suspicious. There's never been a murder on the stations."

"That we know of," I note. "So the Council decides to hide the investigation into Palau's death among the chaff of a suicide review. If anyone asks, we're not looking into a single suspicious suicide, we're looking into a possibly worrisome trend."

"Exactly," says Sean. "But it's all for naught. It appears the suicides, including Palau's, were just that, suicides."

"How do you know that? We haven't finished our investigation."

Sean pauses for a moment, I can tell he's considering his answer. Reluctantly, he admits it.

"You've been reading my logs!"

"Not just yours, everyones—on every team." He says it casually, as if I should have expected he or someone else would be reviewing our personal logs.

"What the...? How did you get access? What the heck happened to Privacy First?" It occurred to me there might be other entries in my personal logs, information about Cecelia and Kami I'd rather he not know. "My entire personal history has been fodder for some Council voyeurism? God dammit, Sean!"

"The Council..."

"Don't talk to me about the Council. We're friends. You should have told me you were spying on me. Looking through my life. Creeping in the ether to vacuum up my thoughts. We've known each other our entire adult lives."

"You know I couldn't tell you," Sean fires back, his indignant, self-righteous attitude incinerating a cloud of shame before it can form. "And I didn't read your fucking secrets, just the stuff about the suicide study. I don't give a good god damn who you're fucking or where you're getting your bootleg booze. This isn't a game. We needed to know if there was any possibility Palau was killed. If someone killed him it would mean one or more Council members had taken things into their own hands. We'd have to root that out, quash it. Society functions because the Council is united for the greater good. This isn't like the politics of the planet where elected officials serve their own self-interests. The Council exists to serve society, period. A divided Council would be disastrous for the stations and humanity."

Sean's always believed in the Council's service to Cits and the greater good. Even if he found out a Council member went rogue, he'd simply rationalize it as a single bad apple in an orchard of altruism. I recognize he has a big picture view. He's read all the logs, not just my ideas. If there were something to be found, he would have connected the dots. I'm not sure I wouldn't have done the same thing if I were in his place, but I'm still pissed and there's no way I'm giving him a full pardon for treating me like just another Cit.

"Eff you. You're totally not forgiven."

"I'm an asshole, I know," Sean quips. "But on the upside, it doesn't appear any of the suicides were anything more than just that—suicides."

"So you've read all the logs from everyone on every station?" I ask.

"Yep, finished getting caught up just before we docked. Trust me, there is nothing in anyone's notes to indicate these suicides are more than suicides, including Palau. That's good news. An increase in suicides Cit's will accept, but murder, not so much."

"What is wrong with us that we think more suicides is good news?"

Sean smiles, one of his trademark, toothy, Irish grins. "Well, compared to the alternative."

My mind drifts to Kami and her involvement in all of this. I really wish Lento hadn't told her.

"What if someone was willing to trade the information to save someone else? Say someone who *is* critical wants to protect someone who isn't. Could they leverage what they know to keep someone else out of trouble?"

Sean's gaze turns intense as he reaches a long, left arm across the table and places a hand on my shoulder.

"Don't go there, Jason," he says, sounding worried. "This path will not lead where you hope. The Palau incident resulted in a pretty heated debate among Council members. Several people wanted to immediately deport him—a first for the Council and I'm not talking about sending him to the CAZ. People wanted to drop him in the Open Lands for putting the stations at risk. They don't take kindly to extortion and they're even less forgiving when they feel the future of the stations are in jeopardy. In the end, precedent, cooler heads and Palau's ability to contribute to a solution saved him. You are not Palau. Best case, you'll be locked in a room on Gemini or some other station until a solution is found. Worst—the more radical elements of the Council sway enough people and you're deported. It would set new precedent on the stations, a deportation for a minor offense—knowing more than you should—but it's not out of the realm of possibility, dude."

I understand the implication, or perhaps it's a threat. I'm not a scientist, doctor, or analyst. Nothing in my skillset is going to help find a cure for our female birth deficit. Heck, I'm not sure I even understand why it's happening. If the Council finds out I'm all of a sudden in the loop, there won't be much Sean can do to influence the debate about what to do with me.

"Tell me you understand the issue," Sean adds.

"I understand," I reply, offering my right hand in an old school gesture. "I'll never speak of it again. Now we just have to save humanity."

Sean shakes my hand like we've seen in so many old movies.

"Not we, dude," Sean replies. "Just me."

Sean walks away and I consider shooting Kami a message. The rest of my evening is a shit show with a stop back at the office, log reviews, and a weekly, virtual gaming session with mates on other stations. I forgo the message, figuring she'll let me know if she wants to get together. Tonight I need to decompress with friends and Activision's recent Call of Duty: Open Lands release.

CHAPTER THIRTY-NINE

Kami Lee

I wake to find Kornel standing at the end of my bed beneath my name, Kami Lee, OSU, his brow tense, cutting fresh wrinkles into an aged portrait as his finger scrolls through a digital readout floating in the air between us. I can't tell what it says because there's a piercing sound just behind and slightly above my eyes like a hammer pounding nails into frozen ground, making everything blurry and forcing me to close them briefly while I catch my breath. I can see Earth from a nearby window, the tan sphere speckled with black and patches of blue, looking nothing like the early twentieth century photos I'd seen during Eco-History classes. The Aries omnipresent low hum lingers, although louder and less soothing than usual.

My left arm aches just below the elbow, an uncomfortable pressure building for several seconds before subsiding, followed by pinching in the forearm. I reach for the sting, clumsily jabbing a finger over the area to scratch whatever is biting me. It's a cuff, something designed to deliver medications and monitor my health. Then I realize where I am...the Med Bay. How the heck did I get here?

Lento notices me moving and closes the virtual screen.

"Hey kiddo. Nice to see you awake," he says, making his way from the foot of the bed around to my right. "Do you remember what happened?"

The last thing I remember is walking down the corridor feeling like awful. There was a momentary hot flash, then blinding lights overhead imploding into a single, shining star amid increasingly inky blackness. I think I fell or tripped. The memories before and after are there, blanketed in a dense fog, indistinct shadows dancing across a screen.

"I'm not sure. Everything is a bit, um, hazy," I mutter incomprehensibly. My throat is dry and my mouth doesn't seem to want to work properly. "Hazy," I repeat.

"That's to be expected," Kornel replies. "The memories will return as soon as the drugs in your system are fully neutralized."

Drugs? What drugs? I ask. It takes a minute watching Lento stand without reacting for me to realize no words came out of my mouth. "Speech," I say with some effort.

"Yes, that too will clear up shortly. You've been under for almost 24 hours while the neutralizing agent did its work. You should be back to normal in another hour or so, but until then don't try to get out of bed because your legs may not work the way you expect. You've missed most of today in the Med Bay. It's a small price to pay for letting your body heal itself—with the help of some decent pharmacology, of course."

"What day?" This time my voice performs as expected, albeit with some effort and sounding like I've got a cotton ball stuffed down my throat.

"Sunday. It's Sunday. The poison was a paralytic, Procurium, designed to attack the central nervous system, cutting the link between the brain and pretty much everything else—extremities, speech, heart, lungs—eventually resulting in suffocation and cardiac arrest. It's basically a synthetic combination of three drugs commonly used during intubation. We use it conservatively to slow the body's processes during long surgeries—never in the quantity you took."

"Who?"

"Well, I've been here since I got the call—over 24 hours—so at this point I know as much as you do. Thankfully, there are no lasting effects. You'll remember exactly *who*, if not *how* soon enough."

I'm starting to remember and not thrilled about what's coming back. I recall the suicides not being quite as clear cut as I initially thought, and Lento possibly being involved. But there is no way he'd want me dead. Part of the conspiracy, maybe, but not a killer in his own right. I'm not sure what to share while there are still gaps in my memory.

"Your boss and Parker stopped by. They said they'll be back today when you're awake. Any idea who'd want to kill you?"

Kill me? Nobody would want to kill me. Unless...I raise my left arm to review the notes on my ComLink, but it's missing. "Where?" I mutter.

Lento motions toward a small shelf on the other side of the bed.

"There."

As I reach for it, a sharp pain shoots into my arm followed by another into my head, as if someone jabbed a needle into my temple. It lingers, causing me to fall back onto the pillow and close my eyes for a moment.

Lento reaches over and places his right hand on my forehead, gently massaging my temple and scalp. It is surprisingly effective, like kneading out a muscle cramp, his warm hand and nimble fingers pushing an unseen anesthetic into my aching skull.

"This too will pass shortly," he whispers. I let him continue, feeling the pain fade into memory until I can open my eyes without it crushing me.

"Can you hand me my ComLink?" I ask, hoarsely. "And some water?"

Lento walks around the bed, collecting the ComLink and a glass of water from the wall dispenser on the way. He places the ComLink on my wrist below the Med Cuff...I can feel it power up when it recognizes my DNA. I take a couple small swallows of water, leaving my left arm flat on the bed while the ComLink finishes booting. I'm not thirsty, but my throat is as dry as the Open Lands. "Thank you," I say, handing back the cup. "How did I get here?"

"Parker, actually," Lento says, sounding a little surprised. I don't think he cares for Parker much, putting him in the majority. "He contacted the Med Techs and gave them your location. For a grumpy, self-righteous, bigot he has his moments."

"How did Parker know to send the Med Techs?" My voice still sounds like I swallowed a sponge, but at least the words are coherent.

"Not sure. He wasn't sharing a lot of details when he was here earlier—totally out of character for Parker," Lento quips.

I tap a couple keys on my ComLink to bring up the logs. The last thing sent was an unfinished message to Parker about Gothard Hong. Right. I remember standing in the corridor after a meeting...an interview. Ocasio, Doctor Ocasio, she was the last person I saw before reality collapsed around me. It was an interview for Jason, but she was also a referral from Lento.

Another swipe brings me to the investigative log. I scan it, hoping to jog my memory, but it doesn't make sense. There are notes, but they aren't mine—at least I don't recall recording them. There is something off about the language, it's not me. It's no more my voice than the one I'm using now. My records are clean and professional, but littered with theories and detail. These are vague, fact-centric, and devoid of insight. The last few paragraphs read like they were written by the Aries AI.

The interview of Dr. Ocasio yielded no additional information to indicate the suicides under review and specifically those of Neil Palau or Derek Ocasio were anomalous. Dr. Ocasio treated Mr. Palau for stress related to work which she stated manifested itself as nightmares. His accusations of malpractice related to his psychological pathology were unfounded and there is no evidence to suggest otherwise. Dr. Ocasio noted that Palau's stressful work environment led him to bouts of depression. Although she accepted responsibility for insufficiently recognizing the extent of Palau's mental state, she recognized his accusations had put her in a position where she was unable to provide further help.

Dr. Ocasio stated that her son, who otherwise presented as a normal young adult with station-adaptation issues, could suffer from occasional, non-violent mood swings resulting in short periods of self-isolation; however, she did not identify the mood swings with potential suicidal tendencies at the time. She was not treating Derek and there is not a record of him seeking treatment from other sources save referrals to support groups made after convictions. Dr. Ocasio stated her son did not speak to her about whether he was considering suicide, nor did he indicate an inability to cope; however, she said she identified post-act the signs of depression and believed had she spent more time with Derek she would have known to refer him for counseling.

Signs of depression and potential suicidal tendencies appear to have been apparent but unrecognized in both the Palau and Ocasio suicides, which is consistent with previous studies relative to the outward display of anxiety among suicidal males.

That is crap. There is nothing about those three paragraphs that even remotely sounds like something I'd write. They are overly clinical and lack observations about Ocasio's mannerisms, body language, and tone. We aren't trained to simply observe and record—we're supposed to think and consider, hypothesize and test, question results. There are no references to alternatives in those notes. Someone altered my logs—someone who didn't think I'd be around to dispute them.

Consistent with previous studies. That phrase stabs at something behind my left eye, forcing me to pinch it closed to stave off the returning flash of pain. Parker sent me a copy of a previous study—something to do with male-female suicide rates. I open one eye enough to tap into my ComLink. Here it is, from Parker: "Males and females committed suicide at the same rate, however, men displayed signs of depression and despondence in greater numbers than women, with men showing more overt signals and indicators." Finally, a memory triggered. There was a mitigation letter missing from Derek's file and a lack of signs of depression in the male suicides; the gender birth gap; Lento's female selection preferences; Plumin's connection to the cases and his failure to mention Palau's project. It comes flooding back, a river of memories and doubt. That's what I was recording when I went down—the logs that are now missing.

"Something wrong?" Kornel asks, noticing the look on my face.

I want to tell him…tell him I remember what I was doing before I dropped, but he's wrapped up in this somehow. Perhaps he's just influencing selections at the direction of the Council, but I can't take the chance. If he's not involved in the suicides, he may share whatever I tell him with the Council and I'm not sure I want the one body with sufficient access to alter logs to know of my suspicions. Whether the Council is involved or not, telling Kornel anything might make him a target. Luckily, I'm saved from having to answer when Parker barrels through the virtual privacy curtain.

"Hey kid! How's it hangin'?" Parker shouts as the frosted heads of Med Techs and patients attached to ghostly bodies turn from behind the virtual curtain toward his voice. "Wow, do you look like shit!"

Lento looks at Parker like the disapproving father who's just seen his daughter with the station bad boy. As usual, Parker doesn't notice or just doesn't care. "You know you're famous, right? Well, not yet, but you will be if they let this shit leak."

It takes me a second to pick up. Of course I'm famous. I'm the first victim of an attempted murder on a station since, well, ever. It's not quite the recognition I'd hoped for.

"That's great," I mumble. "Now we just need someone to arrest for it. Then they can be famous for being the first to try to kill me." My speech has improved and my throat is beginning to clear.

"Oh, that's right. You've been nappin' your ass off for the last day or so." Parker looks toward Lento. "So, are we going to pull that Cuff crap off or shall we keep pumping her full of whatever counteracting drug you people decided she needed at the time but obviously doesn't need now?"

Lento pauses for a moment, probably wondering just how hard he should push back. Pulling up the virtual chart again and scanning through the readings, he finally relents.

"It appears the offending agent is out of your system. But that doesn't mean you're fully recovered." Lento pauses as he makes his way over to the left side of the bed. He peers up at Parker as he removes the Med Cuff, adding, "You need to take it easy, Kami. Limit your interactions *and* visitors."

"We took some chick into custody last night," Parker says, again ignoring Lento's not so subtle suggestion.

"Who?"

"Why don't we wait until there are fewer ears in the vicinity before we discuss further. I'm not sure the Council wants this out just yet." Parker smiles knowingly and I look at Lento.

"I get it. I'm leaving," Lento acknowledges. "But I'm serious about taking it easy. Your body has been through a trauma. You almost died. You need time to heal."

"When can I get out of here?" I ask as Lento heads through the virtual screen.

"I'll sign you out now, even though I know you won't listen to a…" His words trail off down the hall.

"What's this about an arrest?" I ask, turning to Parker who has taken a position at my bedside.

"I really shouldn't say until Carl arrives," Parker says, grinning.

"Don't be a jerk, Parker," I say, hoping he takes it as a request rather than a challenge. "Who did they arrest?"

"Indra Ocasio," Carl's voice booms, filling the room enough that I think I feel the bed vibrate.

Carl Lavoie is the head of the Orbital Sheriff's Unit and is commonly known as the toughest SOB on Aries—he is *the* Sheriff. He worked as a Law Keeper in his late teens in the Open Lands—'Law Keeper' was what they called those individuals badass enough to take on the growing criminal syndicates. By age 20 he'd already put down more violent criminals than most people knew existed. He transitioned to the US-Canada CAZ the year before the wall was finished in 2068, and was immediately recruited into the Zone Enforcement Bureau, eventually becoming Deputy Bureau Chief. He was offered the opportunity to set up the Orbital Sheriff station network and run the Aries OSU in 2079. He's important enough to have his own chapter in the Primary History Studies curriculum.

Carl is in his early sixties, but he looks a dozen years older. He says every year in the Open Lands was like three on Aries, and every year in the CAZ was like two and it shows. His full head of gray hair matches his thick mustache, which has grown to the point where it hides his mouth entirely. At a colossal 6-foot, 3-inches, his lean, sinewy frame still obvious through his tan jumpsuit towers above most of us. He takes my hand as he stands beside the bed, his long, boney fingers so dwarfing my own they look like the hands of a child.

"How are ya, kid?" He says, but unlike with Parker, I don't wince inside when Carl calls me kid.

"Good, sir. Who poisoned me?"

"Y'all not interested in small talk?" Carl speaks like a character from an old western, slow with a gravelly drawl as if someone recently sanded the inside of his throat. "Well, me, neither. Turns out it was your therapist, Doctor Indra Ocasio. Although she claims not to remember any of it."

Ocasio? The light flips on almost instantly. "The tea. She insisted I drink it. She's not my therapist and I hate tea."

Carl chuckles. "Best to stick with your instincts in the future. This is the reason we have an OSU, by the way. The Council initially considered no law enforcement presence on the stations, but being more practical than delusional and knowing there would always be some type of crime even if it's mostly petty, they opted for at least a small LE presence. Crime is part of being human."

"But why? Why would she poison me?"

"We're not sure and she's not talking. The first time we questioned her, shortly after you were picked up, she didn't mention anything other than she'd met with you a few minutes earlier. Her office was the last place you reported to The Center, so it was a natural first stop. Once the Med Bay identified the toxin and method of delivery, and determined how fast it acted on the nervous system, she was left as the only suspect. We got a writ for her detainment and searched her place where we found the poison in her inventory and the cup still in her office. A second analysis of the cup showed traces of the same substance, so we detained her pending your, um, *outcome*—it was touch and go there for a while. We hooked her up to a Neuro-Analyzer and questioned her again after we finished the search and she again swore she wasn't involved. The Neuro confirmed she was telling the truth, but the physical evidence is overwhelming. We got a writ for her logs and we're analyzing data from her ComLink now."

"So she's denying it?"

"Not exactly," Parker pipes in. "The chick just plain doesn't remember any of it. She claims you arrived, exchanged some information about her son, uh…" Parker taps on his ComLink.

"Derek Ocasio," I say.

"Yeah, Derek Ocasio and a Neil Palau," Parker says, "Then you split and that was it. She truly doesn't remember poisoning you."

I'm not sure how I arrived at the precipice of infamy with so little solid information—the first attempted murder in station history, lying in a Med Bay with the remnants of a drug floating about my system, a spotty memory of recent events, and a horrible feeling there is something about this I'm missing.

"Is this part of that Council investigation y'all workin'? The suicide thing?" Carl asks with a note of disapproval.

Of course it is! I want to shout, but decide to down play it in case Parker or Carl end up being involved. It's unlikely, but given recent events, I'm not taking any chances.

"Possibly. I was following up on an earlier interview by one of the others on the team, Jason Plumin—just confirming some information he received yesterday." It's almost a lie, but not quite. "Who found me?"

"Well, I fucking did, kid," Parker proudly announces. "Sort of, anyway. It was your text, the one about Gothard Hong. It didn't look complete, not quite your normal genius banter. I checked your location and vitals—you were in shit shape and turning worse, so I expedited the Med Techs. If they'd taken another minute to get there, you'd be dead, dead, dead."

Certain station leadership, the Council, and law enforcement can call up live-time location and health-related information on station Cits. Normally it takes a warrant, but if you're in the LE community and someone with access believes there might be an issue, they can pull the data without waiting for the Council's okay. It's highly intrusive and violates every aspect of Privacy First, but in this case the access and Parker's willingness to push the envelope on its employment served me well. Funny, I thought the Council's and the OSU's ability to monitor me at will was a downside of the job—Parker turned it into a life-saving measure.

"Parker, shut up," Carl admonishes. "The point is, Parker basically saved your life and you're insane if you think he's going to let you forget it."

"Thanks, Parker. I owe you one."

"Well, you owe me like three," Parker replies. "I ran that name, Gothard Hong. He's one of your suicides."

"Yes, I know."

"Well, you won't have much luck talking to anyone about him. He was pretty much a loner, no family aboard, few friends…"

"Any record of infractions?" I apologize for cutting in.

"None," Parker notes while pushing the file to a virtual Viz at the end of the bed. He starts scrolling through the list of known and possible associates. Most of them are dated and there are even fewer recent contacts. There's nothing there except a lonely life writing books nobody actually reads.

"Wait," I interrupt, noticing a name. "Scroll back."

Parker scrolls back to a list of acquaintances, people Gothard Hong went to school with. There it is, top of the list: Jason Plumin. "He knew Plumin."

"Who's Jason Plumin?" Parker asks.

Carl knows Jason and doesn't much care for him. I'm beginning to side with Carl. Our obvious physical compatibility notwithstanding, Jason is at the center of this thing. "Jason's part of the suicide team," I reply to Parker.

"Well, he's about the only person who still spoke with Hong, although I wouldn't say they were besties. The contacts are sparse and short, maybe once a month up until Hong committed suicide. I can't see how them knowing each other is relevant, unless there's something I'm not seeing?"

The relevance is Jason knew Gothard Hong. The relevance is he didn't mention his relationship with Hong when we reviewed the list. He knows most of the people on our list and he had access to Derek Ocasio's records. He would need help to delete Dr. Ocasio's letter and alter my logs, which means he is not in it alone.

I should tell Carl about Lento and Plumin, but I'm not positive I fully understand what's going on, yet. Right now, I just have a bunch of connections to a Station Rep, a doctor, a robot-voice feeding me information, and Council-sanctioned bias in migration selections, as well as too many questions. I still doubt Kornel is involved with the killings, if they are killings, which I'm still not sure of. But his role on the migration selection committee puts him in the middle of whatever this is. If it gets out he's involved in a conspiracy it will ruin him—the man who basically raised me without hesitation.

And then there is the issue of Jason being the guy I'm sleeping with. I'm sure explaining to Carl I might have to arrest my sexual partner for his involvement in these suicides and—oh, yeah—possibly having me poisoned, will go over spectacularly. Jason appears to be mired in whatever is going on—the suicides, a Council cover up, omitting relevant information—and those are just the things I know about. I suppose about the only person left to talk to is Brandi, but she's not exactly a fan. She doesn't appear to have any connection to Doctor Ocasio directly or indirectly—aside from writing a letter for Derek as a courtesy—and there's no way she'd be able to modify digital logs or delete case records. She just migrated a few years ago, so she's not invested in Aries like Parker or potentially in the leadership loop like Carl. I hate to say it, but despite robot voice's warning, Brandi might be the only person I can trust.

CHAPTER FORTY

Brandi Mikkelson

I hate coming to the Med Bay, even when I'm here to see someone else. It's full of people whose immune systems have been protected from the rigors of planet-borne pathogens to the point they cannot handle feeling even the slightest bit out of sorts. The first sign of an ache or sniffle sends them running for medical attention. I get it. Living in close quarters necessitates a certain hyper vigilance, but for fuck's sake, suck it up already and wear a mask like people in the CAZ. All this Med Bay molly-coddling every time there's a hint of discomfort is creating a species of human unfit for life.

"Hi Kami. How are you feeling?" I ask, noticing she looks more pale than usual, even under the ultraviolet, vitamin-D fortified Med Bay lights.

"Brandi. Nice to see you. I'm a lot better. One more test and I'm outta here."

Kami's voice has a slightly nasally sound, like she's getting over a cold. She's sitting up in bed, elevated about 45 degrees from horizontal with two pillows propped up behind her. There's a virtual screen floating at eye level between her and the digital walls that make up her room. I wait for a moment as she swipes down to scroll through the last of the data. I can't see what she's reading—she has the back side pixelated for privacy.

"Good timing. Parker and Lavoie Just left," Kami adds as the screen disappears.

The Med Bay isn't crowded, just a few Med Techs, three patients including Kami who both look perfectly fine to me, and a bored looking doctor reviewing diagnostic computer code at a table toward the center of the bay. Doctors are still a nice resource, but they aren't nearly as vital as they once were. Computer algorithms do most of the heavy lifting, diagnosing patient woes and controlling robots during surgical procedures. Doctors will still monitor the process, review records, scrutinize treatments, and confirm results, but this is more for patients who are uncomfortable with a computer treating them—something fewer and fewer people have a problem with. Since the Council has only shared a limited bit of tech with the surface, migrants who are not used to programmable healthcare are the most common to request a sentient physician. Gens born into station life rarely if ever consult a living, breathing clinician. Older doctors who migrated from the planet, like Lento, are stuck on practicing medicine; however, the new cadre of medicos enhances the code behind diagnostic and surgical applications to improve accuracy and efficiency. At this point they are more programmers than physicians.

"Jason was supposed to meet me here, but I guess he's running late." Kami's face twitches, not enough that most people would notice, but it's there. "Something wrong?"

"There is something I'd like to talk about before Jason gets here."

Talk? Kami and I aren't besties, not even close. In fact, I'd describe our interactions over the last few days as cool bordering on confrontational. We haven't been overtly rude to each other, but I know my talent for pissing people off far exceeds any ability I have to make friends. I might not be the last person I thought she'd be sharing intimate details of her love life with, but I'm sure I'm toward the bottom of the list and I'm fine with the ranking. Nothing interests me less than talking about her and Jason hooking up.

"If this is about you and Jason, I already know and it's fine. I don't care and your secret is safe with me for as long as you care to keep it."

Kami looks unexpectedly surprised at the revelation. Her face turns from hospital pale to a shade of pink even I hadn't expected and her mouth widens as if a heavy weight is dangling from her chin. Several seconds pass before she pipes in with questions.

"Who? What? How did you know?" she stutters.

"It's not a big deal. Unless you've pissed off the gossip mongers, nobody actually cares. It's perhaps a little out of the ordinary given the age difference and our working together and may even be out of character given your reputation, but I doubt it will even register if anyone else finds out. Worst case, your boss might school you on the dangers of engaging in a sexual relationship with a coworker—you know, potential bias, workplace conflict, in-house sexual tensions, inappropriate sexual encounters while on duty, stuff like that." I mention the last one just to see if I can get a rise out of her. It works.

"On duty? What the heck is that supposed to mean?" Kami defensively fires back.

I allow a sarcastic smile to spread across my lips. "Well, who knows what's going to happen in the throes of passion?"

The color in Kami's face normalizes as she realizes I'm pulling her chain. She's bright for what passes as a sheltered child on the stations. She didn't grow up in the harsh, sometimes brutal Zones, where the early development of a thick skin and perfecting a comeback jibe were part and parcel to survival. Her recovery is still quicker than most Gens, including our intern who I once left silent, mouth gaping, grasping for a response to an assessment of her boyfriend. It took 24 hours for her to formulate a reply, explaining she didn't believe her boyfriend needed that kind of reassurance.

"How did you find out?" Kami asks.

"Jason."

"He told you?" Kami seems genuinely surprised.

"Well, he didn't phone me the morning after if that's what you're worried about. I cornered him during the last meeting and verbally beat it out of him." It's a lie, but a small one. I just asked and Jason offered up the info. But there's no need to make Kami feel she's made a huge mistake, as much as I'd like to get another dig in right now. "Besides, he was not forthcoming with details," I add. "He wanted to keep this quiet until after we turn in the report."

Kami doesn't say anything for a long minute. I wonder if she's considering the longevity of her relationship, or the trust that was betrayed. She's smart enough to figure shit out, but inexperienced. I'm in mid-thought when she interrupts.

"I think Jason has something to do with the suicides."

Holy crap! It's the first thought that pops into my head. Perhaps I was wrong and she isn't inexperienced after all. She can't be considering a bright future if she thinks Jason is killing people, which, by the way, um, *where the fuck did that come from?* It's about now I feel I should put that last thought into words. "Where the fuck is that coming from?"

Kami sits up, exhaling slowly and audibly as if banishing unseen tension to a far away place where it can't interfere with her explanation. Her story is peppered with brief starts and stops as she lays out facts and observations in support of her theory that Jason is somehow involved in the suicides—Jason's connection to many of the deaths, including Gothard Hong, which he failed to mention; his knowing what time she was meeting with Ocasio; his access to Derek Ocasio's records; Jason's knowledge of the now deleted letter from Doctor Ocasio about her son being on the autism spectrum, a mitigating circumstance that would have weighed heavy in any sentencing decisions; and his awareness of Palau's genetics project and failure to mention it. She tells me about finding her logs altered when she woke, the original notes replaced with less salacious—*my word, not hers*—details. When she finishes, she leans back into the pillows as if the help she needed carrying some heavy load has finally arrived.

There's a lingering silence and I get the feeling she's considering sharing something more. I wonder if I should tell her about Jason's meeting with someone close to the Council. It seems prudent and relevant given her suspicions. In order for her hypothesis to pan out, Jason needs someone who can alter records, someone on or connected to the Council, which he has. In fact, he was supposed to be meeting with his contact yesterday.

"The thing is, he just doesn't seem the type," Kami says, her eyes betraying the exhaustion of the last 24 hours. "There must be something I'm missing, right?"

"Why?" I ask. "Why would he kill people and cover up evidence?"

"Why," Kami repeats, her head nodding in agreement as if she knows the answer. I get the feeling she has a theory or perhaps more than a theory, but she's holding back. I decide not to press the question.

"I suppose now is as good a time as any to tell you about Jason's contact on the Council," I say, deciding it's not fair to keep it to myself any longer.

"He has a contact?" Kami asks with a balanced mix of surprise and reconciliation.

I take a seat beside her on the bed, resting my knee on the mattress.

"I heard from a very reliable source that he was meeting with someone he knows on the Council yesterday. I have no idea what they were discussing, but it's a good bet it has something to do with our little project." I know good and well his contact is a Council Clerk, not a Council Member, but since a C-Clerk might also be able to alter logs, it's not strictly relevant.

"That explains how he could delete Ocasio's letter and alter my logs." Kami's eyes widen and I can see her connecting this information with the rest of what she knows. "It's still circumstantial, but a lot less so than before. Do you know if they actually met?"

"I don't know for sure, but I'd say it's highly likely based on the information I received."

Kami thinks about it for a moment, running her hand through her long, black hair and pulling the strands so they splay atop the pillows. The contrast bursts from the bright, white cases, momentarily distracting me. It takes a second to refocus. When I do, I explain that I should have more information later today or Monday at the latest. I leave Marta's name out of it, knowing she'll contact me as soon as she hears something. She'll want to show just how well-connected she is to the Council and station business.

Of course, I don't actually believe any of Kami's theories. Jason has as much chance of being involved in making murders look like suicides as I have of becoming a Council member. I haven't known him long—only about three years—but he's not the type to be involved in killing people. On the other hand, he is keeping some things secret, which while I'm sure has nothing to do with suicides, could be an attempt to ingratiate himself to the Council in the hopes of getting some kind of a Clerk appointment, or perhaps even Ambassador posting. Therefore, I don't see any harm in playing along with Kami's delusional theory. Maybe it will force him to reconsider cutting me out.

"You know," I start, pausing for affect. "It sounds like you might be right. He obviously knows more than he's sharing and these secret meetings with Council POCs..." *shit, Marta-speak creeping in again,* "with Council points of contact, are damn curious. Seems like he's neck deep in whatever is going on. It might even be why the council assigned him to this investigation. What better way to keep an eye on our progress than from the inside? He could report back or even steer our results with bullshit information and omissions."

"Yeah, it's the only explanation," Kami acknowledges, nodding in agreement. "All the evidence points to him. I'm not sure how deep he's in, but he's definitely in. How could I have been so stupid?"

"Don't beat yourself up. It's not stupidity." I rest my hand on her thigh. The white synthetic blanket between us does little to hide the heat coming off her skin and the lean muscle of her quadriceps. "It's human nature. We can't help who we're attracted to. There was no way to know he was involved in any of this."

Kami sits up again, pulling her hair to one side over her right shoulder and letting it drape gently across her breast. I can just barely see it's outline beneath her silky, black gloss. When she instinctively places her hand on mine, it doesn't feel sexual. She's looking past me, not at me—not reciprocating as I'd hoped, just commiserating from afar.

"How can we find out who he met with and what they discussed?" she finally asks.

"I'm not sure," I reply, leaving my hand where it is and wondering if she's a late bloomer or just too involved in the moment to realize what it means. "My contact might have some of that information, but we won't know for several hours." I'm confident Marta will have the answers, but there's no need to prematurely seed Kami's expectations. "One question that still remains is how did he poison you? You said Dr. Ocasio never met him, so he couldn't have coerced her."

As I ask the question a message comes through on Kami's ComLink.

"It's Parker," she says, reading from the small, physical screen rather than putting up the full-size virtual display. "He says there are no indications of drugs in Ocasio's system and that she still denies she poisoned me—all consistent with her Neuro results. They are going to resume questioning as soon as they finish the forensics on her cloud files and analysis of her Pharma acquisition logs. He wants me to stop by tomorrow if I'm released this afternoon."

"Well, we need to get you out of here, then."

"What do we do about Jason?" Kami asks.

"Nothing. At least not until we have enough information to detain him. We'll need to act like everything is normal, continue with our investigation and only keep him in the loop on the most mundane facts. I'll touch base with my contact to see if there is any more information about who he met with on the Council and you check on the progress of the Ocasio interrogation. We'll touch base tomorrow." I sound convincing, even though I don't actually believe Jason has anything to do with killing people. He's an opportunist, not a murderer or a conspirator.

"Ready for that last test?" the Med Tech asks, poking his head in through the digital curtain. "We'll need to move you into another area."

"Jesus, what the hell happened?" Jason walks in through the virtual screen as the Tech is transferring Kami to a Magna Chair. "I came over as soon as I heard."

The look of concern on Kami's face is fleeting, morphing back to trusting coworker and lover before anyone but me notices. "Just a little accident," she says, adding a disarming smile.

"A little accident? I heard you passed out."

"We need to get to this last test if you want to get out of here," the Tech announces.

"You heard the boss," says Kami. "Can I catch up with you later?"

"Of course," Jason replies with what I register as a confused lilt.

The entire thing plays out like a scene from a low budget love story. Jason waits until Kami is through the virtual curtain and can't hear our voices to start in with the questions.

"What happened?"

"Apparently she was poisoned by the doctor you sent her to see," I say with a little too much glee in my voice.

"Poisoned? By Ocasio? How? Why?"

His single-word confusion strikes me as sincere—were I a better person, I'd feel sorry for him. Instead, I find myself enjoying the exchange a tad too much. But as I don't believe he's guilty of anything more than fucking the wrong girl, I'll let him in on our little secret.

"I'm not sure we have those answers, yet. But you should know Kami believes you're in on it."

As expected, Jason looks stunned. I suppose I should feel bad for betraying Kami's trust. But what did she expect? I've known Jason for almost three years and I've known her for all of about five days. Outside of her imagination, Jason is nothing more than a do-gooder trying to get ahead. I have no doubt we'll find out he met with some C-Clerk to confirm information he discovered during one of the interviews, something he'll share eventually, framing it as if without said key piece of information the entire suicide study would be useless. Thus securing for himself some notoriety leading to an offer to become part of the Council's circle of trust. As I said, he's an opportunist, not a killer.

"Why on Aries would she think I'm involved?" Upon seeing the subtle grin I'm sporting, Jason adds, "And why do I think you had something to do with it?"

"Well," I start. "Let's just say I didn't dissuade her." I share the short version with Jason, giving him most of the highlights: he's connected to many of the deaths—as am I, by the way—and he knew Gothard Hong and didn't share with us; he arranged for Kami to meet with Ocasio in his place; and apparently he deleted a letter from Derek Ocasio's mother. I round out the story with a not so subtle accusation that he's been meeting with people close to the Council behind our backs, people who might have the necessary access to alter logs.

Jason stands there for a moment, shocked into silence for the first time since I've known him. When he finally recovers, he replies to what I presume he sees as the most egregious claim, that he is untrustworthy because he's meeting with people without telling us.

"I didn't meet with anyone from the Council behind anyone's back," he argues. "I met with an old friend to confirm some information about Palau. I didn't share it because I didn't want to muddy the waters with unfounded accusations. It had nothing to do with the suicides, anyway."

I'm struck he prioritized his Council contact over him trying to have Kami killed. He must not think the accusation is serious enough to warrant an explanation. It's telling, perhaps because Jason believes it is more important to address the question about his honor than the one about his being a murderer, the latter being so outlandish as to not faze him.

Jason sits down on the side of the bed where I sat a few minutes earlier with Kami.

"Palau's coworkers said he was working on Genetic Balancing Reviews—which turns out to be Gender Balancing Reviews. I wanted to find out if it was a project assigned by the Council, so I asked a friend. Turns out it was not. It was self-assigned and not any big deal. And, yeah, I knew Gothard Hong, but not well. We'd talk about once a month because he was working on a book that included some legal-ease and he needed clarification about terms and laws. We were in primary school at the same time, but I hardly knew him. I didn't leave it out, I forgot to mention it."

I see him struggling, explaining away Kami's concerns with perfectly reasonable explanations. Under normal circumstances, I'd let him ramble on for a while before interrupting, but I'm bored and need to meet Alex at the HMC soon.

"Chill out. I didn't say I believed her. I personally don't care why you did or didn't tell us anything. But I'm an equal partner in this report and I'll be damned if you're going to get the lion's share of the credit. I want opportunities just like you." I register a feigned look of surprise forming on his face. "Oh, don't even think about going there. We both know you'd like to parlay this into a Clerk spot or something bigger, which is fine, so long as it doesn't look like I was simply a passive member of the team."

"Okay," says Jason, the surprised look replaced by two fingers rubbing his forehead. "So I planned to turn this waste of time effort into a future. I wasn't going to cut you out or minimize your role. But I also don't want this thing dragging on into the next millennia. There is nothing to these suicides and our plugging along hoping to find something is a waste of time. I'd rather drop this in the Council's lap with a nice bow and move on."

"On that count we are in agreement," I snap back, recognizing that not even the virtual curtain is sufficient to muffle our increasing volume. "About the only person who thinks there is something going on is your girlfriend—oh, and she thinks you're involved."

There's a long silence as we each consider our next move. Jason is up now and pacing, his hands clasped behind his back. I remain standing in the corner, arms crossed, hoping to convey the message that I am not backing down. I can't tell for sure if he's moving toward further defiance or capitulation, but something about his demeanor, the way his head hangs and his shoulders slump tells me it's the latter.

"I'll talk to her," he relents. "How she got the idea that I would kill people is beyond me. I don't suppose she mentioned *why* she thinks I'd be randomly making murders look like suicides?"

"No, only that you're involved and likely part of a conspiracy."

"A conspiracy. Great," says Jason beneath the two pink lines which now grace his forehead.

I should probably attempt to postpone any Kami-Jason hookup until I have time to draft this report to the Council. Having them at odds will keep Kami busy trying to prove her wild hypothesis and put Jason off his game thinking about how to explain things.

"So what now?" I ask. "You're going to stick around until she's back and confront her here? Not the most private place to have a conversation about you killing people, is it?" I make the statement with a sarcastic lilt, a subtle attempt to get him to postpone and give me time to talk to Marta about what she's heard.

"No, I'll wait until later," Jason confirms. "I suppose there's no hurry as long as I'm not sitting in an interrogation room."

CHAPTER FORTY-ONE

Jason Plumin

"Hi," I say as the door on Cecelia's HabU swooshes open. "Thanks for making time on a Sunday."

"Get in here and stop being an ass, Jason," Cecelia replies with her usual, unfiltered style. Her raw honesty is comforting at a time of too many secrets.

"I'm just saying, it's not our normal Tuesday."

Cecelia leans in to kiss me and I return the favor, allowing her warm, wet tongue to caress mine in a familiar dance. Sean's warning not to tell anyone notwithstanding, given all the revelations of the past few days, I need someone I trust.

In this particular situation, Kami would be my first choice since Lento also told her about the gender stuff. But since she currently thinks I'm running around killing people and making it look like suicides, it seems like a bad idea to share details about my conversation with Sean. Cecelia is my go-to for advice, despite her unwillingness to commit to a public relationship.

"Do you want a drink? I've got a bottle of bootleg bourbon from that tech in the Aries dynamics plant," she asks as I head toward the table and bench seats jutting out from a wall.

"Sure, I'd love some." I know that tech, a genius at recreating early twenty-first century liquors...not that I'd know for sure, since I've never actually tasted early twenty-first century whiskey. But Cecelia says it's pretty close.

Cecelia walks to a spot on the adjoining wall with a built-in digital display and taps in a short code, causing a panel a couple feet away to slide upward. On the now visible shelf is a nondescript bottle filled three-quarters full of a deep amber liquid and two glasses. She grabs all three and sets them on the dinette. Cecelia sits on the opposite side and pours two-fingers worth in each glass, sliding one across the table toward me and taking up the other for herself.

"Cheers," she says, holding her glass up toward me.

"Cheers," I reply with a clink, tapping my glass to hers before taking a healthy swallow followed by an extended and labored exhale as the liquid burns my throat. "Mmm. That's good," I say in a bourbon-induced, gravelly voice. I notice Cecelia is not affected by her initial swallow.

"So to what do I owe the pleasure of this visit two days early? I know it isn't just for the sex, as great as it is," Cecelia asks.

"True, but yeah. It's this suicide study. I need someone I trust won't go talking to the press and you're the first person I thought of." *Actually, Kami was first, but it's a small fib.*

"Ooh, mysterious. Shit, you didn't find out these suicides were actually murders, did you?" Cecelia pauses for a minute. I can see her considering alternatives. "Or is it just some sexual tension with one or more of your teammates? Did you hook up with someone?" I can't tell if she's serious or just being her normal, slightly cynical and perpetually sarcastic self.

I consider the relationship with Kami for a quick minute and decide to leave it out of the conversation for the time being. There's no need to add a distraction to an already distracting situation. Besides, I'm not positive how Cecelia will react. She's been fairly honest about our long term prospects, even encouraging me to find someone my own age. But there are times I feel she might not be totally okay with me moving on to something serious with someone else. Then again, I read women about as well as I read Mandarin, so there's little chance I'm interpreting her signals accurately.

"No," I start, "as far as I can tell the suicides are exactly what they appear to be. I even received confirmation from a friend Council Clerk. Apparently all the stations are coming to the same conclusion—the increase in suicides is simply an increase in suicides, not an inter-station murder spree." Cecelia pours me a bit more bourbon.

"Oh, then it's the hookup. Which one was it, the Orbital Sheriff's Deputy or the slightly gritty, migrant PersRep? I hope it's the latter, the one with the tough, no bullshit sign painted across her chest. But knowing your need to fix and protect people, I'm guessing it's the young, Asian Deputy—she strikes me as slightly broken in some way."

"Jesus, Cecelia," I say before taking another healthy swallow of bourbon, relieved at how much smoother it goes down. "It's neither of those. I'm not sleeping with Brandi and Kami isn't broken." I consider the statement as soon as it passes my lips, realizing I may have slipped up. I decide to leave it lay, hoping Cecelia doesn't pick up on the omission about Kami. "There's information," I continue, "which might prove embarrassing or worse if it became public knowledge. The Council's involved, as well as a number of scientists and doctors, maybe even a few analysts."

Cecelia finishes her first pour and tips the bottle again, adding another two fingers to both our glasses. She's serious when she leans in across the table and takes my hand in hers, apologizing and encouraging me to go on.

The whiskey is going down easier with each swallow, causing a warm, euphoric sensation in my head and nerves. Not given to excessive alcohol consumption and especially not liquor, the feeling is one I've only felt a couple times in my life. It relaxes me enough to tell Cecelia the entire story—the information from Lento, Sean's confirmation of the Council's complicity, the race to find a solution and the potential impact if they fail. I leave out the part about Lento telling Kami, but include Kami's belief I'm involved with killing people, an admission that makes Cecelia laugh out loud and question whether I'm capable of even killing off the drink in front of me, which I do just to prove a point. By the time I finish, I'm sufficiently drunk but still considering taking another sip of the glass Cecelia just refilled.

"Well, C? Some thoughts would be helpful about now. What do you think I should do?"

Cecelia is quiet throughout the story, save questioning my machismo when I brought up Kami's hypothesis. She sits back in her chair, lifting the glass to her lips to take a sip. It's small, barely perceptible. The room behind her has started gently rotating, Cecelia's image softening into the utilitarian background. Her first words are whispers, as if she's trying to keep from being overheard.

"First of all, Sean is correct. You can't tell anyone. You shouldn't have told me. This isn't something to fuck around with, Jason. You've investigated yourself into the middle of a shit storm. Do you have any idea what might happen if the Council finds out you know their secret —a secret, by the way, that would set off a panic among the Cits?"

"Yeah, they'll kill me. I know," I blurt, sounding far more sarcastic than I intend.

"No! You jackass," Cecelia snaps back! "It will be much worse than death, much more painful. If you're lucky they might lock you into a private room, somewhere people can't find you where you can wait it out until there is a solution. More likely you'll end up on the surface, probably in the Open Lands, since the last thing the Council wants is the CAZ politicians finding out the stations are potentially unsustainable, giving those corrupt, greedy fucks the upper hand. But before they banish you, they will to want to know everyone you told and everyone who told you. Lento will be fine, he's been around long enough that he knows how the game is played *and* he's needed to help solve this mess. But anyone else not part of discovering a cure is going with you. They're not going to kill you, but you'll wish they had."

I take slug of liquor. This time I don't wait for Cecelia, reaching for the bottle and pouring more than a couple fingers worth into my glass and a bit onto the table.

"I'm wouldn't tell anyone who knows." The sentence seems coherent bouncing around my head, but in play the grammar and slurred words sound more like English is my second language. "You know what I mean."

Cecelia must have noticed something unintended because her next question catches me off guard. "Jason," she starts slowly. "Who else did you tell? Who else knows? And don't lie to me."

I cross my arms, forgetting that I'm still holding the mostly full glass of bourbon until it spills onto the front of my uniform. "Shit," I say, taking another sip before setting it on the table.

Cecelia slides to the front of her seat. "Jason, who else knows about the gender problem aboard the stations?"

This time I process the question exactly as intended, considering whether to answer and if so, whether to lie. I'm not sure Cecelia can tell when I'm lying. Probably not, but I've never lied to her before so I have no benchmark. I could easily toss out a denial, claiming I haven't told anyone but her, which would be true while also avoiding the bigger question of who else knows. She's already said I shouldn't have even told her, a fat thank-you-very-much for cluing her in on the news of the century. It's information she can use, maybe deciding to return to the CAZ before the stations become a shit show. Of course, that's ridiculous. Nobody is going to voluntarily return to the planet without setting off serious alarm bells. To even consider…

"Jason!" Cecelia whisper-shouts, bringing me back into the moment. "Focus. Who else knows?"

It must be the booze because I don't care if she finds out. I don't care if she finds out Lento told Kami. I don't care if she finds out Kami and I are sleeping together, or were sleeping together before she thought I might be killing people. So I tell her, "Kami. Kami Lee knows and we're sleeping…together," I snap, a deep sense of regret blanketing my boozy confession.

Cecelia is quiet, her mouth open like a fish gasping for air. She must be considering the admission, wondering if it's serious, trying to figure out her next move. As she sits back into the chair, I start to wonder if she's ever going to speak.

"Sorry I didn't tell you about Kami sooner."

"You're an idiot," Cecelia says, shaking her head. "I don't care that you hooked up with the young Deputy. I care that she knows something that could end her future and get her expelled to the planet. I care that the two of you have gotten yourselves into a situation where the only way out is to stay silent until there is a cure, hoping somebody doesn't find out you know. How much do you trust Sean?"

"Absolutely," I blurt out, recognizing my slurred speech and frat boy loyalty makes me sound like a moron. Feeling the need for a clarification, I add, "I trust Sean. He isn't gonna tell anyone on the Council."

"And you're sure you haven't told anyone else? There isn't anyone else who knows?"

I think about it for a second, my brain swimming in bourbon, wondering if anyone else gave an indication of being in the loop. The people who worked with Neil Palau might have suspected something, but they didn't even know the true nature of Palau's work. 'Genetic Rebalancing' is what they called it, which could mean anything. There isn't anyone I can think of who might have a clue about the problems rolling down this track.

"I haven't told anyone but you. And I can't think of anyone else who knows. But there's more."

"What more?" Cecelia asks, seeming exasperated.

"The Council must suspect cuz they ordered the suicide reviews. Sean said they noticed the uptick in suicides, ordered the investigations to confirm they were legit, not murders. He also said the Council knew about Neil Palau's work in the lab. Sean was not concerned with the results…from Aries or other stations. He said everything pointed to normal uptick, and they had Palau under control."

"Under control? What does that even mean?" Cecelia asks.

I regurgitate what I know about Palau's work along with a tiny bit of vomit into my throat. Another sip washes down the foul, acidic taste before explaining Palau's research includes not only Aries but the entire station network. I describe how the Council knew about Palau's work and suspected he would release the information to the general public, which is why they offered to bring him onto the team. Only he committed suicide before he could accept.

"The problem now isn't the Council, it's Kami. She thinks there's more to it. She believes the suicides aren't suicides and that I'm involved with killing people. She thinks I tried to have her killed."

"That's ridiculous," Cecelia exclaims!

"I know, but she's convinced there's more to these suicides than we know and that I'm part of the conspiracy. What's more, Brandi hasn't exactly been dissuading her."

"What do you mean?" Cecelia asks.

"She's been subtly encouraging Kami's paranoia about me. She thinks it's a big joke. I'm going to talk to Kami and probably her advocate, Kornel Lento. This is nuts."

My head is a mix of Jell-O encased thoughts jiggling to a blurry shimmer. Cecelia stands. Without speaking she collects the bottle and two glasses and sets them on the shelf. I can't help think about how stunning she looks as she lifts me from the seat and presses the actuator on the wall to lower the bed, or how screwed I am as she slides the zipper down my uniform and reaches in to caress my chest. I don't remember lying down, or Cecelia removing my clothes. We make love, a mix of foggy memory and soft moans giving way to sweat-soaked bodies and tangled sheets. The last thing I recall is her head on my chest and bright, red hair draped across my right arm. I drift off to sleep hoping today was just a dream.

CHAPTER FORTY-TWO

Kami Lee

Monday's have always been my favorite day of the week, until now. Every Monday holds the promise of a new beginning, a chance to start off the week right with a solid coffee, time on a treadmill at the HMC, and a crisp, new plan. Normally by Friday things have gone off schedule enough to require reconsideration, but Monday's are usually days of optimism, except when you have a lingering headache from being poisoned. To cap it off, I'm meeting with Parker in a few minutes —in fact, I'm leaning against the wall outside the Aries OSU right now psyching myself up. I wish there were another option, but I need to discuss the Ocasio interview with him. I feel a tinge bad for that thought after he saved my life and showed up at the Med Lab, but one visit to my death bed does not erase a year's worth of inappropriate jokes.

I'd be lying if I said I weren't relieved to see Jason was gone by the time my last test concluded yesterday. I didn't want to see him, but I am also surprised he didn't call last night to check up on me. Perhaps he sensed something was wrong, or maybe Brandi told him to give me some space. There were two messages from Kornel, one last night and another this morning—I was asleep for both.

We're supposed to have our initial findings about the suicides into the Council by tomorrow and I've still got a lot of unanswered questions. I haven't reviewed Jason and Brandi's rough draft, either. I suspect it describes the suicides as nothing more than they seem— lonely, desperate people unable to cope in space deciding non-existence is better than space existence. Despite her concern, I doubt Brandi is prepared to jump on the conspiracy bandwagon, especially in a document going to the Council. After all, what do I have other than a few unfounded suspicions, an old suicide study, and a Station Rep who knew most of the male victims, had access to their records, failed to disclose information about ALab genetics projects, and according to Brandi has a Council contact who could alter my personal logs. That actually sounds like a lot when I think about it—it's just not hard evidence. A weapon would be nice. Or digital prints. Something physical.

After a few minutes I decide I can't put off the meeting with Parker any longer. I'm looking forward to finding out what he knows, but I need to balance my thirst for knowledge with the persistent, low-grade ache between my temples. I pop two of the pain relievers the Med Lab sent home and walk through the OSU door, crossing the room where Mike the administrative assistant offers a tentative 'good morning,' before I enter Parker's dominion.

Parker is standing in front of a raised desk, a virtual screen hovering at eye level and his hands resting on a new X1 virtual keyboard with enhanced synaptic response. His foot is tapping the floor to a beat I cannot hear through the barely visible auditory plugs in his ears, something with a quick, snappy tempo from the way his shoeless toes are dancing. Parker is from a time when footwear in the office was mostly optional. He'd rather feel the semi-firm cushioning of the 3-D printed faux rock pad beneath his socked soles than constrict his feet with state of the art station loafers. Personally, I think it's nothing more than an eighty-two year old man's way of reminding people he's been around longer than most of us and isn't going to change.

"Is there anyone besides me who doesn't have the new X1?" I ask, knowing he probably can't hear a word I'm saying.

"What?" shouts Parker. "You'll have to speak up! I can't hear you!" He devilishly grins, then pops the plugs from his ears, dropping them into a pocket on the front of his jumpsuit.

"I asked how I get one of the new X1s."

"Oh, well they only go to people doing actual work. Young, Asian know-it-alls with record-high test scores have to wait until the X1 is obsolete," Parker replies. I should have known he'd know about my test scores.

I consider responding with my own sarcastic quip, but I don't want this to digress into the inevitable tit-for-tat it is sure to become once we get started. Instead, I attempt to ingratiate myself by asking, "What were you listening to?"

"Brain Drain by Mud Fingers. Classic rock and roll from my wild youth. The late-2030s were a great time to be into music. I'm guessing you haven't heard of them, you just having sprung from puberty."

In fact, I hadn't heard of the Mud Fingers. My guess is they are some obscure band that nobody but Parker actually listened to, even in the 2030s. He has this way of coming up with ambiguous and usually irrelevant things from the past, stuff people couldn't actually verify. Many records of things produced between the two pandemics and deemed inconsequential were purged after TwoGP, unknown bands, sitcoms, and political speeches made by Hollywood actors being the first to go. For some reason people decided if it was created between the start of OneGP and the end of TwoGP, it probably wasn't worth keeping. Of course, this is the era in which Parker draws most of his material.

"But I didn't ask you to stop by to talk about the best music ever," Parker adds. "They finished the analysis of Dr. Ocasio's logs and let me just say it was a pleasure cataloging their findings." Parker is sporting one of his 'If only you knew what I knew,' smiles, lips upturned to show both uppers and lowers, eyes wide, and bushy brows raised. He's elated at having both a secret and an audience with whom to share it.

"Well?" It's all I can muster while rubbing my temple, my headache having migrated from front to back.

"Look at this."

Parker taps a key on the virtual keyboard *with its damn synaptic response*, switching to a double-sided display to allow us both to see what's on screen. It takes a minute to register the images, a woman and a man, naked and engaged in what can only be described as animal love—passionate and violent at the same time. The man, probably in his mid to late thirties and in reasonably good shape is standing behind the woman aggressively thrusting, forcing the woman draped over a table to hold the end to keep from banging into it. She appears to be in some pain, but also thoroughly immersed in the moment. It's at that point, in what appears to be the middle of rapture, I realize where they're at—it's Dr. Ocasio's office.

"Is that?" I start, unable to finish.

"Yep, the doc in all her glory. There are a couple dozen of those videos with perhaps a third as many men all engaged in carnal knowledge. Ocasio admitted to having drugged them with synthetic Benzos. Powerful, dissolves quickly in the bloodstream and heightens one's susceptibility to..."

"Suggestion," I interrupt, the video still running. "Has she admitted drugging me, yet?"

"Nope," Parker replies, still watching. "She swears she has no memory of poisoning you."

I consider his reply, allowing it to ferment for a moment. What if she really doesn't remember? What if someone used the Benzos on her, instructed her to poison me, then replaced the memory? It's plausible. It doesn't totally answer the question of why someone would want me dead—although I'm still guessing it has something to do with this current project—but it certainly explains why she doesn't remember. Jason could easily have slipped over there before I arrived and set up the entire thing. If he's willing to kill men who've committed various infractions, the leap to cover it up isn't that great.

"Did they find any drugs in Ocasio's system?" I ask.

"Nope, again." It takes another few seconds for Parker to understand the implication. When he does, he adds, "By the time we processed her for drugs the Benzos would have been long out of her system. Several hours passed between when you were transported to the Med Lab and we detained Ocasio."

Yeah, the drugs would be long gone by then with no way to extract the true memories.

"Wait," Parker starts. "I haven't told you the best part."

Great, there's a best part.

"Apparently Neil Palau, one of your suicides, was right when he accused Ocasio of, well, whatever he accused her of doing. He's in several of the videos making animal noises and doing things I thought were impossible for anyone over thirty. Afterward, they get dressed, Ocasio implants a new memory, and he goes home to his wife none the wiser. It's fantastic stuff. Video and audio. Do you want to see it?"

"No, thank you. I'll take your word for it." I'm starting to wonder how many of these videos Parker watched.

"I guess that helps confirm Palau committed suicide. He was having legitimate nightmares, which is a solid sign if there ever was one," Parker adds.

Palau's emotional problems coupled with lack of sleep, a guilty finding in the Ocasio accusation incident, and job stress does put him in the high risk category. But the genetics project he was working at the time of his death continues to bother me, like tiny, jabbing pins reminding me to stay awake. There has to be a connection, I'm just not seeing it.

"How did she get the drugs in their system?" I ask.

"Once we showed her the videos and stills, she opened up like a breached hull. In some cases, she prescribed other medication and just switched the pills at the office, others inhaled what she called 'calming agents' during session—and I know this last one will surprise the crap out of you—she also put the Benzos in their tea, although in some cases it was coffee or water, but you get my point."

"Neil Palau was drugged, forced to have sex with his therapist, then has nightmares about it afterwards. He describes his nightmares to his therapist, who then drugs him again and has sex with him. Ocasio is one messed up chick. Did any of her patients remember anything?"

"Nope," Parker replies. "We interviewed everyone in the videos, men and women, nobody remembered a thing. Some of them were married, but not all. A couple were disappointed, said they wished she just offered up the sex. They would have happily complied. Not all of those were single, either."

"Wait, men and women?"

"Yep," Parker replies, this time with his patented devious grin. "Don't worry, we didn't find you in any of the videos."

"She tried to poison me, not screw me," I blurt out.

"Well, just to make sure, I watched every minute of every recording, cataloging each detail. I didn't want you caught off guard during some future proceeding."

"I don't suppose you were able to find out the status of the suicide studies on the other stations? I mean with all that video time."

Parker motions over one of the virtual keys and I watch as the screen hovering between us turns opaque, switching to single-side viewing mode. He then taps a few more keys to bring up his notes.

"There are investigations on every station, all at the behest of the Council. Everyone is reporting an increase in suicides, but none are seeing anything out of the ordinary. I didn't talk to every OSU, but the ones I did didn't think there was anything anomalous, save for a change in the percentage of suicides by gender. And get this, the Deputy assigned from each station seems to be someone newer to the unit—someone young like you. Not sure if that's significant or not."

I'm not sure either. Could be they wanted someone new, hoping they wouldn't uncover anything. Or if it went bad, they could blame it on the lack of experience. Or maybe they just wanted a fresh, untainted set of eyes on the analysis. It's hard to say.

"What change in suicides by gender?" I ask, recalling the statement buried in the middle of his explanation.

Parker scrolls down the screen, reading his notes as he goes. He describes how suicides are up across all the stations, as much as 50 percent year-over-year, and the ratio of males to females has also been going up. "It appears more men than women are committing suicide these days. There's probably a joke in there, somewhere," he adds.

Parker goes on to note there is nothing to suggest foul play, at least within his circle. He's been around long enough to establish a well-connected crony network throughout the various OSUs. But since many of them aren't involved directly with the suicide reviews, they are only privy to the investigation if they are asked for data.

"There's one more thing," Parker adds. "Your *friend*, Jason, met with someone in the private docking bay on Saturday. I'm not sure who, there's no log on file. The meeting lasted just over an hour."

There's an implication in the way he says *friend*, but I refuse to dignify it with a response.

"What time?" I wonder, considering that was the same day I interviewed Ocasio.

"What time was he in the docking bay?" Parker asks, looking confused. Apparently he's already moved on to the next salacious detail in his notes.

"Yes. What time was he in the docking bay? When did he leave?"

Parker scrolls up the screen looking for the date-time stamps. "Late afternoon, around 16:00 according to the docking report."

"Who could dock without leaving a record?"

"Oh, Council members, for one," Parker answers without hesitation. "Ambassadors and Clerks. Possibly someone from the planet whose travel the Council wants to conceal for some reason, like a politician."

The common denominator in each of those scenarios is the Council. It has to be the contact Brandi mentioned. Perhaps Jason had to follow up with a progress report after trying to kill me earlier in the day? He wouldn't want to talk remotely about something as sensitive as murder.

I need to talk to Lento. He can't be involved, not in trying to kill me, and he probably knows someone I can trust on the Council—someone I can talk to about Jason without him finding out.

"Where to next?" Parker asks.

"My suicide team is meeting this morning to discuss our findings. I imagine they'll want to finalize any theories for our report."

Parker taps the virtual keyboard, shutting down both it and the display. "Well, that should be fun."

CHAPTER FORTY-THREE

Jason Plumin

"I'm starting to get the feeling Anna doesn't actually like me," I mention to Brandi as I sit down at the conference table.

"Well, Jason, why do you suppose that is?" Brandi replies without looking away from whatever she's doing on her computer. "Perhaps it has something to do with you being an asshole and telling her she could be eligible for one of the few 'flex Roles?' She knows there's no such thing as a *flex Role*, but continues to ask people about it—me, Botha, her boyfriend, parents, random visitors to the office, the gummy dispenser, the Eight Ball she found in my bottom drawer. It's like a child wanting to believe in Santa Clause even after her parents come clean with the facts because they're tired of some phony, fat bastard in a red suit getting credit for their gifts. There is no Santa Clause and there is no flex Role."

"Well, when you put it that way, I suppose I deserve a little animosity flung in my direction."

I ask Brandi about Kami, seeing she has not arrived, yet.

Brandi looks up from her MiniComp, "Since you don't know the answer, I suppose it's safe to assume she is still avoiding you?"

"I haven't actually tried to contact her since yesterday," I reply. "You're the one who suggested giving her some space. I'm just following the advice of a wise, worldly woman."

"Do me a favor and save whatever conversation you're planning for after the meeting. The last thing I need is to listen to you try to recover your relationship from the bottom of the conspiracy well."

"Thanks, I'll keep that in mind," I reply.

"Speaking of the meeting," Brandi starts. "I actually started drafting the report last night. You should take a read, add whatever you think I missed."

I set my MiniComp on the table and boot to the report. It's well written and pretty much done, save for a few minor details Brandi doesn't know and won't be included. It's short, only five pages including a cover sheet, half-page executive summary, tables listing suicide names, locations, and particulars, and our conclusion. I can't help but be impressed with the thoroughness and writing style—bottom line up front and supporting material in the body. The only thing I'd like to change is the cover, which currently reads, 'Investigation conducted by: Brandi Mikkelson, Jason Plumin and Kami Lee.' Clearly my name should be listed first.

"Very nicely done. I like the style and the conclusion." I read the conclusion from the first paragraph of the Executive Summary: "The investigative team—*thank you for not calling us the suicide crew, by the way*. The investigative team concludes that while suicides are up year-over-year across multiple years, there is no evidence to suggest the increase is the result of nefarious acts. Furthermore, the team recommends the Council order a review in coordination with the Psyche lab to explore cause and effect related to suicides and determine whether the increase is the result of avoidable stimuli."

It doesn't get much clearer than that, which is exactly what I tell Brandi. "Nice job and I totally agree."

"As much as I'd like to give Kami's suspicions about you some credence," Brandi starts with a wry smile, "I just don't see the evidence the way she does."

"You know we need to discuss this with her at some point. Her name *is* on the report."

"Why don't you let me handle that," Brandi replies. "I think at this point, my relationship with the girl is on more solid ground than yours. Besides, it'll be fun to watch her reaction when I tell her I know all about your connection to the many suicides, including your rather suspicious contact with Gothard Hong and the Council. Speaking of which, you never did explain what Genetic Balancing Reviews are or what Palau found out."

There really isn't an option here. I can't tell Brandi about the DupleX report, or the fact that without a solution the human race is doomed. There's no way to keep secret who I told if the Council questions me—five minutes on a Neuro-Analyzer and they'll have the truth and with it a list of everyone I've put in jeopardy. Brandi needs to know as little as possible.

"It was actually nothing," I lie. "The Council didn't order the study, but they also didn't care about it. My contact said they got the results just after Palau's suicide. It revealed slight fluctuations in the gender of babies based on the relative position of the Earth to the sun during the course of a normalized year."

"Huh?" Brandi says, a contorted look on her face, head cocked to one side.

"Think of it like this," I start. "Since the stations are in synchronous geostationary orbit above specific points on the Earth, they suffer from the same issues as the planet relative to revolution and rotation. The stations are essentially extensions of the planet where the sun is concerned. Palau was studying the effects of solar radiation on births, whether it impacted a child's gender. Apparently he found that at the time of conception, depending on where the Earth was in relation to the sun, as well as the location above a specific point on the planet, there are small variations in the number of male or female babies conceived. Since there are fluctuations on the planet, he surmised we'd experience those same fluctuations on the stations, which over time normalize the population."

"Ah, I see." Brandi says. "So we see fluctuations in the number of male and female children born based on the date and time they were conceived. So what?"

"Exactly," I reply. "The fluctuations are apparently a normal function of orbital position at conception, something the Council considered. However, Palau's study suggested we could influence the number of babies being born of a specific gender by regulating procreation and implantation."

"He was advocating telling people when they could fuck?" Brandi replies, capping the question with a laugh. "That'll going to go over really well. And not for nothing, but to what end?"

"That's just it. There isn't a reason to control gender production. It was all theoretical—a 'what if' scenario, namely, 'What if we had to do this, could we?' The Council filed it away hoping to never need it."

"It sounds like a complete waste of time to me. No wonder Palau committed suicide. His life was spent studying things that will never happen, proffering irrelevant suggestions, and writing reports nobody cares about. If I were an Analyst, I'd probably kill myself, too."

I'm actually feeling pretty good about that explanation. It's total bullshit, of course. There absolutely is a problem with gender at birth and Palau stumbled right into the middle of it. If it got out, there'd be panic and chaos. It would change everything on the stations, not to mention the impact on the CAZ-station dynamic. There would be no place left to survive long term. Either way, Palau's study isn't what killed him and I can't share any of it with Brandi, so enough said.

"We still need to convince Kami this is the right path," I suggest. "How do you plan to get her on our page?"

Brandi's devilish smile scares me a little. "I have my ways of convincing people they're crazy without making it seem hopeless. A little girl-girl time and she'll be begging to come on board the good ship Mickelson."

"Speaking of that, perhaps we can discuss the cover page a bit. Specifically, the order of the names," I say cautiously, not wanting to trigger anything primal.

Brandi laughs like a teenager, full and with abandon. "I thought you'd enjoy that. I think Mickelson, Plumin, Lee has a nice ring to it. We can shorten it to MickPlumLee."

"I was thinking the order should reflect our relative time-in-grade, as it were. Perhaps in descending order of experience?"

"I'll just bet," Brandi shoots back. There's something about her tone —it's playful, not serious. Her eyes are wide and she's got this half grin wanting to break into a full blown smile. "Or reverse alphabetical order," suggests Brandi.

"I'm picking up what you're putting down. We can list your name first, provided I can add a sentence at the beginning of the draft. Something along the lines of, 'The investigative team, working in partnership, blah, blah blah.' Just so it doesn't seem like any one of us was in charge."

Brandi volunteers to consider changing the order of our names in the report. Just as I'm wondering what she'll want in return, she says, "But you need to make sure whatever windfall happens you don't forget your friends. I'd prefer not to be stuck on Aries my entire career."

"Of course!" I reply, wondering if I sound overly enthusiastic.

"Now what are you going to do about your relationship with Kami?" asks Brandi, feigning concern but unable to conceal a tinge of sarcasm.

I've actually given this quite a bit of thought. I really like her, not just because the sex is good, but she wears this combination of brilliant-understated-woman slash girl-with-a-dark-side like it's a custom fit sari, revealing just enough to keep people interested without seeming overly slutty. She's obviously bright, if not somewhat inexperienced, and, I mean, who doesn't like a girl who thinks one is capable of not only murder, but conspiracy to boot. It's all a delicate auric balance, but she pulls it off.

Then again, she does think I'm capable of killing people and conspiring with others, which places a moderately sized hurdle around the whole trust issue—it being the foundation of a healthy relationship. I mean how can we possibly move forward from, *I think you're a liar and a killer?* It's true, the only direction to go from here is up, but there will always be that awkwardness hanging out there. Not that I'm presuming we have a future even if she didn't suspect me of the most heinous crime on the stations.

If I'm going repair anything, I need Lento on my side. If I do that and remove the specter of me being a murderer, there's a chance we can get back to the place we were a few days ago.

"I'll talk to her in a few days," I tell Brandi. "Maybe a week, as soon as I talk to her Advocate. I'm guessing the team approach will go over better than one-on-one."

"There is nothing a girl likes more than being confronted by her most trusted parental figure and the guy she thinks is offing people and making it look like suicide," Brandi says, smiling.

"Perhaps you're right. Maybe I'll go back to my original plan and let it sit until this project is over."

"*That* sounds like the best idea," replies Brandi.

"Speaking of which, would you mind if I add some edits to the document?" I ask, still trying to sound conciliatory, but planning to modify it whether she wants me to or not. "I'd like to add a few details from the interviews."

"Sure. You have access in the joint log. Once we finish hammering out the details, we'll submit and brief the Council." Brandi pauses momentarily. "And before you ask, 'yes', your name can be first in the 'From' block."

CHAPTER FORTY-FOUR

Jason Plumin

It's well past 20:00 when I arrive at Lento's office only to find it vacant. I let myself in via the ID pad on the outside of the unit when he doesn't answer. It recognizes my biometrics immediately, inviting me in, *Welcome, Jason.* I know I told Brandi I'd sit on this until after the suicide study, but I need someone on my side when I talk to Kami.

I didn't expect Lento to be here this late, but I was hoping. I was held up editing the report and then by my boss, the latter to discuss crime metrics and Council policies. Apparently I'd missed a staff meeting in the last few days and all the important banter that comes with it. Tom was his usual good natured self, breezing through the new inter-station travel policy and other relevant news in record time before moving on to sports for which I'm woefully under aware.

Standing here now, I can't decide whether to leave a note or make an appointment for tomorrow morning. The relationship I share with Lento is less-than-cordial to say the least, but we do share a mutual interest. An appointment will give him sufficient warning and a chance to avoid me. I could also head over to his HabU tonight, where Mrs. Dr. Lento could join the discussion about how to get back into Kami's pants. Probably not a good idea, either. I settle on leaving a note.

I can't help notice how sterile Lento's office looks even for the stations. Save for the retro, pocket-sized pad of paper and pencil on the table, his desk is as barren as a blank computer screen. The paper-pencil combo notwithstanding, there is nothing in the room to identify Dr. Kornel Lento as the user. There aren't any photos or kitschy remembrances—even the ALab geeks kept odd mementos of their past. Patel had a small statuette of Ganesha, his plump torso and flat buttocks anchored to the surface to keep the extended trunk and arms from toppling forward. Annie, the new replacement, taped a small photo of a sunset over the ocean torn from a book to the wall behind her virtual screen—an image I'm certain she's never seen in person. I don't recall Glen having anything in his workspace, save for a slightly surly attitude. Perhaps it's only people of a certain age who forgo personal reminders at work?

Lento's old school note taking gives me an idea. Instead of an appointment he can avoid, I'll leave him a note he'll read a few minutes before I arrive. This way he'll be forewarned without having sufficient time to bolt. It's his own fault for being such an unapproachable ass.

I want to sound earnest without seeming weak. I think if he suspects vulnerability, he'll assume insincerity. I take a seat behind his desk, in the same chair in which he sat a couple days ago and spilled the information about the DupleX report and migration preferences. I shudder remembering the conversation.

I pick up the pencil, gently gripping it between my thumb and first two fingers in an awkward, retro embrace. We practiced with pencils in primary school, since they are still used on the planet for various tasks. The CAZ—and certainly the Open Areas—do not enjoy the same level of tech as the stations. Although they use computers, there is still a large portion of the population using electronic pencils and synthetic paper to jot down notes to colleagues and pass information they don't want stored digitally.

Lento's pencil is the real deal, not one of the electronic versions. It's rigid, painted yellow and topped with a pink eraser. This one is only a few inches long, it's owner having sharpened it down to a point more than once, removing at least two-thirds of the material over time. It feels different from the electronic pencils we used in primary school, all optimized to be five inches in length with smooth, slightly rubberized sides and a tip that never dulls. This one has ridges running longitudinally from tip to eraser and real wood making it firm and softer than it's sheathed metallic cousin. I'm tempted to dig my thumb nail into the side, but decide against it. It's the first time I've seen one outside of a photo or video. He must have come by a stash somewhere, because there aren't enough trees left on Earth to manufacture these to order, not to mention no facilities willing to invest the time and materials to produce them.

Unlike Lento's pencil, the paper is neither authentic nor retro. The synthetic version, bound in a small three-and-a-half by five-and-a-half inch notepad is the same material we trained with years ago. The light blue lines pop from the paper's stark white surface, reflecting the lights to the point of it being slightly uncomfortable to look at. It feels how I imagine real paper must have felt, chalky and crisp to the touch, but with an almost imperceptibly sweet smell added during processing to placate the senses. I guess even Lento has trouble finding things made of wood from a planet suffering from a lack of vegetation.

I flip to the first page of the notepad and start to write, "Kornel…" *Shit, don't use his first name. We are not on a first name basis.* I tear the sheet from the notebook, place it crumpled into my pocket and start over.

"Lento…" *that's better,* "Lento - Would like to discuss Kami…" Ugh. Nope, too specific and passive. He'll be formulating theories almost immediately. Besides, I don't know for sure what Kami's shared with him. Another wadded up piece of paper in my pocket and a fresh sheet before me.

"Lento - Will be by at 07:00 to discuss…" to discuss what? What will pique his interest without prompting him to leave in the minutes before I get here? I can't say 'Kami'. 'Conspiracy?' Ha! Definitely not. Oh, how about, "…to discuss Palau autopsy results." That will set him solidly wanting to be here. He'll be motivated to defend his findings, not wanting to let a Station Rep with only a modicum of mandatory primary school medical training pick apart his methods. His ego will be his undoing. Queue deep-throated, evil laugh peppered with presumptuous triumph.

I'm pretty proud of myself, note written, leaning back in Lento's chair, one foot on his desk, bathing in my creativity. I feel pretty good, right up until someone shatters the silence and my hubris with a knock on the door. Instinctively, I drop my foot to the floor and get up to let in whoever is waiting, until I realize first, this isn't my office, and second, nobody knocks anymore. It has to be someone older, stuck in a past where knocking was commonplace. Perhaps one of Lento's older friends from IPI? If that were the case, they'd know he's not in his office this late, which means whoever it is might know I'm here, or know someone is here. That means they knocked because they don't want a record of having been here. But why? I don't suppose there is any way around this—I'm going to have to open the door.

CHAPTER FORTY-FIVE

The Collective

I know Jason's in there, probably wondering if he should answer or not. I can almost feel him a few inches away, just on the other side of the door trying to figure out who's here and debating whether or not to answer. He's weighing his options, of which there are really only two: open the door or not, the latter an unrealistic alternative as he can't hide in there forever. He will realize this sooner or later, hopefully sooner, because only someone who knows he's in there would knock. Someone who thought Lento was in the office would just scan, unless they were old school.

I'll have to bio-scan into the space if he doesn't open the door, but it will leave a record and I don't want to be bothered with coordinating a log modification. I was ready when Jason's name came across my ComLink with the timestamp of him entering Lento's office. I grabbed an old stash of pills and a bottle of spiked, bootlegged hooch I've kept despite not needing it for the last few years, walking a circuitous and speedy route from my HabU. The last minute knock was a judgment call. Altering an entry log requires time—several extra steps and contact with an anonymous source supplied by the Collective. I'd be bumping up against Jason's discovery tomorrow morning. If he doesn't answer, I'll have no choice. "So, answer the fucking door, Jason," I whisper to myself.

I'd been tracking Jason's movements for months at the behest of the Collective. He was involved in several cases which could prove embarrassing were he to start putting the pieces together—which he had. His role on the team investigating suicides makes things more complicated. Perhaps there's some way to use that to my advantage?

He was depressed. All those interviews and heart wrenching stories from loved ones about their troubled and deceased family. It would push anyone over the edge.

I'm about to knock again when the door slides open, making a sound like the tearing of a sheet of paper. "What the fuck are you doing here?" I ask.

Jason is startled, his open mouth and wide eyes echoing a combination of surprise and confusion. He's searching for a question he's unable to ask. I glance both directions, checking for other people in the corridor—I don't expect to see anyone in the Med Lab admin hallway at this hour—then I step inside, forcing Jason to stumble back a half pace to make room. It takes him another long minute to get it together.

"I said, what the fuck are you doing here?"

"I'm…" Jason stutters. "I need to speak to Lento?" It's more of a question than a statement, like he's polling to see if that answer will work.

I walk around the table, taking a seat in Lento's chair and examining the note. "I see. But something tells me it has nothing to do with Palau's autopsy results."

Jason approaches the desk, placing one hand on the back of the chair across from me in order to steady himself. "How did you know I was here?"

I can't just tell him I'm a member of a society whose goal it is to ensure the longevity of the human race and I've been tracking him because he's dangerously close to figuring out what we're doing. He might become suspicious. I opt for a subject change.

"You can't just fuck a judge and an Orbital Sheriff's deputy at the same time and expect it to stay secret."

It works, at least temporarily. The look of shock on Jason's face returns.

"Sit down," I demand. "I brought booze."

I place the bottle full of a potent mixture of genetically modified sleeping aids and bootlegged, high octane liquor on the table as Jason flops down in the seat across from me, wrapping his left hand around the bottle. In a single motion he flips the cap up and downs a full quarter of the tainted liquid, almost tipping as he leans back into the chair.

"So you're pissed," he says, sounding a little worried.

"You're fucking right I'm pissed," I scold. Always better to feign righteous indignation in the face of potential confrontation.

Jason reaches for the bottle, but I pull it away. It's a vain attempt made with already slowing reflexes. I pour myself a small amount, leaving the glass on the table and pushing the bottle back toward Jason with a subtle hint to help himself. He willingly, if not subconsciously, complies with several more considerable swallows.

"You know everything there is to know," Jason says, his speech already beginning to slur from the pharma in the liquor. I keep the spiked whiskey for just these occasions, when I need someone compliant.

"Of course I do. I'm not an idiot," I respond, careful not to temper my superiority. "You might as well take another swallow. It won't make a difference in the end."

"Three end?" He slurs, struggling as much with the words as he does to right himself in the chair.

"Yes, the end. I not only know everything, I know more than you. I know life on the stations is slipping away, breeding itself into nonexistence." He looks up and I see even now he thinks he's got the answers. "Yes, you also have that bit of information. The DupleX report. But it's much worse than you or Lento could possibly imagine. This issue is not a few years in the making—the Collective has been aware of it for at least 15 years. We've understood for over a decade that without proactive intervention, the population on the stations will become irreversibly male dominated within 25 years. It won't matter if every permitted station birth is female and Lento's little team selects only females for replacement, there isn't enough birth and migration capacity to replace the number of double 'X' chromosomes needed to repair the damage. None of which actually matters, because the scientists are no closer to a solution than they were a few years ago. The Collective provides the proactive intervention needed to stave off what seems inevitable by helping to reduce the male population, making them look like suicides."

Jason's face lights up like a dimmed bulb tempered by the influence of booze and high-potency sleeping pharma. He tries to speak, but he can barely lift his head at this point. The only thing that comes out is something that sounds like, "yeoman." I think I get it.

"Women? Women suicides?" His head bobs, barely able to keep himself upright. "Yes, occasionally we are forced to eliminate females, but it is rare. The others were actual suicides—even a few of the men didn't need any help."

He's fighting the pharma. There's labor on his face as he struggles to stay in the moment, his drooping, watery eyes trying to focus on some singular stationary object, a small bit of saliva peeking from the corner of his mouth, his head bobbing forward with each effort to lift it upright. It's impressive, but ultimately futile.

He tries to say something, but only the hissing of a faint whisper passes his lips. I stand and lean my ear close to his mouth to see if I can decipher the message. The words I hear are, "Find me."

He wants to know how I found him. It's a fair question. But considering he must know his fate, I'm a little surprised this is his last request.

"You scanned into Lento's office. You should have knocked. Then again, you weren't trying to keep off the record." He gently slumps forward onto the desk, laying his head down as if to take a nap. I run my fingers through his hair until his labored breathing abruptly stops a minute later. He's gone.

I collect the whiskey, replacing it with an almost empty flask sans the pharma and press Jason's hand to it, cementing his prints and DNA on the container. I doubt they'll examine the liquid within, but why take the chance. Substituting clean, albeit unsanctioned booze is far better than risking Kornel running tests at the suicide crew's behest. I rest the small, clear bottle with a few leftover pharma pills next to his right hand. Anyone examining the scene will presume he downed the pills with the liquor, slowly shutting down his respiratory system.

There are two partially completed, wadded up pieces of paper in Jason's outside breast pocket. Apparently, he put a lot of thought into what he wanted to say, trashing his mistakes along the way. It won't do to have someone find them, so first order of business is disposing of these.

Next, I turn my attention to the note he left Lento. I read it aloud, "Lento - Will be by at 07:00 to discuss Palau autopsy results. Jason P." No, that won't do at all. I think something remorseful, maybe discussing the impact the investigation is having on his personal life and his connections to the victims. Something like, "Dr. Lento - Please tell Kami I'm sorry…"

CHAPTER FORTY-SIX

Brandi Mikkelson

"Brandi, what are you doing here?" Kami asks. She looks as surprised to see me as I was to get a message from Lento to meet him at his office. He must have texted us both. "What are you doing here?" Kami asks again.

"Lento. He said to meet him here." I was on my way to the HMC expecting a normal, early morning, lower body Tuesday lift session with Alex, then Lento's message came through on my ComLink. The only thing I could think was he wanted to talk about Kami, as implausible as that sounds given I don't know Lento well at all.

"What are you doing here?" I ask.

"Kornel…um, Dr. Lento messaged me a few minutes ago. What can he possibly want this early on a Tuesday?"

"Don't ask me. You're his surrogate daughter." It comes out harsher than I intend.

Kami takes a long minute, staring down the corridor as if searching for an answer. "Who isn't here?" She finally asks.

"What do you mean, 'Who isn't here?' A lot of people aren't here." I pause for a moment before realizing, "Jason." Plumin isn't here. If Lento contacted both Kami and I, he would certainly have contacted Plumin.

"Jason," Kami says. "Maybe he's already here?"

It's possible, but I doubt it. His HabU is further from Lento's office in the Med Lab than the HMC where I came from. It would take him at least five minutes more to make it here. Even if he got the call before me, Lento would have called Kami first, which is why she arrived at the same time I did. The chances Jason made it here before us are so slim as to be not worth considering.

"Hey, before we go in," I start, just in case Plumin is in the office. "I talked to someone about Jason's contact on the Council. I'd planned to share it with you after yesterday's catch up meeting, but you were a no-show."

"Yeah. I had a couple things to do," Kami replies.

"You were right. He definitely has access and the ability to alter logs. That Council contact is actually a Council Clerk, a friend named Sean." The name is from Marta, the rest is total bullshit. "I was told Jason checked on the status of the suicide studies on the other stations. He apparently asked about the Council's intention requesting them. His contact, the Sean guy, reported to the Council he believed Plumin was acting suspiciously and seemed like he was under what he described as 'significant strain.' Plumin apparently discussed a relationship, one of some concern. Honestly, except for you and a few rumors, I didn't even know Jason had 'relationships.'"

Kami doesn't say anything. I haven't mentioned sharing her Plumin-the-murderer theory with Jason. There's no need muddying her clarity with actual facts. There is some benefit to having them at odds. While they're thinking about each other, they're not trying to figure out how to spin this thing to their benefit.

"There's more," I add. "The C-Clerk..." *damn it, Marta,* "the Council Clerk supposedly reported that Jason asked a lot of questions about how the Council might handle someone with potentially sensitive information. He was specifically interested in their process for dealing with a Cit who may have committed a crime. Could such an individual trade knowledge for leniency? Would there be a situation where someone in a critical role could protect someone in a less critical role?"

Kami looks contemplative, staring down the corridor in silence.

"The sensitive information has to be his involvement in the suicides," she offers. "I'm convinced they were murdered. Maybe not all of them, but definitely most of the males. Maybe he's not doing the actual killing but knows who is and wants to trade his involvement for leniency. Either way, he's culpable and I fell for it."

I'm still not convinced he's killing anyone, but seeing this play out does provide a respite from the mundane. I realize immediately what it says about me as a person and I'm okay with it. I wasn't born on the stations, I worked to get here. Nobody handed me anything and I'll be damned if I'm not going to take any advantage I can get. The only fight worth fighting is the one I win.

"He fooled a lot of people, Kami," I say.

CHAPTER FORTY-SEVEN

Kami

I place my thumb on the Identification Pad outside Lento's office and the door swooshes open, announcing me to its sole occupant, Kornel Lento.

"Kami," he says, walking toward me with his arms outstretched. He wraps them around me in the fatherly hug that always means bad news. A few feet away sits a body slumped over the desk, its back to the door.

"I'm so sorry," says Kornel, his voice barely audible above my pounding heart. I'm familiar with the signs of adrenaline response: auditory system stunted, breathing shallow, blood diverted to the core, processing minute visual clues, like the fact it's definitely a male with his head on the desk near a mostly drained bottle and an almost empty pill container. I've never been good with the retreat part of the fight-or-flight equation.

"It's Jason, isn't it?" I ask, pulling away from Kornel and moving toward the desk. Of course it's Jason. I don't need to see his face, which is turned away. The hair and build are a match. It even smells like him, triggering a memory of our last night together and the morning after. *Jason*, I think to myself, *you were in the middle of some serious shit.*

"I'm not quite finished with the autopsy, yet, but it appears to be suicide," Kornel breaks in, snapping me back from the warmth of my hallucinatory bed.

"Autopsy?" I ask, glancing back to see Kornel and remembering Brandi is still standing in the doorway.

"Of course," Kornel replies. "I figured you'd want the same protocol as with the Birmingham suicide. Absolute confirmation. I even took scene photos prior to disturbing anything. I can send you everything if you want—but there isn't much to see."

"No…" I start to reply, then I'm stymied by a wave of unexpected, emotion-laced energy.

"Yes, Doc. That'd be great," Brandi pipes in.

My clarity returning with my training, I ask Kornel to also send me the photos, as well as any conclusions and findings as soon as they are available. "What do you have so far suggesting suicide?"

Kornel pulls his small notebook and a pencil from the left breast pocket of his jumper. The notebook is different from the last one, green instead of red, and the pencil is definitely newer, although only moderately so. "Burn through that other notebook already?" I ask, before he finishes opening to one of the first pages.

"That's what I was going to tell you," Lento replies. "Mr. Plumin left a hand-written note. He used my notebook, the one I left on the desk. It's been packaged in case it becomes evidence."

"A note?" Brandi asks. "Who the fuck leaves a hand-written note?"

"Here," Lento says, tapping a couple keys on his ComLink before making a swiping motion. "I scanned it. It's pretty straightforward."

I read the note aloud, "Dr. Lento - Please tell Kami I'm sorry. I didn't mean for it to go this far. I've spent the last three years trying to make up for a bad decision, one I'd hoped wouldn't come back to haunt me. But here I sit, waiting for the Council to catch up to me—an inevitability looming over an uncertain future. If there was any way to change what I've done—what I've had to do to keep the secret—I would. My only regret is having met Kami too late."

"Holy shit. You were right," Brandi replies first.

"Right about what?" asks Lento.

It's not the best time to brief Kornel on the myriad evidence, circumstantial or not. "Was there any DNA on the note?" I ask, hoping to move him off the subject.

Kornel swipes up on his ComLink, then flips a couple pages into his notebook. "Only Mr. Plumin's." There's a long pause, an uncomfortable silence begging to be filled. Kornel recognizes it first, adding, "He really didn't seem the type. But then again, who does?"

"There was that incident about ten years ago when he held himself up in his HabU for several days. They ended up calling in a Wellness Specialist." Brandi tosses the information out so casually as to catch both Kornel and I off guard.

"A WelSpec?" I ask.

"Well, it's just a rumor I heard shortly after migrating," Brandi replies. "Supposedly, Jason had a breakdown a few years after Role training. The Algorithm flagged his behavior as anomalous—lack of movement, no food gummy distributions, drop off in logged HMC time, failure to respond to wellness pings. Someone on the Med Lab Psyche team reviewed the referral and dispatched a WelSpec to make sure he hadn't, well…"

"Committed suicide," Kornel answers, finishing a thought we all shared.

"Jeez. What happened to Privacy First?" I ask.

"Well, the rumor isn't exactly accurate," Kornel explains. "The Algorithm can't assess people's activity for patterns which seem abnormal. There needs to be a corresponding report filed by an actual human."

"I don't understand?" I say, turning toward Kornel and away from the body—Jason's body.

Kornel takes a deep breath, as if preparing to deliver a lengthy oration. "Initially, Privacy First applied to any and all monitoring. As time went on, people spent more time aboard the stations and suicides ticked up. The Council recognized the value in limited metadata collection and adjusted the Algorithm to check for indicators of mental distress within the data. It's rare to see referrals, even today, unless someone's behavior—their pattern of life—changes suddenly and dramatically *and* someone files a report. The Algorithm only collects and analyzes metadata. Without a personal report, there is no way to correlate the data with an individual. That's why it's impossible to intervene in suicides where signs are not logged or reported by someone who knows the potential victim. I'd guess someone Mr. Plumin knew filed a report."

"Okay, so he attempted suicide once before?" I ask.

"The records would be sealed," Brandi starts, motioning to Kornel. "But you can file a request as part of an inquiry into his death."

Kornel is already tapping out the request on his ComLink by the time Brandi finishes her thought. "I'm not sure how long it will take to hear back."

"Did you do a DNA scan?" I ask, not hopeful.

"Yes, although it's not SOP where suicide is indicated," Kornel replies without checking his notes. He pauses momentarily, perhaps realizing he might sound insensitive given my relationship with Jason. "Nevertheless," he finally continues, "I anticipated you'd want all the bases covered with this one, especially considering the project you're working. Unfortunately—or perhaps, fortunately—a full DNA scan of the office revealed nothing out of the ordinary. A total of five people were in the office: You, me, and a couple people who stopped by yesterday to see me…and Mr. Plumin, of course. Nobody else."

"And the bottle?" I ask, noticing it again on the table.

"I analyzed a sample, as well the pharma," Kornel replies. "The liquid is some kind of bootleg whiskey, potent stuff and widely available on the black market, as are the pills. The latter are a sleep aid, Lemborexant. It's available from the Med Lab, except this isn't prescription strength, it's an extremely potent, hybrid synthetic. Taken with the alcohol, the effect is, well, exactly what we'd expect."

"So, it was a suicide," says Brandi, running her thumb across Jason's temple and stroking his hair before adding, "Like the others." The action strikes me as disturbing and out of character.

"It would appear so," replies Kornel, not noticing Brandi's odd behavior.

"Why here?" I ask. "In your office. It's not like you were friends. In fact, I'd suggest the opposite."

Kornel looks up at me from his notebook. I can't tell what he's thinking, but his glaring look vaguely reminds me of when I'd ask embarrassing questions of strangers as a child—an attempt to quell an inappropriate pre-adolescent. I glare back, sporting my best eyebrow raise in the hopes of conveying my own confusion. What?

"I'm not sure why he'd come here," Kornel finally responds, turning his head to break eye contact and speak to Brandi. "He scanned in at 20:26 and as near as I can tell was the only person to enter last night. There were no other entries in the logs and there's no physical evidence to suggest anyone else was here."

"So, he came here to commit suicide and that's it."

Kornel is rarely short with me, but this time he doesn't attempt to disguise his impatience. "I'm simply highlighting what the evidence suggests. Entry logs show a single scan, there is no DNA or physical evidence to suggest anyone else was in the office, and he left a note expressing remorse. There is an empty bottle of booze on the table next to a partially empty bag of pharma designed to put someone out for an extended period of time. I'll finish the physical exam when we are done here, including the toxicology and let you know if I come up with anything else—but yes, it does in fact appear he came here to commit suicide."

Brandi seems to note the tension, stepping toward the door. "Well, I don't see how I can be any more use here. Kami, stop by this evening and we can discuss where we're heading and any other concerns." She doesn't linger, adding, "Thanks, Doc," as she heads through the doorway.

"I'm sorry, Kami," Lento says as soon as the door swooshes shut.

"There's no need. I know you're going to do your job. I shouldn't question your competency. What was with the evil eye earlier?" I ask, remembering the glare. "It felt like I'd just mentioned someone's facial goiter and you were attempting to change the subject."

"There's something I wanted to tell you earlier. Mr. Plumin may have had a reason for committing suicide and it might be partially my fault," Kornel says as the door to his office opens behind him.

Two Med Techs, both men—*because ever since Kornel told me about the issues with female births I notice gender more keenly*—both men stand on the other side of the entry waiting to transport Jason to the Med Lab. Their uniforms match ours, neatly pressed, one-piece jumpsuits bearing their last names and Role emblems. One of them, the younger of the two, is carrying a small, rectangular device about the size of a pack of playing cards. The taller, lighter-haired tech announces they are here to transport the body.

"Of course," Kornel confirms, motioning them toward Jason as we both shift to the other side of the room.

They are surprisingly gentle, deploying the gravity gurney from the playing card pack and lifting Jason onto the virtual transport platform in one motion, as if they've had some practice moving suicides. Jason rests on his back, visible for only a few seconds before they activate the electronic body bag. Someone who didn't know they were Med Techs could easily assume they were transporting a large, shimmering, rectangular box, any evidence of a human form hidden beneath the ones and zeros of programmable covers. It's like he's already been erased.

I break the silence as they exit the office, "What do you mean it might be your fault?"

Kornel looks pensive, perhaps a little ashamed as he explains how he inadvertently shared with Jason the information about the DupleX report and station-based births.

"Why would you of all people share that information with Jason? You didn't even like him."

"Now that's not fair," replies Kornel, tilting his head ever so slightly to the right to exaggerate his wounded psyche. I shoot him a look, the one that indicates he's lying to himself, causing him to back pedal. "Okay, perhaps I didn't exactly enjoy the guy's company. But I didn't want him dead, either. And in answer to your question, it was an accident…the way he found out."

"An accident?" I ask.

"Yes. He came to see me on Saturday, angry about something I'd supposedly done to *you*, actually. He figured I needed a solid berating for making you complicit in your father's suicide. He was pretty pissed and chivalrous, if I can use that word to describe anyone these days. I thought you'd shared what I said about our commission offering preferential treatment to females during replacement migrations. I was wrong."

"So you decided to share the biggest secret on the stations with him as what, a consolation prize?" I regret my tone as soon as the words leave my mouth. It's only now I realize Kornel's intent has always been good—good for the stations, the Citizens, and most of all me. He's as much a father as I've ever had and deserves better. The wounded look on his face reminds me I can be as big a jerk as anyone.

"Wait," something in my head clicks into place. "You shared the secret. You told him about the gender disparity."

"Yes," Kornel replies, having recovered from his wound. "He was genuinely surprised, as expected. Speechless, in fact. I made him swear not to tell anyone else, although I have no idea if he did or didn't keep that promise. Either way, he was under a lot of pressure, what with the investigation and knowing the fate of humanity lies in the breakthroughs of a half dozen people."

Something doesn't make sense. If Jason was surprised to hear about the gender issues, he couldn't be part of some Council conspiracy. If he's *not* part of a conspiracy, then why was he involved in making murders look like suicides? And why would Jason confront Kornel on Thursday about my father's death, then try to kill me two days later? During the week he's a swashbuckling, Station Rep boyfriend and on the weekends he's a cold blooded killer, all while balancing his part in a conspiracy to kill men and make it look like suicide. *Yes, I'm convinced they were killed, it's the only thing I'm sure of at this point.* No, if he was part of the conspiracy, he wouldn't have been surprised when Kornel told him about it. And you can't tell me he committed suicide two days later.

"You're sure Jason was surprised when you told him about the birth issues and your team's selection of females?" I ask, making sure I didn't miss anything.

"I'm positive," confirms Kornel. "He was stunned. There is no way Mr. Plumin knew about it before I shared it with him."

I'm convinced Kornel isn't part of killing anyone and making it look like suicide. He may be complicit in covering up bad news and manipulating selections that are supposed to be dictated by the Algorithm, but he's not a killer. I still need to hear it from him.

"I'm going to ask you something and I need you to answer honestly. I'm not judging your decisions or loyalties, but I need to know the truth."

"Ominous, but okay," Kornel replies.

"I'm serious." I pause, considering how best to phrase it to illicit a response without triggering ego-bruised sarcasm. "I understand you're attempting to buy time to correct the gender imbalance by selecting females for migration. Are you also aware of a parallel project designed to reduce the number of males on Aries, making their murders look like suicides?"

The look on Kornel's face, mouth open, head shaking, breathless, tells me he can't believe what I'm asking. His response confirms it. "Are you crazy?"

"Hear me out. What if in addition to replacing male deaths with females from the planet—*your* team's task—there is also a Council-sanctioned effort to remove males from the stations? If replacing men with women for migration has even a small impact, an increase in male deaths would make an even greater impression, buying more time to find a solution."

"Kami, the Council doesn't kill people," Kornel insists. He cannot imagine a Council that would eliminate its enemies, much less random men.

"Just consider it for a moment. I think Jason knew about the suicides and was covering it up—or at least I did, until you told me he was surprised to learn about DupleX report. But either way, even if he didn't know about the issues, there is enough evidence to suggest a number of the suicides in our investigation, especially the male suicides, are not suicides at all, but murders made to look like it. And who has the power and access to not only make murder look like suicide, but alter personal logs and attempt to kill OSU deputy? The Council."

"That is insane!" Kornel charges. "I'm telling you the Council doesn't do things like that. The Council doesn't kill people. They sanction, censure, confine, and deport. But they do not under any circumstances kill. It's a tenet of our founding. No killing."

"Maybe so. But I'm telling you a number of those suicides are murders, including probably Jason's." The word *murder* sends a shiver down my spine causing an involuntary flutter. But that's what they are, cold blooded killings, or in the least, forced suicides, which isn't much of a difference, and not just one, but multiple, across every station.

"I hear what you're saying," replies Kornel, "but it's just not possible. There must be another explanation. The Council may manipulate migrations, but they *do not* kill."

I understand his reluctance to believe the all-powerful, benevolent Council might not be capable of sacrificing some people for the long term good of others. He came from a planet where the politicians practiced the art of deception for more than 250 years with few checks on their corruption. Unfortunately, there isn't another explanation. The Council has to be behind the murder-suicides.

"So what's next?" Kornel asks.

I honestly don't know. I need to find and speak with Jason's Council Clerk contact, Sean. He's the only one who can confirm what Jason knew and when. I'm just not sure how to identify him. It's not like they have a database of Council Clerks floating on the inter webs. Maybe Parker can find out his last name and IP.

"I suppose," I start, looking at Kornel, "I'll have to pull together enough evidence about the Council's role in these suicides to convince you. I mean, once you're convinced, an avid Council defender, I can be confident everyone else will believe me."

Kornel places a firm hand on my shoulder. "I love you, kiddo, and I hope you're wrong. But if not, I'm not sure I can protect you from the Council."

CHAPTER FORTY-EIGHT

Kami

I message Parker on the way back to my HabU to see if he can find a last name for Jason's Council Clerk contact, Sean. I ask him to keep it between us, to which he replies in what might be described as both condescending and sarcastic, "Kami, you know me." I'm sure he will mention the request to Carl Lavoie, our boss. Can't be helped. I need to talk to that Council Clerk.

I've also started recording my notes in a secure log separate from the main server—I'm tapping into it now. If someone can alter my personal log, they might be able to make other changes. I'm not sure which information to trust and which to assume has been modified. It's not protocol and I'm sure Lavoie will say something when he finds out, but what else am I going to do? I can't simply go to Lavoie and claim my logs were changed. Worst case, he'd say I'm nuts, remembering things different, a result of the trauma of almost being killed. Even if he believes me, he'll think it was Ocasio, who isn't talking or can't remember. There's no way he'll allow me to pursue an alternative, namely the Council, given the scant evidence I've collected thus far.

Evidence. Ha. Not so much evidence as deductions. What do I know for sure? I know Dr. Ocasio tried to kill me and can't remember—the Neuro Analyzer confirmed as much—which means someone else was controlling her and wants me dead. Lento is prioritizing female selections for migration. The stations are not sustainable. Then there are theories: The uptick in suicides is unnatural, there's a coordinated effort to eliminate men, the Council may be involved, Jason was into some bad shit.

It's times like these I'm grateful for a self-regulated black market and bootleg vodka. I keep it in a chilled slide-out next to the coffee dispenser—I'd be lying if I said I'd never been tempted to combine the two first thing in the morning. The bottle, full of the clearest liquid imaginable, blemish-free like the reinforced glass surrounding a recreation sphere, begins frosting over as soon as I pull it from its resting place. I pour half a glass, stuff the bottle back in its refrigerated cubby, and take a healthy swallow on my way to the bed I left deployed this morning. The vodka is icy cold and comfortingly warm going down, like a peppermint candy Kornel gave me once as a child only with more of a bite and less cloying sweetness.

Jason. The bed reminds me of him, lying next to me when I couldn't sleep. He met with Sean the afternoon I was poisoned. Brandi confirmed it, he wanted to trade his involvement for leniency. But something about it gnaws at me, a dwarf chipping away at a corner of doubt. What did Brandi say Jason asked? *Would there be a situation where someone in a critical role could protect someone in a less than critical role?* That doesn't sound like someone trying to save the themself. It sounds like someone attempting to save someone else.

I swipe the photos Kornel sent of his office onto a virtual screen hoping to see something, anything to confirm my suspicion that Jason didn't commit suicide. There is one of the entire room, a panorama from the entry showing Kornel's spartan office, Jason slumped over the desk and Kornel's empty chair. The liquor bottle is close to his left hand, but the pills aren't visible from this angle. Jason is facing away from the entry on the side of the desk he'd sit if he were meeting with Kornel. That would require him to reach across the desk for the pencil and notepad. Jason didn't maintain any deference to Kornel—in fact, I didn't get the impression he had much respect for him. Why would he sit on the opposite side of the table unless there was someone already sitting at Kornel's desk?

Speaking of which, Kornel's name is flashing on my ComLink. I take another quick sip of vodka before tapping to display his image and swiping it onto a virtual screen next to the photos. "Hi da..." I catch myself before finishing the word. "Hi Kornel. Do you have something?"

Kornel looks tired, more than I've seen him in quite a while. I'm guessing it has less to do with this case and more to do with worrying about his adopted daughter. "I expedited the lab tests and autopsy... thought you'd want to know of any findings sooner rather than later.

How are you holding up?"

He's still the closest thing to a father I've ever known. Kornel would spend time with us even when my own father was alive, taking us on tours of the various labs and telling us stories about what earth was like before the pandemics. But at this moment, information is more valuable than sympathy.

"I'm fine," I reply. "What did you find?"

"A couple things. First, there was no other DNA in the office or on the bottle. The alcohol would have nullified anything left on the lip of the bottle, or if someone was there, they brought their own glass. Either way, the rest of the room was devoid of DNA, save ours, Jason's and that of a couple people who stopped by the office yesterday— neither of which were in the vicinity at the time of death. There was some DNA on the deceased, namely Brandi's after she touched him and that of another female with whom he likely engaged in sexual intercourse, given the various locations of deposited DNA. The toxicology…"

"Wait," I interrupt. "Sexual intercourse? With who?"

"Uh, well, I thought it was you, actually," Kornel stutters. "Based on your reaction, I guess I'm wrong?"

"Yeah, definitely wrong. I haven't seen Jason since Sunday morning and I know for a fact he showered after, uh." I notice Kornel look away and decide further explanation is unnecessary. "Any ideas about other candidates?"

"Well, it's definitely female. Since I thought it was you, I hadn't planned on running a check against known Cit samples, but I'll add it to the queue. It will take some time to get the results of the database search, but I doubt it will make much of a difference."

"What do you mean?" I ask.

"Well, first of all they would have to apply to be parents or have migrated in the last year in order for Aries to collect their DNA. Privacy First prohibits the station from maintaining DNA profiles for more than 90 days after migration—they're only for initial screening. Plus, unless they had sex in the office before he died, I don't see how who he fornicated with in the hours prior to his death is relevant."

Brandi said Jason might be seeing someone, but she didn't think the rumors were true. I didn't mention it to her, but I assumed Jason was talking about me when he met with Sean. Maybe there was someone else—well, obviously there was someone else. "Let me know when the DNA results are in."

Kornel's digitized image sits motionless for several seconds, as if he's waiting for me to give him the okay to continue. Eventually, he picks up where he left off.

"Right. Well, DNA notwithstanding, there is little doubt he killed himself. The toxicology showed increased levels of modified sleeping pharma, potent stuff. When mixed with the alcohol it caused his respiratory system to shut down. He knew what he was doing. The combination of drugs and booze—also highly enriched—would have impacted his speech and motor functions almost immediately and led to total respiratory failure within minutes."

"So, he wrote the note before he took the pills," I say, mostly to myself.

"Yes," replies Kornel. "He wouldn't have had time to do so otherwise."

"Anything else?"

While Kornel glances down, presumably at the small notebook he uses to keep notes, I scan through the office photos on the other screen. Everything looks normal, except for where Jason is sitting. But that might just be my imagination running a bit wild. Jason's body position on the desk fits with his passing out, the bottle of booze and pills are where we'd expect for a right-handed pill swallower, and the note…

"Did you touch the note before you photographed it?" I ask.

Kornel looks up from his notebook with one of his 'Are you kidding?' expressions, complete with protruding eyebrows, cocked head, and raised corner of the mouth. "No, this is not my first go around the chicken coop." I'm certain I'm supposed to process the folksy expression with a visual, but none comes to mind.

The note sits a few inches beyond Jason's hand toward the other side of the desk, but it's askew as if written by a left-handed person, angled so the bottom edge points toward his right hand. It's possible he pushed it when he laid his head on the table, but Kornel said Jason would have simply fallen asleep rather than pass out suddenly. It's unlikely he would have pushed the paper away then pulled his arms back toward his head. Even if I accept the push the note theory, there is no explanation for the pencil, which is clearly inserted into the rings of the small notebook from left to right, the way a left-handed person might insert it after they finished writing.

I'd like to compare the handwriting, but handwritten documents are extremely rare these days. What did Brandi say? *'Who the fuck leaves a handwritten note?'* I'm about to set it aside as a lost cause when I recall a class Jason taught during my last year of role training. It's hard to believe that was only a year ago. Jason was making the point that while violent crime is non-existent on Aries—as well as every other station—petty crimes still occur, including on occasion the tagging of certain spaces by exuberant teens. He scribbled onto the virtual blackboard a number of phrases he'd seen electrostatically painted onto various surfaces. I know I still have the record in my archives and do a quick search, finding it attached to the topic, 'Common Crimes' in the folder hierarchy. I swipe Jason's scribblings next to the photo of the note, which is next to Kornel's still talking face.

"Why are you asking if I moved the note?" he asks.

I ignore the question. The handwriting on the suicide note doesn't match the phrases Jason jotted down just over a year ago. The records from the virtual blackboard show a clear right-slant to the letters and words on the screen, as if they are leaning into a heavy wind. The words are choppy, peppered with starts and stops, breaks in the middle between letters, as if someone with little cursive practice strung together individual letters in a failed attempt at the style. In contrast, the suicide note has no lean whatsoever, its uniform letters stand tall, fluidly flowing from one to the next. It was written by someone with some experience in cursive.

"How many people on Aries write in cursive?" I ask.

"I'm sure a lot of people learned cursive..." Kornel replies. "All the migrant adults, for example, and everyone who came aboard during IPI. But I doubt anyone still uses it—other than old doctors."

Migrant adults. Someone schooled on the planet and migrated as an adult.

"What?" I ask, having missed what Kornel just said.

"I said I received the information from the records request."

I'm quite certain I have no idea what he's talking about and say as much.

"The one about Mr. Plumin's earlier attempted suicide."

"Right," I recall. Brandi mentioned that Jason attempted suicide several years ago.

"The rumors of his depression were quite possibly exaggerated. He wasn't randomly flagged by the algorithm based on a reported concern about antisocial behavior. Apparently a friend called in a wellness check as a practical joke during some major gaming event. Once the 'concern' was logged, the algorithm reviewed his metadata and assigned a WelSpec to visit Mr. Plumin. The caller later confessed to making the report in an attempt to get Mr. Plumin to..." Kornel glances down at his notepad, flipping a couple pages up. "An attempt to get him to 'blow a mission on Saturn.' It was some kind of competition…"

"Do you know who called in the wellness check?" I interrupt.

Kornel flips a few more pages in his notebook before answering. "Someone named Sean."

Sean. "Is there a last name?"

"Not in the report," Kornel replies. "And it's doubtful the name would have been released to Mr. Plumin, either. As far as he was concerned, it would have appeared to be a standard wellness check."

I'm about to ask Kornel if he can do some digging and try to find a last name for Sean when I'm pinged by someone at my door. Brandi's image appears on the screen.

"Hey, can I message you back? Someone's here."

"Sure," answers Kornel. "Do you want to stop by later? Bhavna would love to see you and your brother. I'm happy to coordinate with…"

"Yeah, I'd love to," I respond before he can finish. I actually wouldn't love to, but I can manufacture an excuse later. Something involving work usually does the trick.

"Okay, we'll…"

These are the last words I hear when I shut down the video feed. I grab the nearly empty tumbler of vodka from the table beside the bed and head for the door, leaving the window with the scene photos active.

CHAPTER FORTY-NINE

Kami

"Good timing," I say as the door swishes open. "I have something to show you." I walk over to the bed and press the button to stow it, tables and chairs replacing whatever memories it's collected over the last few days. The dinette, although less comfortable, won't be as awkward as reviewing evidence with Brandi while propped up against two pillows on sheets I'd shared with Jason a few days ago.

"Kami, before we get started, do you have another one of those?" Brandi asks, nodding toward the vodka.

"Of course, over there next to the coffee dispenser. It's a slide out." I extend my hand with the half empty vodka glass, a subtle hint for a refill. "There are a few inconsistencies in Jason's suicide, if that's what it was."

Brandi walks through the virtual screen of suicide scene photos, causing the pixels to popcorn into millions of ball bearing-sized dots that almost immediately re-coalesce into a photo of Jason slumped over the desk, the note he drafted visible toward the top of the image. Brandi takes a seat across from me, sliding the ice cold vodka in my direction.

"Cheers," she says, holding her glass in the air before downing the vodka in one shot. "Mmm. That's good. You're going to have to share your supplier."

I lift my glass, then set it back down. I'm not in the mood to celebrate anything just yet.

"Look here. See the note?" I tap on my ComLink to zoom in on the suicide note, rotating it in the process so it's upright. "This is the note Jason is supposed to have left."

I tap out a few more commands and swipe the virtual blackboard records up next to the note. "This is a series of notes Jason wrote during a lecture a little over a year ago. See the difference? The suicide note is all wrong, it's fluid, flowing, and there is a definite slant to the letters—it was clearly written by someone who learned cursive as a child, someone who grew up on the surface. And look at this…"

A few more swipes stows the blackboard images and changes the zoom on the photo of Jason in Kornel's office, making the entire scene visible. "The notebook is on the left side of his body and the pencil is inserted from the left, like a left-handed person would do. And look at the body. He's on the side of the desk someone would sit if they were meeting with Kornel—or if someone else was already sitting in Kornel's seat."

"So you think someone else wrote the note?" Brandi asks, her tone betraying her disbelief.

"I think someone killed him, wrote the note and staged it to look like a suicide. Perhaps someone else involved in the conspiracy who felt Jason was a liability."

"That's insane," replies Brandi. "There are plausible explanations for everything you've shown me. Jason could have been jotting things on the virtual blackboard in a hurry, but wasn't rushed in writing his last words. Remember, he did spend almost ten years on the planet, over half of which would have included time in primary education practicing cursive. And who knows why he sat with his back to the door instead of in Lento's seat. Maybe he didn't want the message to be misinterpreted. He did write the note *to* Dr. Lento—perhaps sitting on the opposite side of the desk was his way of psychologically putting Lento across from him. And let's not forget he was committing suicide. The last thing he'd be concerned about is where the notebook and pencil ended up when he laid his head on the table." Brandi pauses for a long second before adding, "Oh, and he has a history, remember? He apparently attempted this once before."

"Kornel's records request was honored. Jason never tried to commit suicide. It was all some kind of practical joke."

"A joke?" Brandi's eyebrows raise and she shakes her head as she processes this new information. "Well, either way, there's never actually been a violent crime, much less a murder on any station. I can't believe this is the first."

"Until Ocasio tried to kill me." I take a healthy swig of vodka before launching into this next part. "And I don't think Jason is the first."

I lay out everything I know for Brandi, including the Kornel's reveal about the DupleX report and the current gender disparity which is only going to get worse, and that Jason knew about both. I describe the project Neil Palau was working, the one Jason didn't tell us about, and my theory about its connection to the birth issues. Whoever deleted Ocasio's letter about her son from the official logs and altered my records had high level access, Council-level access. Then there are the past studies which prove men and women commit suicide at roughly the same rate and the increase in suicides year-over-year for the last few years. I remind her what she told me about Jason and his Clerk friend, his question about trading information to protect someone, which appears to me to be an attempt to protect someone else.

"I thought both Jason and Kornel were in on it," I say, "and in a way, they are—but I doubt either of them kill someone, even to save humanity." I hesitate, deciding whether to share this next part. It puts Kornel at risk, but I don't see any other way to add credibility to the argument. "The Council," I start, "is already taking steps to mitigate the gender disparities by giving priority to female selections during migration. Kornel told me as much. The next logical step is to eliminate men, allowing for more female selections than the normal replacement process allows. All of this is designed to buy time to develop a solution. The problem is a solution might be years away and even if they *only* select females for migration, it's not enough to stem the inevitable shift to a primarily male population. The Council needs to reduce the number of males on board—they *need* to kill men." Pausing for a moment to give Brandi time to digest the information, I raise my glass. "Cheers and welcome to the conspiracy," I say, taking another sizable swig. It stopped burning my throat—usually a sign I've had enough.

Brandi sits silently staring at the screen. It's a lot to process.

"The only thing I can't figure out," I add, "is Deputy Finn. He's male, but other than that his death just doesn't make sense. All of the other men—except Jason of course—had a conviction on their record, a violation in their past. Finn was a deputy."

"Kami, how are you?" Brandi asks.

It's an odd, out of the blue question, but now that I think about it, I do feel a bit off. Not like when Ocasio poisoned me, not sick, exactly, but calm. "I'm good," I respond tentatively, because despite the brain dump of evidence and hypotheses, the implications of a Council conspiracy to kill males and make it look like suicides, I do feel surprisingly…well.

"Glad to hear it," Brandi replies. "I'm surprised it took as long as it did. Both times I dosed. Ocasio with Benzos her reaction was much quicker. I'm guessing it took you longer because I had to dissolve the pill in the vodka, then wait for you to drink it. Perhaps the alcohol has an effect on the reaction time. I'll have to remember that…for the future. Of course it doesn't help that you drink like a girl, sipping away bit by bit. Who drinks like that? For fucks sake, just shoot that bitch already.

I reach for the glass with what remains of the vodka. I'm not sure why. It's not that I don't want it—in fact, it's just the opposite. I want to down the rest of it. Only I didn't know I wanted it until Brandi suggested it. I realize as I swallow the remaining vodka that it's me and not me at the same time.

On cue, Brandi asks, "What does it feel like? Doing things because you want to but knowing it's not really your desire being acted out? Your body and mind are simply reacting to what I tell you."

"It feels oddly calming and extremely disturbing at the same time," I say in response.

"The cool thing is you don't just react to verbal cues. Remember when I touched your hand in the Med Lab?" Brandi asks.

"No," I reply, because I honestly don't remember.

"Well, it doesn't really matter. I was hoping to make a connection, but apparently it was lost on you. My point is I can get a reaction to my actions." Brandi stands and leans across the dinette, moving in closer than I'd normally be comfortable. The first thing I notice is her hot, humid breath on my lower lip. It's warm and inviting and I find myself involuntarily leaning in. I open my mouth, feeling for her lips with my tongue, hovering for a brief moment while I search, my inhale matched to her exhale. I can't stop myself—I don't want to stop myself as her tongue finds mine and we dance for a moment in silence. My heart is still racing when she pulls away, leaving me with a fleeting feeling of wanting that dissipates as quickly as it built.

Brandi sits back, looking at me in silence.

"Yeah," she finally sighs. "Unfortunately, I've never actually tried Benzos myself. Not that I need them. But it might be fun to simply react to someone's touch, to lose control and along with it any baggage keeping me from enjoying the moment. Is it scary or confusing? Do you feel anything?" she asks.

"It's not scary," I reply. "It's exciting and erotic." I can't believe I'm telling her these things. The responses are involuntary. It's not that I have to answer, I *want* to answer. Brandi confirms my unspoken hypothesis.

"Truth and desire are part of the Benzo package. You can't help but answer because you *desire* to answer, and when you speak you can't help but tell the truth. It's a quality I wish people had without the drug."

Brandi's legs are touching mine beneath the table, the top side of her Aries-issue canvas sneaker gently stroking my right calf. It's like this is fun for her, some kind of game. She's reveling in the control.

"Unfortunately, I have to kill you."

"Unfortunately?" I ask.

"Indeed. Personally, I'd prefer to let you live. You're somewhat attractive, if not naively exhausting, and your termination hasn't been sanctioned by the Collective. There is an over-arching rule—well, more of an understanding, really—we don't kill women. There are exceptions, of course, but they are few and generally require explicit permission, which I did not get in your case. None of this would be necessary if you hadn't figured out a lot more than I gave you credit for, or if Ocasio had done a better job—that would have eliminated two loose ends. You didn't drink all the tea, did you?"

"No," I respond, remembering what was left in the cup. "I don't like tea."

"That was a miscalculation on my part. I assumed everyone of Asian descent enjoyed tea. I'll need to revisit my biases. Although I think Ocasio's incompetence might also have had something to do with it. She's not used to killing people and she didn't know what she was doing at the time. I'm the one who suggested adding the Procurium to the tea to enhance the flavor. She initially mentioned the potential downsides, namely death, but she was on Benzos at the time and happy to comply. I should have had her add it to her tea, too. But I couldn't take the chance she might succumb before finishing with you.

"Speaking of which, did you see the photos and videos? That woman is a total freak, even by my standards. I'm pretty sure if I hadn't killed Neil Palau, he eventually would have done it himself. He was a hot mess by the time I caught up with him—not sleeping, overwhelmed with anxiety about his little self-assigned project. In the end he couldn't even fuck is wife because of what Ocasio was doing to him. It was more of a mercy killing than anything."

Brandi takes a deep breath, as if waiting for me to ask a question, then asks it herself, "I suppose you're wondering who else is involved?"

"Yes," I respond, adding, "Jason and Kornel, for example?"

Brandi laughs out loud, leaning back in the seat and tilting her head toward the ceiling in what seems fake but sounds ominously genuine. She's enjoying this.

"Well, Kornel is involved. His team is one of many on the stations selecting women over men for migration. But he has no idea about the work going on behind the scenes. Dr. Lento is part of the *Council's* plan to buy time, as insufficient as it is. Your theory depends on the Council killing people. If the Council writ large was aware of what Plumin or Palau or anyone else knew, they wouldn't kill them. They don't have the backbone for those decisions. They'd either bring them into the loop, sequester them somewhere, or deport them. The Council doesn't kill people. Thankfully, there is at least one person on the Council with foresight, wisdom and the guts to do what it takes to beat back the inevitable. It's that Council member who formed the Collective many years ago and set forth our charter: eliminate males to exponentially increase the value of modified recruiting and make a difference in the gender balance."

"You don't know who it is," I comment.

"No, I don't," she responds, her tone changing to one of anger. "In fact, I don't even know how many it is. It might be one person or half the Council. I know not everyone is involved or there'd be no need for all the secrecy. Perhaps the rest of the Council will get on board someday. Maybe they'll vote to enact a lottery, males entered and the winners removed from society at a rate to keep pace with the birth disparities. But until then we'll keep doing our job, unsung heroes in the fight to save humanity."

"Jason?" I ask.

"Oh, right, Jason Plumin." Her calm enjoyment has returned. "You know I've known him since I migrated, right? We've never fucked—he's not my type, as you well know by now. But I did like him. I also would have been happy to kill him, but I didn't, which is why I suspect he actually did commit suicide, despite your overwhelming evidence."

So, Brandi was not the one he had sex with prior to his death. There's someone else.

"I suppose there could be others on board Aries doing what I'm doing, but it's unlikely. I've reviewed the data and if there were others the numbers would be much higher. The Collective generally doesn't overlap and even if they did, we wouldn't know it. Anonymity is what powers the organization. If someone does fuck up, they can't dime out the rest of us."

Brandi pauses briefly to retrieve the chilled vodka from its hiding place. Despite willing my hand to reach across the table, it does not move. I'm hyper-focused, each finger viewed through a telescope. Nothing happens until I'm jolted back by the clink of bottle on glass chiming like the sound of a bell tolling for the dead.

"Besides, why would anyone kill Jason? He didn't really know anything, save for what Lento told him. Jason didn't suspect a conspiracy, like you do. He believed the suicides were a normal part of station life. I had no idea he knew about the DupleX report until you told me, and I doubt he knew about it until Lento confessed. The report *Jason* agreed to send to the Council indicates the increase in suicides is the normal effect of prolonged station habitation by people unable to cope with the psychological rigors. There was no reason for me to kill him.

"No, Jason was not involved and had no idea about the Collective. In fact, I think he was in love with you. He wanted to protect you from blowback should someone find out all you know. He said he would to discuss it with Lento, hoping to mend things with you. It's sad, really."

I watch as Brandi tops up two-finger pours into each of our glasses.

"As nice a guy as he was and as much as I genuinely liked him, I can't say I'm sad he's gone. Your death might have put him on a path to discovery, resulting in tough decisions—leave him be and risk exposure or kill him and invite additional focus on suicides. This way your suicide makes more sense. A girl who suffered the recent loss of her lover and has a family history of suicide takes her own life out of overwhelming grief."

Brandi tips the glass and downs the vodka in a single swallow, tacking it to the table with what seems like exaggerated force. My glass remains untouched. I'm not interested in drinking it.

"By the way, there's a reason the Finn death doesn't fit with the others, and it's not because Deputy Michael Finn was an accident. I killed him. There wasn't any particular reason, other than he was a fat, pompous ass bag who enjoyed bullying people into doing whatever he wanted...and because it was rather poetic. In my three years onboard I'd seen him throw his authority around like he was an untouchable Council member. He enjoyed catching people in mistakes and shitting on anyone he didn't like. He'd spent the last months bragging about retirement and all the things he wasn't going to do, a plan he called, 'Sponge Time', because he intended to sponge off station resources for the next twenty years. Most of the suicides I enabled were for the Collective. Don't get me wrong, I enjoyed them all the same, but Finn was personal. An unsanctioned disposal. A masterful means of supplementing Derek Ocasio's removal that saved an unimaginable amount of Aries resources and provided access to Dr. Ocasio's Benzos. The execution was artful, yielding rewards you are only now experiencing."

"You want that?" Brandi asks motioning toward the glass of vodka sitting in front of me.

"No," I respond.

"Yes, in fact you do. Drink up."

I pull the glass toward my mouth for a sip, but stop when Brandi comments, "Not like that. Drink it like an adult. Do the shot."

A brief instant passes when I'm aware of a wish to put the glass down. It's fleeting, quickly replaced by a contradictory, compelling desire to drink. I up end the glass, bursting into a coughing fit as the burning liquid slides down my throat.

"You're such a girl," Brandi comments. "That's why you have to commit suicide; although, if I'm being honest, I also don't want you around. I could bring you on board, make you part of the Collective— at least, I think I can do that. I mean, if someone can handle me why can't I handle a subcontractor? But the truth is I'm a solo actor, a lone wolf hunting weaker prey and making the herd stronger. Plus, I just don't want to share the glory.

"Do you know why the Council allows suicides? They don't care about our investigation, not really. They're hoping we find no link between suicides and anything preventable. Suicides are a necessary part of the cycle, an opportunity to ensure genetic variability. They don't care if half the station commits suicide, as long as they can replace them with people from the surface. People with a diverse genetic makeup. People uncompromised by the rigors of space, strengthened by planet life. People like me. So sure, I could probably recruit you into our exclusive club, our Collective, but I'd be tainting the gene pool with your Gen ideals and sensitivities, your self-righteous judgments grounded in nothing more than sandy entitlement. Only migrants can make these decisions. We have the character to do what's needed when others falter, an unwavering commitment to remove the lives necessary for the greater good, and nobody is better at it than me."

The more Brandi speaks the more I realize the inevitable truth—not that I'm going to die, which does seem to be inevitable at this point—but that Brandi is without a doubt absolutely fucking nuts. I wish I'd recognized it earlier, before I let her in and offered her a drink. I mean, who shoots vodka anymore? She's so obviously crazy it's impressive she's been able to keep it under wraps for as long as she has. Present circumstances being what they are, given the choice between dying and having to listen to anymore of her crap, I'll take the former.

"I know what you're thinking," Brandi continues. "You're thinking there must be a way out of this. There must be an alternative to suicide…"

Nope, not what I was thinking.

"…Well, you're wrong. I've considered the options, the impact on the Collective and our goals, and of course my personal preference, which, when you think about it, is all that matters. There is no other way. And I'm bored with this conversation."

CHAPTER FIFTY

Kami

"Well, let's get this over…"

Brandi is about to tell me to do something I'll accept as my own idea when there's a knock on the door. It's a welcome alternative to whatever suggestion she was going to make. She doesn't finish her thought. Rather, she looks toward the door without speaking. I can't move, or I'd answer it. Someone is better than no one at this point.

"Should I answer that?" Brandi asks after a second, longer but still soft knock.

"Yes," I say without hesitation.

"Yeah, I thought you'd say that. Why don't we see who it is first? Call up the door cam on your ComLink."

I tap the screen of my ComLink and swipe to put the image flat against the wall. It's a woman in her mid to late forties with the reddest hair I've ever seen. It's short, cut above the collar, and messy in a way that looks planned. She's not nervously glancing up and down the corridor, or attempting to hide from the camera, she's just standing there, calmly waiting for someone to answer. I don't recognize her, but I think Brandi does.

"What is she doing here? Were you expecting a visitor?"

"No. I don't know her," I answer, as if I've been programmed with a specific set of responses.

"Well, I suppose we'll let her in. You'll behave. We're just two girls drowning the recent loss of a friend in some vodka. You'll answer any question she asks without giving her reason to believe you're in jeopardy, even if you have to lie. Do you understand?"

"Yes," I respond.

Brandi glances back to remind me to close the cam viewer as she heads toward the door. I can't see them from this angle, but I can hear their voices as Brandi greets the woman with the fiery red hair.

"Ms. Ryan, now is not the best time. We were just…"

Ms. Ryan seems to ignore Brandi, stepping into my HabU and walking to where I'm seated before Brandi can finish her thought.

"Yes, yes I know," she says, her petite frame and emerald eyes looking down at me. "What did you give her?"

"I don't know what you mean?" replies Brandi, returning to stand behind the seat she previously occupied across the dinette. I can't tell if the look on her face is one of confusion or shock, possibly a little of both. She obviously wasn't expecting anyone else to join us. On the other hand, I'm happy for the additional company if it keeps me from committing suicide.

"Don't play coy," Ms. Ryan chastises. "Did you think you were alone on Aries?"

Ms. Ryan stands at the head of the table, but her small stature—I'd guess she's no more than 5-feet 2-inches tall—prevents her from towering above either of us. Brandi is only a couple inches taller, but has about 20 pounds of solid muscle on the demur Ms. Ryan. Should this turn into a brawl, I have no doubt Brandi will destroy her.

"I'm here to stop you from making another huge mistake," barks Ryan.

"Listen, Judge…," Brandi starts, her voice peppered with confusion.

It finally clicks, she's Cecelia Ryan. She's well known on Aries, one of the original judges to migrate late during Initial Population Integration. I haven't met her, but the deputies at the OSU have no problem discussing her qualifications at every opportunity.

"Don't *Judge* me. You're lucky I haven't informed the Collective about your recent adventures into idiocy. Killing a Sheriff's Deputy in a charged field array. What the fuck?"

"He was an asshole," Brandi shoots back, defiantly.

"Because he called you mean names and didn't let you play in his sandbox? It was an emotional response followed by an unsanctioned disposal that threatened to draw attention to the Collective. Then you drugged a Psyche in order to kill Lee here—setting up the first attempted murder in station history—*and* you altered her logs to cover up what she knew. Also unsanctioned, I might add. Only she didn't die, did she? It was only a matter of time before she figured out her records were changed and there's literally a handful of people with that kind of access, all of whom are on the Council. Then there's the female you suicided last year without approval. Now what, you're going to kill this one and make it look like a suicide? Do you really think people are going to believe an OSU Deputy who was recently the victim in an attempted murder would then turn around and commit suicide a few days later? Now *that* won't draw any unnecessary attention."

Brandi's silence betrays her intimidation. The rise and fall of her chest beneath her uniform has slowed and deepened. She's exerting effort to keep it under control. Her jaw muscles are twitching almost imperceptibly, and her lips are pressed together so tight you'd have trouble slipping a piece of paper from Kornel's notebook between them. Her face has become a poster for shock and awe. She's afraid of the Judge.

"Now sit down. We're going to need to rethink this," Ryan adds.

Brandi seems compliant, but the look on her face says she hasn't fully resigned her authority to Ryan. I'd guess she's holding it together long enough to figure out how to deal with this new problem. It sounds like Brandi's been straying off the reservation. All of which I assess as she retakes her seat across from me.

"Sweetheart, be a dear and add a seat to the dinette, please," says Ryan.

I tap my ComLink and access the HabU controls causing a stool to extend from the floor where Ryan was standing a half-second earlier. She sits down between the two of us, a powerful woman in a child-sized body taming a lunatic.

"Who are you, exactly?" Brandi asks as Ryan pours a shot of vodka into Brandi's glass.

The Judge takes a sip before answering, "I'm you before there was a you."

"That's not possible. I migrated because someone was eliminated. I was recruited almost immediately..."

"Yes, yes by someone you haven't seen since," Ryan interrupts, again, forcing Brandi's eyes to form an annoyed squint—she really doesn't like being shut down. "The Collective has been around since the beginning, since IPI. We understood the Council's pacifist, quixotic attitude would prevent it from taking radical steps to solve equally radical problems. Even before the DupleX report, we recognized the need for a sub-Council. The Collective was born of a recognition that the Council was incapable of dealing with the things that destroy life—

the truly scary stuff—and we've been doing that for the last quarter of a century. Those rumors you hear about the Council deporting people to the Open Lands or the CAZ in order to shut them up, or destroy media narratives with alternate facts, or influence station leadership to limit travel, it's all bullshit. The Council doesn't have the backbone to do any of that, which is where the Collective steps up. The Council may be unwilling to kill people to save humanity, but the Collective will always do what's necessary."

This woman is at least as screwed up as Brandi, who at this point seems as confused as I am. If I can't believe what I'm hearing, I'm even more stunned by Brandi's silence. I have a reason, I'm half drugged up, but this is a new reaction from Brandi. I keep expecting her to haul off and clock Ryan, but she just sits there, stone faced.

"Seriously, did you think you were the first Collective asset to be placed on Aries?" Ryan continues. "We've known about the problems with female births and the resulting male over-population for over a decade. It was the Collective who decided more was needed to stave off disaster until a solution could be found. Someone had to come before you. Who do you suppose that might have been?"

I'm not sure Brandi's ever considered the possibility that someone actually came before her, or that this Collective was formed long before there were any problems. She knew she had predecessors, but I get the feeling she thought she was the first to be doing the Collective's killing on Aries. In her mind anyone before her was not good enough.

"You? *You* were *me*?" Brandi finally replies, stunned by the revelation but maintaining a defiant tone.

"Yes, me," Ryan snaps back, sounding more like a scolding parent. "And your impulsive, lone wolf reactions are threatening to undo everything we've accomplished. If it weren't for you, Plumin would still be alive."

I'm struck by the confirmation. I suspected Jason didn't commit suicide, but the wave of remorse washing over me serves as a not so delicate reminder that I was wrong about him. Knowing he died because of Brandi makes it especially painful.

"*You* killed Plumin?" Brandi asks.

"Yes, I killed him. He was getting too close. He confided in me Sunday night about his contact with a Council Clerk and his conversation with Dr. Lento. He was torn up over his relationship with Ms. Lee. He also mentioned how you'd been toying with her, encouraging her suspicions about him. It's all a big game to you, isn't it?"

"It's not a game!" Brandi bristles. "Just because I like to play with my food doesn't mean I don't take the mission seriously."

"Well," Ryan snaps back, "Jason was going to figure it out sooner or later. It was only a matter of time before he and Ms. Lee realized they were actually on the same side and compared notes. I shared what he told me with the Collective, so it was no surprise when the order came through. Now he's dead, all because you like to *play with your fucking food*."

"Oh, I'm sorry dear," says Ryan, turning toward me. "That was insensitive of me. I know you two were sleeping together. Nobody knows better than I what it means to lose Jason. He was an amazing lover, someone whose company I truly enjoyed. I'm going to miss him. I can only imagine how you must feel given the intensity of your brief relationship."

"You and Plumin?" Brandi asks incredulously.

"Yes, me. Although I imagine you already suspected as much after you accessed Jason's call logs on Saturday." Ryan says it so casually, Brandi is momentarily caught off guard.

"How…" Brandi starts.

"Because my status within the Collective is greater than yours. But none of that matters now. It's time we figure out what to do about our little problem."

Ryan looks toward me, placing a hand on mine on the table.

"I told you, I've got that one figured out," Brandi exclaims, angry at being cut off again.

"Oh, not that problem. I'm talking about you," Ryan says in a flat, emotionless tone while turning back toward Brandi.

Brandi's eyes widen as if she's seeing the sunrise for the first time. She knows what Ryan means, her face changing from shock to fiery rage. Brandi starts to stand, pushing out from the table where she's wedged between the seat and the underside of the dinette. She's trapped, something that takes another second for her to figure out. There's a momentary flash in her eyes, an epiphanic resolution, but it's an instant too late.

Ryan, still holding my left hand in her right, whips her other arm around like a snake striking prey. I've never seen anyone move so fast and least of all a woman of her age. The needle penetrates into Brandi's neck, catching her mid-attack. The sting forces her to jerk away, banging her head against the wall. She regains her balance, slamming both palms against her seat and pushing toward Ryan before realizing she's lost control of her motor functions. I can't tell if the drug is fast acting or was simply injected directly into the bloodstream, but the effect is almost instantaneous. Brandi's head lay on the table a second later.

CHAPTER FIFTY-ONE

Kami

"Kami, I'm going to give you something to counteract the Benzos. We could wait until they wash out of your system in another hour or so, but we just don't have that kind of time." Ryan's voice is steady and eerily soothing, right up until she adds, "If you do anything stupid, I *will* kill you."

She pulls a small syringe from a pocket within her uniform, flicks the vial a couple times and delicately slides it into the side of my neck. It's so subtle as to be barely noticeable. There's also no immediate reaction, no shock to my system to indicate I've regained free will. It's a non-event, one which I wouldn't even be aware if Ryan didn't ask how I was feeling.

"Pissed…and grateful," I answer without the placid vexation that accompanied my previous replies. "You killed Jason," I add. It's the first thing I can think to say.

"Yes."

"Why?" I know what she told Brandi, but I want to hear her answer now that Brandi's gone.

"I tried to help you—tried putting you on the right path. But you didn't want to believe someone on your team could be compromised. Then when you finally accepted the possibility, you focused on the wrong person—Jason. I warned you Mikkelson was a concern. All you had to do was your job."

"It was you," I reply, struck by how stupid I am. "You're the robot voice."

Ryan takes a deep breath before answering, exhaling with enough force as to form ripples in her glass of vodka. "Yes. But I didn't count on Ms. Mikkelson being so impetuous or having Benzos. In retrospect, I probably should have stepped in earlier. But these things take time to coordinate—one doesn't just kill a female on the stations without approval from the Collective."

I'm sitting here, hearing everything she's saying, replaying our conversations and I still can't believe it. It was all a lie. Brandi manipulated every step. She killed all those men. Except Jason— Cecelia Ryan killed Jason.

"Why? Why Jason?"

"As I said, he was getting too close. He wasn't involved until Lento confided in him about the migration selections. Even then he didn't understand the connections to the suicides. He believed his friend, Sean, when he told him the two were unrelated. Left alone, I think I could have swayed him, but you and Brandi just wouldn't drop it. She kept pushing your buttons in some perverse game of cat and mouse, and you continued to cycle between believing Jason was involved and wondering if he was just an unwitting pawn. Eventually, you and he would have made up and started discussing the suicides. You would have figured out there was more going on than a simple attempt to buy time. You might not have identified the Collective, but I'm sure you would have reached out to Jason's Clerk contact, which would have made its way back to the Council. Things might have become uncomfortable for those Council members who support the Collective's efforts." Ryan pauses for a moment, a subtle smile betraying a fond memory. "I apologize. I know you were in love with him. So was I. You can't spend as much time with someone in and out of bed as Jason and I and not love them. If it helps, it was one of the most difficult things I've ever had to do."

"It doesn't help and I wasn't in love with him any more than you were." I'm doing my best to maintain the same level of dispassionate control I see in Ryan, but it's not easy. It's true, Jason meant a lot to me, even when I thought he might be part of a conspiracy, but to call it love is a stretch. It had only been a few days and a couple nights—good nights, but not earth shattering enough to make me believe he was the one. I'm pissed because he was killed, because of me and Brandi. He had no idea what he was in the middle of, he just wanted to set things straight with me. If I had been a little less gullible, a bit more aware, I would have seen the way Brandi played me and could have confided in Jason from the beginning. He's dead because I didn't love him, not because I did.

"Well, none of that matters now," Ryan replies, cold and dispassionate. "We still have two problems."

"I suppose I'm one of those."

"Here's the issue. I can't let you walk into the corridor, down the hall to the OSU office, and report what you know. There's a reason the Council doesn't want this information in the public domain. If people found out, there would be chaos. The Council may lack the fortitude required to make tough decisions, but they are generally on the mark when it comes to understanding social dynamics. If I allow you to leave, it will mean an end to everything we've accomplished so far—everything we've done to buy time."

"And the other problem?" I ask.

"I need to replace Brandi."

This is the first time I've taken notice of Brandi since her head smacked the dinette. I was so caught up with regaining control and Ryan's explanations, it didn't occur to me to check to see if Brandi is dead. Part of me presumed she was and given Ryan is now talking about replacing her, I suppose I'm correct.

"Not that Brandi will be easy to replace," Ryan continues. "She was extremely good in her role."

"We're not talking about her role as a PersRep, are we?" I ask.

"No, although she wasn't bad at that one either. I'm talking about her role within the Collective. Brandi excelled at solving problems, particularly problems involving people who needed to be sacrificed for the rest of humanity. But she could also be impulsive, prone to making decisions without considering the consequences, taking action to correct problems which didn't require a solution. She enjoyed the process a little too much. We would have called her 'flawed' back in the day."

"We just call her insane, now," I comment.

"It's all semantics and quite frankly, irrelevant. What *is* relevant is the Collective is down one operative and I believe you'd make a solid addition to the team."

"Why would I consider joining your little club, other than the inevitable fact that you're going to kill me, ."

"Funny you should use the word *inevitable*. Because you know what else is inevitable? The end of humankind. The DupleX problem is significant and simply replacing naturally occurring accidents and suicides with female migrants isn't going to work. There just isn't enough volume to hold back the tidal wave of testosterone building aboard the stations. It's not a choice between doing nothing and doing something, because even the something we're doing will result in the stations becoming unsustainable. We have to do more—the Collective has to do more."

"I get it," I reply. "Kornel…Dr. Lento explained the issue. We need to migrate females in order to maintain the population balance."

"That's not enough," Ryan corrects. "Lento only knows what the Council told him, which is only enough to guarantee his complicity and keep him silent. When we discovered the disparities over a decade ago, we assumed we'd have plenty of time. There wasn't much data, but what there was suggested the radiation did not affect all women— viable breeding stock remained. It didn't take long to figure out the problem wasn't limited to only a few women—all females are affected. The radiation rapidly changes DNA at a molecular level, causing an inability to produce female children. We aid the process by bringing women aboard and the Collective reduces the number of males, but unless the migrants are pregnant when they arrive or conceive within a few weeks, neither of which guarantees a female child, they are little more than stones to balance the gender scales. Without the Collective there won't be enough time to find a solution."

"That sounds like a justification to me," I say and mean it. "You want a reason to kill people and you've got one. It doesn't make it right. Those men have families, people who care about them. I'm sure given the option, they'd choose to relocate to one of the CAZ rather than die aboard Aries, Gemini, or any other station."

"Where they and their families can die a slower death? It's not a choice anyone wants to make, but it has to be done. We need to maintain a male-female balance in order to keep this from becoming uncorrectable. What we are doing today isn't enough, we need to do more."

"You mean kill more."

Ryan disapproves of my answer, shaking her head. "It's not like we're killing the most upstanding members of our society. These people have problems, they've committed offenses and in some cases they've skirted responsibility for their actions because of connections they have on the Council and elsewhere. We are removing people the Council should have removed had they any balls. It says something when a woman who gets pregnant without the requisite authorization can be deported but a peeping Tom pedophile like Birmingham is allowed to travel from station to station untethered, taking advantage of his position to coerce young men into doing vile things."

"And Jason? What was his crime?" I ask, painting the question with a sarcastic lilt.

"Collateral damage," Ryan replies without hesitation. "He was an unfortunate victim of Brandi's hubris. He and the others Brandi manipulated—Ocasio and the OSU deputy, Finn—they were anomalies caused by an unstable recruit. A situation which has been corrected."

"And me? Am I another anomaly?"

"No, you're an opportunity," Ryan quips. "You can make sure that only the right people pay for our survival. You have a chance to be part of something bigger, a Collective with a single goal: save humanity. You can call the shots, choose the sacrifices, implement corrections, and make a difference. You'll be one of the unsung heroes of our time, honored in death for being bold when others cowered."

"And if I refuse?" I ask, convinced there is an as yet unmentioned plan behind Ryan's lunacy.

Ryan is silent for a moment, perhaps trying to decide if I'm a lost cause. "There's something I want to show you." She taps her ComLink, then swipes the result into the air over Brandi's lifeless body.

It takes a minute to deconstruct the pixelated image. It's a person, someone sitting against a wall, a male with his head in his hands. The room is dark, a handrail mounted a foot above the man's head, the walls lit only by the various panels on its face. There's a small screen on an adjacent wall next to a door with a square window the size of two hands placed side-by-side. It's not until the man lifts his head toward the camera and the ambient red light drives the shadows from his face that I recognize him.

"Where is my brother?"

Ryan reaches toward the image and makes a motion, zooming in on Christopher's face. "He's safe. He thinks he was picked up for his drug hobby. It's not serious enough to get him deported, but will definitely result in a long stint in group, which is probably why he looks so dejected. It's hard to remain high in group."

"He *thinks* he's been detained?"

"Two of my associates escorted him to the airlock you see here hoping to inform him it was all a huge mistake. The Collective may be exclusive, but it is not small. We have women on every station, some assigned direct action like Brandi, others providing information and support. The point is we can get to anyone."

"So, I'm not so much being recruited as drafted."

"Drafted into an elite organization whose mission is to save humanity," Ryan replies, motioning toward the image. "Starting with your brother and Dr. Lento. The terms are simple. Suicide those you deem unworthy, as well as anyone whose name appears on your ComLink. There are only two rules: deaths must appear natural—suicides, accidents, no-trace disappearances—and no women. The Collective must approve any female target in advance. We do not want to draw attention to ourselves."

"And what about this woman?" I ask, nodding toward Brandi.

"If you're asking whether I got permission, the answer is 'yes.' Her removal was sanctioned. If you're wondering what I'm going to do with her, well, I'd rather keep that to myself. She will disappear, seemingly having hitched a ride on a shuttle to the surface." Ryan pauses, her lips forming a coy smile. "There will be a nice note."

Acknowledgment

I'd like to thank my Beta readers, Jeannette, Ali and Mike. A couple of you actually read the story more than once, which is either a testament to your commitment or an indication of premature short-term memory loss. Either way, your advice and feedback made for a better book.

Just like my first novel, this book draws on absolutely nothing from my past employment in the USIC. However, unlike the first book, which I ended up sending for pre-publication review after disclosing it during a five-year reinvestigation, I will not be sending this one through the same process just to appease an investigator who didn't bother to read it but still threatened to wield the tiny bit of power he holds over security clearances.

About the Author

Robert J. Richey

Robert J. Richey wrote creatively for the U.S. Intelligence Community. His first book, Two Monkeys, One Tale, is an exploration of expat life in the land of milk and Hindi. Robert taught for a U.S. Intelligence Community academy and has officiated two weddings—one of which stuck. He's been published in Good Old Boat Magazine, The Times of India and Peace Nepal Academy's annual magazine. According to a financially motivated source with questionable reliability whose past reporting is uncorroborated, Robert is a heck of a nice guy.

Praise for The Author

Best travel book I've read on India! I can't remember when I last laughed so hard while reading something, while being educated at the same time, and when that something is a look at life in India (through an American's eyes), you know it's worth reading.

- KSJanna on Amazon.com

Fun Travel Reading. I thoroughly enjoyed this opportunity to live vicariously through COS Robert J. Richey and his wife as they embarked on their adventure to India.

- James R. Fee on Amazon.com

An Invaluable Resource. Robert J Richey's "Two Monkeys, One Tale: Expats in India" is an invaluable resource for anyone traveling to India. You need not be an expat to make use of the insights and advice contained herein. Richey's writing style delivers a wealth of information sprinkled with humor and wit.

- Christopher Charney on Amazon.com

www.ingramcontent.com/pod-product-compliance
Lightning Source LLC
Chambersburg PA
CBHW070613300726
48975CB00006B/1808